THE SUN BLESSED PRINCE

THE SUN BLESSED PRINCE

LINDSEY BYRD

Random House Canada

PUBLISHED BY RANDOM HOUSE CANADA

 Published in 2025 by Random House Canada, a division of Penguin Random House Canada Limited, Toronto, and simultaneously in the United Kingdom by Tor UK, an imprint of Pan Macmillan, London.

Random House Canada, an imprint of Penguin Random House Canada Limited
320 Front Street West, Suite 1400
Toronto, Ontario, M5V 3B6, Canada
penguinrandomhouse.ca

The authorized representative in the EU for product safety and compliance is Penguin Random House Ireland, Morrison Chambers, 32 Nassau Street, Dublin D02 YH68, Ireland. https://eu-contact.penguin.ie

Library and Archives Canada Cataloguing in Publication

Title: The sun blessed prince / Lindsey Byrd.
Names: Byrd, Lindsey, author.
Identifiers: Canadiana (print) 2024044809X | Canadiana (ebook) 20240452844 | ISBN 9781039012462 (softcover) | ISBN 9781039012479 (EPUB)
Subjects: LCGFT: Queer fiction. | LCGFT: Romance fiction. | LCGFT: Fantasy fiction. | LCGFT: Novels.
Classification: LCC PS3602.Y73 S86 2025 | DDC 813/.6—dc23

Cover design: Neil Lang
Image credits: Shutterstock
Typeset in Goudy Old Style by Jouve (UK), Milton Keynes

Printed in the United States of America

1st Printing

To all those who have questioned
the meaning of life and death

Author's note

This book came about during a very difficult part of my life – and, indeed, in many people's lives. A product of Covid lockdowns, I spent much of 2020–21 thinking about life and death and what it meant to be truly alive. The mythology I built here spawns from countless hours of reflection, and a deep hope that global access to effective healthcare and equitable social services is something that might one day become a reality. I am incredibly grateful to everyone in my personal and professional life who helped this book come to fruition. I could not have done it without the support of each of you. Thank you, all.

The Sun Blessed Prince is a lyrical and character-driven queer fantasy, which begins on a hotly contested battlefield. Some of the scenes in this book are intense. Though not written for shock value and handled with requisite care, readers may be sensitive to some aspects of the story. These scenes include discussions of unviable pregnancy and potential miscarriage, bigotry, child abuse (implied) and child death (not explicit), ableism, torture (including medical torture), induced self-harm (brief), forced incarceration, intense scenes of anxiety and discussions of trauma.

PART I

Life was born to a great barren nothingness. He emerged, shapeless and undefined, and he longed to fill all the empty spaces. First came the ground that became known as Earth. It was hard and firm and cold. Life cast light upon the Earth as a great and powerful sun, giving birth to every colour Life could imagine. Blues, reds, yellows, and all those in between. The colours combined and shifted and changed. They swirled and danced about. They became warm under the glow of his power and cool in Earth's shadows. 'But the Earth is too hard,' Life decided, so he made Water too.

And Water filled Earth's empty spaces. It slithered between every available crack. Then it split and separated each crevasse, turning the Earth soupy and soft. If Earth complained, then Water fought with it. It threw itself up against all of Earth's sharp edges and smoothed each jagged point. Water could go anywhere it pleased, and it encouraged Earth to join it on its adventures. And with Life's help, it did. Life helped craft the Earth, moulding it into forms that Water filled and helped animate. Life would find them settled in one place or another, and he would ask: 'What are you? What is this?' And they would reply: 'I am now Grass,' or 'I am now Tree.' And for a time, this was pleasant. For a time, this was good. Water and Earth worked together, and together they found new ways to take shape, and new ways to explore the great world that had started from nothing.

– *The Origins of the Gods*, Anonymous

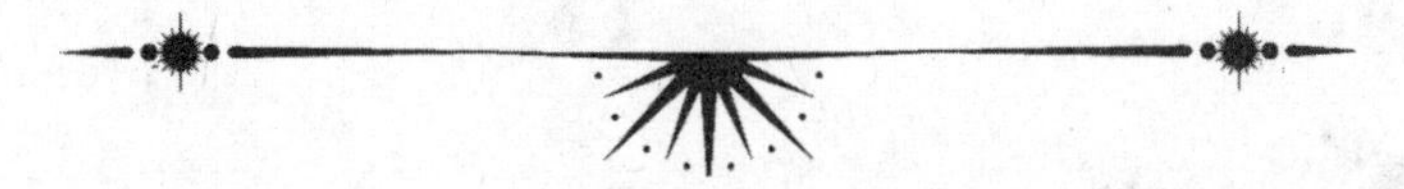

CHAPTER ONE

Elician

The battlefield is always chaotic. Even on a good day, when their defence is strong and their lines remain unbroken, Elician can only just manage to keep track of Lio. His presence is a constant balm in the violence as he blocks a sword here or an arrow there. Never straying far. They have fought this war for three years at each other's sides, and knowing where Lio is has become instinct. Elician does not need to look. He knows, with perfect clarity, Lio is there.

The melees never last long into the afternoon. It is too hot. But they start early, and the battles often stretch for hours as one relief group after another reinforces the front lines. Today, the humidity is impossible to ignore, even for the most steadfast of soldiers. They choke in their armour, gasping for breath between one strike and the next. And so, when Elician first sees a flash of streaking white, lithe and impossibly agile, he thinks the creature is an illusion, or perhaps his battle-weary brain playing tricks. For no nightcat would ever appear in a place like this.

Lio yells his name. Elician twists – an enemy soldier, dressed in tattered grey rags and clinking chainmail, swings a blade towards his head. Their swords clang loudly. Elician pivots on his heel. He ducks low. He yanks his blade up in a fierce diagonal, killing the man between one hot breath and the next. The body falls and – there it is again. A flash of white. Not the beast he had first imagined but a young man, bare-chested and pale, twisting away from the violence of the battle. With no armour to protect him, the man's skin shimmers in the high sun of the day. His hands cover his ears, as if that could possibly be enough to muffle the sound of the fighting. His head whips back and forth, mouth open in a wordless scream. There is dirt and blood splashed across the naked expanse of his chest. Elician takes one step towards him, bewildered by his appearance – then a new soldier appears in his peripheral vision.

Elician turns. Blocks. Looks back. The figure is gone, swallowed by the melee. If he had kept standing still like that, he would have been killed in an instant. Elician does not see his body amongst the collapsed forms littering the ground, but there is no time to search. The battle has not been called off yet and Elician cannot afford the distraction.

Blinking the sweat from his eyes, he adjusts his grip and his stance, then continues to fight. An hour passes. Another. His muscles burn hotter than the packed earth beneath his feet; he breathes in short bursts. The melee is agonizing in its refusal to submit to the muggy summer sun.

But eventually, it does.

A horn blows from the Alelunen encampment to the west, signalling to the enemy troops to regroup and retreat. Elician catches himself mid-swing, diverting an attack that would have taken his closest opponent's head off. The blade slices harmlessly through the air, but he must catch his weight on a hastily planted left foot as his balance shifts to accommodate the new position. His opponent stumbles backwards, staring at Elician in horror once she realizes how close she came to dying today. She raises her sword uncertainly, but Elician shakes his head. 'That's enough,' he tells her, speaking in her own language to make sure he is fully understood.

Finally, a second horn blows from the east. Elician's uncle, Anslian, has conceded the field. The battle is over. Both armies have been ordered to retreat, but the woman Elician could have killed is still hesitating. Her eyes fall to the shimmering golden sun that shines proudly on Elician's chest plate. Someone has already managed to dent it once today. But the sigil is too obvious to be obscured. 'You're . . . you're the Soleben Prince,' the Alelunen soldier identifies slowly.

'Yes,' Elician agrees. 'I promise, you may try to kill me tomorrow.' He pulls off his helmet and drags a hand across his brow. It is easy to ignore the sweat during the fight, but in the first moments of the aftermath Elician is hyperaware of each dribbling bead. He turns back towards the east. Lio is there, hand still on his sword, looking over Elician's shoulder towards the woman who should have already begun her retreat. 'She's not going to attack again,' Elician murmurs to his friend. He pats Lio's metal-clad shoulder. 'Come on.'

'You're too trusting, Your Highness,' Lio tells him. But he follows Elician to camp, only looking back a few times to ensure the would-be heroine has not decided to take it upon herself to make one final effort to end the crown prince's life.

'I'm too tired,' Elician corrects valiantly. If he can avoid killing one more person today, then he will take it. He is sick of feeling lives snuffing out at the end of his sword. He has done his fair share of death-dealing during the melee. Soon, he will need to stand before his uncle and recount every pertinent detail.

Clearing his nose, he leans a little closer to his friend, murmuring something he knows he will not include in his report. 'I thought I saw something today,' he says, swiping more sweat off his overheated brow. 'On the battlefield.'

'There were plenty of *somethings* on the battlefield,' Lio says.

'No, not like this one, Wilion. This one was different.' He smiles conspiratorially. 'This one was a nightcat.'

Lio and Elician help each other remove their armour after they are given permission to retire from the command tent. Ordinarily, Elician would not be expected to assist his friend. But Lio's fingers are clumsy and tired after the hours of conflict and Elician has no interest in prolonging this process for decorum's sake alone. The initial after-battle reports had lasted long enough for Elician to start feeling truly uncomfortable. Sweat had begun to pool at his chest, and his head had spun dizzily as the humid air made each choking breath even harder to inhale. He is desperate to shake off each layer like a beast shedding its fur.

Lio's nostrils flare as he takes a closer look at the vicious dent at the centre of Elician's breastplate, one that has crushed the shimmering golden sun inwards towards his heart. 'You're lucky this isn't worse,' Lio gripes, tossing the very expensive and finely made plate to the side for repair. 'You're equally lucky that no one in Alelune seems capable of aiming a damn *arrow*. Any competent archer can sight you from four hundred paces away with all this glittering nonsense.'

More than a few archers *had* aimed and nearly struck true, but Elician wisely does not inform his friend of that. Instead, he finishes unknotting the messy tangles of Lio's left arm guard and teases, 'At least I'm the prettiest target on the field.'

Lio is not amused. He swats a mosquito as it lands on Elician's chest, killing it with a bit more force than necessary. It drives the air from Elician's lungs, and Lio doesn't even bother to apologize as he brushes the insect to the ground and stomps on it for good measure. Another flies close to Elician's ear. Elician swats it against his neck with a few creative curses that would have earned him a sharp rebuke had they been back at court.

On Elician's desk a camp attendant has already set out a bowl of scented water. Lavender and lemongrass are the best remedies to keep the bugs away. That the infusion also washes off the sweat and grime from the melee is a bonus he's grateful to have. He sets to cleaning off his skin while Lio wages a much smaller war against the mosquitos at his back. 'What were you saying about nightcats earlier?' Lio asks, swatting and slapping away.

'I thought I saw one, is all,' Elician replies idly. It would have been a beautiful thing to behold if it had been real. His uncle Anslian, High General of the Soleben army and Second Son of Soleb, has always said nightcats don't exist, and Elician has yet to see one in the wild. However, the other soldiers at camp *always* tell their own stories about the creatures prowling through the woods. Nightcats are never heard, not until the moment of attack, and they disappear whenever someone turns to look. But the camp insists they're white as snow, and gone in a flash, taking with them anyone who strays too far from the fire lines. As knowledgeable as his uncle is, Elician much prefers the stories to reality.

'Should I be worried you're seeing things when you fight?' Lio asks as Elician finishes cleaning and steps back to dry himself.

'Probably not,' Elician replies, sliding his fingers through his black curls in a vague attempt to assess the damage. Bad. It is bad. His fingers snag on a knot almost immediately. Sitting on the raised bed in the back of his tent, he tries valiantly to beat his curls into submission while Lio takes his turn at the bowl for a wash. But Elician's hair and his helmet do not get along, and the result of this fight is almost assured. *I should cut them all off*, he thinks. *But Mother will despair if I do.* 'It was a trick of the light,' he continues when Lio's silence weighs heavily between them. 'That's all.'

'Did you eat today?' Lio asks shortly.

'You saw me eat.' Elician takes up a comb in the hopes of gaining ground. His scalp screeches its despair.

'I saw you put food on your plate, and I saw your plate empty. The middle bit I'm less certain about.'

'Alas.' Elician tries it from another angle. Then another. 'Making . . . food . . . magically *disappear*' – the comb flexes almost to a breaking point – 'is *not* one of my talents.' *Snap.* Lio snorts, and

Elician glares at the flimsy piece of wood that had promised wonders beyond its ability.

'No, your talents clearly remain elsewhere,' Lio says. 'Shall I put a new comb down on your requisition report? How shall we explain it to your uncle, I wonder?'

Elician has no desire to explain the incompatibility of his hair maintenance with the army to anyone, least of all his uncle. Anslian had successfully won the territories on the Bask River's west bank from Alelune, their only continental neighbour, twenty years ago. And when Alelune had regrouped and declared its intention to reclaim the land it had lost, Anslian had remained high general of the Soleben army. He is a hero, and too many people have died today for him to be worrying about whether his nephew's hair is in good order. Their requisitions report should prioritize other matters. He tells Lio as much.

Lio opens the drawers of Elician's dresser and finds them clothes to wear for the evening. Outside, he can hear the other soldiers preparing for a night of food, drink and laughter. Despite Alelune's best efforts, Soleb hasn't lost any ground. Tonight is a night to be proud of. Especially after a long, hot day. The smell of food wafts through the air, something thick and hearty. Elician's stomach gurgles as he begins to dress. Lio is faster than he is. His sweat-darkened blond hair, straight as the arrows that keep missing Elician's heart, is already tied back. *Bastard.*

Mostly dressed, Lio reaches for his discarded armour and plucks a carefully folded strip of cloth from the pile. The shimmering purple-and-burgundy scarf is neatly embroidered with a perfect celestial map in gold and silver threads. He unfolds it, then refolds it with meticulous precision before slipping it beneath his shirt above his heart. 'Have you received any new letters from Adalei?' Elician asks slowly as Lio finishes his ritual. The same ritual he's done from the moment Elician's cousin pressed that scarf into his hands the day they left for war.

'This morning,' Lio admits, reaching now for his sword and fastening it to the belt around his waist. 'Fredian was managing mail call.' He glances towards Elician, his lips twisting in an annoying leer of a grin. 'He asked how you were doing.' Elician flushes at the young soldier's name, then scowls. He tugs on his change of clothes, thrusting his arms through the sleeves of his linen tunic and turning his back on his friend in the process. 'It wouldn't kill you to talk to the man.'

'If only it would,' Elician mutters darkly. There is a small cache by his bed. He opens the lid to retrieve the heavy golden sun pendant which lies inside. 'And it isn't *talking* that Fredian wants to do.'

'He's not asking you to marry him, just . . .' Lio makes a crude gesture.

'If you can't even say the word, then maybe you shouldn't be doing it either.'

Lio's cheeks turn positively scarlet at the insinuation as he sputters 'I haven't!' even as one hand returns to the hidden cloth at his heart. 'I wouldn't! I promised her I wouldn't!' Perhaps more importantly, he would never get permission to marry Adalei if he was seen sleeping about the army camp. And unlike Elician's comb, that is something Uncle Anslian would deem *most* important for him to know.

'I made promises too.' Elician loops the chain over his head. Its weight tries to pull his neck into a bend, but he is used to it. He knows how to stand straight even under the burden of his royal birthright.

'They're stupid promises.'

Maybe they are. Elician shrugs. *But they're all I have.* He has a few more years left before his lack of interest in camp dalliances will earn him more than an amused grin and comments on piety. He intends to milk those for all they are worth.

'Fredian is a good lad. Good family too. He–'

'He's perfectly *fine.*' There had been nothing wrong with any of the suitors – formal or otherwise – Elician had met. The women were exceptionally *appropriate*, the men had legacies to be admired, and the soldiers were blunt, offering to help him clear his head after a long day of fighting. Every offer had been *fine*. And he had wanted none of them. He has more than enough loved ones in his life that will die before he will. He has no intention of adding another to that tally, not if he can help it. And the mere thought of opening himself up to any kind of physical intimacy . . . That runs the risk of emotions getting involved. He knows better than that.

'You're lonely,' Lio accuses.

'How can I be lonely?' Elician asks. 'I have you.'

Lio scowls. 'You're my best friend, and I'll serve you until the day I die, but you *know* that isn't what I'm talking about. I'm not going to *be* at your side for ever and–'

'Yes. I know.' He does not need their incompatible life spans spelled out. He never has. Thoroughly done with the conversation now, Elician gestures towards the tent flap. 'Let's get some food . . . and go to the river. You can tell me what Adalei wrote you.'

Lio agrees. He does not have much of a choice in it anyway. They head out into the camp proper, passing the injured, the weary and the still strong. Elician offers words to anyone who notices his presence. Polite and repeated phrases easily ignored. He avoids Fredian's eyes when he collects his stew, and quickly leads Lio towards the river. It's a full moon tonight. The world bathes in shimmering silvery-blue, and at the camp's edge the terrain stretches out, hinting at possibilities yet to be seen.

The Bask River runs north and south, splitting their continent in two, Alelune on one side, Soleb on the other. Their countries have been fighting over ownership of this river since long before history was recorded. No one knows who struck first, but it has not mattered as the centuries have slipped by. The first god, Life, formed and gave birth to the world right at this spot, long before the water came and the river formed. Neither country will allow the other to claim this sacred site for themselves. It is both countries' birthright and heritage.

Elician can feel it in the air as he approaches the Bask. He can feel it in the sound of the waves. This place radiates a kind of peace unlike anywhere Elician has ever been. As if Life himself is entreating all those who could listen: *this place should be protected.* And they *will* protect it, eternally, from their enemies across the river. Soleb will never relinquish its claim to the waterway, and Alelune equally refuses to contemplate a life without the river in its domain.

The Bask simply feels *right.* It flows calmly and with great certainty. Its depths contain endless fish to feed their troops. And it bears witness to blessed occasions, such as when sharks and breeding whales use the river to transition from one sea to the next. The great migratory periods are some of the few times the war comes to a pause. No one wishes to disturb these oceanic wonders on their path of travel. It is one of the only things any Alelunen or Soleben soldier can agree on.

When Elician had first been enlisted and arrived at this camp, his uncle had posted him as a whale-watcher, to sound the alarm the moment one was seen. He and Lio had spent months practising swordplay and observing the water as they listened to the older and more experienced soldiers fight. In those early days, announcing a sighting felt like the only way he could save anyone's life. Call the alarm and the fighting stopped. Swords were returned to their sheaths. Music, calming and peaceful, echoed from one campfire to the next. Whale-watching is an honour that he has outgrown now, but not one he will ever forget.

The Bask splashes against its rocky shores as they approach. A cursory glance confirms there are no whales tonight. It is the wrong season for it. A shame. Sitting down at the river's edge, Elician pulls off his boots and sinks his toes into the soothing waves. He brings his bowl to his lips and eats slowly, languidly, relaxing for the first time all day. 'Fen would love it here,' Lio says, sitting at his side. Elician hums thoughtfully. His adopted sister, fourteen and malcontent, would likely love anywhere that didn't force her to continue her education. 'All that anger,' Lio goes on. 'She could win the war in a night.'

Elician snorts. Nods. The camp songs echo louder. This far away, the lyrics are muffled but he recognizes the beat. His fingers tap along to it absently. *You came – you died! You thought that you could take our lives, but Life is at our side! You came – you died!* The taunting never endears them to the Alelunen soldiers camped on the other side of the battlefield, in the Grünewald.

'We should come up with a different song,' Elician suggests, exhausted by the nightly recitation. *Do they really need to waste their energy on this?*

'You're the poet.' Lio shrugs. 'You–' He stops. Frowns. Elician sits up, listening. A noise. Quiet, muffled, but . . . *there*. An eroded shelf not far from the river's edge and a shadow subtly moving in the darkness. Lio stands, drawing his blade. Elician sets his bowl to one side and joins him. They walk closer and the hitched breathing that had first drawn their attention grows ever so slightly louder.

Elician peers over Lio's shoulder just as they reach the overhang, and when the hiding creature finally comes into sight, Elician laughs. 'Look, Lio. It's my cat.'

Half-naked and pale as the moon, the huddled form is that of a man not much younger than Elician or Lio. His long brown hair hangs limply in a tangled mess around his face, but there is the slightest bit of stubble on his chin, like it has just started to grow in. He wipes his eyes to hide tears and Elician's heart wrenches. *A new recruit?* Quite possibly. Most soldiers have bad reactions on their first day in the melee.

If he is a new recruit, though, he is not one of theirs. No Soleben soldier would be as pale as this, skin all but glowing white in the moonlight. Sun-kissed skin is a badge of honour for their people, with designs burned into their skin whenever possible. But in Alelune, the less time spent outside, the better. Elician glances towards the Alelune camp. They could, conceivably, lead the recruit back across the battlefield and send him on his way. It would be an awful business to do it without getting spotted though. And his uncle would not be pleased if they were seen. He would want to know why *they* were the ones to do it, and what they were even doing so far from the encampment in the first place. Elician has no desire to give up the few minutes of peace he can wrangle each night. He does not want to receive another lecture regarding propriety either.

None of that matters now.

'How did he make it *here*?' Lio asks, speaking Elician's thoughts out loud. 'Did *all* of our sentries truly miss him?' A worrying question of security to be considered later, for sure. 'Where are his clothes?' he continues. The younger man is not naked, exactly. If he were Soleben, the tatty trousers would have at least been moderately appropriate summer wear. But even at the height of the hottest days of the year, Alelunens do not care much for displays of 'indecency'. Bare-chested, bare-footed and disreputable as he is, this soldier may as well be a beggar.

'Battlefield initiation gone wrong?' Elician guesses awkwardly.

'I didn't think they had the sense of humour for something like that.'

'Anything's possible.' Elician crouches. He rarely has the opportunity to practise Lunae with anyone. A few lines here or there during battle, certainly, but the chance for a full conversation does not come frequently. His countrymen hate the floating vowels of their closest neighbours. Lunae is a language that seems to imply its meaning rather than indicate any degree of specificity. Worse yet, learning it requires mastering the most subtle of nuances between vowel sounds. Elician struggled to learn it as a child, preferring Soleben or his mother's tongue, Glaikan. There is a kind of perfection found amongst the hard consonants and dedicated finality to those languages, something Lunae's lilting lyricism cannot quite manage on its own.

Lunae's subtle vowels are often the first to fall under the assault of a Soleben accent, mangled beyond recognition. But, with great care, Elician resurrects them from the dead. 'Don't worry,' he says as best he can. 'We're not going to hurt you.' The Alelunen's eyes flicker down to the pendant swaying on Elician's chest, then snap to his face with such rigid attention it is almost enough to drive the air from the prince's lungs. He frowns, unused to such piercing focus from anyone not under his command. 'How did you get here?' he asks.

Pale limbs unfold themselves one at a time. The Alelunen's arms slide off his knees. His legs twist as his weight shifts. He tilts himself forward.

He is handsome, Elician supposes, for an Alelunen. Appallingly thin, all things considered, but there is a peculiar cut to his nose and jaw that Elician can appreciate. It would be a shame to kill him if it turns out he is not a wayward new recruit but a spy or something worse. Some of the Alelunen's hair shifts, revealing a dark shape along the curve of his right cheek. *Dirt?* No. Something else.

Elician's memory tingles with recognition. A half-formed thought starts to take shape even as he leans back on his heels. But the Alelunen is already moving, his left hand snapping forward – Lio intercedes. He snatches the recruit's wrist with his bare hand and promptly falls to the ground.

Dead.

Elician's breath catches in his throat. For a moment, he does not understand. He looks, stupidly, for an arrow or a blade or anything he could have missed. When the answer comes, Elician nearly chokes on his next inhale. A Reaper.

Both taller and heavier than the would-be assassin, Lio's collapse had dragged the other man to the ground. But the Reaper wastes little time wriggling free. He gets back to his feet and charges at Elician once more, hands outstretched. Elician takes half a step back, instinct howling at him to defend himself even as he realizes the inevitable. He left his sword back in his tent. Lio's is too far away. There is no other way for this to end. The Reaper reaches towards him, his deadly touch crossing the distance between them, and Elician shoves him backwards. *Hard.*

The Reaper trips over his own feet but manages to stay upright. He seems to be preparing for a second assault when his eyes go to Elician's bare hands. He falls eerily still, staring at Elician's sun-dark skin. Elician had made direct contact. He should have died. Had Elician been anyone else, he would have.

'I'm a Giver,' Elician confirms, exhaustion coursing through him. 'You can't kill me. No one can.' A Reaper's touch means death. But a Giver is imbued with the power of the god of life. Only the gods can kill their kind. Nothing else. Elician glances back towards camp. They are still alone. There are no other witnesses. Good. 'But,' he growls out, aiming one finger at his best friend's body, '*he* really hates it when I bring him back.' It is impermissible. Frowned upon for many reasons and considered taboo. Whole histories have been written about how pulling people away from Death leads to nothing but suffering. And yet, Elician kneels. He presses his palm to Lio's throat and *wills* him to return.

Immediately, his friend lurches beneath his touch and Elician feels relief flood his bloodstream like a bitter high. Lio gasps for air, rolling to one side and coughing as he tries to catch his breath. 'Welcome back,' Elician mutters.

'*Fuck.*' Lio braces himself on his hands and knees. 'Did you— What happened?'

'You died,' Elician replies, dry as dirt. Lio curses again. And again. Elician leaves him to it, turning back to the Reaper, whose confusion has given way to wonder. He meanders closer, one hand outstretched towards Elician. Not out of malice, necessarily, simply to test a theory. His eyes are wide, lips parted, stunned and curious. Elician takes his hand. Holds it long enough to make it clear that neither is going to die from the contact, then asks, 'What are you doing here?'

The Reaper does not reply. When that fails, he leans back on one foot and slashes his other hand towards Elician's face, sharp nails nearly catching him in the eye in the process.

Elician ducks, twisting the man's wrist in his hand to manoeuvre the Reaper down to the ground. 'Give me your belt,' he snaps at Lio, then quickly works to bind the Reaper's hands behind his body once he has it. 'You really are a damned cat,' Elician gripes once he is done. Bound for now, he tugs his captive up onto his knees and steps back to get a better look at him. 'What's your name?' he asks, temper rising.

The Reaper hisses something, some nonsense thing that sounds like it was intended as a word but has turned furious and unintelligible instead. 'Cat it is, then,' Elician decides. It is simple enough for now and he does not have the energy to come up with something better. *What to do?* There is nowhere in the tent-city of their army that a Reaper can be properly restrained. The closest true city, with a proper prison system, is Altas. But, once there, Cat would need to be kept in solitary confinement and isolation. The guards would not be able to manage him otherwise. If he were to break out of the cell, he could murder anyone who dared try to stop him with barely a flick of his wrist. Sending him back to Alelune, though, is not an option. He knows Elician is a Giver now. And *that* information cannot be known. Not yet.

'What is he even doing out here?' Lio asks, fetching his sword from the ground and holding it uselessly in front of him. 'It's forbidden for Reapers to fight.'

'It's forbidden for Givers to fight too,' Elician reminds him, rubbing his face again as if the sensation alone would provide an answer. He is *exhausted*. After the endless hours of the melee . . . he had just wanted to get clean. Eat some food. Sleep, even. He does not have the energy to deal with this too.

'You aren't resurrecting or healing anyone!' Lio protests. Elician's hand drops to his side. Even Cat looks unimpressed at that proclamation. A proclamation that Elician had not even thought the failed assassin could understand. They both look at Lio, incredulous in the face of Lio's own, very recent, resurrection. And Lio has the audacity to argue. 'We're not on the battlefield now,' he snaps. 'And a Reaper is as much a liability to the Alelunen army as he is to ours. *Especially* like that.' He waves a hand at Cat's half-naked body. He's not wrong. Any Reaper, in any capacity, is a liability in combat. He is a danger to both armies merely by existing.

'He's a danger to himself too,' Elician murmurs. Someone with his powers cannot die a proper death. He could have been stabbed or sliced by hundreds of blades earlier today, and each wound would have healed. Even fatal blows would have eventually led to him standing up and walking away. But Elician knows from experience that just because something heals quickly does not mean there is no pain.

There is a good chance this violent, vicious assassin – surely sent by Queen Alenée of Alelune – really had been crying by the river, caught in the same post-battle shock as any new recruit. And his attack – almost successful, all things considered – had been a crime of opportunity. He could not possibly have known Soleb's crown prince would be here, now. Which means . . . something.

Elician sighs. *It means something.* His sluggish brain is simply not willing to work it out at the moment. 'He can't stay here.' That much is certain. He rubs his face again, trying to form his scattered thoughts into logic. 'We could take him to Kreuzfurt,' he offers. Though the fortified town is three weeks' journey by horseback.

'He tried to kill you,' Lio says slowly. 'He *did* kill me.'

'Yes, but you're better now.'

'Joy.' Lio's unhappiness is palpable. Elician ducks his head even as Lio keeps talking, growling out each word with increasing frustration. 'But even if we do take him there, what exactly do you think is going to happen? It might hold others of his kind, but do you think he'll just play nice with all the Soleben Givers and Reapers with no thoughts of escape?'

'I think,' Elician says, kneeling down to look the Reaper in the eye, 'that the guards patrolling Kreuzfurt are the only ones capable of keeping our Cat here from wandering off. They are uniquely qualified to handle those with his powers. And if he *does* decide to tell anyone what he knows about me being a Giver, that information isn't going to get very far. Marina will put a stop to it immediately.' He expects hostility, violence, even a few curses or condemnations, but the Reaper stays silent. The brief moment of clarity that had come at Lio's earlier bombastic declaration seems to have passed and he regards them both with almost passive nonchalance. If anything, his attention is solely on Elician's hands, as if he is trying to work out exactly where his planning went so wrong.

Slowly, Elician reaches for Cat's face. He ignores how the Reaper flinches back and presses his thumb against the man's cheek. He rubs back and forth, smearing a concealing unguent that had disguised the black stain seared into his skin. 'I thought nothing could leave a permanent mark on your kind,' Lio murmurs at his back.

Elician nods, continuing to reveal the stain. 'Marina told me it was something the scientists in Alelune had invented to make sure that anyone who crossed paths with a Reaper would know what they were.'

Lio shivers. 'Alelune likes its experiments.'

That it does . . . Clearing his throat, Elician returns to Lunae to ask, 'Tell me, Cat, what would you prefer? I cannot let you go. So, either I take you to Altas to be held in solitary confinement, or I bring you to Kreuzfurt – where you can wait out the rest of the war with your own kind.' Both are life sentences in their own way. The war always picks up again, for one reason or another. The last break in tensions only lasted seventeen years, and that was following a particularly aggressive forty-year campaign. This recent assault is only three years in the making. There is no guarantee when Cat will be returned to his own people, but at least one option comes with human contact and the possibility of a life worth living.

It is more than most assassins get.

'Can he even speak?' Lio asks in their native tongue when the Reaper stays silent.

'Altas,' Elician repeats in Lunae, holding up his left hand. 'Or Kreuzfurt.' He holds up his right. Slowly, the Reaper's head tilts towards Elician's right hand. 'Kreuzfurt it is. Lio, could you go fetch my uncle?'

'You want me to "go fetch" the high general of the army?' Lio scowls, already lowering his sword.

'Well, we need his permission to go.' They need more than that, but it would be a start. None of them are going to get much sleep tonight, it seems. At least they will not have to fight on the front lines in the morning. And good things, no matter how small, should always be celebrated.

CHAPTER TWO

Cat

Cat keeps his head down as the prince pleads his case to Lord Anslian, Second Son of Soleb and high general of the Soleben army.

Lio had escorted the esteemed lord to the bank of the Bask River with no other guard or soldier accompanying them. *It makes no sense – he should have a guard.* Instead, despite the fierce scowl that slashes across Anslian's face, he had come at Lio's request and allowed himself to be brought before an enemy Reaper. *My Queen would never have permitted such a thing,* Cat thinks. *She values her safety too much for that.*

But Anslian had come. And now he stands within striking distance as Prince Elician makes a very impassioned case designed to save Cat's life.

Cat does not listen to Elician's diatribe. He had for a few minutes, puzzling over what the prince hoped to gain by bringing him to Kreuzfurt, but Anslian's presence is more distracting than the prince's precise Soleben pronunciation.

There has never been a shortage of stories about Anslian in Alelune. Even when Cat had been living in the Reaper cells, news of the man had flowed like water. Anslian was both a great commander and an opportunistic *villain*. He secured the west bank of the Bask River for Soleb twenty years ago only because he managed to take Alelune's prince consort, Marias, hostage. Legends of Anslian's military victories have always been told with an infuriating mix of scathing contempt and grudging respect. He may have been a dishonourable fiend for how he ended *that* war, but he's managed to hold Altas and the Bask ever since. No one could deny that the man is a brilliant tactician. In truth, from all the stories Cat has heard, Anslian should have been a giant. Easily the size of mountains. But he stands before them now as nothing more than human. It is more disappointing than Cat had anticipated.

Anslian shares a few features with the crown prince. They are both dark-haired, though Elician's curls are more pronounced than Anslian's. Their beards are similar, groomed to a careful neatness. Elician's skin is darker, with a particularly unique tan line on his cheeks from where his helmet curves over his face. Anslian's skin, by contrast, seems to burn rather than darken, and it flakes along his brow over a particularly bright red patch.

The crown prince lists his reasons for not sending Cat back to Alelune as if he is giving a governmental address. He seems to be putting a lot of effort into the attempt, though Cat cannot work out why Anslian would bother to listen in the first place. Cat's queen would have punished someone arguing with her like this a long time ago.

'Has he said anything?' Anslian asks.

'No,' the prince replies. 'But that doesn't really matter at this point. What we *do* with him is the problem.'

'I think it matters quite a lot what he does or doesn't know,' Anslian argues. Cat tugs at his wrists, testing the leather strap wrapped around them. It does not budge. 'For Queen Alenée to send an actual *Reaper* into battle is an escalation. What if there are more?'

'Are there more?' Lio asks Cat directly. He repeats the question a moment later in heavily accented Lunae. Cat tilts his head back to look at the soldier. Blond but dark-eyed, skin deeply tanned from long hours in the sun, Lio is slightly taller than the prince. Broader too. He stands with a more grounded stance, one hand resting on his sword in warning. It has been many years since someone has stabbed Cat. He is not interested in experiencing it again.

He shakes his head. No more Reapers were sent.

'And we should trust him?' Anslian sneers. Cat almost sneers back, but there is no point. Their decision, whatever it is, is not one that is going to take his opinion into account. He failed his mission. What happens from here is out of his control.

'I want to bring him to Kreuzfurt,' Elician says. 'To Marina and the House of the Unwanting. She'll find out if he does have anything to hide, and they'll be better equipped at handling him.'

'The House of the Unwanting is not a jail cell. He is an assassin, an *Alelunen* assassin. You are rewarding your attempted murderer with a comfortable room and a garden to walk through. Do not use mercy as an excuse for stupidity.'

'I won't torture a man just because I don't know what else to do with him. Kreuzfurt is designed to maintain our kind – Givers and Reapers both. Shy of burying him alive or tossing him into the Bask with weights around his ankles, there is no convenient way to maintain him here in camp – and it is too great a risk for everyone involved to keep him locked away in Altas.'

Cat freezes at the mention of drowning. He glances to the left. The Bask River had stalled his panicked flight earlier. Probably for the best, all things considered. He had not been thinking straight. But the sight of the water had not helped ease the anxiety the battle had caused. All it had done was make him remember the last time he had tried swimming anywhere. The water filling his lungs, reaching desperately for something that had seemed so worth it at the time, a question being asked–

He really does not want to drown again.

Elician's hand touches his shoulder. It rests there, heavy and secure. 'And since I am not planning to torture any prisoner in our care, Kreuzfurt is the only logical choice.'

Cat drags his attention away from the river. He meets Lord Anslian's eyes. Not unlike the main disciplinarian in the cells, his eyes are sharply focused, narrowed with distrust and disgust in equal measure.

'You were his intended target, yes?' Anslian asks slowly. If the stories about him are to be believed, Anslian has never had a problem with torture. Cat tugs again at the bindings around his wrists. They do not move.

'He . . . hasn't admitted to such a thing.'

'Do we *need* him to admit that?' Lio spits out. 'He still tried it.'

'I'm not going to blame him for a crime of opportunity,' Elician replies shortly.

'And yet,' his uncle says, 'if he had succeeded in killing you, then you would have been removed from the battlefield and the line of succession. And now, if you take him to Kreuzfurt, you are still removed from the battlefield.'

'But at least not the line of succession,' Elician teases. His hand tightens around Cat's shoulder. 'I'm not throwing him into the Bask.'

'I am *not* asking you to torture the thing. But he *is* an Alelunen Reaper, and the only way he would have got here is if their damn queen allowed it. So, I want to know exactly what Queen Alenée hoped to gain by sending a Reaper into the melee when the gods themselves have forbidden such things. And if it *was* just to get a chance at killing you, then *why*?'

To be fair, Cat had never intended to end up on the battlefield. He sighs, curling forward as the three Solebens argue over him. His queen will be furious when she finds out; her commanders were supposed to release him *after* the melee. It is easier to cross into Soleb under the cover of darkness. He could have found the prince . . . Anslian . . . and all the rest far easier from that point onwards. She had given the troop commander specific instructions, and those instructions had been spectacularly ignored. The barrel Cat had been in had been confused for a supply barrel, and he had been kicked and rolled and tossed into the fight long before anyone realized the mistake they had made. The Alelunen general, Leferge, had been screaming obscenities at the chaos on the field, and the rest of the disaster had unfurled simply because Cat had been trying desperately not to touch anyone.

The noise and sudden bright light of the sun had overwhelmed every sensation he had. And there had been so much *death*. He had never been surrounded by that many people dying all at once before, each life snuffing out like a snapped thread in the back of his mind.

Lord Anslian walks closer. Elician shifts somewhat, preventing Cat from trying to take advantage of the proximity. All it would take is pitching forward. A brush of skin. The slightest bit of contact. *Not even that*, Cat thinks as the man continues to draw near. *But . . . it doesn't matter.* Elician can raise the dead. Even if Cat could take down the general, Elician would simply revive him. Cat had thought it was illegal to do such a thing in Soleb, but that must have been wrong. Another lie he had been told.

A lie that came with its own kind of curiosity, though. Cat had never felt someone coming back before.

He knows what it feels like when someone dies. He has seen Death herself more times than he would care to count, taking souls with her to be remade and reformed. It had never occurred to him that he would feel something when the inverse occurred. When someone used their god-given power to force a soul back into the body it had left behind.

In the brief moments when Elician had touched Lio, Cat's senses had come alive. He had felt the resurrection taking place, even before he understood what was happening. It had coursed through his body, a hand reaching down his throat, pulling the air from his lungs, choking him and emptying him, leaving him raw and open, ready to inhale once more. The sensation had grated, and it had soothed, a reminder that whenever breath is gone, something will always strain to fill in the empty spaces left behind. Lio had returned from the dead, and Cat had stared in stunned wonder, half expecting the god of life to appear right at his side. But there had been no one else, only Elician and the dear friend he had refused to let die.

'Tell me the real reason you want to take him to the House of the Unwanting,' Anslian beseeches quietly, as if he intends for Elician to be the only one capable of hearing him. But Cat has spent more than half his life listening to whispers. He can hear perfectly fine.

He can even hear Elician's whispered reply, words recited like a quote. 'All life is sacred, Uncle. That's what we learn at temple, isn't it? That all lives deserve to be protected and saved whenever possible?' Elician's hand tightens on Cat's shoulder again, as if to share an understanding over something. Cat, however, is too unused to such things to grasp the meaning.

'Elician–'

'I don't have a choice when it comes to fighting this war. I'm here because I'm my father's heir. I fight those soldiers because that's what you and Father have decided is best for our country. But I do have a choice in *this*.'

'He is an enemy. He tried to kill you,' the general protests.

Elician shrugs, impossibly calm. 'That doesn't matter,' he states. '*All* life is sacred, even his.'

He is a fool, Cat thinks. It cannot be that simple. His life ceased to truly matter the day he had died and become a Reaper. He knows what he is worth, and *sacred* does not come close.

'I don't care if he was sent to kill me,' the prince continues. 'There are a thousand soldiers in the Grünewald who try to kill me every other day. The only thing I care about is that he is a Reaper. As you said before: the gods forbid our kind on the battlefield. He was never supposed to be there to begin with.'

And neither was I – four words left utterly unsaid, but words Cat hears within the silence as Elician abruptly seals his lips. Cat does not know the prince well enough to know if those words were his intention, but they echo as loud as the armies' war horns.

'He should be someplace else,' Elician finishes.

Lord Anslian cups Elician's cheek. He angles the prince's head down and kisses his brow. 'Take Lio with you,' he says, no longer bothering to be quiet.

'Uncle?'

He pats Elician's cheek, smiling sadly. 'You're tired. Both of you are. As my daughter consistently reminds me, neither of you have taken any leave since you arrived. Three years is a long time without reprieve. So, take it. Go to Kreuzfurt. Deliver this . . . thing to Marina and then return.' His eyes crinkle at the corners, forming lines that reach out to his hair. 'There is no time for you to go to the capital, but you could take the Long Road back. And you could write to your loved ones from Kreuzfurt . . . or help each other write letters to loved ones, if that's what you need to earn their affections.'

Both Elician and Lio sputter at that last comment. They talk over themselves, offering excuses and protests.

'I never once–'

'That's not–'

Anslian laughs. It does not quite sound happy. 'I'm sure.' He pats Elician's cheek once more, then steps away. 'Go. If anyone asks what you're doing, tell them you're taking the list of the dead to read into remembrance. Marina can plan the ceremony for you once you get to Kreuzfurt. Be back in three months at the latest . . . and find some clothes for your pet *Cat* before you go. Gloves, too. Otherwise, it will kill anything it touches regardless of intent, including your horse.'

Cat frowns, not understanding.

What horse?

It is on the tip of his tongue to ask, but he holds it back. Waiting, watching, bound. It does not matter if he says anything out loud: they will do what they want regardless of whether he speaks or not.

Lord Anslian returns to camp. Lio leaves to get supplies. Cat shifts about to sit more comfortably as Elician paces. *Impatient*, Cat thinks derisively. Soleb is the Sun Kingdom, filled with golden imagery and great idolatrous affection for Life in all his glittering glory. Their people are fast-paced, quick-thinking and bad at foreseeing consequences.

Very bad indeed, it seems. Elician's pretty speech about all life being sacred had been almost too idealistic to bear.

'The place we're going,' Elician says suddenly in Lunae, turning on his heel and running a hand over his curls. Something must snag in his first pass because he grimaces and starts retying the short mess of curls at the base of his neck. 'Have you heard of it? Kreuzfurt?'

Yes. He has heard many stories about Kreuzfurt, some too wonderful to believe. Always spoken furtively and hushed, like a secret.

Elician clears his throat, then hurries on, not waiting or expecting Cat to reply. 'There are two Houses, one for Givers and one for Reapers: the House of the Wanting and the House of the Unwanting. Marina is the head of the House of the Unwanting, where all the Reapers of Soleb live. She's from Alelune, just like you. Though she came here a long time ago. She's . . . she serves as a cleric at the Kingsclave when it's in session.'

For the first time, Elician's knowledge of Cat's tongue shows its weakness. *Kingsclave* is a distinctly Soleben word, one he had directly translated rather than using the Lunae equivalent. It is a word their people would never use, for Alelune has no king, only a queen. *Always* a queen. One whose own title translates better as *Moon Blessed*, as she serves as their god's chosen speaker. No Alelunen would ever call the summit where Alelune and Soleb meet to discuss treaties under the banner of truce a *Kingsclave*. Not when their own word, *Blessedsafe*, holds far more meaning. But Soleb enjoys their insults.

The last time the two countries had met on the neutral grounds of the *Kingsclave* to discuss terms had been to sign the Marias Compromise and return the hostage prince consort to Alelune. Twenty years later, that night still weighs heavily on his people. They have never forgiven Soleb for that either.

'Marina is sworn to neutrality,' Elician continues. 'She'll be good to you.'

Marina. The name is an echo of a promise half forgotten. Ranio Ragden had told him about Marina. About Kreuzfurt. About Elician, even. *A sweet boy, too kind for his own good, and shy. But he'll grow out of that one day, I'm sure.* Ranio's description, nearly eight years out of date, still seems accurate. But whatever shyness Elician once had, there is a self-confidence in him that is now undeniable. Even with his linguistic missteps, he continues to speak in Lunae. More than that, though, Cat cannot understand why Elician has made the choices he has made tonight. There is no reason Soleb's crown prince could not toss him in a box, or a pit, or a prison cell. This trip to Kreuzfurt is beyond what rationally needs to be done. And yet the prince has convinced himself of the need for it anyway. Because of his lessons in temple. And apparently that had been enough to convince Anslian of it too.

Elician asks him, 'Do you have a family? Loved ones? People who will miss you?'

He does. He has never truly been alone. He waits for the prince to make up his own mind, to say what he needs to say to clear whatever part of his conscience is aching over the decision of sending Cat to . . . live comfortably in a religious commune. 'When the war is over, truly over, or when I'm king – I'll ensure you can go wherever you need to go. I swear it.'

You can't make that promise, Cat thinks, well used to broken promises and pretty lies. But Elician seems truly earnest in his intention. Cat nods his understanding, and Elician grins. He sits down at Cat's side, leaning back to stare up at the sky. The moon is bright and full tonight. Gorgeous. Cat has no idea how long it will take before he ends up back in Alelune. Someone will likely come fetch him sooner or later if he takes too long to finish his task. His queen will be disappointed that he did not manage to kill the prince, but at least he tried. He tilts his head up towards the sky. *At least I saw the moon.*

Elician's arm is warm against his and the silence that settles between them is surprisingly comfortable. Elician stops trying to fill it with meaningless prattle, and Cat leans into the excess heat coming off the Sun Kingdom's prince.

Lio returns eventually. He brings with him two massive horses, fully kitted out with saddles, saddlebags and accoutrements. They tower over Lio like hulking monsters, limbs thick and menacing. Their bodies are dark brown, almost black, but their manes and tails are as pale as marble.

'Those are not our horses,' Elician says in Soleben, eyeing the beasts trailing behind Lio by their reins.

'No, they aren't,' Lio agrees, patting the largest of the pair. 'I'm not trusting him on his own, which means he needs to ride double. With you – since I don't fancy dying again, thanks.' He unloops a satchel from around his neck and shoulders, tossing it to the ground by their feet. 'It'll be too much strain on the horses to ride double for too long though, so we'll have to switch off. Which means our usual mounts just earned a nice long stay out at pasture while we're riding these all the way to Kreuzfurt.'

'You couldn't have found a cart to go with them? It would have been so much more convenient.'

'Sure, but we're still banned from taking a cart, and everyone at camp knows it.'

'Seriously?' Exasperation drains off Elician's tongue. 'Even now?'

'Pretty sure it's a lifetime ban written into *law* at this point. I doubt your father is ever going to forgive us for the *embarrassment* we caused him. This was the best I could do.'

'Did you bribe someone?'

'Fredian. You owe him dinner – a *proper dinner* – when we get back.' The prince sputters, making a sound Cat has never heard before as he devolves into Soleben so rapid that Cat cannot keep up. Lio is not paying attention. Instead, he turns to Cat properly and says, in rather broken Lunae, 'Sorry, you much small than other man.' Lio opens the satchel and reveals a set of clothes. 'Did that I could. Good luck.'

'I'm not having *dinner* with Fredian,' Elician says in Soleben as he unbinds Cat's wrists. In Lunae, he commands, 'Get dressed.' Then he goes back to arguing with his friend in their native tongue. Something about carts and racing and how *it was all in good fun.*

Cat dresses. The clothes fastenings are simple enough to figure out, but he understands Lio's broken warning far better as he begins slipping them on. The off-white braies should only reach his knees but instead kiss his ankles. The trousers need to be rolled up. A pair of strings secure them around his hips, but the fabric bunches unpleasantly at his waist as a result. The linen undershirt and tunic both sag. The neckline on his tunic nearly slips off one shoulder. He puts his feet into the boots Lio has found for him, but they slide backwards and forwards, his toes not even close to touching the ends. The gloves he has are perhaps the only items that fit him well. They are still too big, but only slightly.

It is not the worst he has ever worn.

But it comes close.

He imagines, suddenly, what his queen would think if she saw him like this. He flushes with embarrassment, tugging awkwardly at the sleeves. The movement catches attention, interrupting the pair from their heated debate. Lio snorts indelicately behind his hand, but Elician clears his throat. He tries lying again, saying, 'We'll . . . see what we can do on the way to make it better,' and Cat hisses beneath his breath in frustration.

But there is no response to his ire. They do not recognize the sound.

'We'll cross the river tonight and find a place beyond the east bank,' Elician says. He sighs and curses while looking at the towering monster of a horse. 'This is going to be *exceptionally* uncomfortable, Lio.'

'Deal with it,' Lio mutters. 'You're the one who wants to take a Reaper assassin all the way across the country.'

'Do you have a better idea?' Elician snaps.

'You mean morally better. Do I have a morally better plan? And the answer is no. But I still don't like it.'

'Noted.' Elician holds out his hand towards Cat. 'Do you need a boost?'

Cat does not move. Gently, Elician wraps his fingers around Cat's bare wrist and tries to guide him towards the grotesque beast of a creature. Cat digs his heels in. He yanks his arm back. Ranio had put him on a horse once. *It will be all right,* he'd said, *don't worry.*

'It will be all right,' Elician promises him too, daring to smile like he means it. 'There truly are worse places to stay than in Kreuzfurt.'

No.

Cat hisses rather than speaking the refusal, the noise sharp and fast. Elician hesitates. Frowns. Cat hisses again. Even opens his mouth to speak the refutation outright, the first words he would have uttered here, but then the horse moves. Its head sways, ears flick. Cat stumbles backwards and Elician tugs him forward. It is useless to fight. Cat has never won at anything when he's fought back, but he scratches and kicks anyway. He yanks himself free and – trips in the *stupid boots.*

He hits the ground. Rolls. He tries to get up; his feet slither from the boots and that is fine. He can run without them if he has to. But an arm wraps around his waist and his hands are getting tied again. He thrashes and tries to break free. Someone hoists him up and over, tossing him like a sack of grain onto the horse's rump. He pitches forward, gravity yanking him down. Cat closes his eyes before the contact, hissing an apology no one understands, and his chin bounces off the poor thing's rear.

The world gives way beneath him. The horse collapses. Someone curses and starts shouting. Cat cannot understand the words, too busy trying to find a way to sit up. Hands grab at his shoulders, and he throws his head back. Another curse. 'Wait! Wait, Cat, I'm trying to–' He's rearranged on the ground away from the horse. 'That was my fault,' the stupidest prince in the world says, kneeling before him. 'I didn't think that . . . It was an accident.' Lio says something in the background, but Cat is not listening. 'You're afraid of killing her, is that it?' Elician asks.

Cat hisses his incredulity into the air. He *did* kill her. She was a hideous, unnecessary thing, but now she lies dead on her side, saddle still attached just like Ranio's. He glances off to the left, half expecting Ranio's corpse to be lying there in brutal refrain. But it's only Lio, standing awkwardly by the dead horse, and Elician, looking far too sad indeed.

The prince holds up his palm. 'Look, look, Cat. Watch.' He presses one hand against the horse's flank and – it happens again. A pull of air, a yanking of attention, a shiver shaking the far corner of Cat's mind, and then: the horse is alive. She huffs. Stands. Shakes her head and her braided mane. She extends one leg and rubs her face against it. Lifts her tail and farts.

Elician turns back towards Cat. His hand, that magic touch, capable of undoing every horror Cat could contemplate, reaches for him. 'When was the last time you touched something and it didn't die?' he asks. He cups the back of Cat's head. Pulls him close. Cat's brow rests against Elician's neck. He closes his eyes and breathes in. Lavender and lemongrass. Like the perfume his father used to wear.

'I won't let anything happen to you,' Elician swears. 'I will not allow anything you do to permanently hurt anyone, or any*thing*, that travels with us.' His fingers stroke through Cat's hair. Soft, soothing. Unreal. 'If you get on that horse, I promise you, it will be all right.'

Trust me, Ranio had whispered, reaching through the bars of Cat's cage. *The prince in Soleb . . . he's not much older than you, but he's a lot like you in many ways. I'll bring you to him, if you want. You could have a different life there. But you have to trust me to help you escape.*

'If you climb onto that saddle *appropriately*,' Elician says, 'you won't risk touching her. I'll sit right behind you.' He keeps hold of Cat's head, but he leans back far enough to meet his eyes. 'Trust me,' he beseeches one final time.

Cat nods.

Then, carefully, with the prince's help, he gets on the horse.

CHAPTER THREE

Elician

Elician has never taken someone prisoner before. It is not something his instructors taught him as he trained to join the war effort. Prisoner exchanges are rare. Once both sides have issued a retreat order, then the conflict is meant to be over for the day. It is simply too much fuss to try to take someone hostage.

Despite this, his uncle Anslian had done it once. He had been named a hero for managing to take Marias, Alelune's prince consort, as a hostage. For dragging him from the east bank of the Bask River all the way to Soleb's capital city, Himmelsheim. Elician even remembers standing next to his mother in the throne room as the Alelune ambassador negotiated the terms of Marias's release. Elician had not been allowed to travel with the party to the Kingsclave when the transfer finally took place, but there had been months of negotiations before then.

Marias had been well treated, of course; no one would have been foolish enough to risk his health and well-being. But he had been caught in the first place because of an injury in the melee. Elician remembers how strange it had seemed to see such a fuss being made over a thin, pale-faced man who said little in his defence and sat slumped in his chair, left leg wrapped in thick bandages from his ankle to knee. All Marias had wanted was to go home to be with his infant son. It had seemed like a reasonable request. Young Elician had even told him so. Marias had smiled at him, and Elician had been escorted out of the room. He never saw the prince consort again.

By capturing Marias and brokering his eventual return in what became known as the Marias Compromise, Anslian secured the west bank of the Bask and the whole of Altas from Alelune. In return, Alelune had the safe return of their prince consort and an agreement that no lands past what they'd conceded would be pursued by Soleb. It had been a resounding victory for Soleb, and a brutal embarrassment for Alelune. Queen Alenée divorced and replaced Marias in the years that followed. For seventeen years, there had been peace. *Long enough for new soldiers to be born and raised,* Anslian had scoffed when Queen Alenée declared war. She wanted Altas back. And the Bask. And all the land beyond that shore. Three years since the war had begun anew, and she had not stopped trying.

Although Elician has never taken a prisoner before, considering the legacy he has inherited, he rather thinks he is doing it wrong. He has not taken a prince hostage here. The thin waif of the failed assassin is not going to end any wars any time soon. If anything, if anyone discovers that Queen Alenée had resorted to using a Reaper to end her troubles, it would only encourage Soleb's armies to march deeper into Alelune territory. They did not have to stop at securing control over the river, after all. Soleb leaving the fertile lands to the west had been a stipulation of the Marias Compromise – a proviso they no longer needed to heed after Queen Alenée broke the terms of their agreement with her assault.

No one can know what the Queen had tried to achieve with her Reaper. It would just make the war worse.

That still does not mean Elician knows what he is doing.

He is lucky the Reaper is small enough to fit the makeshift two-person saddle Lio had rigged together for them both. And despite his complaints, Elician does see the wisdom in taking draft horses instead of their Trakehner mares. At over sixteen hands, these horses can more easily manage the weight of their riders and their gear. They will do well on the mountain passes leading to Kreuzfurt too, having been bred to manage the difficult terrain.

It is still not the most comfortable ride to be had. Elician brackets his prisoner between his arms as he guides his horse through the city of Altas and towards the great river crossing ahead. He can feel every breath the Reaper takes. *Surely,* Elician thinks miserably, *even prisoners deserve more privacy than this.*

They ride through Altas late at night, passing the streets that clash in architectural confusion, this building built under Soleben rule, that one under Alelunen, one right after another. Arches and curves lean against straight geometric latticework, gold and silver accenting the exteriors as people talk to each other in the chaotic dialect born from a mix of both languages used as one.

Elician hides his sun pendant beneath his tunic as they ride east over the bridge that connects the two halves of the city together. Civilians laugh and chat with one another as they pass. No one pays them any mind ostensibly, but Altasians are good at hiding their attention. Elician *feels* watched, even if he cannot prove it. The people of Altas are well used to changing allegiances and accepting a new rule of law whenever their city falls. Their loyalty is rarely, if ever, assured.

Crossing the city is like holding a breath too long. Expectation of the eventual release and anticipation for the inevitable conclusion whirl about to an almost painful degree. By the time they cross the bridge from the west side of Altas to the east, his nerves are thoroughly frazzled. *It's been a long day,* he thinks dully. *I'm tired.*

The rest area they find almost an hour later is flat, surrounded by large beech trees, and far enough off the road to ensure some modicum of privacy. Elician helps Cat down from the horse but is barely aware of going through the motions of setting up camp for the night. His uncle would have likely had a system in place for managing a prisoner, but Elician has no idea what might be best. He ties Cat's wrists and ankles, hopes that is good enough, and curls up next to his saddle.

For the first time in months, he doesn't dream at all.

It is almost refreshing.

In the morning, he wakes not to the sound of whistles and drums, but to Lio humming a camp song as he cooks breakfast. Their prisoner has been fed – 'Two bowls of porridge and three apples. He's got a better appetite than you've ever managed' – and Elician eats slowly as Lio prepares their horses for travel.

Elician is not sure what etiquette is appropriate for interacting with your hostage, but he is uncomfortable with saying nothing. He considers his options, eventually asking: 'Did you sleep well?' Cat glances at him, frowning. When Elician repeats the question in Lunae, he is given an even more incredulous look. Embarrassment flushes through Elician's body. He winces and looks away, muttering an apology as he finishes eating. He still cannot quite meet Cat's eyes as he cleans up, and when they head out an hour later, he is still not certain what it is he is meant to say, or if he should say anything at all.

For much of the first week, the routine stays the same. They travel slowly, but not silently. Lio seems particularly interested in pointing out every red-rumped swallow and unique foliage configuration he sees, which leads Elician to point out interesting things *he* sees as well. They make an informal game with transient rules on who can spot which first. Winner would not cook dinner that night. Elician won the first three days, Lio won the fourth, and by the fifth Cat had begun pointing out any new creature or species that he saw too. Elician would verbalize the sighting and take credit as Lio scowled at them both.

'He's only helping you because you're a shit cook,' Lio says when he catches Cat pointing out a black-bellied warbler.

'By that logic, you should be willing to let me win too,' Elician replies sweetly, even if it is the truth. He had seen Cat's nose crinkling up at the fish Elician had tried making the night before, and even though Cat generally ate anything and everything placed before him, he certainly had not gone out of his way to eat more that evening. Elician would've been offended if he was not simply grateful that their prisoner was doing more than sitting quietly and following directions.

He is sure he is tying the ropes around Cat's wrists and ankles improperly. Too loose, or too easy to shake free. Cat never seems interested in taking advantage of that prospect though, and Elician cannot understand *why*. He tries talking to him, testing phrases in both Soleben and Lunae. He's almost certain Cat understands Soleben, for all he refuses to answer in it. But Elician cannot exactly be considered verbose when it comes to Lunae either. Cat refuses to speak, explain his intentions or interact with them beyond the vague miming of polite obedience.

They reach Great Dawn Pass just before sunset on their eighth day and aim for a traveller's point that promises a glorious view in the morning. Constructed along the saddle of two rocky peaks, the pass provides a near-panoramic view of the countryside. It's a stubborn slope down but one of the few convenient ways to reach both the capital city of Himmelsheim to the north and the road to Kreuzfurt still further east.

Their good luck, though, seems to falter as they reach their evening resting point. Elician smells the group before he hears them, smoke and spices rising through the air and making his mouth water. Then a lute's plucking confirms what he had been hoping had just been a sign of hunger: a large party of travellers are already well encamped in the only convenient resting point for the next three hours. Old men and women, families with their children. Elician pats his chest to make sure his pendant is still tucked under his tunic and meets Lio's eyes as his friend slows his horse to walk side by side.

'The pass is too steep to descend at night,' Lio says. Elician glances back the way they came. It had been steep on the way up too. Elician has marched this pass enough times to know the point is the best rest area to be found. He has never had a prisoner with him though. Especially one he wasn't too keen on allowing near the local civilian population.

This is a bad idea, Elician thinks, returning his attention to the travellers. 'He hasn't been much trouble so far,' he says. The circumstances are far from ideal, but if they break their horses' legs trying to descend at night, their journey is only going to get worse. Lio grimaces, then nods.

'I'll tell them he's sick,' he offers, then jerks his head to a somewhat less crowded area to the left of the party. 'Keep him there.' Riding ahead, he dismounts and speaks to an old man sitting on the edge of the fire who seems to be the leader of the assembly.

The man looks between them all, then nods, waving his hand. 'There is space enough,' the old man calls out. 'Come, come!'

'Please don't hurt anyone,' Elician murmurs into Cat's ear. He adjusts, then dismounts. He guides the horse to the area Lio had mentioned and helps Cat get down. Settling him on the ground, he gets a blanket from his saddle bags and quickly wraps it around Cat's shoulders.

He goes to pull away when one of Cat's bound hands twists and slips free from the blanket. It snatches at Elician's sleeve with a weak grip, holding him in place. Meeting Elician's eyes for the first time since they met, Cat speaks. 'I was sent to kill you and your family, Prince, not your people.' His words are accented – a bit too rounded along the top, vowels dragging just a touch longer than is proper – but the syntax and grammar are flawless. Elician had suspected, but the confirmation that Cat can speak Soleben perfectly fine still manages to surprise him.

He glances back over his shoulder. Lio is talking with the group, keeping them back most likely. The large draft horse that had been tasked with bearing both Elician and Cat is lazily chewing on her bridle, sighing like a disappointed grandparent and adjusting her weight even as she starts sniffing at the compact earth beneath her hooves. 'So you *are* an assassin,' Elician says.

Cat presses his lips together and releases Elician's sleeve. He shuffles his hands back behind his blanket in an almost polite show of respect in an already damaged situation. Head down, in the dark, the circular black scar on his cheek is almost unnoticeable. Elician waits a moment longer for something else to be shared, but Cat seems reluctant to become a budding conversationalist. Turning back to his task, Elician gets the horse and camp settled for the night.

His prisoner stays quiet. Not quite a facsimile of a soldier who fell ill and is at death's door, desperate for a trip to Kreuzfurt in order to save his life, but at least not running away into the woods.

Elician says, 'You could, you know. Flee.' *Anslian,* Elician thinks, *probably never gave Prince Marias such suggestions.* He glances back towards the crowd. A child shrieks in delirious laughter, running away from another child in some kind of game. There is food being prepared. Elician had smelled it earlier, and if he squints through the bodies along the fire, he can almost make out someone dutifully tending to a cook pot. Lio is crouched down next to the old man, who has finally taken his seat. They're discussing something with intense concentration. Elician tries to read their lips—

'Flee where?' Cat asks. The words come at a delay, so long after Elician's that he hadn't expected a response.

'You could go home.' Though it would trigger all the things Elician had been trying to avoid when he first came up with the plan to bring Cat to Kreuzfurt. Cat would tell someone *why* he failed, Alelune would spread word that Elician was a Giver . . . and that would be enough to destabilize the monarchy that Cat was sent to unravel. Suggesting Cat leave is foolish. A waste. Elician sighs. *But it'd be so much easier if everyone just* knew *what I was and I didn't have to keep pretending anymore.*

'Home is a cell underground,' Cat says flatly. Elician flinches at the reminder. He glances at Cat's pretty face. The Reaper isn't looking at him, but up at the sky. The stars aren't out yet, and just for a moment he almost seems wistful. 'If going home meant a change in circumstance, I would go back, but there is no point now.'

'What change in circumstance?'

Cat tilts his head slightly, emulating his namesake to eerie effect. 'I was offered freedom in exchange for your lives,' he replies slowly, unblinking eyes burning into Elician's soul. 'Of all the people on the list . . . you seemed most important. But you cannot die. And so the task will never be complete. Why bother killing anyone else in your family? It won't free mine.'

'Queen Alenée offered to free you and your family . . . if you killed me?' Elician asks, numb at the thought of it. Someone laughs behind them. A whoop of delight that quickly gains timely echoes. Elician glances towards the group, then back to his prisoner.

'You're worried I'll hurt them,' Cat observes, ignoring Elician's question. He nods slightly towards the party. 'I have no reason to kill them. So, I won't.' A grimace crosses the Reaper's face as he tugs the blanket around his shoulders to hide his hands and body from sight. 'Not on purpose.'

That's the trouble with being a Reaper, though. It does not need to be on purpose. All it takes is a touch.

'Sir?'

Elician looks up. A heavily pregnant woman approaches slowly, a bowl in each hand. She smiles politely, dipping her head in greeting. 'We thought you might be hungry. And we had more than enough to share.' Standing, Elician closes the distance between them. He thanks her kindly before crouching and setting the bowls on the ground. One by Cat's side, the other near the fire he had been trying to tend to. 'Your friend said you're going to Kreuzfurt.'

'Yes,' Elician replies, awkwardly standing between her and Cat and not entirely sure what he should be doing with himself. Rarely has Elician had the opportunity to talk to somebody without Lio or someone else there to serve as a shield.

'I . . .' She bites her lip. Lowers her voice. 'Do you know much about it? Kreuzfurt?'

'Yes.' In the firelight, he takes in her face. Her clothes. One hand rests on the swell of her stomach. His awareness wraps around her, reaching out for more beyond what his eyes are telling him. Information slides in through his thoughts as if he had conducted a physical examination himself. She is tired, dizzy even. Her ankles hurt. Her feet ache from hours of walking. And worse, much worse, he senses something he has no business knowing at all. 'Are you worried about your child?' he asks.

She bites her lip again and moves closer, tripping clumsily over a stone at the edge of their fire pit. Elician catches her before she falls and guides her gently to the ground. 'Oh, sorry, sorry!' She gasps, leaning on him as she lifts one foot and tries rolling her ankle.

'It's all right,' he soothes, skin prickling as he touches her hands. Too late, his senses are already turning towards every ache and pain, every abnormality, every flaw. She'll notice before too long: a sudden lack of any problem at all. He has already begun healing her without conscious thought, and the longer they stay in contact . . . the better off she will be. He should pull away. Immediately. It's what his father would have him do. 'Can I see?' he asks as he helps her sit down, prolonging the contact needed to help her and vaguely keeping track of each soothed muscle and strained tendon that rights itself beneath his touch.

'I . . . It's not that bad, but . . .'

'I just want to make sure.'

She nods her assent, and he makes a good show of checking her ankle, as if the act of massaging it is all it takes to heal the joint.

'Oh, it feels better already.'

'My cousin used to say I had magic hands.' He smiles, and she laughs, missing the joke but relaxing as he continues to gently rub his thumbs into her skin. Behind him, Elician can feel Cat's gaze on the back of his neck. But his prisoner does not speak again.

'They don't help with pregnancies at Kreuzfurt,' the woman says suddenly. 'Do they?'

'No,' Elician replies. 'Givers aren't allowed to give life, no matter the circumstances. They cannot call it into existence. Until a babe draws its first breath it is not yet considered a life fully formed. Givers are forbidden to interfere.'

'So, if there was something wrong . . .' She rubs her stomach again, anxiously. He wonders how often she's done that. 'They wouldn't help?'

Not only would Zinnitzia, the head cleric of the Givers of Kreuzfurt, not help, but she would give a long and detailed argument for why such help would be an affront to the gods themselves. While technically only the royal family are legally forbidden from being healed or resurrected, Zinnitzia's management of Kreuzfurt is far more draconian than that. She would never allow any of the Givers in her charge to help this woman or her child. Until the moment the child is born, it remains potential only. And Givers have long since been forbidden to enter the realm of potential as far as new life is concerned.

'What's your name?' Elician asks.

'Kassandra.'

This is a bad idea, Elician thinks, pressing just a little harder on the ankle in his grasp, willing his senses farther along until he can sense the fragile life inside her struggling to survive. 'Where is the father?' It's a terrible question to ask, in truth. Hardly appropriate on the face of it, and worse: the father could well be a soldier on the very warfront that he himself has abandoned – just so he can travel to the very place that would deny her the care she desperately needs.

But she flushes instead of wincing, lowering her voice into a fast-paced ramble. 'It's . . . complicated. It's . . . well, one of the Travelling Givers was doing their rotation through Altas, and I went just for a routine check-up. Might as well, right? Sometimes it's months before a Giver comes to the city. Especially with the war on – and I didn't really think anything of it. He asked me if there was anything he could do, and I just asked. My wife and I always wanted children, but I didn't want to . . . do what needed to be done, if you know what I mean.' He does. 'And the Giver, he said it would only take a moment. He just had to touch my stomach and then . . . well, it certainly took less time than *the usual method*.' She laughs, but it is a broken, anxious sound.

'There was no attendant?' Elician asks. Travelling Givers always came with guards meant to monitor and watch all proceedings.

'They stepped out, there was a fuss with someone in the line outside and . . . I had a moment of opportunity, so I took it.' For all the anxiety that came with telling the tale, she concludes it almost in defiance. She meets his eyes, lips pursed, jaw clenched, preparing for a verdict he would never have it in him to pass.

'May the sun shine on your lives,' he offers, giving the prayer by rote. Her shoulders relax, but the anxiety has yet to fade.

'I know it's illegal,' she says, 'and I guessed no one at Kreuzfurt would openly be able to help. But . . .' She is worried. She should be.

A Giver can start the process. Can help encourage an egg to grow, to travel through the body and latch on to the womb. The child would be a perfect genetic copy of the mother, in all ways. She could even be born healthy and happy. But so much can go wrong, and to ensure the child survived . . . that Giver would need to be there, constantly monitoring growth and development and healing all the imperfections that threatened viability along the way. But Travelling Givers were only ever in towns for a few weeks at best before moving along to the next town in need.

Kassandra has never received the care her daughter requires.

Elician feels the child inside her. Malformed and struggling to survive with a heart too weak to carry on. He can *sense* the other Giver's presence there. A subtle kind of fluctuating energy that had provided a spark of life, and nothing more. He drowns that energy with his own. *Be well,* he wishes. *Live. Live, and be well.* The child twitches, limbs adjusting. Kassandra flinches, her ankle jerking in his hand. But he is already done. He lets her pull away even as she stares down at herself.

'I . . . I've never felt her move before, but . . .' She reaches for him, takes his hand and presses it to her stomach. 'Can you feel that?' The babe moves again, stretching an arm that had for so long been bent in the wrong position. Better still: he senses her heart, finally beating as it should.

'I feel it,' he murmurs. 'Is she your first?'

'Yes, yes, I–' She breaks off, distracted. Consumed by the shock and awe of hope where despair had always lurked.

'It's normal to be nervous,' he reassures her. 'Where are you going – is it very far?'

'Himmelsheim. My wife – we have a house there now, all ready for us – I was so scared when I hadn't felt her move. I thought . . . I thought I'd done something wrong. I was going to go to the temple once I got to the city. Pray as hard as I could.'

'You probably still should,' he says, wincing slightly. 'It's always best to thank Life for his gifts. And she will be his gift.' And without another Giver to check on the child's progress, she really will need a god's help. Elician has done what he can, and she's far enough along to give him hope. But the future is never certain.

'Yes. Yes, I . . . I . . . Gods, I was really scared. And now she's . . .'

'Well, maybe you should trip on a firepit more often,' he suggests, smiling as best he can. 'Seems like it has good effects from time to time.'

Kassandra laughs, and he helps her back to her feet. Her ankle no longer hurts. 'Good luck with your own journey too. I hope your friend gets the treatment he needs.' He'd almost forgotten about

Cat's fake illness, but he manages to school the confusion off his face before it grows too obvious. Dipping his head, he says his goodbyes, and waits as she walks back to the camp.

Elician watches her go. Then, silently, collects the food she had brought. *If anyone finds out what you are,* his father has reminded him time and time again, *you'll have put all of Soleb at risk. No one in this country is worth saving if it keeps you from the crown. Not Lio, and certainly not some stranger on the street. There is no choice here. You are a prince first. Not a Giver. Act like it.*

He's saved a life tonight. More than one, really. Kassandra and her wife would have been devastated at the loss of the child. He could feel her love and desire and hope in every breath she had taken. And the wife, whoever they may be, has gone all the way to the capital to make a better life for their fledging family far away from the border war at Altas. He has saved a family.

And yet, it – like taking Cat prisoner in the first place – still feels like a mistake.

CHAPTER FOUR

Cat

Elician avoids speaking to Lio when he finally returns to them. He eats his soup, then curls on his side, falling into a restless sleep. He twitches and jerks, waking in startled gasps before forcing his eyes closed to try, try again. Cat spends the night watching Lio watching Elician. Cat wonders how much he saw. If he too had seen the pregnant woman falling into Elician's arms, and Elician's lengthy pause, bare skin pressed to her own.

When the sky starts to turn, Lio sighs loudly. He wakes Elician for a quick breakfast, then encourages them to pack and slip away from the rest area while all the other travellers are still asleep. The sun peeks above the horizon just as they guide their horses to the crest of the saddle between Great Dawn Pass, and the view truly is remarkable. A windowpane of stained glass shatters across the sky. Blues, purples, reds and golds cascade along the heavens, painting clouds with their majesty and the landscape with their love. It is breathtaking.

Cat has never seen something so sublime.

They pause there, crisp morning air warming as the sun rises, and embrace the glory of Soleb's precious god of life. Cat cannot bring himself to begrudge the Solebens their prayers. It is a view worth praying over.

Lio restarts their journey when the sun rises high enough to no longer be quite as spectacular as fresh dawn. He also, finally, loses his patience with waiting. 'What happened with that lady last night?'

Cat hears Elician's breath hitch at his back. His arms tense on instinct, then relax slowly. Elician explains everything: Kassandra and her soup, the fall, the conversation – the healing that is apparently forbidden. 'Why is it forbidden?' Cat asks.

Lio startles. He swivels on his saddle, needing to stand up in his stirrups to manage it. 'You *speak*?'

When I want to, Cat thinks, pressing his lips together. It's a show of petulance that would have got him in trouble in Alelune. Something that would have infuriated his brother, and all his brother's entourage. If Cat were feeling particularly petty, he would liken Lio to that gaggle of sycophants. The trouble is, despite the near worshipful attention Lio bestows on his beloved prince, he genuinely seems to care about Elician. Lio worries and frets over each of Elician's moods as if it were more than an obligation or necessity for political advancement, where Cat's brother's followers seek only to manipulate and control.

Cat knew someone, once, who had Lio's penchant for loyalty, and he isn't petty enough to diminish true friendship or commitment when it dares to rear its head.

'We spoke some last night,' Elician informs his friend.

'Did he tell you why he killed me?' Lio demands.

'You were in the way,' Cat replies. It is difficult to turn in the saddle to look at the prince. They sit too close. When he rotates in his seat, his shoulder brushes Elician's chest, and his face is barely a handspan from the prince's – crossing a boundary of impropriety that any self-respecting Alelunen would balk at. He feels Elician's warm breath across his cheeks. Sees his lips too close, the carefully maintained beard that curves lovingly around his chin and jaw. 'Why is healing someone forbidden?' Cat asks again.

Lio squawks, indignant at his initial response, but Cat doesn't pay the man much mind. Elician is answering his question, calm and serene. 'Healing isn't forbidden at all. But resurrection or bringing something to life, such as with a baby, is.' His tone doesn't match the tension in his body. He glosses over how the strongest, most impressive power a Giver has – the literal opposite of everything a Reaper is known for – is something that is rejected by a law his own father enforces.

'The baby is not brought to life; it is already there,' Cat says slowly.

'It is a cultural difference, perhaps,' Elician replies. 'Until first breath, it is not yet considered alive. Any action taken to it, then, is an act of bringing it to life. Givers cannot interfere.'

'Why did you do it, then? Heal or . . . give life to her child?' Cat asks. It is not what he means to ask. *Why rebel? Why ignore the edict you are meant to live by? Why not turn away?* Answers to those questions would be closer to what he wants to hear. But instead, he simply qualifies his question with, 'Why her?'

Elician's dark lashes flick downwards, half shielding his brown eyes from view. He frowns. The corners of his lips dip into the soft edges of his beard. 'Why not her?' he asks in turn.

To answer a question with a question is a lazy form of rhetoric that should never be utilized as a defence, the Queen of Alelune had once told Cat. He had just murdered someone on her orders. Her court had averted their eyes, pretending they could not see him, for he was not meant to be seen or acknowledged. He had died to become a Reaper, and dead things do not gain the privileges of the living. He is denied their attention, their understanding, their consideration. And no one would ever admit to seeing his face. *If you are incapable of saying what you mean,* his queen had said, ignoring a room that ignored him in turn, *then don't say anything at all.*

And yet.

Why not her?

Cat adjusts his seat. Returns to facing forward. Elician doesn't seem to expect an answer, and Cat has none to give him. The question he asked is the only answer that matters. It lingers. Festers.

Kassandra was no one. Her clothes were poor, her intentions less than honourable. She had admitted to breaking some kind of Soleben law that barely makes sense to Cat but everyone else seems to take hypocritically seriously depending on the circumstance. She had admitted it to a prince she had not been able to recognize, which only confuses Cat further. *Why* had she not recognized her prince? Why had Elician hidden his pendant, kept to himself, talked like someone lesser? Lower? Her impact on the world is and will be minimal . . . and yet he had chosen to help her anyway.

It was illegal, and it clearly could have consequences.

He had done it still. Cat's queen would have condemned such an act.

'Look,' Elician says, pointing out over Cat's shoulder with his right hand. 'A pileated tree hopper.'

It is a green bird, with a blood-red crown and spindly little legs. It hops vertically up and down the trunk of a large fir, tilting its head this way and that, listening for bugs. 'Damn it,' Lio curses, falling back into the casual ease of a game that he lets Elician win.

'Is it common for you,' Cat murmurs, low enough that Lio won't overhear as he rides ahead, 'to heal people like that?'

'No,' Elician replies, just as quiet. 'Perhaps you're a bad influence on me.' That sounds like a joke, though Cat cannot find any trace of humour in the tone. 'I've healed more people since I met you than in three years of war.'

'You never healed those soldiers? Truly?'

'Truly.'

'So why break the rules now?'

Lio points out a matted grey land sparrow. An imaginary point is tallied on a scoreboard that no one pays too much attention to. The numbers are as transient as the prince's slipping judicial devotion.

Cat's question is too close to the last one Elician dodged. Cat does not expect a response. He doesn't deserve one.

And yet, in the brief moments before that pileated tree hopper flaps its green wings and flutters back into view, Elician replies anyway. 'Because I'm tired of seeing people in pain. Just once, I want everyone to get the happy endings they deserve.'

'Will you be in trouble?'

'If anyone should find out, undoubtedly.'

What kind of punishments does Soleb enact? He cannot imagine Elician being frogmarched into a dark cell. Held down by his wrists, ordered to obey and submit as a burning coal approaches his face to mark him to all the world as an outsider meant to be feared.

Once, long ago, Ranio Ragden had promised Cat a life beyond the bars of the Reaper cells he had made his home. Sitting in silence, ignoring the game that Elician and Lio play with an almost forced delight, he ponders the question that he has never dared to speak out loud.

If everything we do for the country means only imprisonment or pain, is it worth it?

He doubts the prince knows the answer to that question, but more than that: Cat fears hearing denial on the prince's tongue. At least in the fragile space granted by the unknowing, some form of hope still remains. He is, he realizes, much like Kassandra in that.

Lio, however, holds no such hesitation. He scoffs loudly, turning in his saddle to look at his prince. 'What kind of king do you want to be, Elician? The kind who knowingly allows his ailing subject to continue on until they suffer heartbreak and loss? Or the kind who helps them despite the risk to himself?'

'What good is it to help one person now if it means I cannot help others in the future?' Elician asks shortly.

'Because you *can* help her now,' Lio replies, just as short. 'And you do not know what will happen later. You did good, Your Highness.

You always do good, and it's why I will support you regardless of your crown.'

'It doesn't feel good enough.'

'Does it need to feel good, to be good?' Cat asks, startling himself by asking the question out loud. Elician meets his eyes, lips parting in surprise. But his words seem to have failed him. He can only stare down at Cat while Lio sighs loudly.

'I can't believe I'm saying this, but listen to the assassin,' Lio says. 'It doesn't matter if it feels good or not. Do it because it is right, then worry about what happens next when it comes. It's how we ended up with an assassin to lug around in the first place.'

'And we could always use more of those, I'm sure,' Elician says, finally smiling somewhat. 'Tree hopper.' He jerks his chin towards a branch above their heads.

'Doesn't count!' Lio shouts. 'That's the same one as before.'

'Prove it.' That smile only grows bigger. As if his heart is somehow more at peace with just a few words of support.

He is, Cat thinks, *desperate to make everyone else happy.* It is not what he would have expected; nothing about this experience so far has been what he had expected. He doesn't know how *he* feels about that either.

Their journey drags on beyond the ridges of the mountains separating the west from Soleb's far flatter east. Fewer civilians are found along the roads. Those they do pass are quickly bustling along to whichever home or business they're hoping to reach before nightfall. Their steps only cross for mere moments, and never again at night.

Elician still sleeps poorly. He sits up by the fire, peering out into the woods as if searching for something that never appears. He cuts a fine figure, there, with orange light flickering across his face, threading charming gold in amongst the black of his hair. Cat falls asleep before the prince on most nights. There is little point in trying to stay awake. He meant what he said. He does not know where to go now, and he has no intention of escaping.

He cannot just return to Alelune. It would serve no purpose at all. And yet . . . to wilfully let himself be taken prisoner chafes at a memory best left buried, a pride that has no place in his life as it stands. This is an opportunity. Foolish as it all is. This is an opportunity spawned from the simple fact that he had been sent to kill an unkillable prince. There is nothing else that can be done on that front. Not even he can undo the will of the gods.

Cat lies down each night cognizant of the loose bindings on his wrists and the genuine lack of effort that would be required to run away and never be found. He closes his eyes rather than plotting his escape. And he dreams. He dreams of sunrises over mountainscapes. Birds he doesn't know the names of. A golden prince of Soleb, shrouded in light, smiling as if he has been instructed all his life that smiling is what must be done but still hasn't managed to perfect the trick. He dreams of his family promising that it is all right to leave them behind.

He wakes to a hand at his shoulder. He gasps, jerking back. It's Elician.

The prince crouches at Cat's side, holding up one finger to his lips. *Quiet.* Cat's body stills. His lungs pause, holding in all the air he's swallowed. Carefully, Elician helps sit him up. Lio is still asleep. The fire has burned out. There is light though. Strange light, flickering above them. Elician points up and Cat looks.

The sky is falling.

Thousands of bright streaks stream across the heavens, each star above swiping from right to left as if they have better places to be than their usual celestial homes. 'It's the Gods' Tears,' Elician murmurs softly, glancing quickly to make sure he has not woken Lio.

It is not called that in Alelune. There, the star shower is *Death's*

Rain. It happens every year, but often the summer storms inhibit anyone from seeing the sky beyond the clouds. He has only seen it properly once – long before he became a Reaper. Every other year the storms had blocked out the sky. Even on that night, rolling thunder had crashed for so long that Cat had fallen asleep waiting for something magical to happen. Then, in the hours before dawn, the sky had finally broken, and his father had woken him up to see. It had been glorious.

'It's sacred in Alelune, isn't it?' Elician keeps his voice low. He shifts, his arm settling in against Cat's side. 'We don't celebrate it here, but I remember learning . . . you have a festival for it, don't you?' He seems to be searching for a word, then finds it. '*Tomestange?*'

Cat nods. A night of change.

A night where everyone wears masks and plays pretend. Where some people swap masks and costumes multiple times in the night, slipping in and out of existence on a whim. It was the one night a year he had been allowed to slip from the Reaper cells and mingle amongst the people, so long as every part of him was hidden away; no one could know who or what he was. He could play games and eat good food, and no one would ever know.

He closes his eyes, then rubs his fingers against them. When he opens them again, he looks towards the prince.

'I want to ask you something,' Elician murmurs in Lunae, phrasing academic and precise. 'You don't have to respond in any way, really. But I wanted to ask.' He runs a hand through his disobedient curls. They spring back into position, unrepentant. 'Do you think . . . it would have changed things if you *had* killed me? I mean, do you think it would have ended the war?' He meets Cat's eyes, earnest and hopeful. The prince of his nation, and he almost sounds willing to die for that nation so long as it would help. Starlight streaks across Elician's face.

Cat does not have to answer. There is no need to. He knows full well that it is something that his queen would not approve of. And yet – it is the night of change, and Elician is being too foolish for a response to make any difference at all.

'No,' he murmurs back in Soleben. Elician's lips part and his eyes widen. He leans in like he wants to start talking more immediately, but Cat presses on. His throat is scratchy and his voice is hoarse, still thick from sleep, but he swallows and continues. 'But it is what my queen declared necessary.'

'Do you think it's necessary?'

'I think . . .' Cat pauses. It has been a very long time since he has told anyone outside his family about what he *thinks*. Often, what he thinks are things that will get him into trouble. Better to stay silent than to encourage wrath. But Elician sits across from him with a kind of earnestness that demands honesty. 'I think,' Cat starts again, 'that my queen wanted you dead from the moment your father threw a party the night her son died.' Elician flinches. Cat licks his lips, swallows to wet his dry throat. The conjugation for what he wants to say next is more difficult. He pauses, running the sentence through his head a few times before carefully saying, 'It did not matter if it would have ended the war or not. She wanted you dead. And so, here I am.'

Elician tears his eyes away. He looks up towards the stars. Some slash across the sky quickly, point to point in mere seconds. Others take their time in their journey, spiralling over the arc of the world at their own pace. 'That's . . . fair,' Elician murmurs. 'I remember when we learned of Stello Alest's death.' Cat blinks in surprise. It was the right name and the right title. The heir to the throne of Alelune is always a woman, and her title is always *Stella*. But Alest had not been a woman, and the title had been uncomfortably altered to fit him until a sister could be born. None ever had. And still, despite the irregularity, twelve years after the tragedy, Elician has used both the right title and name without thinking when it is commonly butchered by others. Cat often heard people bemoaning their dear *stella's* death during the festivals, and they were proper Alelunens who knew better.

'We were at a family gathering,' Elician murmurs. 'Close friends and relatives only. Lio and I were in the garden . . . my sister, she wasn't adopted then, her father was still alive, but he was my father's best friend and – it doesn't matter. She was only two or three at the time, and we were swinging her about by her arms when the news came. My father announced it. Picked my sister up and tossed her in the air to make her laugh. Everyone started cheering and clapping and . . . I couldn't understand why everyone was so happy. Just a few years before, we'd signed a treaty with Alelune to ensure Marias could go back and be with his son. And that same son . . . Alest was nine years old when he died a horrible, painful, awful death, and they were celebrating it. I still don't understand why they did.'

'Well, no one in Alelune could understand why you celebrated it either.'

Elician flinches again. He stares up at the sky, jaw clenched and fingers curling at his sides. 'I had a dream, you know. It was foolish, probably. I didn't even fully understand the River Wars back then. Fighting over the place where Life breathed all of existence into being – it felt silly. I thought it was mean that Anslian captured a prince in order to force Alelune to give up the river and . . . I thought everyone would just be happier if we gave it back.'

That does not make sense. Cat shakes his head. *Nothing he says ever makes sense.* Then he asks, slowly, 'You wanted to give the Bask back to Alelune?'

'I wanted to share it. Surely, since it means so much to both of our people, we could share the river?' Elician laughs bitterly. 'I was a child. And then, when the Stello died and everyone celebrated, it felt like there would never be a chance to fix things. That it was beyond something I could do on my own. Then the war started again, and now it's hopeless, I suppose.'

'The Queen has another son.'

'Gillage? He's what . . . thirteen? How many more people will die before he is old enough to sit across the table from me? And would he even want to? At this point, I doubt it.'

'You want this war to end, truly?' Cat asks.

'Almost more than anything else I have ever wanted.'

'What else have you wanted?'

Elician shrugs, bites his lip. He watches the stars and Cat doubts he will say anything more. But he does, eventually. When the crescent moon has shifted in the sky and the stars seem to be streaking less desperately, he says, 'Kreuzfurt . . . it really is a prison, you know. Regardless of what Lio or Anslian said, it *is* a prison. It's just meant for people like us.'

'Cages underground?' Cat asks, unbothered. It is what Alelune does – why should Soleb be different?

'Cages above ground, with invisible bars that you cannot see until you're already behind the padlocked gate. When I'm king, I'll open that gate. Permanently.'

'Then where would you keep me?'

'I told you already: you could go home.' To the underground. To the Reaper cells. To continue following his queen's orders until the day she dies and Gillage takes her place. Then, wherever Gillage sees fit to send him. Probably somewhere worse. 'Or . . . wherever you want, in truth. Once I'm king, all the rest won't matter.'

Cat stares up at the sky. Stars are still falling, and when they cross in front of the moon, it almost looks like they are dancing together, shimmying this way and that across a backdrop of black. Ranio, Brielle . . . even, he suspects, his queen, had wanted better for him. Once.

Elician's fingers twitch, then reach out into the space between them. Cat flinches, pulling back as the prince's hand lingers just above the black scar spanning his cheek. Elician hesitates, fingers curling inwards as he sheepishly murmurs, 'I could try to heal it, if you wanted.'

'No one would be able to know what I was if you did,' Cat points out. Elician seems to like being told useless, obvious things. If Elician were to fulfil this incredible offer, Cat wouldn't need to hide his face each time they passed someone on the street. He wouldn't need to pretend. Not here, and certainly not in Alelune.

'Do you want it gone?'

It has never been something Cat has thought would happen. The moment the scar started to fade, the guards in Alelune's capital city of Alerae branded his cheek once more. Gloved hands pinned his wrists to the ground, his head held still by fingers in his hair. Orders. So many orders. Stop moving. Stop screaming. Just obey. Behave. Do as they say. The same orders, the same trauma, playing on repeat the same as it had every few years since the moment he had first become a Reaper. It is a violence that haunts him in a way nothing else ever has. A violence without end. To remove the scar would only mean that soon it would be reapplied. When the war is over. When he goes back to Alelune, and the cells underground.

And still, he nods.

Elician's fingers are cool, his skin smooth. Cat's eyes flutter. He leans into the touch, breathing through an instinctive panic and relaxing at the simple notion that he *can* be touched at all. By flesh, and not fire. By tender hope, and a heart that seems keen to heal all that is forbidden to be made whole. Elician cups his cheek. Cat almost imagines his magic working too. His skin warms beneath the gentle caress. But when Elician pulls back, Cat can still feel the tight flesh tugging awkwardly at his jaw. The scar is still there. 'It's not . . . it's not a normal wound,' Elician murmurs.

If it were, I'd have healed it instantaneously myself, Cat thinks wearily. He shrugs. It doesn't matter. He had not expected it to work. And perhaps it is better that it hadn't. There will be no need to reapply it . . . at least for another few years. It will take that long for his body to finally adjust. And by then . . . it will be more than time for it to be reapplied. Nothing has changed.

'I'm sorry.'

'You didn't do it.'

'No, I didn't.' For some reason, Elician still looks terribly sad about that. Cat's stomach clenches uncomfortably. He rubs at his face, pushing at the rippled skin with his knuckles.

I don't want to talk about this, he thinks, biting at his bottom lip. 'You know, I wanted to kill you for that party too.'

'I'm sorry.' He apologizes far too much for a prince.

'It wasn't your party,' Cat mutters. 'But . . . I'm glad that when I finally did have a chance to kill you, you didn't die.' This time, Elician smiles, and it's as bright as the sun. Cat shakes his head, stomach squirming at the sight. No one should be that happy about something as unimportant as Cat's opinion. But Elician *is* pleased by it. Brilliantly so.

'Can I ask you something else?' Elician leans closer, licking his lips. His curls slip into his face, partly obscuring one of his eyes. 'What's your name? Really?'

There is no point in telling him. Not now. The name Elician has given him is a meaningless nonsense word, something born from the monsters that stalk the woods in the night, never seen but always feared. If he has to have a name, there is a kind of poetic irony to being called by this one. His queen will not be happy with him, but then again, it has been a long time since he has made her happy. She should be used to the disappointment by now.

Slowly, he holds out his hand. Elician takes it. 'My name is Cat.' It is, after all, a night of change. He can be whoever he wants.

CHAPTER FIVE

Fenlia

A sparrow crashes into the glass wall of the House of the Wanting and falls into the red snapper bushes at the base of the tower. Fen flinches at the tell-tale *thunk*, the noise startling her out of her crying fit. She wipes her eyes, twisting to see where the bird fell. She had thought she would be safe here, hidden amongst the brambles and twigs, to cry with no witnesses or interruptions. But Death likes to take things whenever the opportunity arises. And sometimes that includes little sparrows who do not know better than to fly towards glass towers.

Slowly, turning so her skirt hem comes untucked from beneath her and her knees do not get caught, she rolls to the side and reaches through the prickers and thorns of the shrubbery. Her skin is scratched, but it heals quickly. Ruby-red lines vanish over her sun-darkened flesh. Her fingers wrap around the broken bird's body. She pulls it closer, cupping it to her chest.

Its neck had broken when it hit the windowpane. She turns it between her fingers, remembering her anatomy lessons well. She smooths out its wings, moving each feather gently back into place. Birds are fragile creatures, small and tremulous and weak. Sparrows especially. They die so easily over the smallest of things.

Leaning down, Fen presses her lips to the sparrow's burgundy crown. *Come back*, she wishes. It takes a moment. Then the sparrow's heartbeat flutters within its chest. Its legs start to twitch, its wings shift. She uncups her hands and holds her palm out in front of her, watching as the sparrow gets its bearings. It looks up at her. It chirps.

There is some seed in her pocket. She likes to bring it with her in case she can tempt any of the birds of Kreuzfurt to sit and stay for a while. If it stays, she will feed it some and consider it a new friend. But the sparrow hops on her palm once, twice, then flaps its wings and flies away. She watches until it is out of sight, chirping bright and happy, and oblivious of its recent demise. She wishes it would take her with it next time. Anything would be better than this.

'Still practising on animals?' a voice asks. Fen wipes the remains of her tears from her eyes. She sniffs loudly, indelicately, and wipes again. Then she leans her head back and stares up at the tall, dark-skinned woman walking towards her. Zinnitzia has been the lead cleric of Kreuzfurt's Givers for over a thousand years. She is a humourless woman who suffers no indignities and despises all complaints.

'At least I could bring *that* back to life,' Fen says, crossing her arms over her chest and staying there in the dirt. She has no interest in standing, bowing or showing any sign of decorum. She wants to be left alone.

'Resurrection is not a trifle to be played with,' Zinnitzia tells her. She has told Fen this before. Perhaps she believes saying it over and over again will have a different effect in the end; perhaps there is a magic number of possibilities and one day Fen will have heard her condemnation enough times to finally believe it. If so, Fen imagines there are several centuries' worth of lectures yet to be had between them.

'It was just a bird,' she murmurs. She stares at her knees. Her dress is filthy, the pure white folds of fabric crusted with dust and soil. A streak of green slides across one particular section from where she must have rubbed up against the grass too hard as she crawled into position. She cannot find it in herself to care.

'I'm not talking about the bird,' Zinnitzia informs her.

Fen closes her eyes. She is a Giver. And Givers are meant to heal the sick, tend to the wounded, restore health to those in need and prolong the lives of those desperate for salvation. She is a bad Giver. 'I tried,' she whispers. Her voice cracks. Her fingers tighten around her arms. 'I tried to save her.'

For three weeks, Fen had been working to heal a young girl at the House of the Wanting. She had kept her hands on the child's body. She had held her arm, her face, her shoulders. She had whispered prayers to Life, had begged and pleaded and cried. She had sat there, under the increasingly despairing eyes of the child's parents. And nothing had changed.

'We cannot save every person who comes to us,' Zinnitzia says.

'No one ever dies under your care,' Fen snaps back. 'Or under Ava's, or Lorelei's, or–'

'Yes, you can name the whole House, I'm sure.' Zinnitzia removes a fine linen cloth from the folds of her dress. She dabs the sweat from her brow and then tucks the cloth back into hiding.

'Any of you could have saved that girl,' Fen says.

'She was not given to *us* to heal,' Zinnitzia replies. 'She was *your* charge. It was *your* responsibility.'

'And I failed.' She always fails. In the three years since she first arrived in Kreuzfurt, she has not healed a single person. Not a skinned knee, not a bloody nose, not a cold. Nothing. And now someone has died. A little girl has died.

'And you failed.'

Fen's eyes burn. She blinks hard, desperate to keep the tears back.

'I could have brought her back,' Fen says. 'I could have brought her back and she could have gone home and–'

'We do not resurrect the dead here,' Zinnitzia says. 'All things die in the end. If our god wills it then that is what is to be. We prolong *life*, Fen. We do not stop Death from taking her due.'

Death takes more than her due. Time and time again, Death slips in between the cracks of everything, yanking away all those who least expect it. For all the pilgrims who make their way to Kreuzfurt looking for a chance to live at the House of the Wanting, there are equally those who go to Kreuzfurt's other tower: its second House, the House of the Unwanting. And those individuals never come back.

Fen is no Reaper. She does not kill with a touch, nor does she yearn for the possibility. But if she cannot save anyone, and an ill child is left in her care, then she is no better than a Reaper if they still die as a result. The child should have gone to the other House rather than be cursed to suffer and languish for three weeks because of Fen. No one should be forced to die and *stay dead* in the House of the Wanting. Not when Fen could bring them back, could give them a new life.

'The only people that it's *truly* illegal to resurrect are members of the royal family.' No one wants an immortal on the throne ruling for ever. 'But that child *wasn't* a royal. If I can bring someone back, why shouldn't I?' Fen asks quietly.

'You should read your history more carefully,' Zinnitzia replies. 'Kreuzfurt's own founder, Shawshank, played the game you're playing. And it ended in *chaos*! Cities overrun by a never-receding population, resource shortages that led to continued suffering, illness, plague and–'

'It's one person, not a whole city.'

'It starts with one person, and it ends with a whole city.' Zinnitzia waves her hand, motioning for Fen to get up. 'You and your brother are unique. Resurrecting human beings, pulling their souls back from Death, it comes easily to you. But it isn't the goal a Giver should aspire to; it is something many will never learn. *Healing* is more beneficial and useful than resurrection ever will be. There are possibilities you have not even considered yet, because you spend your time wallowing about your failures in the dirt.'

'What other possibilities *are* there? I've *never* been able to fix things.'

'Just because you've never done something before doesn't mean it's impossible to do so. And just because you *can* do something doesn't mean you *should*. There is much about being a Giver you know nothing about. There are more possibilities than you can imagine, and *this*–' She waves her hand judiciously. 'This will get you nowhere.'

The tears burn hotter in Fen's eyes. She swats at them one final time, then stands. She pats her filthy dress uselessly, tilting her chin up at her mentor in defiance. 'Leitja died four hours ago,' she says. 'She was six years old and was *mine* to fix and I failed. And I'm not going to *apologize for being upset*!'

'Don't,' Zinnitzia replies. 'But do apologize for being sorry for yourself and not bothering to do better. Be upset. Get upset. Move on.'

'It's only been *four hours*!'

'There are one hundred and seventy-eight Givers in Kreuzfurt, Fenlia. Believe what you like, but all of us have lost someone before. We have lost *many* people before. But we live here, work here, in service to the crown and Life himself. All we do is for the betterment of this kingdom, its people and our god. It's an honour, a great responsibility that–'

'I don't want it.' It hurts too much.

Zinnitzia sighs loudly. She shakes her head, then flicks her wrist, physically casting off her arguments. 'Your brother sent a letter,' she says, reaching back into the folds of her dress and pulling out a small roll of paper. She holds it out between them, and Fen takes it. She unrolls it and reads the lines. 'He's coming,' Zinnitzia informs her, even as Fen memorizes the information. 'Dry your tears, change your clothes, and be prepared to receive him. He should arrive by nightfall.'

She stares at the paper and her words tumble out. 'Is he . . . because of this?'

'Don't be stupid,' Zinnitzia says. 'It takes weeks to get to the border from here. He has no idea what you have or have not been doing. He's not coming for *you*, but he is coming. So, go. Get ready.'

'Is the war over?'

'Doubtful. Ask him when he comes.' Zinnitzia takes a step back, then frowns. Her lips purse. Her nose scrunches. 'Fenlia . . . people die. Leitja's death wasn't your fault. It's what our god wanted, that's all.'

Fen's fingers curl into fists. Her brother's letter crinkles in her palm. She spits out a curse and says, 'Then you should have given her to a Reaper and put her out of her misery when she first arrived,' before turning and walking to the residential quarters. Zinnitzia says nothing as she departs. Fen is grateful for the reprieve.

It is late by the time Elician reaches Kreuzfurt. Late enough that Fen had nearly fallen asleep at her bedroom window waiting for him. But as the moon rises high in the sky, the great wooden gate to Kreuzfurt's temple opens and two riders slowly lead their horses in. There are no banners, no horns, no announcements, but it does not matter. No one is permitted into the compound this late. No one, except for a royal retinue.

Even with the stress and anxiety of the day, glee bubbles up at the notion of seeing Elician. Fen quickly adjusts her gown and hair. The dress is one her cousin Adalei had sent her from the capital. All Kreuzfurt Givers must wear white, but the style is left to their discretion. Fen's gown has a bold cut down her front that her other gowns had not dared to attempt. Her arms are bare, allowing her to burn sun patterns onto her skin every few weeks. And best of all, a golden 'v' of embroidery dips down from her hips so her torso seems longer. She feels like a woman in this gown, an adult who cannot be chastised or talked down to by anyone. Not even Zinnitzia.

The hem is slightly too long, a problem that should be resolved in a few months, and one that's easily managed by delicately holding the skirt up in one hand as she walks. She uses both hands to hold it tonight, rushing a bit faster than usual so she can meet her brother at the courtyard below. Glow bugs light her way through the fruit trees and the lemongrass.

Elician and Lio are both standing by Kreuzfurt's entrance. The gates are closed and locked behind them. A stable hand is seeing to their horses. She is the last to arrive. Zinnitzia is already there, as is Marina.

Marina is taller than most women. She wears the standard attire of every Reaper in Soleb: every inch of her skin, besides her face, is hidden behind layers of thick black fabric. Even her hands are shielded with gloves. And she has a hood, sewn to the back of her uniform, that comes up and over her face should she need an extra layer of protection. She rarely does. Marina has lived for two thousand years. She knows how to interact with a world she cannot touch directly.

She bows to Elician. One hand is pressed to her heart in a closed fist, and a small silver ball-bell around her wrist jingles as she bends towards him. All Reapers wear such bells to ensure they can be identified from a long way away and warn all who hear them not to approach. Elician ignores its tinkling entirely, mirroring Marina's bow and leaning in close to say something Fen cannot hear. They rise in unison, and when they do, Elician motions to someone Fen had not seen at first. A young man wearing ill-fitting clothes, trousers rolled up at his ankles and a tunic hanging comically large about his body. He even wears a pair of gloves that seem too large for his hands, and his wrists are bound by a thick coil of rope. *A prisoner?* Fen wonders. *Here?*

'Little eyes and ears should announce themselves if they're going to snoop,' Lio says suddenly, loudly. Fen winces as everyone turns to look at her.

'I am not so little anymore, Wilion,' Fen says, drawing herself up to her full height before meeting her brother's eyes and dipping into a customary bow.

Elician grins and opens his arms wide. 'No, you most certainly aren't. Look at you!' She hurries to him, throwing her arms around his neck. He leans back, picking her up and swinging her through the air. She laughs against his throat, pressing her cheek to his skin. 'I swear to the gods, you're going to be taller than me one day!'

'That's the plan!' she tells him as he settles her back to her feet. He laughs and pats her head, messing up her braid as a few strands slip loose. But as he steps back, his eyes fall towards her neckline and his smile falters.

'What are you *wearing*?'

'Adalei gave it to me,' she snaps, cheeks burning. Her stomach twists. *If he's going to come all this way just to make fun of me–*

Lio steps forward, nearly stomping on Elician's toes, and bows. 'She has wonderful taste,' he says. 'You look lovely, Princess.' She waits for a similar compliment from her brother, but his lips are too pursed to possibly offer such a thing.

She turns towards the stranger loitering at Elician's elbow. No introduction has been provided; he does not greet her himself either. 'Who's this, then?' she asks, tilting her chin up and waiting for a proper explanation.

'Can't you tell?' her brother asks. 'It's a nightcat.' It is most certainly *not* a nightcat. She says as much too.

But before she can argue further, Marina intervenes. 'If we're going to do this,' she says in a deep alto that reverberates in the still night air, 'we're going to do it inside.'

'Do what?' Fen asks, but the party is already in motion. Elician puts an arm around the prisoner's shoulders and leans down to whisper something in his ear. Catching the side of her skirt in her hand, Fen hurries after them.

She expects them to turn towards the House of the Wanting; that is where every royal guest or visitor is brought to. But they do not. Instead, they turn towards the Reaper's tower: the House of the *Un*wanting, with all its unsavoury possibilities within. Fen's mouth dries. She calls her brother's name, but he does not reply.

'Keep going, little princess,' Lio tells her quietly.

'But . . .' Only the dead enter here. The dead or slowly dying.

'Keep going,' he repeats.

Fen shivers and nods. She swallows thickly as they cross the threshold. The House of the Unwanting is cold and dreary, dark and lifeless. It is structurally the same as the House of the Wanting: all the floors match, the glass walls and mirrored decorations all glisten and shine to the same effect as its sister tower. Yet the torches do not seem to shine quite as bright. The shadows they cast feel longer. And, worse: an unpleasant sensation lurks in the air here. A sickly, unnatural otherness prickles at the back of her neck, encouraging her to try to fix what cannot be fixed. What, as Zinnitzia has imparted on her time and time again, she is not *allowed* to fix.

She would much rather take Elician back to the residential quarters, or even the House of the Wanting if they *have* to be in one of the towers. But Marina seems determined on this path, and no one argues with her. The bell on her wrist chimes delicately as she moves, guiding them to a grand room. It matches the gallery where guests wait to be seen in the House of the Wanting.

Fen tries to imagine what such a room could be used for here. Executions, perhaps. Or sacrifices. Whatever it is that people with a natural inclination to kill anything they touch do when they're not meandering Kreuzfurt like a pack of ghouls all in black. Not that she's ever seen it for herself. As a Giver she has never needed to enter this House. As anyone with any kind of sense, she has never wanted to. The farther she can keep herself from the Reapers, the better.

There is a strange smell in the air. She cannot identify it, but it is bitter and sour, like mushrooms growing in the dark crevasse of a cave. Her stomach churns.

She glances at the prisoner walking entirely unbothered at Elician's side. She has never seen an execution before – she has always been forbidden from attending. She has heard stories though. Gruesome stories. *What did he do?* It has to have been something bad. *Something truly bad.* After all, nothing short of true wickedness deserves this place.

They stop walking, right in the centre of the room. Elician unbinds his prisoner's wrists, and Marina turns to stand in front of them both. She reaches for the prisoner's face, bell ringing at her wrist. He flinches, but she ignores it, encircling the jut of his chin with her gloved fingers, silently daring him to complain.

'Were any of your men touched?' she asks as she tilts the prisoner's head this way and that with motions smooth as silk. Her limbs are fluid and agile, and she guides her hand with a painter's flourish, each action precise. As she turns his face, Fen sees a large black scar on one of his cheeks. She had been standing to his left and had not seen it before.

'No,' Elician says, though Fen can no longer remember the question. 'He killed Lio when we first found him, but Lio checked with the physicians before we left. There didn't seem to be anyone who died from a Reaper; all the bodies we collected were obviously killed during the melee proper.'

'He's a *Reaper*?' Fen asks, even as Zinnitzia issues a stinging rebuke at Elician for resurrecting Lio once again. The prisoner flinches at Fen's question. He tries to pull his chin free from Marina's grip, but she is holding on too tight. She does not let him go, merely hisses something under her breath that seems to force him to stillness. Fen dares a step closer, curiosity winning out. 'Did he get *made* on the battlefield?' Reapers only find out they are Reapers after they die for the first time. Waking up in the middle of combat would be a horrifying experience.

'No,' Marina replies. 'No, he's still young, but he's been a Reaper for about eleven or twelve years now.' She says something then in Lunae, the language of their enemy. The vowels slip off her tongue like water in a spring. The prisoner nods, and Marina releases his chin. She pets his hair in response.

'That new?' Elician asks, startled. 'That would mean he . . . would have been a child when he first died.'

'How old *are* you?' Lio asks.

'Twenty,' Marina answers for him, seemingly confident in her assessment. Fen can't see how she could be so certain, but the prisoner doesn't deny the assumption. He offers a vague gesture in agreement and Fen shakes her head.

'But he *can't* be twenty,' Fen says. 'He's so *little*!' Fen will be fifteen in four months, and she is already half a hand taller than the prisoner. He barely comes up to Elician's shoulder and Elician is twenty-three. Every Reaper and Giver who is turned young will continue ageing until they reach full maturity, then their age is locked in place until the gods deem it is time for them to die once more. If he is still this short despite being older . . . he is never going to get any taller. *What a horrible fate.*

Lio snorts loudly, covering his mouth with his hand. He says, 'Size isn't everything,' around a giggle that has Elician snapping at him to be quiet and Zinnitzia rolling her eyes at the ceiling.

'He's slight, malnourished, and used to making himself look small,' Marina says, a hint of exasperation in her tone. 'But with this . . .' She rubs her thumb against the scar. 'I'm certain. It's a shame. If he had died later, he might have had some sort of childhood at least.' She says it with so little emotion, Fen doubts it really is a shame to Marina.

'But how can you *tell?*' Fen asks. 'And why is his face all messed up? Shouldn't he have healed that already?'

'Usually, yes. But this . . . In Alelune they burn the face of a Reaper with the bones of the dead. Those coals infiltrate the skin, and the carbon becomes stained and frozen in their bodies.'

Fen stares, stunned by the news. Her eyes fall to the scar and stay there. Nausea burns in her throat.

'It's a barbaric tradition,' Elician murmurs.

'Fresh skin cells *will* eventually grow and push it out,' Marina continues, 'but it's a very slow process. Slower than usual. Alelune needs to redo the brand every few years to make sure it stays this dark. It's how I guessed his age, and how new a Reaper he is. The circle is not perfect. It's been redone at least five times, but if he had been any older, I'm not sure I *would* have been able to tell one way or another.' She looks at the Reaper as if she expects him to comment, but he doesn't. He stays as quiet as he had been from the outset.

'Can he understand us?' Fen asks.

Lio rolls his eyes with such profound irritation that Fen is startled at the display of impropriety. Usually, he is more polite when in public. 'Oh, he can understand us just fine. And he talks too. But only when he *wants* to.'

'Don't be jealous,' Elician teases.

Fen doesn't understand. 'Why would he be jealous?'

'They didn't get a chance to speak much on the road, that's all,' Elician replies.

'An honour reserved for our prince,' Lio adds with an air of affected disappointment.

'You spoke?' Marina cuts in. All three men turn towards her in unison. 'I have heard stories of the conditions in the Reaper cells. Speaking at all, in any language, was highly discouraged. To the point where the ability to do so any longer was often . . . well, uncertain.'

'How would they stop anyone from speaking?' Fen blurts out before her imagination comes up with several possibilities, some more gruesome than the others. She hopes Marina will provide a far less violent option, but instead she asks the Reaper something in Lunae. Fen has never been good at the language, avoiding her lessons where she can. She has never seen much of a point in the endless hours of conjugation tables and diphthong practice when there are other things to work on. She catches a few of the words, but not the sentence as a whole.

The Alelunen has no such problem, replying with a simple, 'More or less,' that Fen learned very early on in her required lessons. His accent is just slightly different from Marina's, and it helps that he speaks slowly, giving her time to identify and translate the words, even without additional context. Still, she wonders what Marina had asked in the first place.

Lio, though, seems to have understood far better than her. 'That's barbaric,' he repeats in Soleben, all but grinding out each word.

The Reaper glances at him, head tilting as he asks, 'Do you care?' in slow but perfect Soleben.

'I wasn't advocating for your torture either, you know,' Lio responds. 'I didn't like our options, but I still brought you here too.'

'Yes,' he agrees. 'You did.'

'And *why* did you?' Marina asks, cutting to the heart of the problem Fen wants to know the answer to as well.

'He would be a liability on a battlefield,' Elician replies, unflappable and calm. 'It's not like I can just send him off back to Alelune now, can I?' He lifts one hand and settles it at the midpoint of his prisoner's spine. 'He never offered a name, and so we have been calling him Cat.'

Marina shakes her head. 'This is not a Reaper from Soleb, Your Highness, he's an Alelunen Reaper. His loyalties and his life have been dedicated to serving Alelune. Letting him loose in Kreuzfurt is asking for trouble.'

'Are you saying you cannot manage *one* Reaper?' Elician asks.

'I got rid of *you* when you became problematic too, Your Highness.'

Fen gasps at the sarcasm, but Elician laughs.

'The crown got rid of me *for* you, if I remember correctly,' Elician says. 'Besides, maybe you can help endear him to our country. You were Alelunen once, something convinced you to stay . . . besides Zinnitzia's charming company, of course.'

'The world was very different when I came to Soleb for the first time,' she says. 'And I had very different reasons for doing so.' Reasons she rarely discusses. For the longest lived of any Reaper Fen knows of, Marina shows remarkably little interest in talking about her history or why Death has seen fit to let her continue onwards with no end in sight.

'You still chose to stay, and as we've already discussed: sending him back to Alelune may not be in his best interests at this point either.'

'Is he a prisoner or a refugee, Prince?' Zinnitzia asks.

'Both, either. To be decided later,' he replies. 'A choice not yet finalized, and not mine to make in full.'

It is a response that neither Marina nor Zinnitzia looks entirely pleased about. Fen doesn't blame them; she wouldn't want anything to do with this decision either. Her brother may be willing to consider all possibilities, but as far as Fen can tell, there is no benefit or value in being so lax with *Cat*. He is a Reaper. Reapers do not belong in any type of society in the first place, but to be an Alelunen Reaper is far worse than that. He does not belong in Soleb. It is against everything their country has stood for since the moment the River Wars began.

And yet, Marina confers silently with Zinnitzia, and they both bow their heads in assent. The matter is settled, and Marina says, 'He can stay,' as if letting in a violent murderer from their country's greatest enemy is perfectly acceptable.

'If nothing else,' Zinnitzia goes on, 'perhaps he can give Fen something to practise on.'

Fen stares, uncomprehending. 'What do I–'

'You can't seem to figure out how to heal a *living* body. Perhaps trying to heal that scar might give you some insight into how healing things works. Reapers are dead as far as our god is concerned, so healing him would be something like a resurrection . . . one that isn't going to get you cast out as a heretic the more you practise. We don't do *that* here, and we haven't in centuries.'

That nausea comes back up again. Fen shakes her head. 'No, that's—'

'She can start tomorrow. Marina can assess what Cat here knows, and how to fit him into the House of the Unwanting, and Fen can join their lessons.'

'*No!*' Fen is going to be sick. She presses a hand to her mouth and looks at Cat. He meets her eyes, and she is certain there is nothing there. No spark of life, no consciousness or intelligence. He may as well be a puppet dancing on Death's strings.

It is that *look* more than anything else that makes her lose her battle with her stomach. She knows Zinnitzia. Zinnitzia will make her touch that face. Feel it beneath her fingertips so her hands are coated in death and decay. She will call it healing, and Fen will fail him like she failed the six-year-old girl that had been left in her care. She will fail. And she throws up, staining the hem of her pretty dress, as the realization washes over her.

He should have stayed dead. He should have stayed in Alelune. But now he is here. Her responsibility. And she's never wanted any responsibility less.

CHAPTER SIX

Cat

Lio volunteers to escort the adopted Princess of Soleb back to bed. He wraps an arm around her shoulders and steers her towards the door, flagging down one of the House's staff members to let them know about the mess. There is a rush of movement in response. Voices calling this way and that. Cat watches the fuss with a detached bemusement. After meeting Elician, it should not surprise him that *another* member of the royal family is a Giver. While it's true that Princess Fenlia had not been on his list of targets to begin with, he is starting to think his entire mission has been a farce from the outset.

Closing his eyes, his heart lurches at another possibility altogether. *My queen wanted me gone,* he thinks, *and knew I would never return.*

Freedom, in the form of exile.

He tries to remember what his queen had looked like when she gave him the order. She had offered him a boon. An exchange, one that he had taken at face value without asking any additional questions. He had agreed to the terms, knowing the only reason it had been offered was because they were not in public. She never played her hand in public. There were too many eyes, too many people who would later hold those moments against his queen in any way they could. She had been trying to tell him something in that office, and he had not understood until now. He should have. He truly should have.

'You could have handled that more delicately,' Marina suggests, distracting him from the downward spiral. Lio and Fen are long gone. The others are still here. 'Today has not been easy for her.'

Zinnitzia shrugs, says, 'She cannot keep avoiding responsibilities that are unpleasant.' She steps away from the mess on the floor, nose curling at the smell.

'Has Fen been very difficult?' Elician asks. His hand still rests at the back of Cat's spine, thumb shifting in a comforting and absent-minded stroke. A pleasant and warm feeling that Cat has become far too familiar with in the three weeks it took to arrive here.

'Fenlia has undeniable talent,' Zinnitzia informs Elician with the gravitas of a beleaguered parent forced to admit to the good qualities of a child they despise. 'But,' she continues, 'Fenlia has no desire to do anything *with* that talent. She avoids the House of the Wanting at every opportunity, and I believe tonight was the first time she even bothered to cross the threshold of *this* House.'

'That doesn't surprise me,' he murmurs. 'Death has taken much from her already.'

'She's ignorant and oftentimes *hateful*.'

'And you have had three years to help her be better,' Elician points out. His hand leaves the small of Cat's back. Cat misses it on instinct. He leans back into the empty space where the feeling once lay. 'You truly believe that she and Cat would do well together?'

'I suppose that depends on the nature of your Cat,' Zinnitzia says. Cat hates the look she sends him, assessing and prodding. Like his brother's most terrifying toady, Eline de Carsay, whose sole purpose in life had been to ask questions and find out how *everything* truly worked. Cat knows this game well. Stay still, stay quiet, keep his head down and maintain a posture as unthreatening as possible.

Nothing to see here, no need to look.

'He's a good man,' Elician says. It should sound like a lie, but somehow it doesn't. The prince is, disconcertingly enough, being honest. 'He doesn't enjoy killing and was quite terrified of killing our horse. The whole journey here, he did not fight or argue. Not really. He didn't complain. He never tried to run or wander off. He would even help us set up camp in the evenings.'

'My, my, you almost sound smitten, Your Highness,' Zinnitzia says.

Head down, Cat thinks, cheeks burning, *do nothing.*

'Just because I want him to be treated with respect does not mean I'm *smitten* with him,' Elician replies.

'Perhaps, but you sound like you're trying to sell him for adoption or marriage.'

'I want him to be treated well. He has done no irreparable harm since we met.'

'Yes,' Zinnitzia bites out. 'Besides killing Lio. Tell me, Your Highness, how many times have you wrested him from Death's grip? Six? Seven?' From under his lashes, Cat sees Elician flinch. His crossed arms tighten, jaw setting in open defiance. But the venerable Giver matron is not finished. She stalks closer, voice dripping with condemnation. 'Your pathetic attachment to Wilion d'Altas is what *really* will be your undoing, *Your Highness*. You cannot keep bringing him back. There are consequences!'

'I am very aware of what those consequences are, thank you.' In three weeks of travel, Cat has never heard Elician speak like this. Sharp and pointed, his tone stinging like ice on an open wound.

'Are you? Because you–'

'That's enough.' Marina. She had been quiet during the rising argument, loitering on the outside of their group and fading into the background as Cat himself had tried to do. He had almost forgotten she was even there.

Zinnitzia, though, is not prepared to stop. Even with Marina's interjection. She glowers at the aged Reaper. 'You coddle him too much. You know where this kind of thinking leads.' She thrusts a finger towards Elician, turning back to him with fire on her tongue.

'How am I meant to teach your sister not to raise the dead when you seem perfectly content to do it on a whim?'

'On a whim?' Elician asks, temper rising ever more. 'A *whim*? I've been fighting that war for three years, watching dozens – *hundreds* of people die every week, smelling the pits burning their bodies, tasting their ashes in the air, and I have not saved a single one of them. I have not brought a single one of them back from the dead, healed a single shattered bone or mended one avulsion. I have watched men and women throw themselves into that melee and not make it to the other side, and I have done *nothing*. Don't talk to me about *whims* when every day of that war is a constant struggle. When all I want is to put an end to a symphony of agony.' He runs out of air, chest heaving. 'If the gods don't want me to save Wilion's life each time he dies, then they can damn well remove their *fucking* blessing from me at any time. Until then, he stays.'

Zinnitzia looks away. She glares at the puddle of sick on the ground. Her fingers flex as far as they can at her sides, then curl back into fists. 'You shouldn't even be there,' she says eventually. 'War is no place for our kind.'

'You are welcome to try to change my father's mind. But the last time *she* tried' – he waves a hand at Marina – 'she was removed from my household and sent here where she could *stop being in the way*. So, tell me, exactly, how do *you* plan to fix things?'

Zinnitzia says nothing. Perhaps there is nothing to say.

He's exhausted, Cat thinks. A sound builds at the back of his throat. A hiss that would carry an emotion. An urge born from his time in the Reaper cells he'd called his home, where language was stifled but sound was almost permitted if they could be subtle about it. Elician would not understand the noise. Few do. But the hiss stutters past his lips anyway, carrying with it all there is to feel. Worry. Concern. Weariness, and a deep need to rest.

Elician glances at him. His frown deepens for a moment. He does not know how this language works. He cannot repeat the sound back in empathetic unison. But his shoulders do lose some of their tension. His crossed arms fall straight at his sides. 'None of this matters now. I won't change my mind regarding Lio. As for Cat . . . my only intention here is for him to have the option of a life beyond the bars of a cage. Once I'm king we can discuss what the future holds from there.'

'You are too kind to be a king,' Marina murmurs when it seems like Zinnitzia has run out of things to say. 'Your reign will not last long.'

'Perhaps it won't. But it will last long enough for me to make that decision, and I will worry about its length after I wear the crown. I'm not a king yet.'

'You will be,' she swears. 'Come, little brother.' She holds her hand towards Cat. He glances at it, then back to the prince. 'You will see him later, I am sure.'

'Go,' Elician encourages.

'Get some sleep,' Cat says in turn, forcing his thoughts into words the prince will understand. Elician huffs. Smiles in a way that is too forced and unnatural to be beautiful.

'You too.'

Cat won't. He takes a step after Marina. Then another. He glances back at the prince and realizes for the first time: he will miss Elician when he leaves Kreuzfurt to go back to the war. His company had not been bad to have at all.

Marina is exactly as Ranio had described. Her hair is straight, brown and cut sharply at her ears. Her face is long and narrow, her lips thin. She reminds Cat, almost, of his mother. But her skin is not so pale as that. Marina spends time in the sun, her cheeks red from its oppressive glare. But, more importantly, though her face is youthful, it is an illusion. Cat knows it like he knows how to breathe. She is old. Very old. And for all she looks nearly the same age as his queen, he knows she is far older than that.

Marina moves gracefully, her heel and toe perfectly in line with each step. The bell at her wrist chimes as she moves, and she sways with it, each step a dance. There is a sword at her waist. As she walks, her hand on his shoulder, his eyes continue to fall to its hilt. Is it sharp? It must be. What would be the point in carrying a weapon that is dull? Then again, she has no need for such a weapon. She can kill easily with a flick of her hand.

Marina opens a door. She guides him inside. It is dark, he cannot see well, but soon she strikes a match and lights a candle. She illuminates the room, one lantern at a time. He stands there, watching, waiting. There is a bed pressed to one wall. Great windows with long curtains pulled back. A table. Some wooden furniture, dresser drawers and a mirror. He ducks his head to keep his eyes far from the mirror. The floor offers nothing nearly so interesting, thick and carpeted as it is, but he prefers it to his reflection. She says something to someone in the hall, then closes the door.

When she faces him, her expression is stern and unyielding. 'There are things I must know before I give you unfettered access to this place,' Marina says in Lunae so perfect it sounds antiquated. It is different from Elician's delivery, where his accent still shortens the closing vowels, or from Lio, who regularly fumbles both pronunciation and conjugation.

As far as Cat has been able to tell, the people of Soleb do not take kindly to the implicatory nature of his mother tongue. They prefer their static consonants and sharp distinctions. Theirs is a language that demands no questions of its listener. There are twenty different ways to say the word *love*, for instance, and each is used for a specific time or place or purpose. The expected and pro forma love of a parent is different from the devotional love of a child or the budding love of friendship. The love of an inanimate object is different from the love of a living thing. These are a literal people who choose their words carefully and have no need for critical thinking or analysis. They wish for the easy comfort of confirmation, so there can be no doubt.

Marina speaks to him in Lunae, but she does so from the viewpoint of a Soleben. She wants distinction in her understanding, and clarification of the unknown. She asks him about his orders. He explains them without pause. To end the royal family. Elician, Lord Anslian, King Aliamon, Queen Calissia.

'Not Lady Adalei?'

He frowns, trying to remember the name beyond the brief mentions he had overheard from Lio and Elician on the ride to Kreuzfurt. But like Fenlia, she had not been included on the list he had been given. He shrugs. *Maybe she's a Giver too.* The royal family seems full of them.

'Have you killed people on your queen's orders before?' There is no point in telling her the answer to that. He presses his lips tight, and she waits, patient and unyielding. 'Have you killed any *Soleben* subjects on your queen's orders before?' He shakes his head. No. Not on orders. Ranio had died, broken and shattered, but his death had not been purposeful. His death had not been at Queen Alenée's word. Cat's hands still clench at the memory. He stares down at the floor, waiting for her judgement.

Marina's posture is tense and dissatisfied. Her hands rest on her hips, her left very near her sword. 'I will have someone watch you at all times,' she decides at long last. 'If you prove yourself to not be a threat to the people here, that may change. But you should know, Cat, this place is not like Alelune. You may not find peace here.'

He nods.

He doubts peace is something that he would find anywhere. But for the foreseeable future, here is well enough. 'Well then.' Her head dips like she is confirming some imaginary contract, sealing his fate therein. A knock sounds at the door. 'Yes?' she calls out in

Soleben. An elderly man, skin drooping and loose, peers in around its edge. 'Fransen, yes, come in.' He does, pushing the door open even further to reveal a tall stack of black clothing neatly folded in his arms. A silver ball-bell rests on top, tiny enough to hide in a closed fist.

The man walks slowly, feet sliding across the floor rather than lifting. His back is bent forward, and his breaths come in loud inhales that seem to press his lungs right up against his ribs. 'Two uniforms for a new Reaper,' the man says, reedy voice breaking as he leans down to deposit his load on the bed.

'Thank you, Fransen. Fransen, this is Cat. He's just arrived.'

'Good to meet you, then, lad. We estimated your size, but if it does not fit well, let me know, yes? Yes?'

'Yes,' Cat responds dutifully.

'Tomorrow, Fransen will give you a tour of the grounds. The outer gate is open during the day, closed at nightfall. It does not matter if the gate is open *or* closed, you will not cross it, understood?' Marina presses onwards.

'Yes.'

'You'll have access to all the grounds, though do take note that there *are* more than just Givers and Reapers here. We have about thirty to forty guests at all times, some for healing at the House of the Wanting and others who are seeking end-of-life care. You will not approach them. Is that understood?'

'Yes.'

'If Fenlia does join us tomorrow, there are some things I'd like to test you both on; I'll see how well you've grasped certain concepts. But when you are not with me, Fransen will be your . . . let's say, your chaperone.'

Cat frowns. It seems like entirely the wrong word. Though calling him a guard would be somehow worse. The elderly man standing between them does not seem capable of such things. Fransen straightens his back, vertebrae popping and cracking into place. He lets out a quiet *oomph*, and rests one hand against his lower spine. 'You think me incapable?' Fransen asks. Cat glances between him and Marina. He shakes his head. If this is how they want it, he will not argue.

Still, he knows as well as Marina does, as well as Fransen *must* know, that Cat could outrun him. He could knock him over and disappear down the hall before Fransen could manage to scream. He could do any manner of things and Fransen could do nothing to stop him. So *why* Fransen? Lio and Elician had been terrible captors for a myriad of reasons, but to expect Fransen to keep him confined? That is almost insulting. *Is all Soleben security this lax?*

'Unclench your jaw, you're too young to be breaking your teeth over silly things like this,' Fransen says. 'It's a test. Tell him, Marina, before he works himself into a frenzy.'

'It's a test,' she repeats. 'One based on your personality more than anything else.'

Oh. Cat closes his eyes. He breathes in, then out again. *I see.* Invisible bars on invisible cages. Elician had been right. The point of Kreuzfurt is not to be forced into place by someone with more power, it is to lock himself inside and wilfully stay put. He has to choose to let this man be his chaperone, and he has to choose to accept what that means.

'You can try to leave, of course,' Fransen says. 'But how you treat those around you will dictate how you are treated in turn. And if you try to breach the outer gates, you *will* be stopped. They are constantly under watch.' The old man points towards the windows. Beyond the glass, all of Kreuzfurt is laid bare. Its towering external wall, made of thick stone and smeared with smooth plaster, offers no opportunity for climbing. Torches flicker as people walk along its length – guards monitoring all those inside. Cat's fingers twitch, threatening to curl into fists. He lets it go. Elician had provided an accurate description after all. More than he knew. It's a far too familiar sight. 'The only entrance or exit is that front gate. The wall itself has been dug deep into the ground, you cannot tunnel your way under it – and you would be spotted if you tried. You have to use the gate. And if you try to leave without permission, you will be shot by any one of the trained archers that patrol that wall.'

'We do not die,' Cat murmurs in the foreign tongue.

'Not for good, no, but an arrow through the heart will still stop you in your tracks. Your heart can't heal with a shaft through it. And even if the arrow should miss or go clean through – the tips have been laced with enough poison to kill you a hundred times over. You'd be dead before you hit the ground, and you wouldn't regenerate until your body had managed to do away with the poison. It is an entirely unpleasant situation.'

That sounded personal. Cat twists to look back at the old man and asks, 'You tried to leave once?'

'Only once,' he agreed. 'My first year here, in fact. I had a damn fool idea that I would go to the art festival in Himmelsheim. I'd gone every year before my first death and, well, I was determined to go and listen to the music. I donned a perfectly clever disguise, no black cloak or Reaper's bell to be seen – or heard!' He laughs at his own joke before miming a bow and arrow with his old, weathered hands. 'I was shot before I made it one foot past the gate. Believe an old man, yes? It is not worth it. Three weeks in bed trying to fight that poison, dying and waking up again in cycles. I'm too old for that now.' He waves his hand to the side, shaking his head.

'You are not old,' Cat states. Both Fransen and Marina laugh.

'Well spotted,' Marina praises lightly. 'How old *do* you think Fransen is?'

It is difficult to say. Cat looks at him and can see what is obvious. He is frail, his bones are weak, his skin is so thin as to be translucent. Fransen's veins are visible along his neck, and there is discoloration from spending too much time in the Soleben sun. His hair is white and thin, balding in patches along his scalp. But what he looks like and what he *feels* like are entirely different. There is an energy radiating off the man that Cat has long since grown accustomed to feeling. Death has placed her hands on Fransen, but she has only done so in the past few years. Compared to Marina, Fransen feels like a child.

'I've been a Reaper longer than you,' Cat murmurs.

'Quite possibly, yes.' Fransen shrugs. 'My clock didn't have the courtesy of freezing me at peak physical perfection like the majority of you lot. I had the great honour of dying of old age about five years ago. I'm the youngest Reaper here as far as that maths is considered, but I look old enough to be *this* one's great-grandfather. Regardless of that, though, I'm still *your* elder, which means I'm due a certain amount of respect. Understood?

'Yes.'

'Good then, I'll leave you to it. I'll wake you in the morning for the Summer Rituals. You'll want to take part, even if it seems strange.' Fransen dips his head and sees himself out.

Marina waits until he is gone before asking, 'Will Alelune send someone else to kill Elician?'

'I don't know,' Cat replies.

She looks at him, lips tugging down into a deep frown, then nods. 'Get some rest. Have a good waking in the morning.'

Then she is gone, the door closing quietly behind her. There is no sound of a lock securing him into place. Thirteen minutes later, he checks just to see. The door opens seamlessly. There is no one in the hall. *Lock yourself into your own cage,* he thinks bitterly. *Throw away the key.* Slowly, he shuts the door.

Walking back to the bed, he eyes it speculatively for several moments before sitting down on the floor next to it. It will be too soft to sleep on. He knows better than to torment himself with that possibility. Closing his eyes, he swallows down a laugh. It is the first time in months he has been left alone more or less unsupervised. He almost wishes Elician was still near. At least then he would have someone to listen to. The prince did seem to love to chatter aimlessly about anything that crossed his mind. And that had been pleasant, at least. For a while. But this room is quiet and still, and that is fine too. Cat is adaptable. He does not have a choice. It's not like he can die.

CHAPTER SEVEN

Fenlia

Fen wakes up still tired. The sun has just started to filter in through the windows, catching the reflected light off the towers. She squeezes her eyes shut, drawing her summer blanket up over her head. Leitja's wide, childish brown eyes stare back at her from the confines of her imagination. Her hand, tiny and frail, replaces the bunched curl of blankets in Fen's fist. *Why?* Leitja had asked, voice trembling on the cusp of death.

Fen throws herself upright. Her stomach clenches, but her anxiety from the night before had already left it empty. She stumbles from her bed and reaches for the eastward window of her room. Opening it, she sinks against the frame. The sun, hot even at dawn, keeps the air thick and humid. It is already hard to breathe.

Down below, white-clad Givers shuffle out of the residential quarters to the House of the Wanting. The gates will open soon and let the pilgrims and desperate masses in to seek relief. Many will receive that relief. So long as they do not come to her for help.

But no one will get the chance, she thinks. *I failed so badly at being a Giver that Zinnitzia is making me train with a Reaper.* Fat tears pool beneath her eyes. She swats at them desperately and tries to get control of her emotions.

Her adopted father, King Aliamon, has always insisted on the strictest control of emotions. Great displays of anxiety, despair, happiness or glee are strictly forbidden. It is unbecoming for a princess to behave so indecorously.

Fen sniffs loudly. She wipes her face. The sun is reaching even higher and soon she will miss breakfast. *Which House am I supposed to eat at?* The thought sends her tripping into another crying fit.

She doubles over, sobbing into her folded arms, breath hitching in the humid air. It takes a long while for her to bring herself to order. When she does, her face is blotchy and red, and she is determined to never eat another thing so long as she lives. She will just starve; that will make everyone happy.

Pushing herself upright, she spares one last glance at the sprawling view beyond her window. The glass towers loom ugly and disconcerting, with their sleek lines and curved windowpanes, but so too do the interconnecting gardens of Kreuzfurt. Boughs of trees arching downwards, trails leading off towards responsibilities she yearns to ignore. Down amidst the faux cheeriness of pansies and columbine, poppies and rue, a statue of Kreuzfurt's founder, Shawshank, stands imperiously in the centre of a large pond. She catches sight of movement and squints at the man crouching down at the water's edge. She would recognize that dark mane anywhere.

Elician.

Fen tugs on her boots and dress. She brushes her hair with a reckless speed that wrenches knots painfully from her scalp, braiding it as she hurries outside. Triple braids – three on each side – looped together in a tight band is the current fashion, according to Adalei. Adalei had detailed the design in a letter nearly six months ago and Fen had dutifully practised it until she could ensure the loops fell exactly where they should, just at her shoulders. She finishes setting the braids into place just as she enters the garden.

Her brother is still there, collecting stones from the shallows. Once he gets a palmful, he stands up and starts skipping them across the water's surface. He seems to be aiming them at the statue. Of the six he sends out, only one goes far enough to reach it, cracking against the statue's base before sinking with an unsatisfying *plonk*.

'What would Father say of you defacing another statue?' she asks, straightening her back and folding her hands in front of her as politely as she can manage. He glances towards her briefly, then skips another stone. It doesn't go as far.

'I didn't deface the first,' he murmurs. He is still wearing the same clothes as the night before and his curls look more than a little unkempt. Fen can almost hear Adalei sighing at the state of him.

'You need a wash,' she says. He shrugs one shoulder up, then releases another shot. 'What are you doing out here?'

'Avoiding responsibility.' Another stone flies free. This one is the worst throw yet; it *splishes* into the pond, startling a few fish from their early-morning fly-catching.

'Is that why Lio's not with you?'

'Lio's resting.'

'Good.' It is almost impossible to talk to Elician without someone else being present. Lio has been Elician's sworn shield since before he could even *carry* a shield, trained since birth to always step between Elician and anyone who might do him harm. Lio takes the job obnoxiously seriously, going so far as to interrupt arguments if he deems them too explosive. He even tries to calm tempers on Elician's behalf too, playing mediator where he does not belong. He had tried it the night before.

It hadn't made her feel any better.

All around them, Kreuzfurt is still and quiet. There is no one here to pay any attention to them. Not for a while yet, at least. The sun rises higher above them, seeming to slip between the pillars of the towers that make up the Houses of the Wanting and Unwanting. Every morning it rises in the same place, reaching its zenith once it is perfectly centred between the towers themselves. Every evening the moon chases after it from the same location. On and on, a constant cycle of life and death that is as endless as the war on the border. And every day, when the first light touches the mirrored walls of the two towers, each shimmering surface reflects the other, amplifying the glare into a blazing, incomparable white. Its incandescent glow bathes the world in possibility – and utter certainty.

There is no better time to hope for certainties than now. Squaring her shoulders, Fen tilts her chin up. Her brother does not do her the courtesy of looking her way. 'You're going back to the front, right?'

'Yes,' he affirms. He has one stone left. He rolls it between the fingers of one hand, then the other. Back and forth, back and forth.

'When?'

'A week at most. Enough time for the horses to rest and to resupply. I . . . I have to read the names of the dead into remembrance, but it depends on when Marina has the time to clear the hall.' He lets the rock fall into his left hand, then flicks his wrist in a quick snap. It soars beautifully through the air. A perfectly subtle arch that allows the stone to skip across the water all the way to the statue and snap upwards to crack once more against the base. A perfect hit.

'I want to go with you when you leave.'

'All right,' he says evenly.

She blinks. That was too easy. 'All right?'

'You want to go,' he acknowledges, then finally looks at her. 'I know you want to go. But I don't have the power to let you.' The worst part is he does not even sound the slightest bit sorry. He delivers each line as if he is delivering a speech before all of parliament, the lords and ladies sitting to one side, the local representatives on the other. He may as well have read her a verdict from a scroll of carefully assembled parchment, decorated with the fine painted inks imported from Glaika and the Gold Coast.

'You *do* have the power. You said–'

'I said that when I am king, I would give you a place at court. That you would be my representative for Kreuzfurt and serve as my adviser. But until then, only our father has the authority to grant any Giver or Reaper a travel pass.'

'You could ask him to let me go.'

'Have *you* asked him?' She has. Every week when she pens her letters home, she has written, in excruciating detail, a litany of reasons why she should be permitted to return. Once, she even went so far as to tell him that he was dishonouring her real father's memory by forcing her to stay here. He had not deigned to respond to that particular comment in his answering letter, preferring to prattle on about idle matters of no importance.

'He says my education here is paramount.'

'It will be,' Elician dares to agree. The traitor. 'If you truly are going to be my adviser and representative, I need you to pay attention to your lessons.'

'And how are my lessons here going to help you?' she hisses. She steps closer. He is still taller than her, and she is furious that she needs to tilt her chin up to meet his eyes.

Elician takes his time in replying. He presses his chapped lips tight, as if holding back an instinctive response – and she yearns to snatch it from his mouth.

'I've already argued with Zinnitzia,' he says finally, stepping back. 'I don't want to argue with you too.'

'Too late,' she retorts. Then her brows furrow. 'You argued with Zinnitzia? About what?' Elician never raises his voice unless he absolutely has to, and when he does, it can drop the temperature of a room. He is not mean when he is angry. He never resorts to insults or harsh words. Instead, he simply autopsies the problem with a cool and clinical hand, peeling back flesh and dissecting the hearts of men and women without so much as the slightest care over who he's eviscerating. Zinnitzia could do with being autopsied for all her faults. Fen hopes it hurt.

Elician shakes his head, denying her the story with a simple, 'It doesn't matter.'

'Did you argue about resurrection?' It is Zinnitzia's favourite topic to lecture on.

'Yes.'

'Did she tell you what happened with the girl I was supposed to heal? The one who died? The one I could have brought back but–'

'You know it's forbidden.'

The nerve! 'You've brought Lio back like twenty times!'

'Nowhere *near* that high, but that's exactly why I got in trouble. We're not supposed to do it.' Because of chaos. Because apparently the populations of whole cities would roam the earth refusing to die. Zinnitzia needs to stop reading bad literature.

'So, it's fine so long as it's Lio, but I can't bring back one girl who died because I couldn't heal her first?'

'It isn't fine so long as it's Lio, none of it is fine. I made a mistake.'

'You just tripped over his dead body and brought it back to life?' she snaps, grabbing his wrist when it looks like he intends to step back once more. 'Don't say it's a mistake if you don't think it's a mistake. You did it on purpose, so why shouldn't I?'

'Because it's a selfish thing to do. Life gave us the power to stop people from dying and changing before their time. But if you *are* struggling to heal someone, then it's because Death wants their soul. Bringing them back is defying Death – and risking Death's wrath never ends well. I will face those repercussions when they arrive, but you really don't want them for yourself. *Promise me* you'll stop trying to resurrect people.'

'No one cares if I bring back flowers or birds or anything else – it's just people!'

'Yes,' he murmurs. 'It's just people. People and their souls, which you actively pull from Death's grasp each time you bring them back. Flowers and birds have different souls, souls that are more temporary and transient, but humans – the gods do not play games with our souls, and neither should you. *Please* promise me you'll stop trying–'

'But I can't do what all the other Givers do,' she whispers. 'I *can't* heal things and they keep making me try and someone *died*. I can fix *that*, so why can't I just–'

Elician tugs his wrist free from her grasp. He places his hands on her shoulders and leans down ever so slightly to make sure their eyes are finally at the same level. 'It is not your responsibility to stop Death from taking the people put in your care. You are meant to heal them, if you can. If you can't, that isn't your fault.'

'You're only saying that because you just ignore everyone you *could* have saved on the battlefield. How many names are on that list of the dead that are still dead right now because you didn't do anything about it, my prince?' He flinches. Badly. Fen lowers her voice, tempering her tone as she presses on. 'I'm sorry, but it's the truth. You know it is. You can't let anyone know you're a Giver so letting people die is all you can do. But it was my job to help that little girl and I couldn't do it.'

Leitja had been six years old. She didn't deserve to die from a disease that another Giver could have healed. 'Even so,' he murmurs, staring past her once more. 'It was not your fault.'

'Let me join you at the front,' Fen requests again.

He snorts, a loud, ugly sound that does not match his fine features and good manners. He presses a hand to his face, pinching his nose, rubbing at his eyes. 'No one knows I'm a Giver. That's why I'm allowed to even be close enough to *ignore* them while they die. But you know full well Givers aren't allowed on battlefields. What could you possibly hope to achieve there?'

'I can tie bandages,' she suggests. 'Or make soup!'

'You don't even know how to make soup.'

'I COULD LEARN!'

Her brother winces, shushing her as he looks about. There are a few other Givers strolling through the gardens. Even a couple of

Reapers in the distance. Not close enough to hear their bells jingle, but certainly close enough for *them* to hear her shout. She lowers her voice, if not her intensity. 'It could be a *lesson*!' she insists. 'One that might help you one day!'

'When I have a sudden lack of soup during a council meeting? Yes, very helpful, that.'

'I'll fight, then . . . I know how to use a sword; I practised before I came here. I could learn how to do it again.'

'You'll *fight*.' The sound that leaves his mouth now is even more derisive. Cold and condescending, a chilling hint at the temper that she rarely ever sees. 'You'll fight,' he repeats darkly. 'Will killing people on purpose make you feel better, then?'

'No!' she snaps back. 'But neither will me staying here and . . . and what, exactly? Training to heal your pet Reaper?'

She had raised his hackles by daring to suggest she could join him at the front – now his anger transitions to shock. Elician's cheeks flush red and he sputters out the words, 'Cat is *not* my pet.'

'You named him *Cat*,' she reminds him. 'Lio told me that the whole way here you were trying to get him to be your friend. And how could you even *want* to? He's a Reaper!'

Her brother's shoulders slump. His arms hang limply at his sides, and he shakes his head. '*That's* your concern? That he's a Reaper? Not that he is Alelunen, or that he was sent here to kill me, but that he's a *Reaper*?'

To be fair, none of those were exactly points in Cat's favour, but Fen could stomach them a bit more. Well, perhaps not the latter. 'You shouldn't make friends with people trying to kill you either.'

'No,' he murmurs. 'Perhaps not.' He still is not looking at her. She wants to take him by the wrist once more, shake him until he listens to her properly. 'Marina was a part of my household before you even came to the palace,' Elician says. 'She was my guard from the moment I was born to the moment I went to war. She taught you how to wield that sword you apparently want to use to kill people.

And you . . . you've lived *here* for three years, and you truly cannot contemplate the idea of being friends with a Reaper? Of wanting to show them basic human decency?'

'They shouldn't exist.'

'Ah.'

She cannot describe the expression on his face. She cannot read what lies behind that distant look in his eyes, nor what that simple sound seems to imply. But something in that expression makes her hands fidget restlessly. She tugs and pulls at her fingers. She licks her lips and takes another step closer. This time, he does not retreat.

'Death shouldn't exist,' she explains, soft as can be. 'If she never showed up . . . if she had just let Life do what he had wanted from the start, then none of this would have happened. Nothing would die, and Reapers wouldn't exist. And if *they* didn't exist then Life wouldn't have needed any Givers either. Everybody could just be *normal* . . . the same.'

'Normal and deathless. What *are* they teaching in temple these days?' Elician mutters. 'So, let me try to understand. You blame the Reapers for the powers a god has chosen to gift them,' he summarizes. 'And you hate Death and all she stands for because it makes your life very hard? Tell me, little sister, what kind of life would you live? Without Death and all her influence?'

'A better one than this. Leitja would still be here. My parents would still be here. My pets.'

'And what would you eat?'

'What?'

'What would you eat if nothing could die? Or perhaps you wouldn't eat. Or need to eat. Or want to eat. Perhaps that would go away. So, what would you wear, if nothing could die? Perhaps you'd wear nothing. Perhaps nakedness would become acceptable, and we could spend our days full in the sun, burning our skin ever darker to bask in its glory. I suppose it would be cold in the winter, but we cannot die and so what do we care for the chill? Where would we live? Only in stone structures, certainly, but what of our decorations? No wooden frames or canvases, no paint. What instruments would we play? Nothing made of wood, but neither could we burn the furnaces to bend metal for a horn. Tell me, sister, what life would you live in a world where *nothing* dies?'

'Don't be so . . . pedantic. You already said it. No one cares if grass or trees or animals die. It's just us.'

'Just us. And then there's Zinnitzia's warning again. Where everything falls into chaos because the whole balance of the world is thrown off its axis.' Elician jerks his thumb towards the statue of Shawshank. 'That's what he believed. That's what Givers used to do. Make sure that no one ever died.'

It is blasphemy to say what she thinks next. Blasphemy to push the boundaries of principles that generations of scripture have written into hard stone. She says it anyway. 'Maybe he was right, and we shouldn't have stopped raising the dead.' Elician's jaw clenches. 'Maybe,' she presses one final time. 'Maybe if we had continued, we wouldn't have that Death-worshipping cult on the other side of the Bask – and Kreuzfurt would just be a place for these *freaks*, not us. A place to detain those who only know how to kill people and nothing else.'

He meets her eyes. The warmth and love that had sustained their meeting the night before has vanished. Utterly. And no trace of it remains. He looks like a stranger – so cold is his countenance, so distant his affection. Her breath catches in her throat.

'I don't often say this, dear sister, but I'll say it now. I agree with Father. You still have much to learn. And you are exactly where you're meant to be.' Elician turns away. Fen reaches for his wrist, fingers curling around it with her last vestiges of strength. But he jerks from her grasp without even turning to look at her. He walks back towards the Houses of the Wanting and Unwanting and doesn't respond to her calling his name, nor show any sign of having heard her at all.

Fen refuses to follow him back to the Houses. But there are guards patrolling the gates and the walls. They won't let her leave. As the sun rises high in all its bright morning glory, it shines on a world where it seems that – truly – she has nowhere else to go.

CHAPTER EIGHT

Elician

'Stupid,' Elician curses under his breath. *'Fucking stupid.'* He rounds a corner and sees a group of supplicants hurrying on their way towards the House of the Wanting. He rapidly changes direction, shuffling his feet across the cobblestones as deftly as he can to avoid attracting attention. He finds a different path, one far less busy than the first, leading to Kreuzfurt's second tower, and he takes it.

Elician has never liked Kreuzfurt. When Fenlia had first written to him about her loathing of the place, and why living here causes her such unhappiness, he had thought he understood her reasoning. Their thought processes could not have been more different. Fen hates Kreuzfurt because it houses and even gently caters to those chosen by Death. Elician's displeasure stems from a far more personal source.

He marches forward, head down, ignoring the meticulously cared for gardens and trees and pathways. He ignores the dark red sandstone walls, built thick, sturdy and strong. He ignores the glittering glass of the Houses, and the reflected sunbeams that strike the path beneath his feet.

A long time ago, Marina had told him that the Houses had been built and rebuilt several times to ensure the reflections were angled to avoid harm to residents. Rumour had it that one window was particularly lethal; its panes reflected sunbeams that could light fires and even burn the flesh of anyone who accidentally crossed its path. Elician had spent the rest of that visit terrified of stepping in sunbeams and begging Lio to stay inside lest they tempt fate.

Now Elician marches across each bright beam, ignoring the heat and the warnings from years past. He ignores them all.

He is good at ignoring things. He has had many, many years of practice doing just that. It is a skill his sister should learn. It is a skill she should learn quickly.

Elician gazes up at the twin domineering monstrosities of glass, stone and steel. The metal was forged in Altasian furnaces and designed by curious architects, fused into a thick stone base. Each member of the planning team had taken on the seemingly impossible challenge of joining glass and metal in a way no other architect had ever managed before. And this was the result. The Houses are the ugliest buildings in all of Soleb and it is simply too much hassle to knock them down and start again. They stand as testaments to time. He can't wait for the day they shatter.

Taking a deep breath, he enters the House of the Unwanting. A Reaper at the entrance startles when he sees Elician, bowing awkwardly with the wrong hand going to his heart and the wrong foot stepping backwards in a half-kneel. Not enough members of the royal family come to visit the House these days, and the etiquette for greeting them clearly isn't well known. Funny, that. Only a decade ago it would not have been surprising to see one of them here at all times. Elician returns the gesture with a well-practised dip of his head, right fist pressed to his chest. 'Do you know if there's a patient in room seventy-three?' he asks.

'A patient? No, we haven't had one in years,' the Reaper replies, still gaping at him with a kind of stupefied wonder.

'Thank you,' Elician replies, then turns towards the great spiral staircase. It is a long way up. There is a lift powered by weights and pullies and occasionally by blue stones if the need for speed justifies the waste. But that is *only* to be used for those incapable of managing the climb.

Burning blue stones would create an endless stream of energy that could operate the lift without manual labour. But they are mined exclusively in the northernmost territory of Alelune - and their hostile neighbour will do anything to keep the stones out of enemy hands. When Alelune controls Altas, the city acquires the stones by the hundred. And whenever Soleb reclaims the city, it strips it of those much-valued resources to disseminate them throughout the rest of Soleb. But since the Marias Compromise, there has been no access to them at all. Alelune occasionally does business with other countries, but they maintain a provision in all trade agreements that no foreign entity may sell the stones to Soleb. Not even Elician's mother being a Glaikan princess has been enough to convince that nation to break those terms, a fact that has infuriated Elician's father for years.

Elician's legs burn as he climbs flight after flight. He reaches the seventh level, takes a few seconds to catch his breath, then wanders down the curved hall until he finds the right door. It is unlocked, as are most rooms in the Houses. There are no secrets here. The curtains along the back wall are closed, keeping the room in darkness. He walks towards them, deftly drawing them back and turning to look at the room once more. When he turns, a startled curse leaves his lips, one hand rising to cover his mouth.

Cat is here.

Why is Cat here? Elician has purposefully come here to avoid–

No matter. 'I'm sorry,' he says. 'I thought the room was empty. I should have knocked.'

Cat sits on the floor near the bed, one shoulder leaning against the mattress. He wears the harsh black uniform of a Reaper. The silver bell at his wrist jingles with obnoxious gaiety as he unfolds his lean limbs.

'You still apologize too much,' Cat chastises in a tone that seems more excusing than accusing. 'I am still your prisoner.'

'And you still deserve courtesy. I–' Elician shakes his head. He looks around the room. Perfectly clean and in good order. 'Marina, she gave you *this* room to stay in? It's yours now?'

Cat responds with a simple shrug.

He stands there, still and silent. For the first time since they met, Elician almost wishes Cat was gone. He does not say such a thing. He is, after all, very good at ignoring all that bothers him. He practises every day. 'I'm sorry for disturbing you. This . . . was my cousin's room, once. Adalei's. I just wanted to see it.'

'Why?'

Elician smiles, makes a dismissive gesture, changes the subject. 'You know, Lio is upset you never bothered to speak much to him.'

'I know.'

'*Why* didn't you speak to him?'

'I had nothing to say to him.'

'But you do to me?'

'Why did you want to see the room?'

His smile fades. It is harder to look at Cat like this – dressed in a Reaper's garb. Harder still to respond. 'To remind myself she's no longer in it, I suppose.' He can easily imagine his sweet cousin lying in this bed. Her cheeks hollow, skin a sickly yellow wherever it was not marked with bruises that seemed to form at the slightest provocation. He shakes his head to clear the image from his mind, looking at Cat's face instead. It is a far more pleasing sight. 'Adalei was sick, as a child. She stayed here, off and on, for years.' He points to the corner. 'I'd visit every few months, and my parents would make me sit there, while she lay in bed, to make sure I never touched her and *accidentally* saved her life.'

'Is it so easy to do?' Cat asks. 'To heal someone like that?'

'It can be. Much like killing something is for you. A touch of skin and all manner of injuries or impurities get resolved. The whole reason I helped Kassandra when she fell back at Great Dawn Pass was because we touched . . . and I had started healing her before I could stop it. And then, when I realized her child . . .' He sighs, pressing a hand to his face. 'Years of never touching any member of the opposite sex, for fear I'd spontaneously encourage a pregnancy, and now I've wilfully helped one along.'

'You didn't impregnate her,' Cat says slowly. Elician drops his hand to his side.

'I all but guaranteed that child will be born. And if any other Giver bothers to investigate further, they'll likely sense I had something to do with it. We leave a kind of . . . interference marker on those we've touched. Have you ever noticed?'

'The people I touch die.'

Elician winces. 'True.' He'd never thought to see if someone killed by a Reaper had the same marker. The same unconscious *sensation* of divine interference that was unique to each individual wielding their powers. He doubts he will get an opportunity to find out any time soon. There are few good ways to test the theory, after all.

'You've never touched a woman before then?' Cat asks suddenly.

Elician flushes. 'I wore gloves, much like you. Marina was my guard in Himmelsheim. My parents told everyone I wore the gloves for my own protection from her. Just to be safe. My clothes were modified to make sure I never showed any excess skin. And . . . every interaction was scrutinized.'

'Why? Why hide your gift at all?'

'Because a Giver cannot ascend to the throne,' Elician replies dully. 'If I am to be king, I can only reveal what I am *after* I wear the crown. And so all my life is spent pretending to be what I am not.'

'It sounds lonely.'

'It is.' He smiles, though, forcing levity to his tone. 'Lio is the only one who knows outside my family, Marina and Zinnitzia. And so he was the only one that I was allowed to play with as a child. They never trusted that I wouldn't make a mistake . . . or just try to heal her quickly when they couldn't see. And while I sat here in this corner, he was able to sit with my cousin. Hold her hand. Give her comfort when I could not.' It hadn't surprised him when Lio had mentioned his growing affection for Adalei. If anything, Elician had had years of observation dedicated to watching Lio's fondness grow. He would never begrudge his friend any form of happiness.

But sometimes, Elician wonders if there is any chance that he will be able to find something so sweet with another person in his own lifetime. It is a yearning better left dead and buried.

'Why did no other Giver help her, though?' Cat asks. 'Your people seem to use them for everything else.'

'No member of the royal family may be healed or resurrected by a Giver,' Elician recites. 'As the ruling family, our lives cannot be extended "artificially". If we are meant to die, then we will die, and our successors will reign in our stead. When Adalei fell sick, her father chose to send her here so at least if she died, she would do so in the presence of the gods.'

'The gods are everywhere.'

'It's the excuse we told people, anyway,' Elician concedes easily. 'Uncle Anslian arranged for people who were trained in Alelunen medicine to help her. Physicians and scientists . . . Reapers too, of course, if they had learned the trade. Not nearly as taboo as letting a Giver heal her, but not exactly something our family wanted advertised either. It sends the wrong message.' Something about his phrasing makes Cat's face scrunch up. It is perhaps the most expressive Cat has been in weeks.

He asks, with a tone that veers between incredulous and genuinely baffled, 'You don't have medicine in Soleb?' and Elician can do nothing but wave a hand towards the room around them. Towards the walled city just beyond the glass tower walls.

'Givers heal the sick,' Elician spits out. 'There is no need for anything else. Unless you are born royal, of course. We must die because that must be the gods' will.' Cat's expression ricochets from baffled to displeased and then back again. 'Say it,' Elician encourages, almost laughing. 'You see the flaw, don't you? Say it.'

He does. Slowly, quietly, as if he wants to be perfectly certain his translation is correct but still cannot bring himself to believe what it is he is saying. 'Kreuzfurt is too far from most of your people to be of use to them.'

'It is,' Elician agrees. 'And the *extent* of that use changes too. In Alelune you have physicians and surgeons and specific professions dedicated to the medical arts. They treat illnesses, injuries, pain. You have . . . methods. Options. Alternatives. In Soleb, each man, woman and child is taught which herbs do what and how to care for basic injuries. But for anything substantive, they must go to Kreuzfurt – or make do with a Travelling Giver, who moves from city to city on the King's permit.'

'It is . . . inefficient.'

'It is. And there are plenty of problems that can arise as a result. The whole mess with Kassandra and her child came about because of a Travelling Giver. But whenever one is simply not available, healthcare matters are left to the community to do their best. On the battlefield, each member of our army knows how to handle injuries. We are not dependent on five or six practitioners to care for hundreds. Any of us can stitch a wound, fix or mend a broken bone and address the majority of complications.'

'Everyone except you, who may not touch your soldiers.'

'What type of king would I be if I didn't try to help my people?' he asks sardonically. 'I just wear gloves and work the same as the rest of them. So long as no one touches my skin, then everyone can be happy.'

'Everyone except you.'

'Well, that was never up for debate, was it?'

'Why did they let you go to war? They would not let you near your sick cousin, but on a battlefield, there would be a far greater chance of discovery.'

'Because a war started, and I'm meant to be king. What other choice was there? Look, I . . . I had an argument with my sister, and I was not expecting company. I just wanted to see the room and be alone for a while. I should go.'

Go where, though? The gates are now open, and the grounds filling with visitors. Givers and Reapers are hurrying this way and that. The chances of making it out of the House of the Unwanting without running into anyone seem slim. It would be worth it if there was somewhere, anywhere, he could rest without interruption. Yet the walk to the main residential quarters would expose him to any number of people.

Eventually Lio will find him. Then, Elician will need to explain what happened. He doesn't want to. He doesn't want to think about his sister's perspective or debate the theological or historical implications of her desires. 'I just want silence. A bit of peace for a while . . . and I don't know where to get it.'

'Here,' Cat murmurs. Elician's breath hitches. Cat gestures grandly to the open space of the room around them. 'Stay,' he says next, as if Elician had not understood his offer. 'I am very good at being quiet.' Then, settling more comfortably on the floor beside the mattress, Cat adds, 'Who would I even tell?'

Elician should not do this. Lio had warned him about befriending Cat. Zinnitzia had also been wholly unimpressed by the fledging friendship that has formed. His sister clearly loathed the mere idea of it. *Fuck her*, he thinks. He walks across the room and sits on the floor next to the man who tried to kill him.

He closes his eyes and leans his head back against the stone wall. The sounds of life echo outside the windows, along the halls of the House of the Unwanting. He breathes in, then out, and finds himself perfectly at peace in the halls of the dead.

CHAPTER NINE

Cat

Of all the assassins my queen has ever utilized, Cat thinks as the late-afternoon sun transitions from too bright to too oppressive, *I may be the worst yet.* Elician is asleep. His head rests lightly against Cat's shoulder, his arm pressing gently against Cat's own. Warmth radiates off the prince, enough so that the uncomfortable room temperature becomes, suddenly, sweltering.

The black fabric that makes up the Reaper uniform is thick and heavy, and it traps the summer heat. While the exterior seems dry enough, beneath the many layers sweat beads and pools. Marina and Fransen had shown him a way to stave off the heat that morning. They had led him to a room where all the Reapers of Kreuzfurt gather for the morning ablutions – and application of a heat-defying salve. Taking part had been both terrifying and obscene. Never in his life had he been touched as intimately as in those moments and, like Elician, he had very much wished only for a moment of silence and seclusion.

Frustratingly, the lotion does work. The more he sweats the more his skin responds with icy chillness. He shivers on occasion, head swimming from the conflicting sensations. And Elician only makes it worse. Elician leans into Cat's body and Cat's skin tickles in response, making him shiver in a way that cannot possibly be comfortable for the sleeping prince. Yet Elician continues to doze. Unbothered. Unaware.

He's lucky I can't actually kill him, Cat thinks. Elician's right hand is curled in a fist at his side. It twitches, flexing and clenching. As on their journey to Kreuzfurt, Soleb's dear sun-blessed prince sleeps, but not well.

Touch is a rarity in the Reaper cells. The distance between the cages has always been just far enough to make clasping hands impossible at worst, or uncomfortable at best. But before then, before he had been sent there, Cat remembers a time when touch had very much been a part of his life. For all that Solebens believe Alelunens to be stiff, formal and unaffectionate, Cat knows with certainty that those observations are mere hearsay.

Why should anyone in Alelune show affection to a loved one when observed by the enemy? Why should anyone in Alelune reveal the depths of their ardour, when such things are treasures beyond compare? Alelunens are perfectly affectionate with those they care for. But that is the point. It is reserved for those they hold dear.

As for sleeping next to someone, curling against them, seeking protection – Elician may as well be asking for his hand in marriage. Cat doubts his queen would approve of that particular turn of fate. Though the look on her face would be almost worth the shock of such a proposal. *I must humbly beg your pardon, Your Grace. You see, he just wouldn't die.* No, that sounds strangely like something Lio would say. Inappropriate and unacceptable. Like this whole mission.

Brielle would laugh though, if she were to hear that. In the cold dark of the Reaper cells, hers had been the cell next to his, and she had always encouraged him to explore or enjoy being belligerent when it was safe to do so. Never to the guards, or his brother, or any of the people who had power over him. But in the dark, when no one could hear their illicit whispers, she encouraged him to speak his anger into the air. *You have a right to be angry,* she insisted.

Elician's hand spasms again. His head turns against Cat's arm. Cat rests his own hand over Elician's. Through his gloves, he cannot feel Elician's skin, but he knows it is flawless and smooth. Elician has no scars, and few calluses. Despite years of swinging that sword back and forth, Elician's hands are softer than ceremonial silk. It must hurt each time he does it, his hand rubbed raw hour after agonizing hour again and again. *He has a right to be angry too.*

Someone knocks on the door.

Elician jerks awake, his hand sliding free from Cat's. He blinks rapidly, useless apologies falling from his tender lips. 'No need,' Cat murmurs. He stands slowly, stepping around the prince. 'Stay,' he says, as if he has any authority to command him. Elician sits, huddled up against the wall, out of view of the door.

Cat has not opened his own door in years. That privilege has always belonged to another. But he opens this one. The young but elderly Reaper Fransen stands on the other side. 'It seems your lessons have been cancelled for the day,' Fransen informs him simply. 'I thought you might like a more extended tour of the grounds than what was originally planned instead. If you have nothing else you'd rather do?'

'No,' Cat murmurs. 'Nothing else to do.' He will leave Elician to his peace and quiet. He hopes he can finally sleep well and dream better dreams. He deserves better dreams.

Fransen nods and starts to slowly turn away. Cat makes to follow when that fool prince calls out, 'Wait!'

Cat had not thought a man of Fransen's fragility could move as fast as he does, but the other Reaper spins perfectly on the heel of his foot to stare at Elician slowly emerging from Cat's room with all the self-preservation of a moth to a flame.

'Sir,' Elician says, 'would you mind terribly if I joined you both?'

'Your Highness,' Fransen says, seeming to search for the appropriate response and not quite knowing what that should be. 'I could hardly deny you.'

'Thank you,' Elician says stiffly. He runs a hand over his curls, grimacing at what he finds. But he removes a ribbon from the pouch on his belt, and within moments has the entire mess tied back in some semblance of order.

'It won't be quiet,' Cat reminds him.

'Yes,' Elician agrees. 'I know.' He gestures with his hand, and Cat wordlessly follows Fransen once again.

The worst assassin on the continent, he thinks again. *The worst by far.*

Somehow, the order of their little procession is shuffled.

Fransen trails behind Elician and Cat as they walk along the great wall. Once they leave the main centre of the city and step onto the perimeter walk that encircles the farmlands, there is far less head-turning and spying from both the residents and guests of Kreuzfurt. To the few who summon the courage to talk to Elician, he gives the same scripted civil responses. He is here in Kreuzfurt to read names into remembrance, and he is working with Cat and Fransen to prepare for that ceremony. So sorry. He has to go now. May the sun bless their days.

Cat memorizes the way he speaks, the way he holds himself. He carries himself differently from the Queen of Alelune. With her, there is no denying she is a ruler, proud and strong. She walks as if the very ground owes its allegiance to her, and she speaks in a tone that invites no argument. Elician does not possess the sheer power of her presence. None of the courtiers of Alerae would dare to approach her as she traversed the city. These people: they rush to him. They touch him, even. His gloved hands, his arm. One even dares to touch the sun pendant around his neck as if it confers a blessing on its own. He smiles at them all, he charms. He is ruthlessly kind, despite how exhaustion and anxiety has occupied his morning.

'Why do you let them talk to you like that?' Cat asks after they have escaped the crowds.

'If they are here, they are here because they are facing the worst days of their lives. The least I can be is kind.'

'And this . . . ceremony you're doing?'

'Whenever someone dies, their name is added to the Scroll of the Lived and read aloud to confirm it has been recorded appropriately. Then, in the last month of the year, the Reapers of Kreuzfurt will reread all the names on the Scroll in remembrance of all who came before.'

'*All* of the names?' Cat asks. 'From . . . how long ago?'

'From the moment the Scroll was first made.' He gestures around them. 'Since King Shawshank made Kreuzfurt and gave Reapers the task of maintaining our dead.'

'That's . . .'

'Millions of names. It takes most of the month. Soon it will take some of the second month too. This will be faster. I'm just reading the new ones that have accumulated so far. It should take less than an hour.'

'But at the main ceremony, they just . . . read the names, one after another, until it is done?'

Elician nods his assent. 'Usually, a member of the royal family oversees the proceedings. When Adalei was here for treatment, she volunteered for the task. She has requested the honour every year since. You'll get to meet her when she comes at the end of the year. She's lovely.'

So everyone has said. He cannot picture her. He tries to imagine Anslian's harsh features cast in the gentler guise of a woman but finds that the image fails to take proper form. He has never been good at imagining things, though. Far better to see reality than to fantasize over what might never come to pass. He could never have imagined Elician as he really is. 'Why is she not Soleb's heir?' he asks instead. 'She is older than you are, and a woman.' Even as he says it, though, he's relatively certain he's made a mistake. It's been a long time since someone explained Soleben succession to him, and Elician is already shaking his head.

'My father is older than her father, and I am his son. Should I die' – he shares a grin with Cat at that – 'then my uncle Anslian will take my place as heir, and Adalei after him. The right goes to the firstborn regardless of their sex, so even though she's older and a woman – which would matter more in Alelune – here it does not matter. My father is older, and so I take precedence.' He pauses, considering, then asks, 'Why do only women inherit in Alelune?'

'It is only for the monarchy,' Cat corrects. 'And that is to retain the bloodline of the Queen. There can be no question over lineage if a child comes from the Queen's own body. Death chose her line, and so the queens must maintain it.'

'There have been stellos in the past, though.'

'Certainly, but they rarely ever rise to king, and the few times they have – their reigns were always short. A more fitting heir is always found, eventually, to replace them.' Usually at the end of a sword. Alelunens are not shy about ensuring Death's line stays utterly intact. 'There is no way to prove that the King's child is truly their offspring. With a woman, there is no doubt regarding the legitimacy of the child she gives birth to.'

'There's not much trust regarding the fidelity of the King's wife then, I see,' Elician comments wryly.

'Fidelity has little to do with it,' Cat replies. 'She could be the most loyal woman in all of Alelune, and, through no fault of her own, the child still might not be the King's.' The prince winces, grimacing at the insinuation. 'Years ago, there had been suggestions for a change. Talk of keeping a woman in confinement and under constant observation to ensure that only the King's seed quickened.'

'That's awful.'

'Yes. The Queen and her court refused it. I don't think they've come up with any alternatives since.'

'Queen Alenée will have trouble with that then,' Elician says. 'Gillage is also a male heir.'

'Gillage will have a problem, not my queen,' Cat refutes. 'He is the one whose authority and succession will be challenged.'

'Poor boy.' He sounds sincere. Truly sincere.

'No one in all of Alelune would think that of Gillage,' Cat tells him quietly.

'Maybe someone should.'

Behind them, Fransen says something that Cat misses. He turns back. Lio is there, sweaty and out of breath. He must have run after them. He makes no move to keep pace with Elician or Cat, though, offering his arm to Fransen instead. He meets Cat's eyes and jerks his chin upwards in a gesture Cat doesn't understand. If Elician is aware of any of this, he does not show it. He just continues moving forward, and Cat does too.

They walk and keep walking. Cat sees the farms and small huts of Givers and Reapers who have no desire to live and work within their Houses. Their path runs along a wall that provides welcoming shade on their return trip but offers no discernible escape route. Not that Cat is actively looking for one.

Each time his eyes wander for longer than a few seconds in either direction, Elician says something. Often, it is not even something important. He speaks, and Cat loses time just listening. Just responding, quietly, uselessly. Rarely with much to even add to the conversation in general. The tour seems to be becoming less of a tour and more of an opportunity to simply spend time with each other. Elician must realize it too, but he makes no effort to curtail it.

As the city proper comes into view, Cat finds his pace slowing. 'For Fransen,' he offers when Elician notices. He is awarded with a smile, lovely and somehow more distracting than the past few hours of conversation. Fond and sweet and perhaps the most beautiful thing Cat has ever seen.

If his queen were to stand before him now and demand Elician's death, if she had found a way to ensure it could be done, he is not sure he could actually carry it through.

'I don't like killing people I know,' Cat says suddenly. Elician stops walking. Behind them, Fransen and Lio, still doing a passable job of pretending they aren't listening, stop too.

'Do you find it easier to kill people you don't know?' Elician asks.

The method is indeed easy, regardless of how well he knows his victims. He ran into his father's arms and killed him with a hug. He executed criminals accused of high treason with simply a glancing trace of his fingers along the top of their heads. He killed a horse, and then its rider – simply by touching that horse's neck – as they raced desperately towards a border neither would ever cross. Killing is simple for him. It has always been since the day he died and learned exactly what he had become.

'No,' he murmurs. 'I don't like it either way. But when I know someone . . .' His father. Ranio. Now Elician. Lio, even. Poor, disgruntled Lio, who had huffed and sighed and complained for most of their trip, but who had also cooked food that tasted good and teased Elician out of his fits of melancholy. He'd never once begrudged Cat extra servings of their meals, despite the need to plan around such things. 'I'm a terrible assassin.'

'Yes. Though I'll tell you a secret.' Elician leans in close. His breath sends a shivering wave across Cat's skin. 'I'm a terrible guard.' It is true. He is hopeless at it. 'But . . . had you been anyone else, I might have actually needed to step up my duties as a jailor. So . . . thank you for being you.'

He could have ended up in the river. The cell in Altas. Locked in endless torture or endless isolation. The thought terrifies him. '*Could* you have done it?' Cat asks quietly.

'I don't know,' Elician admits. 'But I am grateful I have not had to find out.' He holds out his hand.

Cat takes it and, before he can understand the trajectory of the motion, he finds himself pulled in for a hug. He's held there, pressed against Elician's chest. Cat closes his eyes. Elician's body is warm and solid, his clothing soft where it presses against Cat's cheek. His arm is a tight, supporting brace. Cat breathes in the prince's scent, familiar from their journey, and relaxes into the sensation. He dares to lean into the embrace, to relish it, and even, slowly, brings his other hand up to deepen the hold. But then, too soon, it is over. He's released, his back slapped twice lightly in parting. Then Elician turns and continues on his way, oblivious of the devastation left in his wake.

CHAPTER TEN

Elician

For five hours, Elician managed to avoid being alone with Lio. He had spent that time doing everything in his power to not think about his angry sister, the list of names he needs to read and the tasks that are still set out before him. He thinks he has done an admirable job on all those fronts. Cat had been a beautiful distraction – and Elician had made full use of their easy conversation. But he should not have embraced Cat like that at the end of their walk. He should not have held him so familiarly.

He had expected Lio to slam the door when he eventually cornered Elician in his room after dinner. He had expected stomping feet or some other sign of displeasure. But as Elician awkwardly prepares himself for bed, Lio is a picture of serenity. He closes the door gently, with nary an excess sound. 'Did you talk to Fen before you came to find me?' Elician asks, prolonging the inevitable as he fidgets with the edges of his shirt sleeves.

'Yes,' Lio replies. 'She's upset and has sworn to never speak to you again.'

'That will last a month.'

'Oh, give her at least two. Then she'll go back to sending you three letters a day because she just has so much more to say. I'll see if Adalei can come for a visit. It might cheer her up.'

'Or it might make her more upset.'

'Your sister is, as ever, a quagmire.'

Elician tugs the ribbon from his hair, then starts trying to rake his fingers through the curls. He finds a few knots, but he is determined. He will set it right. He will.

'Elician, the way you looked at Cat . . .' Lio says, chastisement already clear in his tone.

'*What?*'

'Oh, nothing. Just . . . I suppose Fredian is going to be so disappointed, that's all.'

'*Fuck* Fredian. I barely had half a conversation with him before he started making those overtures.' Elician crosses his arms over his chest. The last thing he cares about is *Fredian* of all people. Fredian, who, like almost every single other person who has ever offered to share his bed, has always wanted something out of it. Something that has nothing to do with Elician and everything to do with his crown.

'All right. Fuck Fredian.' Lio is being too patient about this. Far too patient.

Elician sits down on his bed. He stands up. He tugs his medallion off his neck and throws it onto his pillow, then starts pacing his room. It is too small. After weeks on the road, he yearns for the open space of plains, mountains and forests. He could lose himself in those wilds. Perhaps it would be better if he did.

'I like *him*,' Elician says finally. 'Cat.'

'All right.'

'*All right?* He's an Alelunen assassin – he *killed you*!'

'El, I'm going to ask you something, and you're not going to like it.' Lio waits, the pause so dramatic that Elician's skin crawls with anticipation. 'Do you like him because of his personality – or do you like him because he's the first person in your life that isn't a member of your family or inner circle who knows exactly who and what you are?'

Lio is right. Elician does *not* enjoy the question. He doesn't enjoy how it takes the very air from his lungs and leaves him strangled and breathless in a too-small room with too-large windows. He sinks back down to the bed. 'Can it be both?' he asks.

His friend, his only friend in all the world, sits at his side. His shoulder is warm against Elician's, his voice tender and quiet as he gently says, 'Yes, little brother, it *can* be both.' Relief courses through Elician's body. He shivers at the strength of it. 'But' – Lio continues, skewering Elician's relief just as it is born – 'he cannot be with you like this. He's our captive. Even if he eventually does decide to stay here, he doesn't have much of a choice about anything else in his life. And when you embraced him . . . what you did crossed more than a few Alelunen societal norms. You *know* this. But then you ran off to avoid dealing with his reaction.'

'Was he mad?'

'Stunned stupid is a better term for it,' he replies. He pats Elician's knee. Consoling, comforting. 'Still, even if it were culturally acceptable to hold someone that closely, he's been kept in a cage for years. And he was literally sent here to kill you. Right now, he's your *prisoner*. Whether he's protected by being in Kreuzfurt or not, he lacks the status to turn you down.'

Of course. Of course. Elician's shoulders slump. It was even worse than the standard warnings he had received growing up, whenever he had dared to even look at the other children in the palace. He was a prince, and they were not. They had to do anything he asked, and so it was best not to speak with them at all rather than invite the kind of trouble one wrong word might bring. He had to be separate, always, or risk consequences he had not anticipated, or relationships he could not escape.

Lio taps his chin. 'Hey. Listen to me. I'm not telling you to stop talking to him until the end of time. Talk to him, be yourself around him. Be his friend. But it can't be anything more than that until he is free. Until he truly has the freedom to choose if he *wants* to stay in Soleb and can pursue the life he genuinely wants. He can't feel that his ability to return to his people, nor his ability to even live a decent life in general, is dependent on his relationship with you.'

There is no point in arguing that Elician would never hold that threat above Cat's head. The point is made, the terms set and understood. Elician agrees. Lio clasps the back of his neck. Presses a kiss to his forehead in a way Cat would likely find intensely taboo and unacceptable.

'I'm sorry,' Lio says, resting his brow against Elician's in sympathy. 'I truly am. You have no idea how good it was to see you enjoy yourself with another person.'

'You missed a few late-night chats, it's true,' Elician confesses.

'I didn't. I just didn't interrupt.' Panic and shame fight for dominance in Elician's chest. 'There was no point in saying anything until it needed to be said. And you obviously didn't want me to know.'

'I'm sorry.'

'Don't be. But one last thing, all right? I know you and *your* intentions. I don't know his. Just be careful.'

'It's not like he can hurt me.'

Lio scowls and turns away. 'He can. Just not physically,' he says. Standing, he stretches his back and rotates his shoulders absently. 'You've just never had the opportunity to learn how to manage relationships. You make friends easily, El, you always have. But save for me and *possibly* your sister, you have never allowed them to mean anything substantial. And because of that . . . you don't know what kind of pain that can bring. Or what joy.'

'So, stay away?'

'No. Just be careful. That's all. Just be careful.'

So, stay away, Elician decides as Lio leaves for his own room. Staying away would be best. And luckily, he has plenty of practice doing just that.

In the morning, Elician finally commits himself to the task his uncle had given him. He finds Marina and asks for the Hall of Remembrance to be cleared so he can read out four hundred and fifty-two names. These are the dead that have accumulated over the past several weeks of fighting. Notices are sent to Kreuzfurt's residents, and its guests are informed of the ceremony about to take place. They are invited to add names to the litany, and his list grows by several dozen additions.

The parents of little Leitja, the girl Fen had failed to save, are still in the city. He makes time to meet with them too, to sit and listen to them tell stories of their child. He makes no apologies for his sister, but joins them in their grief.

For her part, Fen keeps to her threatened isolation. He sees her only once that day, and she very promptly walks in the opposite direction the moment their eyes meet. He has no interest in chasing her down and so he keeps to his business. He avoids meal hour at the House of the Wanting and passes his time with the Reapers instead. They are a smaller bunch, only a few dozen compared to Kreuzfurt's near two hundred Givers.

Cat is there, of course, sitting next to Fransen and Marina. He does not speak with the others, seeming to prefer watching them silently as he quickly eats any food placed in front of him. He eats so fast that Elician wonders if he even has a preference. But he does not ask, choosing to pass bowls along the table entirely without comment.

Elician thinks about apologizing. He probably should. But Cat catches him watching him at dinner, and the thought dissipates in an instant. Shame should have taken its place, but instead all he is left with is a genuine desire to ask Cat how he is doing. He leaves before he makes things worse.

On the day of the ceremony, Elician does not eat. He arrives early in a purple tunic and golden cloak. He walks through the Hall of Remembrance to make sure that everything is exactly where it needs to be, that each station has the appropriate list of names and that the timing of their individual tasks is marked down.

At the start of the ceremony, the hall will be dark. Only candles will illuminate the circular room. There are no windows, only one very carefully constructed glass aperture at the top of the ceiling, which collects light via a series of mirrors. This is funnelled into a single beam that can illuminate the chamber beneath. But a dark cloth will block that light source until Elician reads the one hundredth name on his list. Then the cloth is gradually drawn back, and as Elician reads on, the light will bounce from mirror to mirror, aided by strategic candlelight where necessary, until the hall appears to bask in the sun's great glory at the exact moment he reads the final name.

The Reapers are never seen at this ceremony. Yet their work is felt throughout, as they adjust mirrors and prisms from secret passageways. Death catering to Life, as Life recalls their dead.

Elician climbs the dais in the centre of the room and sets his list on the prepared lectern. The doors open, and one by one the listeners fill the space. The grieving, the aggrieved, the citizens there to give support. He cannot make out all their faces in the pre-ceremony gloom; they simply meld together as a homogenous presence all focused on him and him alone.

At the back, a lantern is held up. His signal to start.

He does.

There is no introduction, no entreaty, no explanation. To speak any words except for the names is to draw attention from those names. The names are the point and purpose. He reads, and he reads well. He could not save these men and women. He could not grant them life. But here, he can grant them immortality in hearts and minds. Never to be forgotten.

He does not look up. He does not meet the eyes of his people, nor react as the mirrors are employed to fill the room with glistening splendour. His feet ache, his fingers are tight and stiff. Three hundred names. He turns more pages. All before him are silent. Four hundred names.

Someone coughs. The light gets brighter. He reads, even as his mouth feels dry and his attention starts to waver. He transitions from the list of the dead soldiers to the list of the newly deceased. Then one name more remains: 'Leitja Vas Aranas.'

The mirrors shift and they are suddenly bathed in a light so blinding and pure that for a moment, Elician cannot see. The faces of the listeners are blurry, but there at the back he sees a harsh black outline. Cat stands as close to the doors as he possibly can, easily capable of disappearing outside the moment the crowd starts shifting to leave.

Elician wets his lips, breathes deep and finishes his task. 'To all who have died, we will remember you for eternity.' He bows low and deep at the names arrayed before him.

When he looks up, Cat is gone. Elician wishes that he had stayed.

CHAPTER ELEVEN

Fenlia

Elician leaves Kreuzfurt without saying goodbye.

Fen wakes to find a letter slipped under her door, covering several pages of fine stationery borrowed from Marina's desk. She recognizes the letterhead. As she flicks through them, increasingly annoyed that a letter has replaced his parting words, she realizes he has perfected another trick. The stationery is unlined, and yet Elician's rows are even in both height and angle. He may as well have written on a ruler, his script is so exact. But he had never received the harsh remedial lessons of their tutors when it came to perfecting his letterings; that had been an honour reserved for Fenlia alone.

Bastard.

'Dearest Fen,' she reads, sitting back on her bed and affecting her voice in an imperious tone – one which she imagines him using to dictate his latest round of chastisements. 'I must return to the front and find myself unable to give you the goodbyes you deserve to hear in person. Forgive me for this. Forgive me also for–' She falters, fingers clenching around the fragile paper. 'Forgive me also for not being able to grant your wish to leave Kreuzfurt.' Her shoulders slump and her anger wanes as she silently reads on.

I know you are unhappy here, and I know that your fate is one that others in your station also face. You are right to be discontented. And I understand well your desire to be someplace far beyond these city walls. I should have been more receptive, and I am sorry for diminishing your feelings. You deserved better from your brother. I will do better in the future.

While Father reigns, my ability to enact change is limited, but you know well my intentions once the transition has occurred. You, Adalei and Lio have a place in my court, and I will need you when the time comes. For the love I know you bear my father, for his kindness in calling you daughter, I have felt it imprudent to discuss what I shall require of you after his death. There may be many years before such a time comes to pass and I had not found it necessary to intervene or limit you to a path you may not wish to take.

But I see now that has been a mistake, and if you truly long for a place as my adviser on matters of great importance, then I would task you to do so now. I do not live in Kreuzfurt. I do not experience her in the way that you do. When I am king, I intend to change the structure of the city and its inhabitants, but you will be the one who can speak on her behalf. Advise me, Fenlia.

Make me a report, a proper report and not simply a letter of personal grievances. Adalei can provide you instruction on the form and structure should you require it, Zinnitzia and Marina too, should you feel comfortable enough asking for their assistance. Tell me all there is to know about Kreuzfurt: its land, its production capacity, its influence. Tell me of the Reapers and their work. What has been their impact? What truly is their purpose, and if this solution is not adequate, what should be the alternative? Advise me, Fenlia. Do so with care, and patience, and prove to me that you are capable of the due diligence I will require of you when I take the throne.

Zinnitzia and Marina have already set arrangements for you to take on supplementary course work at the House of the Unwanting, course work I understand you loathe and despise. While I cannot remove you from these courses, I would ask that you use them as a cover for further investigation. Take note of your surroundings while you have permission to traverse those halls. Few are given the opportunity to know what occurs within the House of the Unwanting, and your observations will be crucial to my final decisions.

In this, I do include the Reaper, Cat. I have sworn to return him to his people when the war is done, an act that potentially carries great risk for myself and my position. I ask you to understand his character, and his intentions, and to advise me on one matter of great importance: can I trust this man? You know well what we all stand to lose should I choose poorly.

Help me, dear sister. I will need you in order to ensure a future we can both be proud of. There are precious few people I would trust with this, and I trust you to always guide me well.

And know, as soon as I am able, I will see to it you leave Kreuzfurt and will never again be confined behind its walls.

I love you, Fen. I trust you.

Please, trust me too.

~E

He had signed his initial in a great swoop, flicking the end of the letter nearly all the way across the page. She is almost glad that he left without speaking to her in person. If he had looked at her while he said such things, if he had sworn her to his cause, she is not certain she could have maintained the dignity and composure necessary for such a thing. His words embarrass her. He trusts her more than she trusts herself. And she is terrified of letting him down.

Elician had been flawless when he read the names of their people. She had been prepared to hate him for eternity only three days before, and yet he had spoken the names of their dead with care and consideration. It filled her with pride to know that, one day, *he will be our king.*

They had fought. She had said things that would have had Zinnitzia screaming for hours. But despite that, he still wants her to be on his council. He still trusts her enough to assign her this mission, even knowing that she already hates the place she'd be reporting upon.

She wipes her eyes. Sets the letter to the side. Thinks.

She knows some of the details Elician is asking for, but nothing with any true accuracy. She does not know the size and scale of the city in its entirety, nor the crops that are grown in the farmland or their yield, nor the exact figure of how many Givers or Reapers are stationed here. Her greatest source of knowledge comes mainly from her personal experiences: daily lessons in history, mathematics and natural sciences that are offset by long hours training with Zinnitzia.

She is the only *child* Giver or Reaper. Cat is the next youngest, and he is already past the age of majority in both their countries. She does not know much about the lives of their older counterparts, though she presumes *they* do not have schoolwork folded into their schedules. There must be more to their duties.

Someone manages the pigeons and the mail call. Someone informs their guards – who even *are* their guards? – to open the gates at the start of each morning. There is so much more to understand about the city of Kreuzfurt as a whole. And she needs to understand it. Because Elician needs to know about it. And it is her job. *Her job.* She smiles. *Finally.* She is no longer being judged just on her ability to heal.

Fen asks one of the Reapers near the entrance of the House of the Unwanting where to find Cat and is directed up seven flights of stairs. She climbs them, legs burning with discomfort, then finds a room marked with a silver star. The door is half open and she pushes it the rest of the way. Marina is there, sitting on the floor in front of Elician's Alelunen assassin. The curtains behind them are closed, but the room is illuminated by a candle.

Marina twists to look at her and frowns. 'Princess,' she drawls. She does not stand to bow, merely inclines her head ever so slightly. 'Is there something I can do for you?'

'Lessons,' Fen says. 'You . . . you wanted me to come for lessons.'

'More than a week ago,' Marina agrees. 'Have you changed your mind about joining us?'

'Yes.'

The Reaper matriarch squints at her, expression icy with disdain. Slowly, though, she inclines her head. 'Sit.' Fen shuffles closer. Marina and Cat sit cross-legged. Not touching, but close. She mimics their posture, glancing back at Marina, then looks to Cat. He is still grotesquely pale, save for the black scar on his cheek, but he is dressed exactly like any other Reaper in Soleb – all in black with a bell at his wrist and a veiled hood ready to draw up when needed. The bell jingles as Cat shifts his wrist in his lap, alerting to all the world: *Danger! Danger! A Reaper is here!*

'I doubted you would ever come,' Marina admits. 'Did your brother command it of you?'

'Yes,' she replies shortly. Something in this room smells . . . awful. The same horrid scent she had noticed when she first entered the House of the Unwanting nearly two weeks before. 'But I'm here now, aren't I?' She tries to surreptitiously identify the source of the smell, but notices something else instead.

Reapers are meant to cover their skin at all times, the only exception being their faces. (It is rarely necessary to use the hoods to block contact there.) But now, neither Marina nor Cat are wearing gloves. Their bare skin glows, unseemly in the reflected light from the candle. Her stomach clenches at the sight.

'It's been almost three years since you came here and you still don't have much experience with Reapers, do you, Fen?' Marina asks. Fen swallows hard at her mentor's tone. At the implicit accusation. Marina isn't wrong though. Fen has avoided interacting with the Reapers of Kreuzfurt to the best of her ability. Nothing good ever comes from associating with Death. But . . . Elician has trusted her to be able to get him information he can use, so she has to do this. 'Tell me,' Marina entreats, 'what do you know?'

Fen fidgets, replying awkwardly, 'If you touch a Reaper's skin, you die.' It is the best summary she can give.

Marina makes a speculative noise, a short, humming thing there and gone again. She reaches out, traversing the space between them, and touches Fen's exposed wrist. Fen flinches despite knowing better. Reapers cannot kill Givers. Not like that. They are both chosen by the gods, and the gods' chosen ones cannot use their powers upon one another. But she has only *been* a Giver for a little less than three years. For eleven years of her life, she had been taught to listen for the small silver bells at the Reapers' wrists. To cross to the other side of the street. To avoid contact with Reapers at all cost. They are Death's chosen, and Death should have no place in a kingdom devoted to Life. Even when Marina had been serving at court as her brother's guard, training them how to swordfight in the enclosed gardens of Himmelsheim, Fen had physically kept her distance. Fen may be a Giver now. A Reaper's touch may do nothing to her. But even the *thought* of it still terrifies her.

'What do you feel?' Marina asks, uncaring of Fen's concern.

'I don't . . . I don't know.' Marina's skin is cool and dry. That is not what repulses her. Beneath the touch is something more. Something that flutters at the back of Fen's mind. 'It's like trying to press two opposing magnets together.' She shivers, her stomach still clenching nervously. She tries to pull free, but Marina keeps her hand where it is.

'You're not dead,' the matriarch points out needlessly.

Fen scowls. 'I'm not normal though. If a normal person touches a Reaper's skin, they die.'

Finally, Marina settles back. She tilts her head in consideration. 'There are other words that are used to describe us, of course, one more ancient and preferred than the rest, but in this time period "touched" or "divine" seem to be most popular.'

Fen does not like either term. 'Touched' sounds a bit too on the nose, while 'divine' seems almost disrespectful. Their gods, Life and Death, rule over all. *They* are not divine, merely lackeys in a divine game that she does not want to play. 'What's the other word?' she asks.

'Exalted,' Marina replies. She says another word too, likely the Lunae translation, but Cat does not react to either word despite her generosity. 'Tell me, what do you think we teach here, Fenlia?'

The question catches her off guard. She shrugs to buy herself some time, but Marina is far more patient than Zinnitzia. She can remain silent as her quarry writhes in the trap she has set. Sweat beads at the back of Fen's neck. 'You teach how to kill,' she says, already suspecting that is not correct.

'I don't need to teach any Reaper how to do that,' Marina says, almost amused. 'Cat could kill someone when he was a child, from the moment he woke up as a Reaper in Alelune. Reapers are not like Givers. For most Givers, crossing the boundary between life and death is a difficult and complicated matter.' She smiles a little, as if Fen's strange talent makes her useless abilities that much more palatable. 'But for Reapers, the transition is far easier. Life yearns for Death in the end, and Reapers connect the two quite nicely.'

She still cannot understand. 'What do you teach, then?'

'I teach our Reapers how to manage that which is alive.' Marina gestures to the candle still flickering between them. She lowers her hand over it, and Fen watches as her palm toasts above the flame. 'Die,' Marina says. Instantly they are plunged into darkness. The light vanishes at her word alone.

A noise rattles through the air. It is a voice, maybe. A voice that has been turned about and skinned so only its abstract form can be understood. It hitches, like a moaning rasp, three times in succession. Each repetition gets slightly higher in pitch. Marina strikes a match. Her face is illuminated in a subtle orange glow, and so is Cat's. Cat's lips are spread in what could almost be considered a smile, and Fen realizes: he had been laughing. That horrific noise had been a laugh.

Marina lights the wick of the candle and gestures for Cat to give it a try. His lips even quirk a little, like he had been hoping for an opportunity to show off. And now that he's been given leave to do so–

He snaps his thumb and middle finger together and the light winks out between one flicker and the next. It is Marina's turn to laugh now. 'Very clever indeed,' she admits, still chuckling. 'You truly are full of surprises, aren't you?' Marina lights it again.

Fen reaches for it now, frowning as her fingers hover over the flickering candle. Heat licks them, and a subtle pain blossoms along her skin. Drawing back, she rubs her thumb over each tingling tip, soothing the ache, healing the nascent burn before it dares to get worse. 'But fire is not . . . it's not alive.'

'Isn't it?' Marina asks. 'Are the molecules not moving? Does the flame not need sustenance to thrive? Does it not require fuel to keep burning? Can it not move? Who is to say that fire is not a living thing?'

'It cannot think,' Fen refutes.

'Neither does a plant. And yet, is a flower any less alive than you are?'

'I can't make a flower spring up from the ground either, so what does it matter if it's technically alive or not?'

Marina does not seem terribly impressed by her proclamation.

'Have you ever tried?' she asks. 'Making flowers grow?'

She has not. She does not know anyone who has. No one in the temple has mentioned plants. As far as she has seen or heard, Givers work exclusively with animals and humans. There is no in-between or room for alteration. Even Reapers do not seem to accidentally kill plant life they interact with. When they do kill them, it seems to take attention and effort rather than a simple brush of the skin – unlike with people. Plants are just *different*.

Marina clears her throat. 'Life is life. Death is death. And yet there are some things that are alive that need a little death to continue surviving. And some lives are surprisingly stubborn when it comes to accepting a god's influence on their existence.'

'What do you mean?'

'Think of a forest with an unbalanced ecosystem,' Marina replies. 'The death of one tree can ensure the safety of the whole forest – if it's inappropriately taking too many nutrients from the surrounding flora. Reapers can kill that tree to ensure the forest thrives. A thriving forest leads to an increase of food supply which leads to the health and well-being of all lives within and beyond the forest's boundaries. Life comes from death, as it were.' That seems wildly simplistic, and yet Cat is staring at Marina intently, brows furrowed and lips pressed tight. 'Though trees tend to be a bit reluctant to be a part of any kind of change. They seem to like being trees.'

'The trees like being trees?'

Marina nods. 'Perhaps a good starting point for you, Fen, is to think more about what actually is alive and dead. And expand your horizons beyond just people and animals.' She stands, stretching her back and cracking her neck. 'I have an idea. Wait here. I'll be right back.' She crosses the dark carpeted floor, disappearing behind the door without another word.

Fen shuffles a little so she is not pressed so close to Cat. He does not seem to mind or notice. He is too busy staring at the flame. Biting her lip, Fen does the same. Fire is not alive. She knows that. It cannot be alive. And yet, if it is not alive, then how could Marina and Cat affect it? More importantly: 'How did you do that without touching it?' Fen asks. 'I thought you had to touch it.'

Cat stays silent. He does not try to make eye contact, nor does he seem to care about her at all. Frustration burns in Fen's chest. *Why would anyone want to be your friend when you act like this?* she thinks savagely. Then, slower, *Why does Elician?*

If the candle is all Cat cares about, then the candle is all she will focus on too. She adjusts her weight, then settles her fingers to the side of the flickering wick. Not so close this time: only close enough to feel the heat. Its incorporeal presence flutters against her palm. She closes her eyes. Fire moves with the air around it. One as small as this shivers in tandem as she breathes. She exhales and the heat trembles against her skin, then settles.

The small flame rotates around the wick ever so subtly, nibbling at the wax-coated string with one bite at a time. Why? To eat, yes. To sustain itself. It needs to sustain itself somehow to exist. But what is fire? Why does it burn? Why does it need air to survive? Why the heat?

Abruptly, the heat vanishes. She blinks, squinting in the gloom. Without the light from the candle, it is hard to see at first, but there is enough radiant light from under the curtained windows for her to make out Cat eventually. He has moved his hand. Moved it so it is directly parallel to Fen's.

He does not speak. Instead, he stares down at the candle that is quickly growing cool before them. There is nothing to touch. Nothing except the wick. But is it the wick that she should be trying to bring to life? Or something else? Marina had mentioned molecules. But which molecules need to speed up? Which ones need to go faster in order to burst with combustion?

She stares at the wick. She thinks *burn* as hard as she can, willing all her energy to her palm as it cups the wick, as if that will make even the slightest bit of difference. It does not change a thing. The wick stays cold. *Light,* she tries this time. Nothing happens. *Start,* she commands. It stays exactly the same. *Live,* she finally settles on.

There.

At the tip, the black – almost invisible – thread begins to glow.

Slowly at first, and the light is so small. The tiniest of sparks. *Live,* she encourages. *Live.* The spark grows, turning brighter, rounder, bigger, until finally it leaps from hesitant light to active flame. Cat nods slowly. Then snaps his fingers. The light flickers out.

'Hey!' She swats his hand away and cups the wick again. Thinks, again, *Live.* The sparkle of orange comes faster this time. It crests into a flame brighter and more vibrant than before. She grins at him, challenging. He blinks, and the fire dies. Spreading her hands a bit wider now, she throws her energy at the fire. *Live,* she shouts in the back of her mind. *Live!*

Red spears through the candle from tip to tip. It illuminates the inside of the wax, melting the whole body in moments as the fire bursts up like one of the festive rockets that race across the sky every Solar Festival. Flames shoot out at all sides, catching the carpet and spreading faster, out of control.

Fen yelps, legs untangling badly as she attempts to back away from the glowing arc. The hem of her skirt ignites. She slaps at it hysterically, hardly cognizant of Cat or the keening noise that echoes in the back of her head. Stumbling to her feet, she watches in horror as the fire starts reaching for the curtains, the bedding. Cat thrusts his hand towards the flame's centre mass, reaching for the pitiful remains of the candlestick now entirely engulfed. She screams, 'That's not going to–'

The candle's fire snaps out of existence. Cat holds his other hand to the side, and with a great slashing slice of his arm, the whole room descends instantly into darkness as every remaining bit of flame dies. All fires have been suppressed, killed, by Cat's quick hands.

'Good,' Marina says when she re-enters the room. 'Thank you for not burning down the tower.' Fen's not sure which one of them is getting thanked for that. She is the one who started the fire, but Cat is the one who ended it. She almost asks, but then she sees another woman standing just behind Marina. Short and plump, with peachy skin and red cheeks, this woman has short grey curly hair. Her clothes are bland shades of olive green and yellow that hang over her round body like a smock. Fen has seen her before, bustling about the grounds. She had thought she was a guest.

'Marvellous job, really!' the stranger says with astonishing familiarity. 'I haven't seen anyone manage that trick nearly so quickly.' Marina draws back the curtains to inspect the damage to the room.

'Who are you?' Fen asks.

'Elena Morsen, at your service, Your Highness.' She bows low and deep.

Marina kneels by Cat, setting a book to her side that Fen hadn't noticed she had brought with her, and takes his hands in hers. His palms are burned but healing fast, poppy-red blisters fading before their eyes, leaving the skin unblemished and whole.

'Fascinating,' Elena breathes out.

'Did you see what happened?' Fen asks.

'We watched the last few moments, yes,' Marina says, giving Cat's hands a gentle squeeze before pulling away. She hands him the book.

'And you didn't *stop* it?'

'I didn't need to, did I?'

'Would you have?'

The old matriarch sighs. 'If it got much larger, yes. Any other questions?'

Yes. More than a few. Fen's fingers twitch at the phantom memory of the precise moment when flames came alive by her will alone. Heat and possibility sparking into existence just at a thought. 'Why did it get so big? The first time – the first time I did it, I only lit the wick. But *that* . . . Why did it explode like that?'

'I'd say it's because you wanted it more. What do you think?'

'Spite has never healed any of my patients in the House of the Wanting,' Fen mumbles.

'Perhaps a different emotion inspires a different result,' Marina replies vaguely. 'And a different level of affinity. It's not unlike learning archery or swordplay in a way. Some talents simply come easier than others.' Then, clearing her throat, she gestures to the woman she has brought with her. 'Elena is a physician from Crowen who volunteers at Kreuzfurt during the summer, delivering seminars at the House of the Unwanting to those interested in practising the craft.'

'A physician? Why would the House of the Unwanting need a physician?' If someone were ill, they could just go to the House of the Wanting instead.

'Oh, I'm going to enjoy working with you, I think,' Elena announces, clapping her hands together. 'Do you suppose you could practise that trick a bit first though? Get better at controlling those flames? I have something I want to show you, but it will be so much more fun if you can get that trick down properly. Does that work for you, Marina?'

'As you like. Tomorrow, then. Fen, if you still intend to continue these lessons, you and Cat will meet here after eighth bell, and you'll go together to locate each of the stinging bark vines that have started growing around Kreuzfurt. You will find them, Cat will kill them, Fen will burn the remains. When you've mastered that, Elena will take over your training. You'll do what she says, when she says it.'

'Both of us?'

'Problem?'

Not on the surface. It would give her time to watch Cat, as her brother wishes. But Fen still has a question for Marina. What is the point of giving her *these* specific lessons? 'I thought Zinnitzia sent me to this House to learn how to heal things.' How to heal a scar capable of marring a Reaper's face specifically, but she will gladly avoid touching Cat for a while yet if she can get away with it. Even just being near him today has taken most of her nerve.

'Yes,' Marina agrees, 'but perhaps you need to learn something else, to help you achieve your purpose.'

Rage flares through Fen, as hot as the flames Cat has just put out. 'Making a fire is not going to save a little girl from dying,' Fen grinds out. Marina nods, like a puppet on strings. Going through the same tired motions as every other tutor Fen has ever had.

But then, before she can respond, Elena says, 'It will if that little girl is cold.' She picks up the melted remains of the candle Fen had destroyed. Holds it towards her once more. 'Maybe all you need is a little perspective and willingness to try something different. Who knows what new skills you might acquire? After all, you didn't know you could light a fire like this before today either.'

She's right, Fen concedes. And if Elena is right about that, then it begs a different question altogether. If this is knowledge that the House of the Unwanting possesses, then what else do the Reapers know how to do? And more than that, *What else can* I *do too?*

PART II

Water is fluid, and its thoughts are ever changing. Its form ever evolving. And Water always longs for something more. It presses against the vessels Earth crafts for it, moulding its shape again and again. One day, Life heard its voice sighing into the dark night of the world Life had made. It lived now as something else. And so Life asked these forms it had taken, 'I sent you to seek, and seek you did. You made yourself something new, but now you cry. Why do you weep?'

And Grass and Tree, made from Water and Earth, replied, 'You made us seek, and seek we did, but there must be more out there. There must be more we can do?'

But Life had no answers. Life encouraged and created new growth that basked under the rays of his great golden sun. Life was satisfied with each new something to fill the world that came from nothing. But the Water that had slipped into every space it could fill still cried out for more. It wanted more than Life knew how to give.

And so, Death was born.

Death listened to Grass crying and Tree despairing. She heard the pleas of Water deep within each of these souls and she offered them what Life could not. 'Die,' she told Grass. 'Unmake yourself, so that you may then live again.' And Grass did as it was bid. Grass bent down low and undid all the work that it had done to grow in the first place. Water returned to Earth. Earth reclaimed its vessels. Life startled and cried out for Grass to stop, but Death stood before him and would not let him interfere.

– *The Origins of the Gods*, Anonymous

CHAPTER TWELVE

Elician

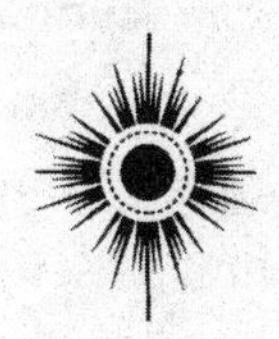

It is a long ride back to the front. Elician had sent news to his uncle, so Anslian knew when to expect them, but time seemed to stretch out endlessly despite the estimate. For much of the first day, Elician and Lio are silent; there is not much conversation to be had. They eat while riding, and dismount only when the horses need to rest. Then, Elician pulls his saddle and bags off his mare's back and lets her roam the tall grass and drink from one of the Bask's longer tributaries. They are making good time, Elician knows that, but that success sits heavy in his stomach. Being free from the constant bloodshed of war is a gift he had not expected to receive. And now that he has experienced it, returning to battle is an exhausting notion.

By the second day, though, Lio rallies admirably. He clears his throat and begins a rambling diatribe that lasts through much of the morning. At noon, he suggests turning back. 'We could tell your uncle your horse lost a shoe,' he offers with a shrug and an easy smile. 'We could stay in Kreuzfurt for a week at least after that; Marina would cover for us. He did say we had *three* months to return. We could stay longer if you wanted.'

Staying longer would mean risking more time spent with Cat. It would mean thinking too much about plans and futures that could not yet exist. Elician could not comfortably hold those thoughts for long; he would never escape their pull if he did. 'We're needed at the front,' he tells Lio instead.

Lio scoffs, shaking his head, and says, 'Your family is asking too much from you,' without even a hint of shame.

Elician can almost hear Marina's lessons from long ago, always ignored but never forgotten. *Givers aren't meant to be on the battlefield. They aren't meant to be around that much death.*

'You're the one who wants to marry into my family,' Elician reminds him lightly. 'That comes with expectations too, you know.'

'Adalei is worth it,' he replies, as serene as a duck in a pond. His cheeks darken as he smiles around the curves of his beloved's name. 'Your cousin is a woman beyond compare.'

Lio does not have a way with words. He has never been able to master any poetic turns of phrase, despite his best efforts. In one very early letter to Adalei, at the start of their courtship, Lio compared her to dirt, explaining *everything good comes from the dirt* as earnestly as any sixteen-year-old boy could. *Sustenance grows from it, it's the foundation everything is built on, and in the summer, it helps cool the worst of the heat. What better thing could there be in the whole world than dirt?*

His family teases Elician for writing love poetry to Adalei on Lio's behalf, but he doubts they understand how much of this necessity Lio creates himself. Elician simply ensures she understands what Lio is trying to say, to avoid her becoming offended at his attempts. The rest . . . is Lio. And Lio has succeeded brilliantly as far as anyone can tell.

For some reason, Adalei is charmed by his best friend, and for longer than anyone would care to admit, Lio has always been equally charmed by her. Dozens of men and women have tried to catch his eye, knowing that a place at Lio's side means a place near the future king of Soleb. Glittering jewels, shimmering robes, chiselled faces and rapturous bodies have all done nothing. Lio's heart has been Adalei's since the day she flung her slipper at a courtier who dared speak out of turn at a banquet.

He proposed to her that night: fourteen years old and without any notion of propriety. *You're just a boy*, she'd told him simply. *I have no interest in children.*

Her reaction had done little to dissuade Lio. He had nodded, accepting her opinion, and simply said, *I won't be* just a boy *for ever.*

Ask me when you're older, then, she suggested.

And he had. Every year since. He had kept up to date with the work she did as an ambassador – and had taught himself the arts that Adalei preferred, so he could help her in her own craft-making. He had served as an official crownsguard on the rare occasions she needed a proper escort during official duties. And he had always made sure that she had time to herself, away from the pestering politicians who chased her down for *one more thing*.

'Do you remember when Adalei let me escort her to the Solar Festival?' he asks now, pulling memories out of the cobwebs in Elician's mind.

His first thought is nowhere near as joyful. That had been the night his father had announced Elician and Lio would finally be sent to the front to join the war efforts. But if Elician scrapes hard enough, he can just conjure the image of Lio and Adalei. Both were dressed in the uniforms of their station, perfectly matching in gold and purple. Adalei's head had been carefully covered by the finest silk scarf, ends delicately wrapping around her neck and trailing over her shoulders. Her eyes were framed with kohl, her lips painted red. She had gallantly allowed Lio to walk her into the ballroom, her hand tucked neatly in the crook of his elbow.

Lio had been so flushed with pleasure at the gesture that he had not heard King Aliamon's war announcement at all. He had kept smiling, dreamy with delight, until Marina dragged Elician from the Festival so he wouldn't disgrace himself before all their assorted guests. Then and only then did Lio realize the calamity that had just befallen them.

A mere month later, they'd ridden out from Himmelsheim to join the war with Marina sent to Kreuzfurt, banished from Elician's household. But Adalei . . . Adalei had finally done what Lio had always dreamed of. She had given him a token, one of her silk headscarves. *Keep it close,* she'd said, pressing it to his hands. *Bring it back when the war is won.*

Elician glances at Lio now, as his hand rests on his chest. Elician knows the scarf lies beneath Lio's tunic, always folded over his heart, over three years from that parting.

He still writes to her every occasion he gets. Adalei always writes back. 'I'm not a child anymore,' Lio says now as if Elician is not very much aware of that fact.

'We haven't been children in a long time,' Elician agrees solemnly.

'When we win this war, I'm going to propose to her again. I'm going to do it right.'

'And she'll say yes,' he says, fighting to smile even as his mood continues to turn ever more sour.

That night, when they finally rest for the evening, Elician lies on his bedroll and imagines Lio's wedding. He imagines blessing the union of the most devoted man in all of Soleb. Knowing that the moment he does, it will mean he will never be able to resurrect Lio from the dead again. *When the war is over,* he thinks, trying to reassure himself, *I won't have to be worried about him. There will be no need to continue to keep him safe from harm.*

Something yowls in the dark of the night. He twists, searching for the animal. But he never sees it. No one ever does.

The attack comes only a day's ride from the front.

Larger groups of civilians had started to become commonplace on the road, shifting in Elician's mind from general travellers to refugees as they appeared more desperate in their flight east. His grip tightens on his reins as he encourages more speed from his horse. There is a fine balance between overworking the beast and reaching maximum efficiency, and he tries to achieve it. He worries all the while as the faces of his people grow grimmer with each passing day.

When he sees his uncle's banners far sooner than expected, he falters, stunned by their presence. He draws his horse up short, stopping it mid-stride. It huffs angrily at him, and even Lio needs to pull around in a circle to make it back to his side. The banners are too far from Altas. If they are here, then the city has fallen. Panic thrums through Elician's veins as he clicks his tongue and urges his mare forward once more. His heart beats faster and faster as he approaches those flickering gold flags set to either side of a great tent.

A soldier holds out a restraining hand as he approaches. Elician reaches beneath his shirt and removes the golden pendant so the sun hangs visibly around his neck. 'I am Prince Elician, son of King Aliamon. Let me through.' Immediately, the soldier bows. Elician dismounts and thrusts the reins into the man's hand as Lio follows behind him. 'Where is my uncle?'

'Inside, Your Highness.'

It is the accent that tips their hand. The words are Soleben, but the accent is from Alelune. Elician stops mid-step and swirls about. Lio has already pulled his sword free from its scabbard. He impales the soldier before Elician reaches him. The tent flaps thrust open and more soldiers come billowing out.

Elician scrambles, hand fumbling for his sword, surprised and wrongfooted. A blade catches him in the side. He gasps as lights flicker across his vision. Lio roars loudly behind him. His consciousness fades as he crashes to the earth. Time blinks forward and he gasps, jerking upright to see bodies lying in a crescent around him. Lio straddles his legs, sword up and defending his prone form from further harm. He must sense Elician stirring, though, because he steps to the side and makes a series of lightning-fast strikes against a pair of assailants to the left.

Rolling to his knees, Elician lurches to his feet. He draws his longsword and falls into step beside his friend. They are outnumbered, and badly so. Grey-clad soldiers continue to flood from the tent in an endless tide. An army of insects focused on one thing and one thing alone.

Elician grits his teeth as he swings his blade towards the enemy. He twists and turns, stabbing at each body that dares throw itself towards him. It is, of course, only a matter of time until one finally manages to strike Lio in the back. Elician hears the harsh hiss of air as it leaves his friend's mouth. He turns to see Lio fumble and falter, stabbed once, twice, *three* times before Elician can even try to get between him and those who would harm him.

'Enough,' someone shouts. He turns but does not recognize the bald man who approaches with all the cadence of a commander. 'Surrender, and you can heal your friend.'

Cold horror crashes through him. He stares uncomprehendingly at the man, the flags, the tent, and the Alelunen soldiers so deep in Soleben territory. His fingers tremble. Lio is bleeding out on the ground beside him, unconscious. Perhaps he is already dead.

Lio's voice echoes through his head. *Do good now, because who knows what comes next?*

He drops his sword to kneel beside Lio and presses his bare hand to Lio's face. *Come back,* he wills. His closest friend, his brother in all things, jerks awake beneath his touch. He gasps for air even as the soldiers rush forward, binding Elician's hands behind his back and thrusting a dark shroud over his head. It's an almost amusing mockery of how he had handled Cat on the way to Kreuzfurt.

He hears Lio start to shout, hears him yelling profanities. It makes Elician smile. His father had told him that he didn't have a choice. He could only be the Prince of Soleb first, Giver second. But this was something his father would never be able to understand.

It *is* a choice, and his loved ones will win every time.

He is mid-laugh when something hard strikes him in the back of the head. His consciousness winks out, and after that, he doesn't know how much time he loses. Only that it is long enough to obscure where he is and how far they have taken him.

CHAPTER THIRTEEN

Fenlia

Fen meets Cat at the entrance to the House of the Unwanting an hour after breakfast. At his side is the oldest Reaper Fen has ever seen, who stands gnarled and knobby, and seems weary about the eyes. They had been talking quietly as she approached, Cat murmuring words Fen did not quite hear. But when they see her, they stop speaking. She tries not to take offence, especially after the old man presses a hand to his heart and bows as best as he's able to.

The wind blows a little as she steps in close to greet them properly. Her nose twitches. *They smell really bad.* Fen sniffs, discreetly rubbing her nose. She tries to be polite about it, though there is an unmissable taint of earthiness around them, which feels unnatural on a human body. Earth, dirt, mushrooms and trees. *Do they even wash?* It is far too impolite to ask.

'I'm Fransen, I'll be leading you about the gardens,' the old man says. 'When we come across those vines Marina wants gone . . . well, then you two will do your business, yes?'

'I know my way around,' Fen argues quietly. 'And I know what stinging bark looks like. I can do it.'

'Maybe you can, but I'm meant to chaperone, so I'm going to chaperone.' Fransen shrugs. He says something that sounds almost like Lunae, and Cat lets out a startled noise of surprise. 'Did I say it right?' A subtle shake of the head, then a much more precise repetition. *Let's go,* Fen translates slowly.

'I don't need a chaperone,' Fen tries one last time, knowing it is futile.

'It's not for you.'

That has her glancing at Cat, but Cat does not bother looking her way. He ducks his head low, and his brown hair blocks out his face as they walk along the walls of Kreuzfurt. Fen's done this circuit before, but this time she pays attention to everything. She memorizes what she sees, intending to consolidate all the information she can into the notebook she has started to keep on her desk.

Kreuzfurt has seven gardens, each with its own kind of purpose and structure, each with its own pond. The ponds vary in size, some small enough to leap over, others impossible to cross in a single bound. Dedicated farmland rests behind the Houses of the Wanting and Unwanting, and enough fruits and vegetables are planted and harvested there to export out of the city. But the gardens still host a mélange of fruits, berries and nuts of their own. One has a line of olive trees, another walnuts.

Fen and Cat follow Fransen as he walks slowly through each garden, pointing out the troublesome vines that Marina wants destroyed. 'That one,' he says, gesturing with the end of his walking stick. 'See its leaves? They're shaped like stars. And the blue is in the centre. That's how you know it's stinging bark.' The vine itself is rough. Thick and corded, it otherwise blends perfectly with the texture of the tree it is wrapped around. Easily overlooked by a casual observer.

Cat pulls off one of his gloves and lightly trails his finger along the edges of one of the vine's leaves. There is no immediate loss of life, but slowly the verdant edges and vibrant blue streaking begin to fade. Colour is sapped from the plant. Water drips to the ground as if it is wringing itself free. The leaves turn crusty and brown, and the transition spreads. From one leaf to another, one stem to another it goes, until the entire vine, from root to farthest tip, is as dry as foliage just before winter.

When it's over, Cat steps back, letting Fen take his place. Her hands hover over the vine. A simple touch of her skin, and it would be enough for this vine to come hurtling back to life. Just as easily as Cat had killed it in the first place. Some things simply long for survival. They fight for it, leaping at the chance to return.

But she does not want to heal this vine. She wants it to burn.

With the candle, she had commanded the wax-coated string to live. But it hadn't been alive in the same way that the vine had. It doesn't yearn to go back to being a nuisance on a tree. *Molecules*, Marina had said. It isn't the vine as it *is* that needs to live. It is everything that makes it whole. Fen pulls on the memory of the day before. On the feeling of the fire bursting into life. That moment of shift, that precipice. Like climbing the stairs up all twelve floors of the Houses of the Wanting or Unwanting, each step winding tension tighter until there is nowhere left for that tension to go but down.

An agonizing ascent, then a sudden freefall.

Sharp pain snaps between her fingers. She opens her eyes as the vine burns.

'I did it . . . *I did it!*' She twists towards Cat, and he smiles somewhat. Half his mouth seems to be tilting upwards while the other awkwardly trails off like an ellipsis leading to a question she had not asked. The expression rests in the space a smile should be, and he nods once, twisting his hand so the bell jingles on his wrist.

'Well done, Princess, well done,' Fransen says. 'On to the next, yes?'

She puffs up her chest in pride and nods. 'This way,' she says. 'I think I saw another one this way.' She leads him along, thinking, *I can't wait to tell Elician what I did,* knowing he would be so proud of her. Knowing, too, that he would want to learn more about this, and that she does as well.

Once Fen understands the trick, starting fires comes naturally. It takes five days to walk through every part of Kreuzfurt, exploring each tree, each pillar, each wide-open area for any lingering trace of stinging bark. Fransen accompanies them through all of it, wearily trailing behind and delaying their progress as they wait for him to catch up.

'Does it hurt to walk?' Cat asks quietly when he sees Fransen rubbing his left knee. He has a low voice, deep and guttural. It scratches at his throat when he talks, too dry and always on the edge of a cough. Rarely does he deign to talk to *her*, but on occasion he will grunt or hiss, or make some other noise or gesture she takes as a response. When he does speak, though, he seems to always say something she had been thinking or considering herself. Fransen's walking had been driving her to distraction, and she is *glad* that someone has finally put into words what she'd struggled to find the most tactful way to say.

Fransen tells them, 'It doesn't really. But for forty years I had a bad knee – had it hacked into pretty good during the River Wars. Ever since waking up a Reaper, it hasn't bothered me at all, and yet I keep feeling like it should. It's the absence that drives me insane more than anything else, I think.' Cat's brows furrow at that. His nose scrunches up. He opens his mouth as if he is going to argue but closes it again while still looking confused. Fransen smiles genially and pats Cat's head like a favoured pet. 'Come along, we're almost done.'

They are. They look very carefully at all the remaining gardens, but none of them see any lingering traces of the vines. Fransen encourages them to do one final walk about the grounds just to make sure, though.

'I don't understand why either of you had to come with me in the first place. I could have just lit them on fire without them dying first.'

'And if it got out of control, how would you have put the fire out?' Fransen *tsks*.

'It wouldn't have got out of control,' she replies. Cat had only needed to intervene twice, and both times she could have stamped on the flames if they had truly become a problem. Fransen does not seem so easily convinced. He sniffs and shrugs one rumpled shoulder up with no further comment. Fen scowls at the ground beneath her feet, asking, 'Have you ever withered vines before?' as they continue their circuit.

'Oh, once or twice, though I wasn't this efficient.'

'And fire, have you seen *that* before?'

'No,' he replies. 'Though Marina and Zinnitzia have been working their craft for far longer. I'm sure they know far more than I do.' She knew that. She tries not to show her disappointment at his lack of knowledge. She really doesn't want to ask Zinnitzia about being a Giver yet. *Sun above, she'd probably lecture me for not paying attention sooner and then give me even* more *homework to do,* Fen thinks in horror. Elician will get his answers eventually. But Fen is resolved to take her time and do it methodically – Zinnitzia just happens to be at the end of her list of things to tackle. It seems more prudent to keep it that way.

On the sixth day of her new training regimen, though, she does not need to wander the grounds of Kreuzfurt snooping for information. Instead, Fransen takes them deep into the House of the Unwanting, circling up through the many staircases until they reach a series of corridors that lead to the House's great library. Elena Morsen has set up a kind of workshop at the far end, and Fransen settles into a large chair by a window as Elena welcomes them over.

He closes his eyes and seems to doze off in moments. Fen walks briskly towards the rows of long desks. Papers and mysterious equipment are spread across every available surface, and she stands as far away from Cat as she can politely get away with, waiting to be acknowledged.

Elena greets them both with a jolly wave, wiping sweaty palms on the front of her tunic before sitting on the edge of her table and shuffling back to let her legs hang. 'Tell me, Princess,' she says, foregoing any preamble, 'what makes something alive?'

'Independent movement,' Fen suggests. She glances at Cat. 'And the ability to reproduce.'

'Good. Cat? Thoughts? Anything else?' He blinks at her, clearly not anticipating the direct question. Fen opens her mouth to give an excuse for him – *he doesn't talk much* – but Cat surprises her with an answer.

'Breathing,' he murmurs, nose scrunching as if he is trying to remember something from long ago. 'Growth. Excretion.'

'Plants don't breathe,' Fen argues. 'So that doesn't count.'

'They do, actually. Alpeur Rangie identified the unique cell structure of what he called a *stoma* on a series of plant samples in 839,' Elena says. 'It's a bit complicated, but the short of it is that plant life takes in gas and releases it in a manner that we'd consider to be breathing. More or less.'

It's an Alelunen name. Alelunen science. Fen bites her lip. *Watch. Learn.* 'But . . . fire doesn't breathe either.' Unless it has a secret stoma too.

'Fire is actually a unique case. You're right in that *it* is technically not alive. But it does all the things that would require life. It moves, it eats, it grows. It needs oxygen to survive so it mimics a need for breathing, and it can even replicate in the sense that it spawns more fire just by its contact. Where it fails is that the fire *itself* is more of a response to something that is happening to a living cell beneath. That cell, and all of its atomic structure, has been given so much excess energy that it ignites. The fire is not alive, but it *is* the result of an action taken upon it.'

'But I told it to live when I started setting fires in the first place,' Fen argues.

'Just because you tell something to do something doesn't mean it will. The *telling* doesn't do much. The intention and the focus you apply to it, however, do a great deal more. If it helps you to think that you're making it live, then who am I to stop you? The fact you did it at all is impressive.' Elena leans backwards across the table to snag a large bag. Dragging it towards her, maps and paperwork skitter in all directions. She pulls a roll of parchment from the bag and lays it out for their perusal. Anatomical drawings fill it from one end to the other, all showing transitions in the process of ageing. 'Now, when it comes to matters of what makes things *alive*, there are some exceptions. Earlier you mentioned reproduction, Princess. But there comes a time in many living things' lives where they are unable to reproduce any longer. In human women, this is seen during what we call final repose.' Cat's head tilts. Fen feels her cheeks burn red even as Elena answers, 'That's when their monthly flows cease. You understand what that is?' She repeats the question in Lunae, but that does not seem to clear things up. Someone taught him about plant breathing and excrement but not *that*, and Fen covers her face with her hands as Elena explains the process in as clinical and academic a manner as Fen has ever heard it.

By the time Fen looks back up, she is horrified to see Cat looking at her as if he expects her to start her flows right before his eyes. Elena clears her throat and continues her lecture before either of them can say anything. 'Final repose can happen for any number of reasons, though. Not just through ageing. Illness, removal of the necessitating organs or other damage to the organic material also apply. Our Queen Calissia is unable to bear more children, for instance. She cannot reproduce. Is she dead?'

'What? No, of course not,' Fen says, scandalized at the mere thought of discussing her adoptive mother and monarch in such a way. 'That's different!'

'How is it different? If you must be able to reproduce to be considered *alive*, then why is she not dead?'

Fen scrambles, desperate to remember terminology. 'Her body continues to live. Her . . . her cells. *Those* reproduce even if she doesn't.'

Elena nods. She grins enthusiastically, speaking quickly now. 'Then, so long as the *cells* that comprise something can continue to exhibit those traits, life exists?'

'Yes,' Fen agrees.

Elena points to Cat. 'If you cut yourself, your body heals, yes?' He nods. 'That is cellular regrowth. You are alive.'

'I'm not,' he tells her, voice cracking badly in the centre. 'Reapers are *dead*–'

Fransen coughs loudly from his place by the window. All three turn towards him, and the aged Reaper adjusts in his seat, eyes still closed, basking in the sun like a contented lizard.

'Reapers *make* things around them dead,' Fransen says. He slowly opens his eyes, looking directly at Cat as he does. 'But you, dear boy, are very much alive.'

'I died,' he insists. 'I drowned.'

'And yet, your cells remake you when you are hurt. They *reproduce*. You *breathe*. You *grow*, and you will continue to grow until you reach a peak level of adulthood. Then, and only then, will you stop. Meanwhile, your blood is replenished, your lungs fill with air, you have movement. You are alive.'

'He's a Reaper,' Fen repeats. 'He isn't a living thing, he's–'

'Why not?' Elena asks.

'Everyone *says*–'

'Maybe everyone is wrong.'

Fen shakes her head. She looks at Cat, then at Fransen. Fransen is frowning ever so slightly in their direction, but Cat's attention is devoted to the anatomy chart on the table. Pictures of humans in various stages of life stare back up at him. Men, women, children, the elderly. All around them are scattered drawings of organs and even cellular structures. A small square near Cat's right hand surrounds five words: cells, homeostasis, reproduction, metabolism, genes. Far more in-depth than anything Fen has ever been taught before. Cat's brows are scrunched tight, his whole face contorted by the ferocity of his thoughts. 'Marina says if you do not eat, you grow weak,' Elena goes on, gently. So gently. 'Your bodies enter a kind of . . . stasis where it neither voids nor grows. It slows much of your ability to develop. But it does not destroy it. When you do eat, you flourish. You grow. You void once more. And so, you *do* have a metabolism, slow as it is. You are still alive, and all life is sacred, Cat. Even yours. Even if you cannot tell it is life, even as you live it.'

He stares at her. Silent. Jaw clenched. Elena says no more. Instead, she reaches for her bag and pulls out two complicated apparatuses made of wood and glass. Both are carelessly set on top of the parchment. She withdraws a small wooden box next and slowly assembles a complex piece of equipment from a glass flask and tubes. Finally, she places a leaf on a slip of glass, under what turns out to be an eyepiece. She instructs Fen to light a small candle and the leaf is suddenly illuminated. Cat is still standing motionless to one side, but at Elena's encouragement, Fen leans down to peer through the newly configured eyepiece.

At first, the brown colouring of the leaf is all she sees. She turns a small focusing screw under Elena's instruction until finally it shows something else. Something she has only ever seen drawn on the strange posters that decorate Zinnitzia's study. 'They're . . . *cells*,' she breathes out, shocked. Small bricklike structures are stacked on top of each other. They are separated only by thin lines. Inside each cell are even smaller structures, circles and loops and whorls that she remembers reading about, and forgetting about, in her homework assignments. Introductions to Alelunen science that no one ever had followed up on. *Good to know what those people think about, but hardly useful for us,* the King had once said. She had never thought she would ever need, or want, to see more.

'They are,' Elena says. 'They're also dead. Can you fix that for us?' Fen glances at where the leaf is being held up, hovers a finger over it and peers down into the tube once more. Slowly, she lowers her finger. *Live,* she thinks as she touches the brittle stem. Softer, gentler, than her command to the vines. Just a bit of encouragement. Plants never need much.

The cells move. They jiggle. They change colours, becoming fleshy and verdant. The interiors start shifting this way and that, wriggling against one another as they metabolize and secure energy from beyond. They become *alive.* 'Let Cat see,' Elena requests. Fen steps back and he shuffles closer. Peering down, a soft hiss whooshes between his teeth in a kind of stunned awe. She wishes she knew why he made that sound. That odd hiss that seems far easier to him than actual words from time to time.

He tugs the glove from his right hand and reaches for the specimen. The verdant leaf slowly wilts, crumbles and decays. The green leaches from its structure. It returns, shrivelled and sad, to the husky brown thing that Elena had first produced. Cat hisses again, softer now. He wiggles his fingers at Fen, and she replaces his touch with her own, willing it back to life. He keeps his eyes focused on the tube, the magnification, watching the play of life and death before him.

He kills the leaf again, has her heal it, then he kills it once more. 'I want to see too,' Fen insists. He does not move, and she shoves his shoulder. Not hard, not in an attempt to overbalance him, but he recoils at the contact – bell shrieking at his wrist. He trips over his feet and throws himself bodily in the opposite direction. Papers and books crash to the ground, and he stays where he falls, frozen in place.

Fen's heart clogs her throat. 'I didn't do anything,' she insists.

Elena steps around her, reaching for Cat. 'No – *wait!*' Cat recoils once more, jerking his bare hand behind him as Elena freezes in place. She is neither Giver nor Reaper. To her, his touch will kill. And Fen had seen her. Seen her reaching, as if she was going to help him. But she *can't*. She'll die. At the window, Fransen begins to move. He stands, then shuffles closer.

'No need to fear me, boy,' Fransen says simply as he steps around both Fen and Elena to wrap his fingers around Cat's ungloved hand and give it a light pull. 'Come, show me what it is you youngsters are getting up to with this newfangled nonsense. I never bothered learning my sciences. Cells and molecules and other Alelunen witchery. Show me what you're doing.' He tugs Cat closer and Elena pats Fransen on the shoulder as she politely cedes the floor. 'Come on, Princess, give us a light, then we'll all take turns. Now, Cat, show me what it looks like when we kill something. There's a good lad. Fascinating. Truly. Come look, Princess. Let's do it again.' Nervous and shivery, Fen glances back into the long tube. She watches the leaf die. Then she heals it. They run through the cycle three more times, then she steps back to let Cat look again. Only, when he does, he moves the leaf out of the way. He looks at his hand beneath the glass, and Elena *carefully* helps adjust the focus so he can see it more clearly.

When it is Fen's turn, he holds his hand still and lets her look. She expects a sign. A mark. Something that shows just how dangerous and physically abhorrent his existence is. But there is nothing. No difference at all. His skin is pale, hers sun-darkened from hours spent basking in its golden glow. But on a cellular level . . . she sees no difference. Not a single one.

'But why do Reapers kill people when they touch them, and I don't?' Fen asks.

'That,' Elena says, 'has nothing to do with science. *That* has everything to do with the gods.' Cat slowly pulls on his right glove. He tucks its edges under the long sleeves of his tunic, then crosses his arms in front of his chest as Elena explains. 'The gods choose who will be a Giver and who a Reaper. It is their divinity that marks you as such.' Fen's teeth clench. It is an utterly unsatisfactory answer. Being *divine* has never done anything good for her, and it has done even less good for Cat.

'*Why?*' she asks again.

'I can only show you what the science says. I can show you the how, but as for the why?' Elena shrugs. She glances at Fransen, who shrugs as well.

'I think it's because we're meant to do something for the gods,' Fransen says. 'It was our original purpose, wasn't it? Givers do Life's work for him, and Reapers do the same for Death. There must be something that they want accomplished and we are the only ones who can do it.'

'But why choose *you*, then?' Fen asks. 'With us, we are younger. Stronger. We won't have the same problems as you because you're . . .'

'Old? And thus I have less value?' Fransen laughs like a bark, loud, snapping exhalations that seep derision. 'Perhaps I can only do what I need to do for my god because I am old. Perhaps no one else can do what I need to do, and that's why I was chosen. Who am I to question that?'

'So that's it. We're just supposed to live out the rest of our lives, waiting to do some unknown task just because the gods decided it?'

'No,' Fransen replies. 'It's too much bother wondering how we achieve our purpose. No, I rather think it's far more logical to simply go on living our lives the same as we did before. If, by doing that, I manage to please the gods, then wonderful. And if not? Then it is beyond my capacity to know or care. I am like this, one way or another, so I may as well enjoy it. Don't you think?'

'How can you possibly *enjoy* being *dead?*'

'Because I'm not. As you've already seen. I may have died to become a Reaper, but I am still so much more than just that. Just as *you* are so much more than your abilities as a Giver.'

Elena clears her throat. 'Abilities that I think you're struggling with, yes?' she asks gently. Fen flushes. She crosses her arms over her chest. She does not need them. She does not want them. It is fine. 'Marina said you can bring dead things back to life, but struggle with *healing* things, or rather: mending and improving the health of things already alive.'

'So?'

'So, tomorrow, we're going to talk about necrotic flesh,' Elena tells her, smiling brightly. 'And I think you're going to enjoy *those* lessons far more.'

CHAPTER FOURTEEN

Elician

Elician has seen the border towns of Alelune before, but none of them compare to the capital city of Alerae. Built entirely of alabaster and limestone, Alerae seems to glisten in otherworldly white. Where Soleb's capital city of Himmelsheim is awash with golden arches and gleaming representations of Life and his great sun, Alelune is its mirror opposite. White stone pillars with silver adornments shimmer gloriously under the full moon of the night. Blue stones, mined from Alelune's north, illuminate the corners of the city. Ornamental arches swoop over each doorway, and great pillars and tall brickwork make up the line of homes and businesses that crowd each city street. Each structure is rectangular and tall with long lines that reach up towards the sky. All dwarfed by the great glistening palace, which casts shadows over any who approach.

The leader of the group that had overtaken them is a tall, hairless man named Nured. He takes a certain kind of pleasure in jerking on the lead attached to Elician's tightly bound wrists. Nured's knots do not slip or weaken, and each snapping pull forces Elician into a half-stumbling jog as he tries to keep pace and not fall. Lio rarely keeps to his feet when his lead is jerked. His stability and balance have been in decline since they crossed the border into Alelune, and he has been losing weight and mobility the longer he is forced to march.

Nured only ever offers meagre portions for them to eat, and water comes once every four hours at best. While Elician's body will regenerate itself as needed, Lio's can only waste away. He trips and falls now at such regular intervals that Elician often needs to barter with their guards for permission to help his friend. Then and only then can he send soothing waves of comfort into Lio's body, supporting him so they can continue to trudge forward.

They are not brought into the palace.

Instead, just before the main gates, Nured opens a door and marches them down a series of steps leading deep beneath the city. Torches with blue flames light the way into the abyss. Elician's thighs burn as they descend. His knees creak unpleasantly, and he needs to steady both himself and Lio when his friend loses his balance again and nearly sends them both tumbling to the bottom.

'I have you,' he whispers, squeezing Lio's arm as one of Nured's underlings shoves him in the back. He nearly falls but manages to hold his balance. 'I have you,' he repeats. They keep walking. Down to where the sun cannot hope to reach them.

The stonework is extraordinary and the craftmanship undeniable, even in the dim lanternlight. Their steps echo almost musically along the carefully built walls. Absurdly, he imagines this to be a wonderful place to play an instrument. The reverberations would hum and echo pleasantly within the stone stairwell. He almost laughs at the thought, but his humour fades when he needs to prevent Lio from falling once more.

Their energy flags as they reach the bottom. Elician sways in exhaustion, squinting at the seemingly endless hall now before them. Cages line the walls with the occasional support pillar dotting the walking space between each cell. He cannot see where the hall ends. It is not lit well enough for that. Another hand shoves Elician in the back. His knees hit the ground this time as a wave of vertigo overcomes him.

Lio reaches for him. 'My prince–' he starts to say, and is promptly struck in turn, right in the same spot. Lio curls over himself, gasping and bracing for another.

'He's not your prince *here*,' Nured sneers.

'Shockingly,' Elician replies, preparing to hoist Lio to his feet once more, 'that's not how monarchies work.' He waits until his friend meets his eyes. 'Ready?' At Lio's nod, they stand together. Lio sways but manages to keep upright. Their legs are shaky beneath them, but they manage to keep walking. Neither is struck again.

Elician peers into the cages as they go. It is dark here, so dark that only one pillar in five seems to display a lit torch. The guards carry their own to illuminate the path, but the gloom feels even more oppressive when he realizes an abyss of shadows lies beyond their small party.

At first, Elician thinks the cages are empty. But then . . . no, there is movement. There's one person per cage, small, curled up and pressed into the darkest corners. They are filthy and ill-kept and Elician's stomach turns at the familiarity. Cat had looked just like them when they first met.

Finally, they stop at a truly empty cage. The door screeches open and both Elician and Lio are shoved – and locked – inside. Nured leads the rest of the entourage away. No questions asked, no information provided. No audience with the Queen. 'What the fuck,' Lio curses, rolling over and trying to assess their situation. Elician's eyes struggle to adjust. When they do, there is precious little to observe.

The ironwork that holds the cages together is sturdy and bolted into the ground. The cages themselves do not reach the ceiling, instead cutting off at a certain height. Elician can stand, but only if he hunches over, his shoulders touching the top and his head tucked low. There are gaps between each cage too. If he stretched an arm out to his neighbour, he would not be able to reach them. Not unless someone reached back as well. He doubts they would.

The people in the neighbouring cages do not look his way. They lie curled on their sides, backs to Lio and Elician, and silent in all things.

Elician presses a palm against his chest in a horrible attempt at calming his too-fast heart, unnerved by the hideous lack of stimulation. The silence is so all-encompassing that he feels a cold sweat break out on his neck. He shivers and tries to take a few steadying breaths, and is saved only when Lio rallies enough to ask, 'Where are we?'

The question echoes, bouncing off the nearest wall and ringing in Elician's ears. Lio had not spoken loudly, but it *felt* booming.

'The Reaper cells,' Elician replies. He thought he had managed to keep his voice down, but it still feels too loud. There is a cloying kind of despair in a place this quiet. During their travels, Elician had often wondered at Cat's refusal to speak. Now, he wonders if Cat ever felt the world beyond this place was overwhelming. Chaotic. He closes his eyes and summons up the memory of that first haphazard sighting in the midst of the battlefield. Cat's hands pressed against his ears, as if somehow he could block out the cacophony of war.

He wonders which is worse.

'They're Reapers?' Lio asks. Elician flinches at the volume.

'Yes,' he confirms, opening his eyes once more to investigate their surroundings with more attention.

They are sitting directly on great slabs of alabaster. But alabaster is a soft stone, easily moulded and carved. He presses his hand against it and feels the grooves and marks of a long habitation. There is a shallow divot at the back of their cage, a small one – perhaps the indentation of a body where it had lain for a long time.

Marina had said Cat had only been a Reaper for eleven or twelve years. Which meant he had first come to the Reaper cells as a child, around eight or nine years old. Elician tries to imagine a child in a place like this.

'No one is going to find us here,' Lio says. The words are too loud, and yet his voice is a balm. He shakes the bars of the cage as if the door will magically open for him. Someone, several cages down, turns towards them, but when their eyes meet, the face ducks down and away.

Alelune did not publicize his capture. He was not brought before the Queen and her court. There is still time for that, but if Alelune wanted to use Elician as a political tool, they would not house him in a place no one goes. If formal talks between Alelune and Soleb begin, Queen Alenée will not admit to having Elician as a prisoner until it gives her an advantage. She will deny his presence. And, if Alelune denies them . . . if there is no proof of life, then death or desertion are the only options his father will have when it comes time for him to explain Elician's absence.

He will never admit I'm a Giver, Elician thinks, blinking into the gloom. *He won't admit I deserted either. It will make us look weak. Him, weak. And if he wants to keep the people motivated enough to endure the fight . . .*

A dead prince serves as better propaganda than a flighty one.

Exhaustion slithers through Elician's body at the thought. He lies down, curling on his side just as this cage's previous occupant once had done. 'I think we should have turned around when we had the chance, Wilion,' Elician murmurs to the cool stone beneath his cheek.

'Yeah. Next time, let's not be in so much of a hurry to rejoin the army,' Lio replies, shuffling close enough for Elician to feel his warmth.

'Next time . . .' Elician should say something. Something funny, lighthearted, something to make it better. All he can think of to say, though, is, 'Next time, let's just go home.'

Lio nods. Pats his shoulder. All they can do now is wait.

CHAPTER FIFTEEN

Fenlia

Elena gives Fenlia and Cat different tasks, then leaves Fransen to supervise as she runs off to address her other responsibilities. She works with many who come to live in the House of the Unwanting. Fen follows her only once, eager to fill her notebook with observations. What she finds is not what she had expected. There are no executions at the House of the Unwanting. There are no screaming wails of agonized souls, clinging desperately to life as a Reaper comes to end their existence once and for all. All the scary stories her peers had told her before she left for Kreuzfurt are . . . false.

Adalei had lived here, once. She knows that. Fen had been too young to visit when Adalei was ill, but she had always pitied and mourned for her cousin's childhood spent behind these glass walls. She had imagined a place of unending sorrow and horror, her cousin valiantly trying to hold on to life even as her surroundings dared to drag her into Death's waiting hands. At court, she remembers King Aliamon arguing with Adalei's father about placing Adalei in the Reapers' care. Lord Anslian had refused to budge. Fen had always thought him cruel for it.

But the House of the Unwanting is not the villainous lair of her nightmares. It is simply a place where people die. Some are elderly and wish only to have someone there when they pass on. Some are young and ill, like Adalei, and tremble at the thought of a Giver intervening – when their life or death should be entirely natural and without interference. Some here believe the powers of Givers and Reapers do not come from the gods, and Fen had thought only fanatics felt that way. She supposes these people must be fanatics. And yet, they still come to the House for something despite these beliefs. Perhaps only to die, but still: for something.

She goes back to the library to study, and she applies herself to her new lessons fully. She reads about anatomical theory and practice, the differences between neurotransmitters and neurons, the histories of the scientists who discovered them all, and the work physicians do when they cannot rely on a Giver to heal the sick with a touch alone. She talks Cat into playing a game of catch with an apple and is desperately amused at how bad he is at it. But once he gets that trick down, they expand to trying their powers on the poor, abused fruit by killing and reviving it in turn.

In truth, it is not proper killing on Cat's part. When he catches the apple, he cradles it between his bare palms, concentrating on it until it starts to decay. Decomposition, she has learned, is a whole separate step from the act of dying. For a Reaper, encouraging something to rot is not as instantaneous a process as ending its life. But he can do it, breaking the apple down to a squishy mess that she winces at the feeling of, but relishes the opportunity to return it to proper firmness: resurrecting it to juicy apple perfection.

'Which book had rotting in it?' she asks as she tosses the apple towards him once more. He catches it, frowning as he turns it over and over in his hands.

'I'm not sure.'

'You were looking at them all last week.'

'Looking, yes.'

'What does that mean?'

Sighing, he holds up the now thoroughly shrivelled fruit and prepares to send it back her way. 'I can't read them.' Fen fumbles on the catch. The rotted apple squishes as her fingers try to close around it and it splits in half, splatting to the library floor.

'You can't *read?*' They are in a library filled with books. They have been looking over anatomy texts and scientific diagrams for nearly three weeks. Elena has assigned them endless bouts of research to conduct, and Marina even *gave* a book to Cat when they first started these lessons. 'How can you *not read?*'

'Soleb uses a different alphabet. And Lunae . . . I haven't *needed* to read anything in that since I was young. It's . . . difficult. I forgot a lot.' Lunae has one of the most obnoxious alphabets that Fen has ever seen, with letters that barely differentiate from each other and are wholly dependent on strange bits of swirling accents or curling serifs to indicate anything from possession to plurality. Soleb, by contrast, has letters that are stark and straight. Words are written with distinct gaps between each independent letter, and these only vary depending on the writer's social class. Nobility cast accents to the left, while lower classes slant their accents towards the right.

'Why didn't you *say* anything?' Fen asks.

Cat shrugs, cheeks tinging red. It strikes her, suddenly, that he's embarrassed. 'There's no point in saying something that does not need to be said,' he mumbles.

'This is something that *needs* to be said.' But something else in that phrasing catches her attention. 'How did you even get away with it? How have you been *learning* anything?'

'I memorize the lessons.'

'You *memorize* – is that how you learned to speak Soleben in the first place? You just *memorized* the whole language? And now during our lessons, you just . . . memorize all this science stuff too?

'Yes.' His shoulders curve inwards at her criticism, like a pill bug preparing to curl up and roll away.

He is brilliant. Genuinely brilliant. But–

'That's a stupid way to learn something.' He curves forward even more. She can barely see his face as his long brown hair curtains before it. 'What if you forget? You need to write things down and read them and . . .'

He appears utterly miserable in the face of her incredulity. Terrified, too, like he is expecting her to do more than point out how dumb he is. Hit him perhaps. Which is stupid on its own. How can anyone be afraid of *her*? She is too useless to hurt anyone.

'I'll teach you,' she offers. It is what Elician would want her to do. And it should not be too hard if he is so good at memorizing things. 'Here.' She grabs one of the books that Elena had given them. Scanning the first page, she sets it aside for something else. They are in a library, there has to be – ah! There. 'It's about nightcats!' She grins. 'Like you. Look–' She reaches for his wrist, and he pulls back in alarm. 'Can you just stop being so scared all the time? *I'm not going to hurt you.*' Cat freezes at her tone, eyes wide, mouth falling open. At the window seat, Fransen chokes on a snore, sniffles loudly, then settles, still asleep.

'You're the one frightened of *me*,' he points out, crossing his arms over his chest and tucking his wrists both out of sight and out of reach.

'*You're* actually capable of hurting people,' Fen snaps. 'What do you think I'm going to do? *Heal* you to death?' She laughs. An unhappy sound. 'I'm not the one who's a threat, but you're the one who always reacts like I'm some kind of monster. I never did anything to you.'

Cat's jaw clenches. His arms tighten around his core. He glances away from her, glaring at an anatomical drawing Elena had pinned up on the library wall. 'You're right,' he grants her with gracious mutiny on his tongue. 'You didn't do anything.' He draws in a breath, long and steady through his nose. When he looks back, it is almost as if he has forced his shoulders to relax by will alone. 'Sorry. Yes. I would like to read.' Rigidly, he reaches for the book she'd found, bell jingling tremulously on his wrist. She refuses to give it up. His cheek twitches. He turns his face to the side, the black scar catching her eye.

She hasn't done anything. But someone did once.

Elena had spent two weeks showing them what dead skin looks like, and Fen had learned the particulars of what she needs to do to heal it. She had watched necrotic flesh piece itself back together again as a result of her ministrations. Her first successful foray into what it means to be a proper Giver healer.

She hadn't done anything to Cat. She was angry at him for pulling away. She was leery still about touching him. But she hadn't tried breaching the barrier between them, even though Elician had bid her to *try*. She wants him to stop acting afraid. It annoys her.

Well then. The King always said you need to give something to take something.

'Do you want it gone – your mark?' she asks him quietly.

He glances back at her. Frowns. He touches his cheek, and she dares herself to step closer, ignoring the strange smell that still radiates from his body, to peer at the scar. The skin is dead. She can heal the dead. She can–

She lifts her hand, reminding herself needlessly, *I'm a Giver, he cannot hurt me,* even though her heart beats wildly in her chest. Cat's fingers fall, granting her space to try. She cups his cheek. The flesh is gnarled and wrinkled beneath her palm. *Live,* she commands in her mind. A useless word of hope-filled intention. Nothing changes beneath her touch. She closes her eyes and tries again. Tries, searching for the right intention, the right connection to a power she still struggles to grasp. *No. Don't just live,* she thinks. *Be free.*

And the skin moves.

It moves, it slides, it changes. She tilts her hand to one side, fascinated, as the black stain does not vanish so much as is pushed from his skin. The blackness falls from Cat's face as if it were a fine coating of dust, staining his shirt and her hand as it leaves his body. The process is slow. Slow and uneven. The apex of the mark heals at a different rate from the bottom and its sides, but it *heals*. The malformed skin becomes smooth as the charcoal is forced from his flesh – until all that is left is a too-pale cheek and a small mole at the corner of his lips.

She lowers her hand. Black stains her fingers. He looks down, then snatches at her wrist with a grip so tight that she yelps. He grabs a carafe of water and upends it all over her palm, splashing liquid against the hard floor of the library but – the soot falls away. He rubs at her hand, and it becomes clean beneath his touch. 'You did it,' Cat murmurs. Awed.

'Yeah,' she realizes at the same time. 'I did.'

'Elician tried,' Cat says. 'He couldn't do it.'

'Don't *lie* to me,' Fen snaps. She tugs at her wrist, but he does not let it go.

'I'm not. I wouldn't. I meant it. Thank you, Fenlia, Princess of Soleb.' It is stiff, formal. He bows his head, and she flushes, finally breaking her hand free. 'Thank you.'

'We should tell Marina, Zinnitzia . . .' she says. He glances at their so-called chaperone, but Fransen is still dozing peacefully, baking in the sun-drenched window seat without a care in the world.

'Yes,' he drawls, rubbing at his face as if to confirm that the scar really is gone.

'And after . . . tomorrow, I'll teach you to read.'

'Why?' he asks. 'There is no need.'

'Because . . .' It seems like something that should be done. It makes her stomach clench uncomfortably that it is something he cannot do. As if that, more than the scar on his face, was the real act of barbarity that Alelune inflicted on its people. *He really hasn't read* anything *for over ten years?* Alelune is supposed to be a country of science and learning and education; they pride themselves on it. Discovering all sorts of things that Soleb would never manage on its own. And yet, Cat cannot read. And that feels . . . wrong.

She cannot say that, of course. The mere thought of saying it makes her blush. Elician had wanted them to be friends, before he'd even asked her if she thought he could trust Cat. *It will be a test,* Fenlia decides. *If he's really someone trustworthy, then he can prove it now. And Elician will be pleased.*

'Elician told me to be your friend,' she tells Cat. 'And *friends* help each other. So you're going to be my friend, and I'm going to teach you how to read.'

He frowns at her, as if he cannot quite work out her intentions either. But he nods. Accepts. Agrees with a faint, 'All right.' Then he rubs his bare cheek once more and says even more quietly, 'I'll be your friend.'

CHAPTER SIXTEEN

Cat

'Do you like it here?' Elena asks Cat as she mixes butter and beeswax in a large bowl. His job is to grind together the active ingredients she calls for with a mortar and pestle, and when he grinds them down finely enough, she adds them to her batch. She has sixteen pots filled with sixteen different ingredients and she calls out names and directions without looking at them. He is only here to follow her commands.

He grinds a bulbous seed that he knows as a snapping ice plant but Elena calls something else entirely, then crushes in a few mint leaves on her order. 'I mean Kreuzfurt, of course,' Elena laughs, 'not here, in this chamber. No one likes helping me in *here*, not even my husband.' She is probably right. The room is hot, stuffy and dark, illuminated only by one glass lantern. There is little ventilation, and the mixture of herbs is too potent, the space too claustrophobic. The only reason Cat is here is because Marina told him it was his turn. Everyone else has already done their part.

It's probably another test, he thinks, squinting at his concoction. Elena is not a Reaper or a Giver. He could kill her in an instant. He does not. There is no point, he has no desire to do so, and the consequences would be extreme. But these Solebens . . . they love their tests.

'You're married?' he asks instead, leaning a bit harder on the pestle, turning it in a full circle.

'Yes, though I rarely get to see him. We both serve the crown in our own ways, and so I make do with what I have. But you, Cat, do you like it here?'

'It's fine.' Kreuzfurt is a place of routines. Routines that are easily memorized and maintained. The gates open, hopeful patients and pilgrims enter, the Givers guide the majority to their House, and only once every few days does someone come looking for a Reaper's care. The halls are filled with laughter and community. Those who do not wish to help patients spend their days working the fields or finding some other kind of productive labour. Any goods or food they produce are sent to the capital, the proceeds from the sale used to maintain Kreuzfurt as a whole. Kreuzfurt could almost be considered idyllic, if the walls did not exist and the guards did not walk the tops with their torches and arrows made of poison. He can understand why Lord Anslian thought this place a refuge, but he knows full well why Elician had called it a prison instead. As beautiful and serene as Kreuzfurt is, no one here is truly free.

He hands her his work, and she dumps it into her bowl, mixing and mixing until she is fully satisfied. 'Fill up the tins, please, about one good scoop each should do it.' He nods and follows her commands until each of the forty tins laid out is filled, lids pressed closed. 'Thank you, dear,' Elena says, helping to move the finished tins into a basket.

They bring the tins to the House of the Unwanting's great hall and set them out for the Reapers to collect on their way through. 'It's very different from Alelune, isn't it?' Elena asks as he arranges each tin in a precise line.

'Yes.'

'Crowen was a part of Alelune when I was still a girl, but it quickly became part of Soleb not long afterwards – and the borders never changed back. My parents never got used to the change. They still cooked with their own creams and cheeses and celebrated *Tomestange*. We'd close the doors and pretend to be Alelunen for the night with some of the other families who stayed after the border moved. Can you imagine that?' He could. He had done almost the inverse when Elician had given him the chance that same night. 'I do miss my parents' quiches and pies . . . I never did learn how to make them right and I've never found anything similar since.'

'Did you become a physician because of them?' he asks quietly.

'Science and art are cornerstones of a good Alelunen life, and in matters of health – well, my parents were quite content to never so much as *look* at a Giver if they could manage it. So, I was raised to appreciate the need for a physician. Most border towns have one, you know: Crowen, Altas, and even further north as well. It's too ingrained in our culture not to want one. I suppose from there . . . I wanted to learn how to heal others too. Besides, I can help more people out there than by staying here year-round. It's impossible for *all* the sick to make the journey to Kreuzfurt.'

'Givers and Reapers truly never leave this place?'

'They do, but only with permission from the King. There is a rotation. Travelling Givers will go from town to town under armed guard and will tend to the ills and concerns of the common folk around Soleb.'

'Why are they guarded?'

'To make sure they don't disappear. A person who can heal anything? Raise the dead? That's a dangerous person to lose track of. A Reaper has a better chance of escape; if they are caught by a baseline human, they just need one opportunity and they could easily kill their captors. But a Giver doesn't quite have that same kind of advantage. There's a greater risk that they could be bound and imprisoned.' Cat rather thinks she's overestimating how easy it would be for a Reaper to overpower someone. If it was so simple, the cells in Alelune would lie empty. But Elena doesn't seem to recognize her faux pas, shrugging and tidying the table with her back to him. She carries on, blissfully unaware. 'The guards are for the Givers' own safety.'

'And to make sure they return?' he presses. She hesitates. Then nods.

'That too.' Elena clears her throat. 'It will be different for Fenlia. Apparently Elician promised her a seat on his council, and the royal court usually has at least one Giver and one Reaper representative. Marina did that for a long while, when Elician was still a child. But in general those representatives are meant to serve as more transient liaisons between Himmelsheim and Kreuzfurt. As far as I know, the plan for Fen is for her to leave here and take up a position in a more permanent capacity after Elician takes the throne. Perhaps she'll even end up as a member of the council at the Kingsclave. But Zinnitzia and Marina would either need to die or cede their seats to permit that – whichever comes first.'

'Fen is too biased to be an honest liaison,' he murmurs.

'She certainly has her biases. You never doubt what that girl is thinking at the very least. Perhaps she'll grow out of it. Though she does seem to be less confrontational with you lately, yes? Or have I got it wrong?'

'No. You're not wrong.' But what Fen wants out of it is still unclear. She has been dogged in her attempts at polite civility and enthusiasm. It is a brand of attention that he isn't used to, equal parts friendly and oppressive. She is loud. Demanding. He misses, sometimes, the familiar comfort and quiet of the cells where all those around him spoke the same language, breathing as one with the same emotions on their lips. He never questioned what he was meant to say or do, there. He had never been confused.

Since coming to Soleb, everything has been confusing. Each new acquaintance more complicated than the last. Elician had been the least offensive of the bunch, despite his frequent breaches of propriety. Cat had never quite minded listening to Elician ramble on about one foolish thought after another. The prince had just been so full of hope. For a while, Elician even made it feel like hope was something worth holding on to. Something precious, rather than a precursor to endless disappointment.

Nudging the final tins in the row back and forth, Cat bites his lip. A door opens at the end of the hall. It is past dawn, the sun is finally rising proudly, and the day is meant to officially begin. All the House's Reapers enter, some in groups and some on their own. They arrive in various states of undress, hair down from their usual Soleben braids, skin exposed, laughing and chatting amongst themselves. Their black tunics, hoods and trousers are carried in bags or tucked under their arms. Two men, bare-chested and tall, always enter the hall arm in arm. Cat watches them under his lashes. One of the men drapes his arm over his fellow's shoulders. He leans over, whispering something in his ear, earning a laugh and a smile and a lingering kiss on his lips.

With a sudden pang that twinges sharper than he anticipated, he thinks of riding with Elician. How his arms had felt around his body. His chin at his shoulder, whispering idle comments or pointing out birds. His breath warm against Cat's skin. His body strong and sturdy–

Elena makes a strange noise to his right. Cat glances at her, finding her laughing, one hand pressed to her lips. '*Fine*, he says,' Elena mimics, giggling nonsensically. 'He says *it's fine* here.'

'I don't understand.' He glances back at the couple moving to their place in line.

'I'm sure you don't, dear.' She pats his sleeve delicately. He wants to ask what she means, but Marina arrives and calls for them to begin. As one, the Reapers form a line and collect their tins. They greet Elena politely, then thank him as he hands them over, one after another.

All the Reapers in Soleb seem to know each other. That is not the case in Alelune. While most Reapers are kept beneath Alerae, Cat knows of at least four other Reaper cells spread across the country. Sometimes those Reapers came to Alerae, transferred for one reason or another, but he knows precious little about any of the others.

Marina had said she thought there were statistically more Reapers in Alelune, simply because that is Death's domain. It makes sense that Soleb has a proportionately larger number of Givers. But even with that knowledge, it feels strange to look into a room and see all the Reapers a country has to offer. Only a few dozen, compared to the hundreds of Alelune. And all of them treat each other with such displays of physical attention, it embarrasses him more than entices him. Even so, when he tries to avert his eyes, the temptation to just look and see and confirm that *yes, it is still there*, builds with uncomfortable instance. And he wonders, sometimes, what it would have been like if he had been brought up in a place like this instead of the cells he had always known.

Hanian 'died' fifty years ago, while sailing to Glaika, but enjoys eating sweet food and has a great boisterous laugh. He spends his time with Io – who died only seven years ago, falling from her horse. But she still adores the damned creatures and tends to the stables whenever she can. Along with Fransen, those three had celebrated the loudest after Cat's cheek had been healed, kissing it and issuing congratulations that Cat had not expected. Yet all the rest had approached Cat too, offering well wishes and embraces to which he had not known how to respond. He'd flushed and stepped away, ducking from their Soleben shows of delight, but not before earning a few kisses to his bare cheek that left him squirming in discomfort. Marina had told some of his well-wishers off when it had happened, but every so often that beautiful couple catches his eye and winks in his direction and his mouth feels too dry as he remembers lessons of propriety that he never thought he'd need to adhere to because who would ever want to touch his skin?

He refuses to learn that particular couple's names. Knowing one thing more about them is simply too much to bear. But he watches them collect their tins, sit at each other's side, comfortable and at ease, utterly unconcerned about their bodies. He wonders, *Will I ever be that shameless?* But he cannot decide if he yearns for an affirmation or not. So, he flushes and takes his own tin instead. Just for something to do with his hands.

Elena leaves. With the product delivered, she has no place in this assembly. She waves goodbye, and he shuffles to his usual place in front of Marina, pulling his tunic off in the process. Fransen is in front of him and, even three months in, he still worries how to approach this task.

'Ready?' Marina asks, opening her tin. Despite spending the pre-dawn hours helping Elena mix the ointment, it still stings his nose. It is too sharp, too acidic by far. It is little wonder its creation is the least liked job at the House. An essential job, certainly, but not particularly fun.

He nods, though he doesn't ever feel ready for this. Then, her hand is on his back. The ointment she applies is bitingly cold. Her touch is gentle but the cold stings, sinking deep within him. His teeth chatter and he twitches forward in a natural attempt to escape. Marina had explained the use of the unguent when he first arrived, and he has used it every day since. As do all Reapers. But the initial contact is still almost overwhelming. Without it, though, they will become too hot in the summer sun – and they must remain robed in their thick black clothing to protect others not of their kind.

The heat won't kill us, Marina had said, shrugging as she handed him his first tin. *But it does make the days excruciating. The exhaustion is unbearable.*

Why wear black – this black – at all? he had asked in turn, rubbing his thumb and forefinger against the too-thick fabric.

Because it is noticeable at a distance, and impossible to ignore. As for this black . . . it's the thickest fabric in Soleb. All of Soleb's people are afraid of us, of us touching them, and us being covered by this keeps them calm. They can trust there will be no contact, even by accident. This ointment does help with the heat. Remember to thank Elena. She developed it just for us.

Cat shivers, spine curving away from Marina's touch. But she is insistent and firm, digging her thumbs into his shoulders and soothing cramped muscles he had not even noticed were getting tense. Careful, fearing he might tear Fransen's far thinner skin, Cat begins the same process. Fransen sighs, humming in contentment as Cat spreads the balm along his back, neck and arms. Once the initial shock passes, the sensation does become somewhat pleasurable, especially as the sun rises higher and the heat of the day becomes cloying in its intensity. He lathers generously, always struggling to find the proper ointment-to-skin ratio. But each time his fingers slip and slide against Fransen's skin, he does better. He improves.

When all the hard-to-reach places are accounted for, the circle breaks. Reapers begin applying the salve to their own chests and legs. Though some, including the devastatingly distracting couple Cat saw before, continue to share in the intimacy of the exchange. They rub their hands over each other's chests, their hips, their necks. Then, when they are done, when their bodies have been tended to, they help each other dress. On go the black trousers, the heavy long-sleeved tunic, the thick boots and gloves. The bells. The sun burns in through the window and Cat shivers at the conflicting feeling of icy skin and choking humidity.

'Thank you, Cat,' Fransen says when they finish. 'You know . . . I think I'm going to sit out in the garden today.' Cat frowns. He has lessons with Elena and Fen in the library. 'Go without me,' Fransen murmurs. 'It will be fine.'

'Are you all right?' Cat asks.

'Yes, yes. It's just such a lovely day.' He takes Cat's hands in his, kissing his knuckles, before slowly ambling away.

Cat's skin tingles at the touch. It always does, even beneath the gloves. Leaving him uncertain if he wants to prolong the contact or pull away. He does remember what it was like before he died. His father hugged him frequently. An arm around his shoulders, a hand in his hair. Whenever Cat had managed to impress his father's seneschal during particularly complex lessons, he remembers the proud clap of a hand to his shoulder. Fingers tightening around his aching muscles. Never more than that – anything more would be considered inappropriate.

Here, it's as if the Solebens are incapable of *not* touching one another. They reach out, tracing fingers and lips to bits of skin whenever the opportunity arises. Holding hands or grasping wrists, leaving kisses against brows, or looping arms around bodies. As if it would kill them to not physically declare to the world all their affections in all their varying degrees.

It's obscene.

It's an indecency that makes his stomach ache. Solebens show their love so freely, and it makes their intentions unclear. If everyone can kiss and hug and touch one another, then how is anyone to understand if those kisses or touches mean *more*?

'Shall you sit with us tomorrow?' asks the tall Reaper Cat refuses to get to know. His eyes drift towards his muscular body, square jaw and direct blue eyes. He imagines for half a second what those hands would feel like rubbing the cooling salve against his skin. Then he definitively shakes his head *no*, collecting empty tins for Elena to reuse in the morning.

'I don't think he's interested, darling,' the other Reaper teases, arms going around his partner's waist. He rests his chin on his companion's shoulder.

'Shame,' the tall Reaper says. They leave together, gorgeous and tactile and unburdened by any concept of impropriety. Cat finishes putting the empty tins back in the basket for Elena to collect. Then he flees to the library to meet Fen. Fen, at least, never makes him feel like *this*.

Abrasive, impatient and rude, Fen flits from idea to idea without thinking too much about the topics that frustrate her the most. But she does not *intend* her rudeness. It seems to just happen, as if she accidentally falls into it without quite realizing what she's saying or doing. He could dislike her more if she intended to be so unkind, but her own disagreeable nature seems to even surprise herself. And once she becomes aware of it . . . well. She has been trying to be nice. As strange as it appears, she has been trying.

Fen is already in the library with Elena when he arrives, going over her latest autopsy results. Last week they had been examining a rat's internal organs as part of their lessons, and Fen had accidentally touched it with the back of her wrist. It woke up, chest still carved open by their instruments. It screeched loudly and Cat had killed it less than a second later, but the sheer shock of it had made Fen cry for hours. Elena had needed to counsel her through much of the week for her to even try again. But she had, eventually, tried again. For someone afraid of failure, and death, Fen seems to be slowly getting used to both. *Even,* he thinks, *the knowledge that they are inevitable.*

He walks steadily towards their usual spot, stopping only when he feels something shift in the air. A chill slides down his back. His teeth chatter. He knows this feeling. Knows it *well.* Jerking back the way he came – he runs. Someone shouts his name, but he ignores it, rushing for the staircase. The feeling washes through him, swift as a river and just as violent. His lungs seem to fill with water. It's a *lie.* His hands scramble for the banister. His feet carry him dutifully forward. He descends towards the gardens, down one flight of stairs, then another, and another. All the way to the bottom where he stumbles and trips across the main hall of the House of the Unwanting.

Fransen's favourite garden is a quiet place with fruit trees and olive vines by a giant pond. He likes to lie amongst the sweet grass and herbs, breathing in the scent of possibility as a gentle breeze flutters. It is not far from the House of the Unwanting. The very edge of the pond is visible from the door.

Cat is not supposed to be running – it draws too much attention – but he does not care who is watching him now. He runs, breathless, choking on water that does not exist. His vision tunnels, then improves. He sees Fransen sitting on a bench overlooking the pond. There is a figure next to him. She turns and meets Cat's eyes. Her mouth moves.

Cat stops. He stands in place. He blinks; she is gone. And he can breathe again. His hands tremble at his sides. 'Cat?' Fen calls from behind him. Maybe she had seen him running. Maybe she too had felt what was about to happen. He hears others now, many others. Footsteps echo like thunderclaps in his head. 'Cat, what's wrong?' Fen shouts. He wonders if it's the first time she has seen this happen. No one else is speaking; they already know. They approach slowly, quietly, afraid to break the tension in the air. 'Cat?' Fen asks again. One of her hands touches his wrist. He flinches away, tucking his arms around his body. Not now. He does not want to be touched now. Not by her. Not by anyone.

'Did you see her?' he asks.

'See who?'

'Death,' Marina suggests. He turns. She and Zinnitzia are approaching together. She has a long black fold of cloth in her arms. Her expression is tender and calm.

'Death?' Fen repeats. Then she turns towards Fransen. 'He's not . . .' She gasps. 'I can't . . . I can't sense him, but he can't be–' Marina approaches their chaperone's body without saying another word. She gently guides him to lie down. 'He's only been a Reaper for a few years. Why would Death make him a Reaper only to take him so soon?'

'Maybe he did what he needed to do,' Cat murmurs. He closes his eyes. Zinnitzia is saying something. Perhaps a prayer. Perhaps something else. There are many Reapers here now, many Givers too.

Some start to cry. Grief strikes, sharp and poignant, as the assembled masses curl into the arms of their loved ones, weeping and huddling close. Some are whispering things, memories, dreams, hopes they had for Fransen that he will never get to complete now.

Cat's fingers curl against his skin. He does not care to listen. He turns and walks away. Fen tries to reach out for him, but he avoids her and keeps walking. Fen resorts to following him instead.

'Did you see her?' she asks. 'Death? What does she look like? I've never seen the gods.'

Cat stops at the steps leading to the House of the Unwanting. He does not know how Givers are made. It has never occurred to him. But he has assumed that Life has to be there at some point, somehow. He turns, glancing back at her. 'You have never seen Life?'

'How many times have you seen Death?' she snaps back, flushing.

'Many times. She's there whenever we die. Properly. At the final moments and the first. When I died my first time, I saw her then. She asked me – it doesn't matter. Yes, I saw her.' Fen stares up at him. She does not seem to understand. She wants a story, an explanation. He has never had to explain it before, though. He is not sure where to start. 'In the Reaper cells in Alerae, whenever one of us died . . . Death always came first. She walked the length of the cells, from the first to the last, and she would stop before whoever she wanted to take. She would speak to them and . . . and then she would disappear and all that would be left was a body.'

Fen shivers, likely horrified. So much about what he is scares her. But this isn't something to be feared; it never has been. He just . . . doesn't know how to explain the joy those moments brought. The sound of a hundred voices crying out in gratitude and jubilation, the tears at being noticed, the hope of a future change. Even one such as this. Fen sees Death as an end to be avoided. She is a child of Life. She will never understand how Death taking a Reaper's hands feels like witnessing freedom at long last.

'What does Death look like?' Fen asks again, voice trembling.

'Not like the paintings or the statues made in her honour,' he replies. 'But . . . like something known but half glimpsed that you have no way of describing. Like a bird that blurs by you in the trees. You know it must be a bird, for what else could it be? So, you imagine it had a head, a beak, a body and a tail, and you imagine it must have been brown because that is the colour of other birds nearby. You didn't see it properly, but you know it must have had that shape. You know it must have had those features. And so, it did. And that's what she is. She appears, and you know she must exist and have a body because you can see her. You can hear her voice, so you must have seen a mouth. She is looking at you, so she must have eyes. She must have a face, but that face . . . sometimes it looks like my mother, other times like the woman who raised me. And other times, like no one I know at all. But in my mind, I see her, and I know she is Death. And I know, more than that, that she knows me. She has always known me, and I have always known her.'

'Because you're a Reaper?'

He shakes his head. Shrugs. 'I don't know.' Then he turns back towards the House of the Unwanting. He leaves her there, climbing the stairs of the tower as fast as he can.

He sits on the floor by his bed and pulls his knees to his chest. Then he smiles and laughs. *Congratulations, Fransen,* he thinks wildly, and tries to remember the words to the songs they'd sing on days when not even those guarding their cells dared to make them fall silent. And when he starts to cry, it is not because he's sad Fransen died. It's because Fransen should have had a chorus of voices singing and celebrating his new beginning. But it is only him, alone in a tower, while all the rest of Kreuzfurt speak Fransen's name, as if holding on to his memory is the only way to cherish his existence.

Night falls and his voice is hoarse from hours of trying to give Fransen the credit he deserves. Someone knocks at his door, and he bids them enter. It is Marina and Elena. They have flowers in their arms and plates of food. 'I was never in the Reaper cells in Alelune; that started after my time,' Marina says. 'But I know Alelune has not changed its response to death.'

'It's the same in Crowen, and Altas too,' Elena says. 'Do you want to celebrate with us?' And he nods, desperate and hopeful, and learns how the people outside the cells thank Death for the changing. And he understands how easy it could be to learn to like it here, with people like them.

CHAPTER SEVENTEEN

Fenlia

Fransen's body is burned, and his ashes are let loose on a breeze which carries them over the wall surrounding Kreuzfurt. For a week, even the Givers wear black out of respect for Fransen's death. They trade stories and memories in his name, and Fen finds the sudden integration between the two Houses both alarming and welcoming. She had never bothered to get to know the Reapers of Kreuzfurt before. They were embodiments of *Death*, and she had wanted nothing to do with them. But here, now, she finds herself chatting with them and learning their names.

Cat mostly avoids the mourning period, scowling and walking in the opposite direction when he sees the Houses mingling. 'It's antithetical to how he perceives what death means,' Elena explains when Fen asks her about it. 'In this, I'd suggest just letting it go.'

She does, but only with great reluctance.

When the mourning period is over and she can reclaim her white uniform, she is surprised by how comfortable it feels after so long in black. She is surprised, too, by how *much* white there is now that her attention has been drawn to it. 'How many Reapers are in Kreuzfurt?' she asks Zinnitzia over breakfast.

Her mentor shrugs, then says, 'Marina would know exactly, but perhaps thirty or so. Forty at most.'

'That's it?'

'You're welcome to go to Alelune to fetch more,' Zinnitzia mutters, tearing into a freshly baked roll. 'Sun knows they have enough of them.' Then, seeming to think her words would be taken as an invitation, she wags her bread in Fen's face. 'Do not do that.'

'I'm not *stupid*.' Besides, one Alelunen Reaper is more than enough. Cat is special. He's a good person. She's not willing to extend a hand of friendship to all the rest. 'Papa once said that the number of Givers and Reapers is pretty stable. That it never really goes up or down much. Do you think a new Reaper will come here, now Fransen is gone?'

'Hard to say. Don't try to rush Death into making any decisions. Whoever the new Reaper is, Death will know before any of us. There is no point in anticipating it.'

'So, who died before I came here?' Fen asks.

Zinnitzia purses her lips. She butters her roll. She says, firmly and stiffly, 'Don't be impertinent,' and nothing more for the rest of the meal. Fen finishes eating, then goes to the library to meet Cat. Elena's still doing rounds about the House today, but no one has replaced Fransen as Cat's chaperone. Fen wonders if it is an oversight. If it isn't, though, it seems at least Marina thinks Cat won't try to do something untoward.

Cat's curled up in one of the window seats next to Elena's usual mess of a workstation. He has one of her anatomy books held open on his lap, and he drags one finger along the words, mouthing each one as if he is not entirely certain he's guessing them correctly.

'How's it going?' she asks, peering over his shoulder. A large drawing of a chest cavity has been carefully etched onto one page. On the other is the swirling, looping script of Lunae. 'That's not *practising*. You already know Lunae.'

'Not very well, apparently,' he mumbles, fingers tightening on the book as if he expects her to pull it away.

'Another reason to keep working on Soleben. If you have to

improve *one*, then you might as well improve that. Besides, Soleben is easier. It's phonetic and you can sound it all out. I don't know how Alelune came up with that alphabet but none of your letters make any sense at all. It's a swirling mess. The *urom* has five different pronunciations! It's *all* memorization. It's insane.'

'I like memorizing things.' He's insane too. She doesn't tell him that. That's rude.

'Have you at least been practising writing too while you've been at it?'

'Why bother?' he asks. 'Who would I write to?'

'My brother,' she suggests. 'I bet he'd like that.' And she could put that in her own report too. Evidence of her good progress. 'You could tell him about what you're doing.'

'He brought me here as a prisoner.'

'Well, tell him you forgive him and thank him because now you're my best friend.' Reforming an Alelunen Reaper might go a long way towards encouraging Elician to get her out of here even sooner. He shrugs noncommittally, and she shakes her head. Sometimes he is truly hopeless. Drifting closer to the table, Fen reads a few of the notes Elena had left behind for the experiment she wants them to conduct. Several candles have been set out and they'll need to angle a few mirrors to increase the light source on the specimen Elena has prepared. 'I wish we could use blue stones for this,' she muses. 'The smoke gets so annoying.'

'You have blue stones?' Cat sits up straighter, closing his book as he meets her eyes.

'Hm? Yeah, course. Well, *I* don't have any. And there aren't a lot here anyway. Just to power the lifts if they're needed. But the palace has a lot of them. They light all the halls, and they warm the baths, and they're *amazing* in the winter when it's almost too cold to breathe. We barely need to use the cocklestoves at all. There are some fancier establishments here or there that have them too, but it *is* really expensive to use them – there's a tax. Most people can't afford the luxury.' She waves her hand towards Elena's experiment. 'Probably why we don't have one for this, but it would make things so much easier.' Cat's lips twist unpleasantly. 'What?' she says in response. 'They're wonderful. You can't deny that.'

'Blue stones don't belong to Soleb, they're Alelunen. Only the Blue Palace can decide who keeps them.'

'How can a *stone* belong to anyone?' Fen retorts. 'They were mined from Alelune, sure, but that doesn't mean they *only* belong there. They're rocks. And they do so much good. Honestly, if *you* didn't hoard them, all things would be better off.'

'They aren't *hoarded*,' Cat insists. 'They're freely given, as gifts. And no one needs to *pay* to use them in Alelune.'

'Wait, you *give* them away?'

'The Blue Palace gives them to the people, so everyone can live well.'

That does not sound right. Alelunens are harsh and unfeeling and don't care for others in the least. Purposefully giving a source of heat and light and *power* to the population contradicts everything Fen knows. Again. Especially because the Blue Palace is *not* the seat of the monarchy in Alelune. Alerae is where the Queen sits, and it makes no sense at all for something as potentially lucrative as the blue stones to be managed by anyone other than the crown. She tells him as much too. 'Besides, how would you know? I thought you lived in a cage?'

'I lived near the mines in the Blue Lands before that,' he replies sharply, the sharpest she has ever heard him speak. Sharp enough that it startles her. She blinks, stunned. It had never occurred to her what his life had been like *before*. Maybe that is how he died, crushed in a mine surrounded by glowing stones. That sounds awful. 'The stones are gifts from the earth to the people of the Blue Lands, and *only* the Blue Palace can decide if those stones are allowed to be given beyond its borders. They're *gifts*,' he insists. 'They don't belong in Soleb.'

'Why not? Don't *we* deserve to live comfortably too?'

'Comfort gained from the theft of another's labour shouldn't be comfort received,' Cat snaps back, fiercely determined about *this* of all things. Fen stares at him, startled beyond measure. For months he had placidly followed along, showing little care or consideration about anything at all. But *this* – this he argues over. 'No one should be *charged* for a blue stone's use,' he insists. 'Comfort isn't a thing that requires a price.'

'You should tell my brother that,' she suggests awkwardly, trying to break the tension. She imagines Elician would agree with Cat wholeheartedly. Because it sounds half mad, naïve, and filled with hope. A wish for a future or a world that glistens bright and perfect with no demons hiding in the corners. 'He'd probably write back pretty quick if you explained this,' she adds. 'He loves getting into philosophical arguments.'

Slowly the tension leaves Cat's shoulders. They slump forward and he sets his book to the side. For several long moments he seems to be rallying his thoughts, before he lets out a long stream of air and asks, 'Would it even be allowed?'

'I'll clear it with Marina,' Fen says with more confidence than she feels. 'Besides . . . I've been waiting for him to write for ages now, and maybe if you wrote to him too, it'd prove we've both made some progress. He'll have to respond quickly if *you* send him something, or it'll be too impolite.' She had not wanted to send her official report on Kreuzfurt to Elician by letter, but she has been giving him brief progress updates. The fact he has not yet responded rankles a bit, but she just *knows* he would say something if Cat wrote. He'd feel *obligated*.

'Does he usually take a while to write to you?' Cat asks, frowning at her.

'Not really. Usually, he sends me a letter right away. It can take a while for them to get here, even with the pigeon post. But he's never taken this long.'

'How long has it been?' he presses.

'Since . . .' Since before he left. The last letter they received from him was the one alerting Zinnitzia to his imminent arrival. Before that had been just an inconsequential response to a complaint Fen had made about the food served at the House of the Wanting. 'Three months,' she breathes out, struggling to get her thoughts into order. 'Since he left . . .'

He should have checked in, telling them he had arrived at the front at the very least. Even if that letter crossed paths with her first missive, he likely would have asked if she intended to accept his mission. *Find out if Cat is trustworthy, learn about Kreuzfurt.* He would have wanted to know. Just to get the confirmation. But . . . nothing. Not a letter. Not a rote response. Not any kind of inquiry at all.

She knows this silence. She's felt it before. When her papa had gone to Alelune on a mission for the King and had never come home.

Cat is looking at her, expression grim. 'You should tell Marina,' he advises quietly.

Fen shakes her head. 'Tell her what?' she asks, not trusting herself to speak the words out loud. She can't. That will make it real. *Elician is a Giver. It isn't like Papa. He can't die. Nothing can hurt him. He's fine. This is just a mistake. A big mistake.*

'Fen . . . if your brother is truly all right, would he have written you a letter by now?'

Yes. Yes, he would have. She feels that answer deep in her chest. Written tightly on the folds of her heart. 'What are you trying to say?' she asks, voice breaking as her hysteria grows.

'Ask Marina or Zinnitzia,' he counsels again.

'Why, Cat?'

'Because something might have gone wrong.' Cat won't meet her eyes. His arms cross tight before his chest, smothering his belled wrist at his side.

'What could have gone wrong?' Fen asks.

'I don't know. But I was sent to kill him, and I didn't. Someone else may have tried.' The panic in her chest roars to an unbearable crescendo. She turns to the door and runs, leaving Cat and their lessons far behind.

She just hopes that, like all the other times before, Marina and Zinnitzia know more about what's happening in the world than she does.

CHAPTER EIGHTEEN
Elician

There is no sunlight in the Reaper cells. Without it, Elician's concept of time slips away. He sleeps in fits and starts in the endless hall of the dead – waking up to near darkness, gasping awake and trembling. He looks, always, to Lio, who has taken to curling up at Elician's side to keep warm. At least their guards remember that Lio is human. They bring him food and a bucket for bodily functions. They don't offer much more than that. None of the Reapers have need of such things. They don't eat. They have nothing to void. *After an extended period of malnutrition, your body will enter a kind of stasis,* Marina had told him once. *It is exceedingly unpleasant. But you will not die.* He had been thirteen years old, curious at what his powers could do. He had never been curious about that again.

Perhaps he should have been.

A bucket has been provided for their cell because Lio is not one of them. Neither Reaper nor Giver, *his* body will function the way a human's body should. He voids, and he cannot help it. He apologizes for his own humanity, shame coursing through him as the smell of his waste turns the air pungent. And sometimes, the mere act of using the bucket is exhausting for Lio, who cannot crouch over it well enough without Elician holding him up. He presses his head against Elician's shoulder, whispering apologies. 'It's not your fault, Lio . . . it's not your fault.'

Elician tries to understand the guards' shifts as best he can, but they seem random. If one walks the length of the room, it takes him so long to return that Elician imagines him gone for hours. He tried to calculate how many once, but the numbers slipped away from him. He kept losing his place, repeating his integers until he conceded defeat. Maybe there is another doorway on the other side of the room. Maybe the guard exits from there, sleeps, and walks all the way back the next day. Or a different guard returns mere hours later.

Time is a game that Elician loses whenever he wakes, and sleep is how he survives.

Exhaustion overtakes him as his mind tries to adapt to the never-ending darkness. He tries to entertain himself, but the world is dark and dull. He cannot focus on Lio or the people in the cages around him. He sleeps, and wakes, and lies on the ground waiting for a new stimulus that never comes. When it does not, he rolls over and sleeps some more.

The next time he wakes, it is to Lio's voice. Lio is a social creature, and the silence of the Reapers around them is a challenge. He tries, actively, to get a response from them, practising his Lunae and testing the limits of his known vocabulary. 'You didn't manage to irritate Cat into speaking,' Elician sighs. 'I doubt you'll succeed here.' Lio glances back at him. Shrugs.

'I was teasing Cat. I don't intend to tease anyone here.' No. That does not sound like something Lio would want to do. 'How are you feeling?' Lio asks him.

'I should be asking you that. I'll be fine. No matter what they do to me. You–'

'Yes. About that.' Lio sighs and runs a hand through his unruly hair. It's finally a tangled mess that matches Elician's misbehaving curls. 'Why am I still alive? They keep letting you heal me . . . fix me. Why?'

'Because you're my brother in all ways that matter,' Elician suggests. 'Because I love you and would bend to their orders to see you live.'

'You shouldn't.'

'I will.'

'Elician.'

'Wilion.'

'You shouldn't do what they want.'

'One day,' Elician murmurs, 'they will offer me a choice I find too unpalatable to contemplate. And on that day, I will refuse. But until then, Lio, I do not want to be here on my own either.'

It is a brutal thing, Elician thinks, *to be loved by me.* Too often Lio has not survived it. Too often, Elician has needed to force him back, even when the gods had chosen for Lio to move along. And even knowing that, Elician knows a further truth: one day Lio will die his final death. Old age will eventually claim Lio's soul and Elician will continue on alone. Givers live long lives. Extending on and on until their god allows them the chance to rest. Only his sister and the community at Kreuzfurt will still be there in the end. And they are the only ones who would understand why their kind shouldn't love those without their *blessings*.

'Stop that,' Lio murmurs. He taps Elician's cheek. Not quite a slap, but close. Elician frowns at his friend. His dearest friend. 'You look like you're about to apologize for being *you*.'

'I should. *You* should regret ever having met me. You have died half a dozen times in my service. You could have lived a life far away from all of this if not for–'

'Aye,' Lio admits. 'I could have. And I would never have met Adalei. Or had the privilege of having you as a brother.' He smiles, bright as sunshine in the dark. 'I don't regret my life with you, and I never will.' *Someday, though,* Elician thinks. *Someday, you might.*

Elician pats Lio's arm reassuringly. He smiles as best he can, yet it is too forced to feel real. 'How did they know about me?' Elician murmurs. Lio leans against his arm, and they stare out into the gloom together. 'How did they know I could heal you?'

'Someone talked. They must have,' Lio replies.

'But who?' Only members of Elician's family, Marina and Zinnitzia are aware of the truth. Cat knows now, certainly, but he wouldn't have had enough time to tell anyone. Their abduction happened too quickly. 'Who betrayed my trust?'

'That way, madness lies,' Lio murmurs softly.

Perhaps it does. But the question spirals within him nevertheless. It haunts him. Even as Lio settles in to get some sleep, Elician's mind spins, working a problem it cannot understand.

A great clanking at one end of the hall announces a new shift in the guard. Elician glances towards them idly, only to sit up straighter when he recognizes Nured. The man is marching towards them at a brisk pace, wielding a torch and trailed by several underlings and . . . what appears to be a child.

They come to a stop outside Elician's cage, and it really is a child. A boy younger, even, than Fen, dressed in a fine dark velvet tunic embroidered with a glistening silver moon and a smattering of stars. His face and hands are as pale as snow. Curly brown hair tumbles to his chin. Nured hovers beside him, one hand on the hilt of his sword as if Elician and Lio could possibly pose a threat from behind their bars.

'*You're* a Giver?' the boy asks. His uneven teeth gleam sharklike beyond the torches.

'Who are you?' Elician asks in turn, though a guess hovers at the tip of his tongue. While most of the party seem to be soldiers, there is a woman amongst them now. She wears a fine puff-shouldered dress that sinks to the floor. She has painted lips and carries a writing slab. A leather strap loops the tray around her neck, so she can more easily take notes on a roll of parchment. This child is someone important if he has all these people and a scribe at his back. And there is only one male child with this much importance in Alelune.

'*I* am the Stello of Alelune,' the boy informs him primly.

He had guessed right. Elician swallows, then greets him by name. 'Stello Gillage.' Crown prince and heir apparent. A loud hissing sounds all around them. Elician flinches. Lio whirls about, head twisting as every cage seems to spring to life in an instant. Their neighbours are all suddenly on their hands and knees. They glare through the bars of their cages, hissing that same noise, like steam from a geyser. It started with only one voice, but the sound multiplies. It travels from one side of the room to the other, growing all the while. A multitude of voices clamouring together, hissing and hissing in unison until the noise echoes and crashes upon them from all directions.

The sudden noise is too much after so much quiet. Elician crushes his hands over his ears. Lio does the same, jerking his head to see the bodies moving in their cages. Nured shouts threats and curses at the Reapers in an attempt to control the din. He slams the flat of his sword against the cages, but the crashing does nothing to halt their unified anger.

Gillage begins shouting now, screeching his own name as if that will make them stop. He snatches a torch from one of his guards and aims it at the Reaper nearest to Elician. The howling screech of his victim as fire burns her flesh overtakes the hissing.

'What the *fuck* are you doing?' Lio throws himself at the bars of the cage. He rattles at the iron even as Elician snatches him by the shoulder to pull him back. 'Stop it!' Lio insists, ignoring Elician entirely. 'You're hurting her!'

Finally, Gillage pulls the torch from the Reaper. The smell of burnt skin fills the air. Immediate crisis over, horror swirls through Elician. He shifts, taking his turn now, reaching instinctively towards the feeling of agonizing pain that radiates from the cell next to his. He cannot touch her; she is too far away. Gillage slams the torch hard against his wrist for even attempting.

'I am the Stello,' Gillage repeats. The hissing does not start up again. The whole room is silent. But all the Reapers watch. They stare at him with unabashed hatred. 'I am the Stello and you – you are a Giver.'

'Yes. What do you want with me?' Elician asks, distracted by the whimpers from the woman just one cage over. He cannot see how badly she's hurt, but he can sense the ruptured skin already starting to heal over. As a Reaper, her pain is temporary. The gods never let their chosen suffer long. But temporary pain is still *pain*.

'*I* want you to disappear,' he says. 'And I want the world to forget you exist.'

For the life of him, Elician cannot recall having ever seen a child speak with such hatred. When he was a boy, there had been no shortage of schoolyard battles between his peers. All the noble children of Himmelsheim had wanted to take Lio's place. Many had made their opinion on Lio's status well known, and their enmity had been evident from the start. One particular group of miscreants had beaten Lio brutally and left him for dead, just to prove a point that Lio was not *good enough* to be at the crown prince's side. Elician knows just how cruel children can be and has never been under any illusion that they are wholly innocent. And yet, he has never seen a child press a flaming torch to a person's body just to watch them burn, and he has never seen a child sneer with such loathsome disdain at a person they had just met. 'My mother,' Gillage continues, 'she wants you here. For now. Until things are ready.'

'Ready for what?' Lio hisses.

'None of your business,' Gillage snaps back. He turns to the woman with the writing pad. 'Eline de Carsay will be responsible for your care here,' Gillage states. Someone else starts hissing now, a few cages down. The sound ricochets, echoing from one cage to the next, threatening to return to its previous cacophony. It settles before Gillage can start wielding his torch and his threats, but it also seems to dissuade the boy-prince from further posturing. 'Enjoy your stay, *Giver*,' Gillage spits out. He marches back the way he came, leading the group of soldiers and guards with him. Eline is the last to follow, still scribbling on her pad, but she looks up as their lights start to wane.

'I look forward to making your acquaintance more thoroughly,' she says. Then she too is gone.

'And they say *Solebens* are the dramatic ones,' Lio gripes as the darkness swirls around them once more. The exchange could not have lasted more than a few minutes, but its aftermath feels cataclysmic. The quiet is also not as oppressive as before. Hissing voices slip from one cage to the next as if messages are being passed. The woman Gillage had burned is still whimpering, burns not wholly healed just yet, and Elician reaches back towards her. He closes his eyes and imagines flesh made anew. He wills everything he has across the span to her cage.

He has no idea if it works, or if her own healing finally manages to take hold. But she stops crying only a few moments later. She sits upright in the gloom, arms around her body. She looks towards Elician, and in perfect – but accented – Soleben, says, 'He is not *our* stello.'

'I don't understand,' he admits, frowning. 'He is Queen Alenée's heir, isn't he?'

'Gillage,' she says forcefully. 'He is not *our* stello.' She points one long finger in their direction. 'You lie in the home of our stello.'

Elician blinks. He looks at Lio, but Lio does not seem to understand any more than he does. When he looks back, he notices that the others are watching too. All around them, Reapers are staring their way. Watching and waiting. Their hissing reproach of Gillage was their first sign of discontent. 'Your stello . . . is a Reaper?' Elician hazards.

Lio asks, 'If this is his cell, then . . . where is he?'

Dark eyes peer back at them through the gap in the bars. Considering. Patient. Then: 'He is serving his queen.'

His queen. The phrasing is precise. Very precise. Precise enough that it triggers a series of thoughts one right after another, like falling leaves after a harsh gust of wind. Elician closes his eyes and lets the leaves fall. The Queen's firstborn, Stello Alest, had drowned in one of the Bask River's tributaries at nine years old. His shattered body was found washed up on the rocks. Elician's family had thrown a party at the news. They had celebrated the child's death, thrilled that Alelune had suffered such a blow, and even as a child, Elician had been horrified by the delight of everyone in the tragic end for a young boy. Prince of the enemy or not.

Nine years old.

A Reaper.

I wanted to kill you for that party too, Cat had said softly, starlight flickering across his pale face.

It has been twelve years since Alest's death. Marina had said Cat had been a Reaper for—

Elician's hand snaps to his mouth.

'My prince?' Lio asks. Elician turns to look at him. He trembles, shaking from his shoulders to his heels. He is not sure if he wishes to laugh or cry or rage.

'Alest,' Elician says. 'Stello Alest . . . he's alive.' Lio frowns, not understanding. Not putting the pieces together yet. Not even when the woman next to them nods and murmurs her assent. 'He's *alive*, Lio,' Elician gasps. He presses a hand to his friend's arm, shaking as the knowledge courses through him.

'What are you talking about?' Lio asks him. His hands wrap around Elician's arms. It is an attempt to steady him, to hold him together. It is not enough.

'Cat,' Elician says, shaking under the weight of the knowledge. '*Cat* is Alest, Stello of Alelune.' Shaking, too, from the horrified *shame* that rises up at the thought.

He had been prattling on about his *oh so sad* reaction to hearing about Alest's death, and how upset he was at his family for throwing a party, right to Cat's face. Cat, who had *been* that terrified nine-year-old boy. Who had drowned and lost his entire world in an instant. Whose own mother had sent him to this place to grow up in the cold and dark, too small to reach through the bars to touch anyone who might have tried reaching back. *It never should have happened.*

Elician's heart aches. He wishes he had choked on those words he said. Wishes he hadn't made a fool of himself. Wishes, more than anything else, that Stello Alest had never drowned that day. Or experienced all that had come after.

Lio squeezes Elician's arms hard enough to make him wince in pain. Elician can do nothing but squeeze back. Lio's eyes are wild and shocked. His mouth falls open.

'Did we . . . did we kidnap their crown prince first?' Lio asks.

Gods damn them, but Elician is relatively certain that is exactly what they've done. For the second time in twenty years, there is a prince of Alelune imprisoned in Soleb.

And it is all his fault.

CHAPTER NINETEEN

Fenlia

No one has heard anything from the front about Elician. Zinnitzia and Marina both write to the high general, Lord Anslian, asking if he's reached them. But they do not hear back. 'We will tell you if we hear anything,' Zinnitzia swears. But Zinnitzia *never* tells Fen anything. She keeps things from Fen all the time and has done so for years since Fen isn't 'trustworthy'. When another three weeks pass with no update, she writes to Anslian directly. He does not respond either.

The only news they *do* receive is about the war. Apparently, Alelune has managed to push the fight right up to the western walls of Altas. 'The city wasn't breached though!' the courier announces when he sees her crestfallen expression. 'High General Anslian pushed them back!'

'And the prince?' she asks. The courier blinks. Shrugs.

'I have no news on our beloved prince. Surely, he was at the head of the fight, though, as always.'

If he was, he would have been part of the courier's story. Some new fanciful embellishment to add to Elician's growing list of accolades. But he hadn't been. There had been no mention at all.

Something is wrong. The thought circulates through her mind, haunting her every waking moment. She writes more letters to

Anslian demanding an update. If the siege really is over, then he must have the time to respond. And yet, still there is no response.

Her fifteenth birthday comes with presents from her adopted father and mother, from Adalei, but nothing from Anslian and nothing from Elician or Lio.

This is the final proof. The final, irrevocable testament to the reality no one will admit to her: something *has* to have happened, because Elician would never have forgotten. Never. No matter what.

Fen walks along the walls of Kreuzfurt, circling around the farmland and the gardens and the towers. She crosses by the gate that travellers can cross with ease but is guarded by those who will not let her pass. They stand above her, patient and waiting, bows at the ready. She keeps walking, anger warring with despair.

Cat finds her after she completes her fourth loop, sliding into place like the shadow at her heels. 'What if he's dead?' she asks him.

'He cannot die,' he replies softly, ignoring how Fransen had proved that even that statement is false.

She does not argue it. It hurts too much. Instead, she asks: 'But how could he have been captured? He never left Soleb!'

'The river can be crossed by boat, at any point.'

'But no one *saw* them do that – or anything else. How can no one have seen them?'

'I don't know.' Of course he does not know. How could he know? Cat has been here the whole time.

Unless. Maybe he does know. Maybe he knew from the start. He is an Alelunen Reaper, an assassin. Maybe this whole thing has been a plan and–

'*Did* you know?' she asks quietly. 'That my brother would go missing?'

Can I trust this man? Elician had asked her. She had started to think, maybe, just maybe, he *could*. But now . . .

Cat is quiet for a long time, walking in line with her, hands tucked into his pockets. 'No,' he says eventually. 'I was not told that there was a plan to capture Elician.'

'What were you told?'

'Other things,' he admits. 'But not about him.'

'He would have done it, you know,' Fen says. 'Let you go after the war. He has all sorts of plans for when he becomes king and . . . he would have done it.' She tilts her chin up. 'He will do it too. Once he gets back . . . from wherever he is.' Confidence returns swiftly, splashing across the shores of her resolve but leaving just as quickly, sliding back to abandon her in a sea of uncertainty.

'Can I ask you something?' he asks. She shrugs, listless. 'Is it *really* necessary for Elician to lie?' The question catches her off guard, distracting her from her ennui. She shakes her head, not understanding. Feet drawing to a halt, she twists to stand and face him directly.

'Lie about what?'

'He's a Giver,' he says. 'But no one knows.'

'He can't ascend to the throne if people know he's a Giver. Shawshank made it a law after he built Kreuzfurt. *Givers*,' she says with as much condemnation as she is physically capable, 'are meant to heal the people of Soleb. That's our job. To help them. The King is obliged by law to turn over any Giver he knows about to Kreuzfurt, to serve the people. But there's . . . The wording is ambiguous. The kings and queens of Soleb are duty-bound to rule and manage *Soleb* first. So, if it's revealed that Elician became a Giver *after* he'd been made king, then he won't have to abdicate. That's why he has to keep it a secret until then – no one can know.'

'People do know, though. You, Lio, Marina and Zinnitzia.'

'I only found out a few years ago. And only after they realized what *I* was.' That had hurt. He had meant the reveal as some form of empathy. She had been upset, crying, screaming about how he couldn't understand how much she did not want this ability. He had sworn he understood, but the words had only stung. The whole of Soleb knew what *she* was. She had stupidly brought a dead animal back to life in front of people, her powers activating without her even realizing it. Everyone knew. But Elician? Elician was able to keep living his life. Go off to fight a war. And he is still eligible to become king just because he's managed to keep it a secret. She swallows back the bitter taste the revelation still leaves in her mouth. *He told me because he trusts me. And I have to prove I'm worth it.*

'You're *sure* no one else knows? Just . . .'

'Family,' she insists. '*Family* knows. And . . . and people who have all sworn themselves to Elician. If anybody says anything about Elician, then King Aliamon will have them executed as oathbreakers.' She remembers the words she had to swear, hand on her heart, the King watching with a sharp eye, and the threat of severe punishment hanging above her should she ever fail. He couldn't kill her if she broke Elician's trust. But he could make it hurt. 'Maybe someone saying something would stop Elician from becoming king, but it wouldn't benefit the tattler any.'

'How would your king know who told the secret?' Cat asks.

'You just don't break an oath,' Fen replies shortly. 'No one does. An oath is sacred.' Then, scrunching up her nose, she squints at Cat. Elician had wanted to know if he could trust Cat, and Cat already knew his secret, but . . . 'You didn't take an oath, did you?' He blinks at her, lips pressed together. She raises a finger, and he holds his hands up as if to fend her off, head ducking slightly. 'Swear my brother fealty,' Fen commands.

Cat does not move and his jaw clenches. His refusal is clear. Fen steps a little closer. 'If you're going to stay here . . . if you're going to be my friend, be someone we can trust and depend on – if you *really* care what happens to Elician, then you have to swear fealty. You can't just know something like that and not do it. It's the *rules*.' The argument sounds weak even to her, but she doesn't know how else to explain the importance of this. Maybe he *did* know something was going to happen to Elician when he left Kreuzfurt. But he couldn't have been involved in that. Not really. The timing was wrong. But from here on out, this is one secret that *could* cause problems. One that everyone had badly overlooked when it came to Cat, and protecting what he knew. She cannot control anything else about this mess, but she *can* control *this*. She can make sure that Elician is safe from this oversight. And she can fulfil her promise to him . . . prove that Cat can be trusted. Because he swore an oath.

'Sorry,' Cat finally gets out. He takes a step back. Then another. Fen can see the exact moment he thinks of turning and running – probably back to the House of the Unwanting and Marina's or Elena's coddling.

Anger runs hot like fire through Fen's body. She snatches Cat by the wrist, locking her fingers around it tightly enough that she can feel his bones move. He flinches and tries to pull free, but Fen has been on the receiving end of grabs just like this. She knows how to dole them out too. He does not escape, and she has no intention of letting him go.

'Swear fealty!' she demands.

He shakes his head, jerking his arm back and clutching at her hand as he tries to loosen her grip. His mouth opens and closes uselessly. She almost lets him go when she sees just how frightened he has become. But she won't relent. It's her job to keep this secret – and her brother – safe. If she cannot fight in the war, or do anything to help find him, she can at least do this.

She likes Cat. He is her *friend*. The first real friend she's made since everyone abandoned her the day she learned what she was. But people make promises without meaning them all the time. A true oath is *different*. An oath is real. Cat will not break it if he makes it. She knows this, knows it like she knows her own soul.

Her fingers tighten, pressing the bell tight against his wrist. There are tears leaking from his eyes. 'Swear fealty!' she demands, even as his knees buckle and he falls to the ground, twisting away. His arm still dangles from her grip. His body: a weight on a string, collapsed to the earth in miserable supplication.

She feels like she is going to cry too, but she cannot. Bruises will form under her grip, but they will heal, and he needs to swear. 'Swear it!' she gasps again, almost begging as a ragged breath is torn from her.

There's shouting, growing closer. Fen turns. Marina is running towards them, sword in hand as if she intends to cut Fen down. Fen jerks back, nearly tripping over her own feet. She drags Cat with her as she steps to the side. He does nothing to stop the motion, folded like a paper doll – limbs akimbo and brow pressed against the dirt.

Marina yells, 'What in the name of the *gods* do you think you're doing?' But Fen cannot let go of Cat's arm. She cannot release it. It is a lifeline and a desperate plea all in one.

'He has to swear fealty to Elician,' she says, lips trembling as she tries to explain. She straightens her back, ignoring the tears streaming down her cheeks. All the fear of the past few weeks bubbles to the surface. 'He has to! He *knows* about him. And if he does not swear . . . Elician will be in *danger*. He has to swear.'

'Let him go,' Marina orders. She steps closer, lowering her sword even as she draws up to Cat. She touches Cat's shoulder, but Fen still does not let go. She squeezes even tighter. The bones of Cat's arm shift. As fragile as glass, she imagines hearing them crack. It doesn't matter. He will heal. Cat is a dead thing, and death is the only impediment she has ever managed to knit back together.

'I am a Soleben princess,' Fen declares, '*you* are a matriarch of Kreuzfurt and cleric to the Kingsclave. You have sworn yourself to my service, and I will *not* be ordered by you.' Marina's lips part and then press together in a firm line. She glares up at Fen as she lowers herself to one knee. She keeps one hand on Cat's shoulder, but her obeisance is still that of the royal family's house guard.

'Your *Highness*,' Marina spits out. 'I humbly request you let Cat go. He's not going to swear any oaths to you or your brother like this, and he's *destroying* Kreuzfurt.'

Fen recoils. Her head snaps up and she looks around. The sweeping arm of Death has reached out in all directions. Leaves have fallen from trees, grass has shrivelled and died, fish are floating belly up in the nearest pond. The nearby statue of Shawshank is crumbling, and the smell of decay suddenly breaches Fen's nose. She throws herself away from Cat, almost retching as the stench hits her nostrils.

She hadn't noticed what Cat was doing. How could she not have noticed? Why else would Marina have appeared so suddenly? The garden around them is being destroyed and what had Marina even been planning to do with her sword? Hack Cat's head off there and then to stop him from perverting the rest of the enclave?

'He wasn't touching it . . .' Fen babbles as Marina shifts from her guard-perfect pose to tuck her arms under Cat's shoulders and haul him upright. 'He wasn't touching *any* of it. *How did he kill all of that without touching anything?*'

'We need to go,' Marina snaps. Fen can hear them now. Other voices. Concerned voices are coming their way.

Zinnitzia is the loudest of them all, practically throwing her voice in a highly affected manner. 'Oh, what could have *possibly* happened?'

Marina takes heed of this warning and moves quickly. Cat's legs do not seem capable of holding him upright; they crumple when Marina tries to get him to his feet. She grits her teeth and lifts him up bodily, throwing him over her shoulder in a dead-man's carry. She hurries them away from the chaos descending on the garden and Fen follows as fast as she can. Her feet slap against the earth as she flees from the scene of the crime. Her heart pounds ruthlessly in her chest. Marina takes twists and turns through the trees, following paths that are still full of life and untouched by Cat's despair.

They come to a part of the garden that Fen has never seen before. It loops behind the House of the Unwanting to a back entrance Fen never knew about. Marina lets herself inside within seconds. From there, she leads them up a series of narrow stairs that exits into the main corridor. Once inside Cat's room, Marina draws the curtains and Fen lights the lanterns with a swish of her hand. Then and only then does Marina slide Cat from her shoulder and let him curl up on the ground, knees tucked to his chest and his terror pungent enough to make Fen's head swim.

Marina turns to Fen almost immediately. She kneels once more, exhibiting a formality she had never previously bothered to display. Fen hates it. She wants to run. She wants to hide. She wishes desperately that she'd never asked for Cat's oath. 'Your Highness, I pray you'll forgive my impertinence if I remind you that Cat is *not* a subject of Soleb,' Marina says with all the dignified courtesy of a noblewoman.

Fen had been there the day Marina had beseeched King Aliamon not to send Elician to war. She had watched as Marina had knelt before Fen's adoptive father and presented her argument in cool, careful tones. She had watched Marina grit her teeth when Aliamon rejected her petition, and as Marina continued despite the King's command. The woman had argued over and over, until the murmurings of the court reached a fever pitch as the assembled lords and ladies balked at her presumption.

Her punishment had been Kreuzfurt. Her place at court, and at Elician's side, irrevocably revoked because she'd dared speak the truth. Elician should not fight in the war. Fen had never understood why Marina had kept arguing when the only one that suffered for her actions was her.

But now Marina kneels before Fen in turn. Beseeching her on behalf of Cat, who did not argue for himself. Who is curled up like a pill bug, mute and trembling violently. 'Cat cannot, and will not, swear fealty to Elician,' Marina continues. 'To do so will compromise who he is.'

'He's still loyal to Alelune, then?' Fen asks sharply. '*Did* he know something was going to happen to Elician?'

'The two points are not connected,' Marina replies. 'He can be loyal to the country and also not know about Elician's disappearance.'

Incredulity overrides all else. 'But why refuse to swear an oath to Elician? *Why*? After everything they did to him, why would he be loyal to them?'

'Your Highness, if I may ask, what *did* Alelune do to him?' Marina asks.

Fen points. Sharp and furious. 'Well, *someone* made it so that all I had to do was grab his wrist before he *collapsed*. He flinches at everyone and everything, he barely talks, he – he's a mess.' Crumpled and terrified after being yelled at and grabbed by a girl five years his junior.

'He's been tortured,' Marina says. 'Imprisoned in the worst, most uncaring conditions for over a decade. And you're right. Someone did do it. But it was not *the country*. The country of Alelune is not responsible.'

'It was their laws, their rules, their choices. They hurt him! Why would he protect them?'

'Because there is far more to Alelune than what a few people currently in power have done to their most vulnerable class,' Marina says. She looks sad. Terribly sad, and exhausted. And yet she kneels to beg Fen's understanding anyway. Kneels between her and Cat, as if Fen is going to snatch him back by the arm and shake him into submission. Fen presses the heels of her palms to her eyes. She sniffs loudly, then wipes her face. She shouldn't have grabbed him. Shouldn't have forced him to stay still.

'He does not have to swear fealty to Elician,' she concedes at long last. 'But he *has* to swear not to tell anyone about Elician. About his secret.'

Marina glances towards Cat. Fen waits. Cat does not move. Marina's shoulders sag. 'I'll bring him to you later, Your Highness,' she says, despondent in the face of Cat's silence.

It is a dismissal, one that chafes badly against Fen's heart. But when she looks at them both, all she can think to do is nod. Nod and flee. Fen has never terrified anyone like she has terrified Cat today. And even though she had done it because she had been rightly protecting her brother . . . she does not like how it feels. She did the right thing. She knows this. And yet it felt so very, very wrong.

CHAPTER TWENTY

Cat

Marina is upset. She closes the door behind Fen, and then stands over Cat. He sits, knees to his chest, arms looped around his head, and waits. It is always best to wait. 'You could have struck her,' Marina says. She paces, angry, agitated. Her sword, in its sheath, clinks impatiently at her side. 'You could have clawed at her dainty little hands like I *know* you did to Elician, *Cat*. You could have slapped her across her mouth, even broken her arm. But you didn't.'

Her steps are loud, thundering even. They echo in the cavern between his ears like the sound of his childhood. The precursor to being dragged out of his cell by guards dressed in protective gear. Hands holding him down, squeezing against his wrists as fire is brought to his face and the corpse-ash ink is forced into his skin. *Hold still. Do as they say. Don't say a word.*

'Thank you for not lashing out at *her*,' Marina says, as if he needs platitudes about his behaviour, 'but I truly wish you had paid a little more attention to the rest of your surroundings in the process.'

The moment Fen had grabbed his arm, his only thought had been to not hurt her. She was a child, but the feeling of her fingers around his wrist was unbearable, the idea of being locked in place with no way out–

'Do you know how *few* people can do what you just did?' Marina continued. 'What it would mean if anyone outside these walls knew that Reapers are *capable* of doing that kind of damage?'

He's lost in memories of dark halls and cages. It's hard for him to follow her words. Echoes cascade in his mind. Voices from years past. Pain. He presses the heels of his palms to his eyes and rubs. Finally, Marina stops pacing. 'I think it is time you and I were honest with each other,' she says, towering over him. 'Eight years ago, a Soleben spy gained access to the Reaper cells in Alerae. He was going to make a report back to the crown on the condition of those cells, and instead came across something he did not expect. A boy, around thirteen years old, living in the dark.' Cat's fingers dig into his scalp. He doesn't want to hear this.

'He was horrified,' Marina goes on. 'While some guards pitied the child, and were kind to some extent, others thought it necessary to beat and brutalize the boy who was apparently a stain on both the house he came from and the country itself. The spy wrote letters to our king and queen, detailing every observation. Then he asked for something. Do you know what he asked for?'

She waits. Waits with a patience that could outlast the gods. Cat lowers his hands. He meets her eyes. 'He asked if I could have a home in Soleb,' Cat replies.

'If you could have a home in Soleb,' she agrees. 'He knew who you were, of course. So did we. And I have known since the moment Elician brought you here.' She had certainly been almost *too* clairvoyant in guessing his age based on the state of his scar. That should have meant something then. It hadn't. But now, he waits for her to say his name. To draw it out like a curse. She does not. She is, painfully, gentle. 'When Ranio tried to take you from Alelune, were you willing?'

'Yes.' He had been terrified, had worried what the impact and influence would mean in the end. But Brielle had encouraged him to go. Cieli . . . all those around him. What life could he have in the Reaper cells? Called out only to conduct murders at his queen's behest. Every year, during the night of change, his mother would let him slip out to be amongst the people. A mask and fine clothing hid who he was from all the world, and every year, when he walked back to meet her at the end of the night, she only looked more despondent. As if she could not understand why he would return, when no one in all the world would have been able to stop him if he left and never came back.

A masked fool had offered. The same fool, most likely, every year he went. They had juggled balls and given Cat salted fruits, then asked Cat if he would like to leave and see the world beyond the city.

I'm supposed to be here, he told that fool each and every year, even though he kept walking to find them. Kept turning his head to see the tricks and treats. *Where else would I go?* he had asked his mother when she finally asked him why he never fled.

And then Ranio had offered a place. A destination. He had held out his hand, and Cat's protests had died on his tongue.

'Ranio failed, obviously,' Marina says. 'How did he die?'

'He fell,' Cat replies. 'We were riding to the border. Someone had noticed I was gone. We were being chased and . . . I lost my balance. I touched the horse and it died. Collapsed. We were thrown and he . . . he broke his neck.' He hadn't even killed the man. Not directly. Cat had knelt at his side, stupefied. Dumbstruck. Altas and the Bask River had both been in sight, just resting on the horizon. He hadn't even tried to resist when his pursuers caught up. Ranio was dead. Where would he be able to go without Ranio leading the way?

'His head was sent to us not long after we lost contact with him. The Alelunen ambassador presented it at court.' Marina takes a deep breath. 'Ranio Ragden was Fenlia's biological father.'

Unexpected pain lances through Cat's chest, forcing the breath from his lungs. His eyes burn with tears. His lungs spasm as they try to maintain air. Ranio's daughter. His *daughter*. He could have hurt her. He could have hurt her *badly*. But he hadn't. *Gods keep me . . .* he hadn't.

'Her father was King Aliamon's dearest friend, and after his death Aliamon took it upon himself to adopt her. To make her his daughter and a true member of his house. A few years later, right around when your mother restarted the war against Soleb, Fen rather publicly brought back a beloved pet from the dead. And, well . . . you know what it's like to be *exalted* and then sent away, don't you?' Marina crouches down, finally at Cat's level. His chest hurts. His skin tingles. She leans towards him. 'The war started in earnest. Elician was sent to the front, where he fought for three years. And then . . . you were given another chance to leave Alelune. What were you *actually* told, Alest?' His name burns in his ears as his heart constricts painfully beneath his ribs.

That's not my name anymore, he wants to say. But it will always be his name. It will always be a part of him. It is why he is even having this conversation at all. For if he were *not* Alest of Alelune, he would simply be a nobody. And he would have sworn himself to Elician the moment Fen asked him to.

Nothing would have held him back. Elician was worth swearing loyalty to. But as much as he had wished to just be Cat, Cat is not the whole of who he is. And Alest of Alelune will never bow his head to Soleb. Not even in this.

'My queen told me that if I killed the royal family, she would let me leave when my task was done.' Everything comes out in a rush. He switches to Lunae halfway through, head aching. 'She said all the Reapers could leave if I did this one task.' She had not said those words publicly. That could not have been allowed. But in her study, just before he had left, she had offered the boon.

It's what you want, isn't it? she had asked. *To leave and not come back? To know your . . . people are safe and still at your side? Do it, then. Kill these people, and in return I will give you what you want most in this world.*

Marina touches the top of his head. She runs her fingers through his hair and counsels him on how to control his rapid breathing. Then, only when he has calmed sufficiently does she continue. 'Did you believe her?'

'I wanted to.' Trusting his queen, his mother, has never been something that comes easy. She says one thing and does another. She makes plans he does not understand. She offers exceptions and possibilities, then reneges on deals and betrays her allies. He could do what she asked. He could find all the loopholes and follow all her orders, and still . . . there would be no guarantee that she'd do what she had promised.

'Your abilities. How long have you known you could kill something without touching it?'

'The last time they burned my face,' he replies, rubbing at his wrist. 'I just wanted them to stop.' Someone knocked him out not long after the first body fell. He had still apologized to his queen when she came to pass judgement on the murder. It had not been on purpose. She had not punished him for it, either. She had simply nodded her head and walked away.

'You could have killed the entire Soleben army the day Elician captured you . . .' She huffs. A humourless laugh. 'You can walk out of Kreuzfurt at any time you want to; you can kill those guards on the wall before they even fire their bows. Why don't you?'

'I – why would I?' He shivers. With the curtains drawn and the sun long past the towers, the ointment on his skin is icy cold.

'Tell me one final thing,' she beseeches, touching his smooth and newly scar-free cheek. 'Do you believe Elician can make a difference on the throne?'

Of all the questions to ask, why that one? Elician is gentle. Thoughtful. Naïve, perhaps. He likes stories and fables and animals. He named Cat after a mythical creature no one ever sees, which features in both their people's histories nevertheless. 'I had thought he was honourable,' Cat sighs, too exhausted, too cold, to argue.

'*Had* thought?' she presses. 'Do you no longer believe that?'

'He's lying. To everyone.' Lying is what royalty does. It is how they stay in power. It is how they maintain that power. Cat's queen lies and cheats and kills whenever it suits her best. She says Reapers are irrelevant to the Alelunen way of life, then she uses them to assassinate anyone who stands in her way. She says, *Stello Alest is dead*, then stands him in her court to execute those who betrayed her. And all the court nods and accepts and holds the lie, lest they be next to feel his touch. And Elician? He had seemed better than that. And yet—'If it is forbidden to become king as a Giver, why should he become king?'

Marina loves Elician. Perhaps she is even blinded by him. He can be blinding. Rarely had there been a time where Cat had not wanted to look at him, listen to him, know what it was that he was thinking. It had been easy to simply lie next to him by a dwindling fire and listen to him talk about one thing or another. When Elician speaks, people listen. It would serve him well as a king if he did ascend the throne.

'Because some laws are made to stop those who could do the most good from ever having a chance to try.' Marina settles one hand on his knee. 'He knows what he is doing by hiding his secret and knows the legacy a Giver on the throne would inherit. Shawshank ruled for generations. A great Giver on the throne of Soleb. He made it so no one ever died within his country's borders, sending Givers far and wide to keep the whole of his people living eternally. And it ended in disaster. Death was furious at being denied and designed a plague to sweep through the country. An illness that no Giver alone could stop, but every Reaper was blamed for causing.'

She grimaces, eyes pinching at the corners. Cat remembers, suddenly, *She is old enough to have been there. To have seen it all.* When she continues, her voice is hoarse. Defeated. 'Shawshank's only method of correction was to undo it. To try to remake the balance of a world he threw off kilter. He sent all the Givers and Reapers in the country as far away from the people as he could, created new laws that governed how and when the exalted should use their talents.' She sneers. 'He let the rumours grow. Let Reapers be blamed for his hubris, for if only Reapers didn't exist or Death herself had just left Soleb alone, everything would have been perfect. But it wasn't. And it isn't. And here we all are. Still in a walled-off enclave, separate from the world. Encouraged to help only a little, and only those strong enough to make the journey here in the first place.'

Marina holds Cat's gaze and says firmly, 'Elician is not another Shawshank. But he knows the story, the fear and the risk. He has a plan for this country's future. And if you ask him next time you see him . . . I imagine he'll tell it to you in far more detail than he told me. His dream has always been peace, *Stello Alest*. And that means peace for Alelune too.'

Cat presses his back against the wall behind him. The ointment on his skin burns in icy retaliation at the excess pressure. 'You have a traitor in the royal family,' he says quietly. Marina's fingers tighten. 'My queen sent me at the advice of a spy of our own. One who detailed Elician's habits, his routes within the Soleben camp. They specified a *Reaper* should be sent to kill him. Of course, he'd heal from any assassin's strike. But sending a Reaper . . . Someone knew about him. And they wanted it revealed.'

Marina shakes her head. 'Maybe that's so, but then why wouldn't they have merely revealed the secret when they had a chance? Elician's secret isn't exposed; he is *gone*.'

'I don't know.' He keeps turning things over in his mind. Twisting the facts this way and that, trying to make it work. 'I wasn't *told*.'

'But you know Alelune is still responsible somehow.'

'Yes.' He can't explain it. Can't put into words *why*, but the feeling is ever present. Sinking into his skin and digging its cold fingers straight through to his heart. There's a traitor in the Soleben royal family, but Alelune is also involved.

'Do you know where Elician is now?'

'I can guess.' If Elician had been publicly brought before Queen

Alenée, all of Soleb would know. Every courier from one end of the continent to the other would be spreading the message as fast as they could. *None of this would have happened if he had simply imprisoned me in Altas,* he thinks, squeezing his eyes shut as tight as he can.

'Will you help us get to him?' Marina asks him.

That would be treason. Worse than simply writing a letter to Elician or expressing fondness. This would be an active step against his queen. Her interests. *But not against my people.* 'I want the Reapers in Alelune freed,' he murmurs. 'All of them.' This is his price. He knows she cannot swear on behalf of the crown, but she can still act. And Marina has priorities of her own. She serves as the matriarch of a House that wants nothing more than its own freedom. And in this, their goals are aligned. Marina holds her hand between them and nods assent. He presses his palm against hers.

'Tell me everything you know,' she commands.

He does.

CHAPTER TWENTY-ONE

Elician

When Elician was eleven years old, Alelune's Moon Prince – Stello Alest – drowned while swimming in a river. The news came while Elician had been chasing fireflies with Lio and baby Fenlia in the courtyard. They were laughing together. Running about and staining their white trousers in the dirt. Elician's hands had snatched at a bug, trapping it between the cage of his fingers. He'd giggled and run to show Fen, just as a herald had announced the Stello's death. His father had laughed, clapping his hands and cheering. He'd shouted the news for all to hear. King Aliamon had plucked Fenlia up from the ground and tossed her in the air, making her shriek in delight.

Elician did not understand his father's glee. A boy had died. A boy younger than him. He looked at Lio, but Lio only frowned and shrugged as trumpets began the calls for a celebration. The rest of the week was filled with revelries. Restaurants filled large glass bottles with water and dropped small figures inside, selling the drink as the *Drowned Prince*. It became a favourite across the capital and can still be found in some particularly patriotic establishments to this day.

Nearly twelve years later, Elician lies in the same cage that had become that hated boy's home, when Death decided his time was not yet done. Lio leans with his back against the bars, hungry and weak. And Brielle, the Reaper in the cage to their left, tells them the story of Stello Alest.

Her voice is low and deep. Elician imagines they, and those in the few cages closest to them, are the only ones who can hear her speak. The Reapers nearby are all watching too. They have been ever since Gillage came and wished Elician would disappear. They watch, and they wait. He does not know what they are waiting for.

Perhaps they too want to hear the story.

'Most Reapers have their first deaths when they're already old,' Brielle tells them. 'They are fully formed, some even wrinkled and frail. Alest . . . he was the youngest I have ever seen claimed. We weren't sure if he would even grow, but he has. Slowly, and likely not as he should have, but he has grown from that day. Despite that, he should have died much later in life. What use does Death have for a child in need of growing? Why damn a boy without giving him a chance to know what it even means to be alive?' Elician shivers at the question, at the thought. He presses his knuckles to his lips as she continues on.

'Queen Alenée divorced Alest's father when he made a mess of the war and still failed to provide her with a proper heir. She married Gillage's father to solidify some support from a restless military. He was a general's son, and it seemed prudent. But still: no daughter to continue her lineage, as is proper.' Brielle laughs, low and rumbling. 'It was Gillage's father who took Alest swimming that day. Gillage's father who let our stello dive into the deep and ignored him as he drowned.'

Murder, Elician surmises easily. Gillage's father had murdered Alest to ensure Gillage took priority. A boy held little weight compared to a girl in Alelune, but a secondborn prince held even less weight than a firstborn. He imagines the new prince consort displaying his devastation when they fished Alest from the depths. He imagines the charade would have been convincing. He would have needed to be so, to escape punishment for the boy's death.

'He was the first one Alest killed when he woke.' Elician sees it clear as day. A small child, lying on the warm stones by the tributary waters. Coughing and struggling to gain air. His stepfather hurrying to appear concerned, touching him and then falling dead the moment his hand made contact with Alest's skin. And the boy, startled and uncertain, would just have sat there, coughing and stunned, as the royal family's retinue of guards and servants panicked and screamed.

He remembers how, on the road to Kreuzfurt, Cat's – Alest's – expressions had at times oscillated from passive acceptance to terror. It is easy to imagine that same face only a decade younger, and so much more confused.

Brielle continues. 'They threw a blanket over him, stuffed him in a sack. They brought him here.' She points to the spot where Elician likes to sleep. The curved stone fit for a body. Where little arms and legs had curled up in a desperate attempt to keep warm. 'He cried for hours, days. The guards didn't know what to do or how to act. He was their stello. But he was now one of us.'

'And then they branded him,' Lio mutters, cracking his knuckles.

Brielle nods. She touches her own scar, the thick black stain of death that marks her as an Alelune Reaper, and as a source of eternal shame. 'They dragged him to the Queen. Released him and told him to go to his father. And when Alest went to him . . .'

'He killed him too,' Elician finishes. He had known the former prince consort had died. He had learned the news in passing, an afterthought swallowed up by the more alarming discussion of Alest's death. He tries to remember what his reaction had been. Grief? Pity? Maybe something closer to acceptance. Marias had loved his son, so perhaps it was a blessing not to live without him.

'His father's bones made the paste for the brand and—'

'*What?*' Lio asks, turning sharply and crawling as close as he can to the bars of the cage.

Brielle frowns, then starts again. 'In Alelune, the father is tasked with one thing: providing the mother with a child. If the child is unsatisfactory, it's the father's fault. In the case of Reapers, it's tradition for the father to be executed, and the bones ground into the paste that marks the brand. Sealing the cause of death into the product of Death itself.'

Elician's fingers touch his own face. He can remember Cat's brand. Alest's brand. The way that it felt beneath his touch when he attempted, and failed, to heal it. A permanent reminder of how Alest had murdered his father simply by running to him when he was scared.

'Marias was a traitor for breeding a Reaper, and so . . .' Brielle shrugs. 'Afterwards, the Queen sent Alest here permanently and Gillage took the title of Stello.'

'What a life for a prince,' Lio whispers.

What a life indeed. Light flickers at one end of the long hall. A guard is approaching. Brielle falls perfectly silent and still. She folds over and keeps her head down. Lio and Elician watch the guard pass before their cage and keep on going, moving down the hall until even the last flickering of his light fades away.

Only when it is safe does Brielle speak again, her quiet voice whispering for them and them alone. 'Gillage does not deserve to be stello. He is a *monster*.' A few quiet hisses of agreement sprinkle in from the cages around them. 'They say the Queen has never confirmed Gillage as her heir.'

'What?' That sounds wrong. Elician sits up a little more. 'Why would she not declare him stello outright?'

'Because he is a monster.'

'He was a toddler when Alest first died. He could not have possibly been a monster then.'

'Mothers know,' Brielle says. 'She knew. Or she would have done it. Declared him as heir. But she did not. Alest is still Stello of Alelune, Reaper or no. He is still our prince.'

Still heir . . . He is still the heir to the Alelune throne despite being a Reaper. So Gillage has no claim until Alest dies for good, and Alest *cannot* really die unless Death herself wills it. *He could live as long as me,* Elician realizes sharply. *He could shape this world as long as I could . . . If the gods give us a chance, we could fix everything, together.*

'Why talk to us now?' Lio asks. 'Why tell us any of this now? We have been here for days.'

'What point would there have been if your stay was merely temporary?' she asks idly. 'But it seems your stay won't be. And so . . .'

'Alest speaks Soleben,' Elician interjects. 'Very well. Did you teach him that?'

'Yes. We taught him all we could, whenever it was safe to speak. The Queen encouraged it, even. She told us to ensure he could understand the world he lived in.'

To train him to one day rule. Elician grinds his teeth. 'Why? Why not let him be free? She is *queen*.'

'And if she is murdered for being kind to her child? He would be here regardless. There was no other option. Not for him. And not for her.'

'Would they?' Lio asks. 'Would someone have killed her for that?'

Brielle seems surprised he would ask at all. 'Of course – to kill an adversary is to gain power. If Death did not want them to die, then the murder would not occur. But if they *did* die . . . well, then it only proves the action just. Queen Alenée had already sacrificed a River War and Altas for Marias. To do more for her son? It would have been suicide.'

She was trapped. Bound. Elician almost laughs at the irony. The heirs of Alelune and Soleb, both exalted and both bound by the laws made to control those blessed by the gods. Both their parents had done what they could, Elician forced to lie each day of his life, holding himself back from true attachment in all things, Alest separated from the world, an education provided between iron bars.

'Did she want him to be free?'

'She did what she could,' Brielle replied. 'It was not always enough. The guards . . . There are consequences if a Reaper attracts attention here. You've seen that already.'

Lio makes a disgusted noise under his breath. It is almost a growl. 'They did that to him?' he asks sharply. 'The guards? Just . . . shoved a stick in a cage and beat him with it?' Before Brielle can answer, he presses on. 'Did they do what Gillage did to you? With the torch? Is that all *normal*? For life down here?'

'Lio . . .' Elician warns.

'He was nine years old,' Lio snaps back. '*Nine.* Fen was only a bit older than that when we realized she was a Giver too. What would you have done if your guards – if *I* – had hurt her because of what she is? Or because she talked out of turn?' A light is coming. An Alelunen guard on their usual rounds.

'*Hush* . . .' someone whispers not far away. 'Be quiet.'

'Getting yourself worked up is not going to save him *now*,' Elician insists, lowering his voice, even though his hands have been clenched ever since the image rose in his mind. Cat's sea-green eyes in a child's face, weeping in terror and loneliness in the cold dark of a cell.

But Lio's always been less restrained than Elician, and when the guard comes close, he ignores how all the Reapers duck and turn away. Lio shouts, 'You put your hands on that child?' And the guard startles at being called out. He turns and squints down at Lio. 'Your *stello*, your *real* stello, the one you assholes buried alive because he had a gift. Did *you* put your hands on him?'

Elician grits his teeth. He shakes his head. He cannot control his friend. He never could. Lio obeys him only because he believes in him, and if he believes in something *more*, Lio will follow that to its end instead.

Lio's hands grip the iron bars. He shakes them – hard. He snarls and spits, taunting until the guard is stupid enough to slap a baton against the cage and tell Lio to shut up. Lio snatches at the baton in the split-second it snaps against the bars, fingers moving with preternatural speed. He wrenches at it with all his strength, tearing it from the man's hand.

More lights are glittering at the end of the hall as Lio's shouting draws attention. More guards are coming. But this one, right now, is furious enough to reach for his keys – to unlock the cell to retrieve his weapon. The moment he does, Lio is on him. He slams the baton hard into the man's body. He beats him and beats him long and hard, shouting and screaming profanities even as Elician crawls from the cage and drags his friend off the man.

'You're going to get us both killed,' Elician growls, throwing Lio to the ground. But it is not an escape Lio wants. It is vengeance he craves, twelve years too late. Lio leaves the first guard only to move on to the next. To save Lio from a beating in turn, Elician joins the fray.

These guards are largely untrained. They may be perfectly capable of wandering up and down a hallway, but they are not soldiers and they are not fighters. Even weak as Lio has become, his adrenaline forces him forward and Elician follows on instinct. Elician swings a torch into one man's face and bludgeons a woman with the still-burning end. He sweeps the legs of the first man, then kicks at his head as hard as he can. It kills the man. An action instantly reversed when Elician's bare skin brushes against his flesh, as the prince turns to face the next one in line. Another kick, a third. Elician backs away to avoid restarting the process all over again.

He swivels to check on Lio and finds the woman he'd pummelled has been knocked out or killed and the two others that had come to assist are being summarily dealt with too. Lio has broken one's arm and is striking the second's throat with a particularly brutal blow from the baton.

Someone has managed to strike Lio's eye. It is bleeding and swollen. Elician heals it with a harsh shove of his palm against the wound. He ignores how Lio hisses, muttering to the guard, 'You fucking deserve this,' even as the cacophony of more guards echoes on all sides.

Reaching down, Elician collects a baton of his own. Lio's rage has not been quelled, and escape is a non-starter. Even from here, Elician can see the next round of fighting is going to involve dozens of men and women. Dozens more than Elician knows they can handle. Taking a deep breath, he does the only thing he knows how to do in such a circumstance.

He plants his feet and makes as much of a stand as his best friend. They fight back to back, defending and protecting and avenging. Elician cannot heal Lio mid-combat, but he feels it when his friend starts to falter. Senses the sharp rise of exhaustion, and instinctively responds to the shift in the fight's rhythm as the melee drags on.

At the border, the battles wage for hours. There are constant waves of fresh troops sent out to provide relief to the ones already there. The first wave is sent out, then the second, then the third. Actual combat is fast, as the human body is only capable of operating at full capacity for short bursts. In the end, victory depends on which army can outlast the other. And Lio, for all the adrenaline that had motivated him from the start, is not in good shape.

Lio doesn't care.

He screams taunts and curses and jeers. He keeps his vicious tongue wagging with insults: *child-beaters, murderers, weaklings*. He grows more creative the more times he is struck. When he knows he will fall eventually but is not yet ready to concede, his insults escalate: 'Limp-dick spermless *cunt*. Ball-less goat-fucking whore! Spineless cow-shit-eating *worm*. Piss-gargling *philanderer*.'

The last one makes Elician laugh hard enough, in his own battle frenzy, that he is entirely distracted when something hard and *excruciating* smacks him right between his teeth. He feels half his mouth shatter at the impact, but he is still laughing when he blacks out. After all, what did Lio even *mean*?

Elician wakes up in more or less one piece. Lio wakes up in *far more* pieces. Many bones have been shattered, his chest crushed. Elician jerks badly when he sees the state of his friend, and it takes him hours to piece him back together. Healing this amount of damage requires more energy than he has to spare, and it takes time to mend each broken bone and torn muscle. Elician needs to eat, to rest, to recover from his own injuries in peace. But Lio does not have the time for him to rest. Elician pushes himself past the exhaustion. By the time he finishes, he is dizzy and close to swooning.

Lio sleeps through it all. Elician is grateful that he does. The pain of waking would have been unbearable. When a guard passes them on the usual route, tentatively walking over the bloodstained alabaster like a nobleman over a mud puddle, Elician bares his teeth and earns a verbal rebuke but nothing more.

They have not gained any friends with the *staff*. Elician does not care. Even if the outcome had been certain from the beginning, he cannot deny how good it had felt to take some of his anger out on something physical. He is surprised that they managed as well as they did, weak and exhausted as they are.

'You shouldn't have done that,' Brielle chides.

'Your stello deserved far more than that besides.'

Brielle is quiet for several moments. She sits with her arms crossed and her knees pulled up to her chest. She watches him, like an owl in a tree. 'Who is that boy to you?'

'Lio?' he asks.

'Yes.'

'My brother, in a way. The only one I've ever known, at least.' He huffs, running a hand through Lio's bloodstained hair. 'I was afraid of everything when I was a child,' Elician tells her. 'My cousin was dying of some disease no one could understand, and my parents were terrified I'd cut myself and someone would see me heal. I wasn't allowed to play with anyone but Lio, because I might make a mistake, and someone might *see*. I was barely allowed to go for a walk on my own in public.' He reaches a knot in Lio's hair. There are always knots, but he has no comb to set it straight. 'So Lio brought the world to me. He played the games I couldn't play and he told me how they felt. He helped me sneak out at night and let me try all the things I couldn't when someone else was watching. He said all the things I couldn't to all the people I had to be polite to. And he . . . he has never liked bullies. No matter who they are. And maybe we shouldn't have done this.' He jerks his chin towards the bloodstained ground and the mess they've made out of everything. 'But Lio wanted to do it, and I will support him until the end. He was there for me every moment I ever needed someone, and I'll be there for him too. And . . . I hope one day someone can do the same for your stello, Brielle. Because he deserves that too.'

The door at the end of the hall opens. More torches come. Elician sighs. He rubs a hand over his face and prepares himself for whatever comes next. He is only a little surprised to see Gillage himself and Nured. Eline is following silently behind with the usual gaggle of guards. He supposes their ruckus had been hard to ignore.

'You haven't been behaving yourselves,' Gillage scolds. The boy's voice has not broken yet. It is still high-pitched and infantile.

For years, Elician has ridden into battle and faced down enemies. When Anslian disciplined him, he had done it with military swiftness. When his father issued commands, he had done it with the firm knowledge that Elician would follow without question. Elician does not even think his mother has ever chastised him like this, wagging her finger to show her displeasure.

Elician cannot help it. He laughs. 'Admittedly, Your Highness' – he struggles to show some modicum of respect – 'there's little entertainment to be had otherwise.'

The boy's button nose scrunches, all pert and dissatisfied. 'You *killed* my men.'

'*Yes.*' Elician applauds. 'Yes, I did.' Then, more soberly, he leans forward. 'Your men saw fit to torture and abuse a child – your older brother – for twelve years. It did not sit well with us.'

Gillage's mouth falls open. His eyes go wide. He glances towards Nured, then straightens his back. Postures, and asks defiantly, 'You did all this for *that thing*?'

'Alest is not a thing,' Elician says, voice low and quiet.

'It's not a person,' Gillage recites. 'You do realize that, right? It's not a *human being*. It's a dead thing walking, nothing more or less.'

'Your *brother* is more human than half the men I have met in my lifetime. He can kill if he wants to, but he does not want to. And I hope one day you understand even a *fraction* of what that's like. To have power over someone, to be able to do anything you want, but choosing to do the right thing anyway – simply because it's *right*.'

Gillage gapes, then glowers. He snarls like a puppy angry that someone has touched his food. He takes a step closer to the cage. Nured mutters a quiet word of warning, but Elician does not hurt children. Neither does Lio. The boy is safe and will remain safe. 'You think that's what *it's* like?' Gillage asks. 'Some sweet little thing? *You're wrong*. It's a murderer. That's all it is, that's all it ever will be. A murderer.'

'And what will you be?' Elician asks. Gillage stares at him, lips parted as if he wants to respond but does not have the words. 'Why are you here, Your Highness?'

The child looks uncertain. He glances back towards Nured and Eline. It is a quick look, but Elician recognizes it. He has seen looks like that before. A subordinate checking in with a superior, or someone who thinks they are in charge looking for guidance from the ventriloquist at their back.

'We will be changing your location,' Eline says, stepping forward. 'Since you cannot behave together, then perhaps separation will do you good.' She tilts her chin at Nured. 'Open the cage.'

Elician expects the man to chafe, to wait for Gillage to give the order instead, but he doesn't. He follows her command with ease, unlocking the cage for the second time in only a few hours. 'Giver,' Gillage commands in his squeaky child's voice. 'Come.'

'I'm a prince, Your Highness,' Elician says. He traces a hand along Lio's wrist. He will panic when he wakes to find Elician gone. Elician glances to his left. Brielle nods subtly in the gloom. She will explain. He hopes it will be enough. 'Perhaps you could show me some of the courtesy I deserve.'

'Come here, and I won't have Nured slit your toy's throat. There's my courtesy.' And *there* is the savagery of the child he first met. The brutal bloodlust that does not coincide at all with what Elician has seen in the boy's older brother. Elician crawls around Lio's body. He slips outside and holds his hands to the side to accept the manacles offered.

The door is closed behind him. Eline smiles brightly. 'I am looking forward to getting to know you better,' she says. 'Come, you will be upstairs. It is a long way.' A rough hand shoves him forward, and Elician glances back. Lio is still asleep.

'See you soon,' he promises. He hopes it is not a lie.

PART III

As Grass disintegrated and returned to Earth and Water, Water cheered, and Earth smiled, and together they built something new. Sometimes this 'new' was more Grass. Sometimes it was something else entirely. Flora and fauna of all shapes and sizes grew from these moments. Life encouraged each new possibility as much as he could. He taught and explained and offered fresh pathways for growth and understanding. And when those paths reached their end, Death offered them a chance to start over. To start anew. Return to the beginning and begin again.

Life watched over it all, shining high in the sky, making the summers hot, guiding all who lived to experience the wonders of existence. He offered warmth and possibility. He offered light.

But wherever Life went, so too did Death. She made her own home in the sky: a moon to block the sun's gaze. She brought forth the winters and the chill, the stillness and the quiet. She pulled waters from the shorelines and dared the living to survive anyway. She dared them to fight her, to fight Death every day they remained on the Earth, to prove they still wanted to thrive. That they still wanted this existence, and nothing more.

And through it all, she tempted the living, offering them the chance to experience something different. Something new. Something more. To die, and live again.

– The Origins of the Gods, Anonymous

CHAPTER TWENTY-TWO

Fenlia

Marina keeps Cat in seclusion for nearly two weeks.

Two weeks, during which Fen dedicates herself to reviving the garden Cat destroyed and avoiding the House of the Unwanting. She runs her hands over the withered grass and along the trees. She hunts down flowers and animals that had been caught up in Cat's path. His powers extended fifty paces in all directions, with not even worms escaping his reach. Other Givers help her too. One, a tall woman named Gerai, is certain that a group of Reapers played a prank on the garden. 'They hate anything nice and beautiful,' she says sadly, stroking the leaves of a drooping lily.

'How could *that* many people be involved and not get caught?' Fen mutters.

'Do you have a better explanation, little princess?' Gerai snaps back. She does not. Not one that she is willing to share, anyway. But from how Marina and Zinnitzia had acted in the immediate aftermath, neither wanted Cat's involvement to be known. And until she knows more, Fen has no intention of telling anyone her suspicions except Elician. One day. Eventually. When everything is right again. She will only tell her brother. He needs to know.

'Maybe they acted out of grief for Fransen?' another Giver suggests. She is the second-youngest Giver of the lot, at fifty-seven years old. She nervously strokes a lizard she has just brought back from the dead, and Gerai puts an arm around her shoulders.

'If it is grief, then they need to learn to respect Life more. To kill all of this because of that? Awful.'

Fen bites her tongue and turns her back. She does what she does best: bring the dead back to life. The other Givers set a slow and steady pace, but Fen is more used to the familiar give and take of Life and Death now. She heals whole sections of the garden while they fuss over one flower or another.

When she is finished, and Kreuzfurt has returned to its former glory, Fen closes herself up in her room. Elena leaves books for her to read, and Fen ignores them. Zinnitzia orders her to behave, and she ignores that too. She practises lighting her candles from afar, focusing on the flame and the flame alone so she does not need to think about Cat, his terror, her actions, or what he did to the garden.

But eventually, Marina requests her presence at the House of the Unwanting. The request comes in the form of a formal missive, following the standard protocols employed when a subject requests service from their liege. 'Petty hag,' Fen growls as she reads over the perfectly embossed calligraphy. She hates that Marina has decided to play at being formal. Hates it enough that, when she answers the summons, she wears the circlet and finery of a Soleben princess.

She meets Marina and Cat in the ceremonial hall they'd used on Cat's first night in Kreuzfurt. Cat steps towards Fen, sliding to one knee in a practised move: something that Marina must have taught him. One hand covers his heart as the other curls into a fist that kisses the ground – as tradition dictates. He utters an oath, perfectly crafted and precise: 'I swear on my life, and the life of my people, I will not betray Prince Elician of Soleb nor any member of his family who work in support of his crown.' His voice does not crack or falter and his accent is relatively muted, as though he has practised enough times in Soleben for the words to flow.

Fen bites her lip, then quickly suppresses the motion. She nods imperiously, raising one hand, and says, 'I thank you for your pledge,' just as Adalei always did when Fen watched her at court. She drops her hand to her side and Cat rises, nodding a little to himself. As if to say, *There, job done.* 'And' – he freezes mid-motion as she continues – 'I'm sorry I hurt you, Cat.' Regardless of what else happened that day, her behaviour to him was the part she regrets most.

'You never have to apologize to me,' he tells her, not quite meeting her eyes.

Marina clears her throat. She steps forward to stand in line with Cat, shoulder to shoulder. 'Your Highness, it is with my deepest condolences that I must inform you of news we received from the capital last night.' Marina, it seems, *will* need a formal apology in order to return to their normal state of affairs. 'After much correspondence with Lord Anslian' – Fen *knew* they had heard back from him. She *knew* it! – 'King Aliamon has declared Elician and Wilion deceased following the Battle of Altas.'

No. *No.* Fen reels backwards. She shakes her head, mouth falling open. 'He's not *dead*.'

'No,' Marina agrees. 'He's most likely very much still alive. But he *is* missing. And, for political reasons, it's more palatable to say that Elician died valiantly in battle than that he is a coward who fled from the fight.'

'Alelune has him. They have to have him . . .'

'There is no proof.'

'There has to *be* proof.'

'His Majesty has done what he could to confirm Elician's position. No one has seen or heard anything to suggest Elician is in Alelune. But–' Marina pauses, taking a deep breath. 'But you may confront the King with your arguments and theories yourself. There will be a state funeral held. And we have been summoned back to Himmelsheim.'

'We – who, exactly?'

'You, Zinnitzia, Cat and myself.'

Fen does not quite manage to hide the horror on her face. She points a finger in Cat's direction. 'He can kill anything just by *thinking* about it.'

'Yes,' Marina agrees. 'And the King is trusting that Cat will not do that. Do you have any doubts about Cat's intentions?'

Plenty. She has plenty. She opens her mouth to list them all, but the words die on her lips. The decision has already been made. She can argue with Marina, but it will do nothing. They will still be leaving. 'Does he know?' she asks. 'Does he know what Cat can really do?'

'Yes,' Marina replies. 'For reasons he declined to share, the King has deemed it worth the risk. It's . . . another test.' Not a very good one, Fen thinks. 'If it pleases Your Highness, I recommend you get ready to leave. It's a long ride to Himmelsheim. We should leave as soon as we are able.' It is said in a tone so saccharine sweet that the words curdle in Fen's ear.

'If it is what my king demands,' she says, scowling ungraciously. Then she turns, just barely managing to keep from stomping out the door.

Fen packs. Slowly, lethargically. She gets her things together and she considers what will come next. She does not have much that she needs to take with her; most of her things are in Himmelsheim, to be sent to her here on her request. So only the essentials are needed. Clothing, brushes, the special underclothes she keeps for her monthly flow. She finishes relatively quickly and changes her footwear.

Elena meets her at her door. But she is not dressed for the road. 'My place is here until the end of the summer,' Elena tells her when she asks. 'Zinnitzia and Marina will be going with you and Cat to Himmelsheim. I just wanted to give you something before you go.' It is a bag of seeds.

'I don't understand.'

'I know you like feeding the birds, but I'm going to ask you not to do that with these,' Elena says, smiling lightly. 'You've been studying biology, anatomy, life and death and everything in between. I want you to try to make these grow, on your own, with nothing except your own power.'

'What? Nothing?'

'Don't plant them. Just hold them and make them grow.'

'Do you really think I can do that?' It still is not healing. But Elena smiles at her and bows.

'I think you can do anything, Your Highness. Good luck, and for what it is worth . . . I am very sorry for your loss.' Tears press against Fen's eyes. She throws her arms around Elena and her teacher holds her close, patting her hair and whispering sweet words in her ear. The moment passes too quickly, but then Fen has to leave.

She drags her luggage to the stable where the others are waiting. She sees Zinnitzia first. Zinnitzia's black hair has been braided and tied into a bun at the back of her head. Her white dress has been exchanged for white trousers and a long tunic that reaches midway down her thighs. She glances over her shoulder as Fen draws near, then jerks her chin to where a pair of draft horses have been hitched to a wagon. 'Did Elician teach you how to drive?'

'Uh . . .'

'Be truthful now,' Zinnitzia insists.

When Elician and Lio were eighteen, they had been a bit too inspired by some of the history lessons they'd been given. They both got it in their heads that they wanted to learn how to race chariots like the kings of old and set about learning how. Lio convinced a group of history fanatics to help recreate all the equipment required. After several months of sneaking around, they had their carts built and the streets cleared. Elician batted his eyes at the guards at each interlocking gate that segmented the capital city not long after, and at three in the morning, they took off racing through the night – driving their chariots as fast as lightning through the city streets. Lio won the race, slapping his reins against his faithful horse's back and pulling ahead just as he crossed the last of Himmelsheim's gates.

The historians judged the final contest and took possession of the illicit chariots when the race was complete, leaving Lio and Elician to slink back up to the palace undetected. They'd almost got away with it too. No one had been in the streets, and the taverns had long since closed. Their bad luck had come almost six months after the fact, when Lord Anslian had gone for a walk along the academics' boulevard and seen Elician's chariot on display. One passing comment that it looked fit for a king had earned him the entire story – and the revocation of Elician's personal freedoms for nearly a year. Neither he nor Lio was permitted to try their hand at driving horses ever again.

But before their lessons had been cancelled, Elician *had* hoisted Fen up onto the bench seat of his practice wagon and shown her what to do.

'Yes, I can drive it,' she admits quietly.

'Well,' Zinnitzia sighs, 'you won't be *racing* this wagon, but you might as well be of use. Put your things in the back, I'll be over in a few minutes. Cat will be riding with you.'

'You're really going to let me drive it?' Fen asks, palms sweaty at the possibility.

'It will be good experience. You might need it one day, and who knows when you'll get another chance to practise?'

Fen opens her mouth. Closes it. Then tries very hard not to look too excited at the possibility as she drags her luggage to the sad little wagon attached to two beautiful draft horses. She wrestles her valise into the back with the rest of their travelling supplies, then hurries to the front to climb up.

The step up is too high for comfort. She must pull herself most of the way using the back of the seat. When Cat finally makes an appearance, Fen holds a hand out to help hoist him up in turn.

Even shorter than her, he clambers clumsily up the wheel spokes, almost crawling into position. Zinnitzia, of course, climbs up with annoyingly perfect grace – the picture of elegance as she slips onto the bench seat. 'Show me your hand position,' she commands as Fen gathers the reins from where they are tethered in the footwell.

'Why are you coming too?' Fen asks as she slips her fingers into position.

'I'm a cleric of the Kingsclave, it's my responsibility to serve as an ambassador at state functions. And besides, do you really believe that I would miss your brother's funeral?'

'He isn't actually dead.'

'Lio might be.' Fen's fingers spasm. The draft horses in front of her snort and huff, heads flicking in annoyance.

And Fransen died after only being a Reaper for a few years, a traitorous voice reminds her. *Why not Elician too?*

'Lighten your grip,' Zinnitzia cautions. 'Show me how you would turn.' She quizzes Fen for a few more moments before eventually nodding and transferring onto her own horse. They leave Kreuzfurt not long after, passing through the gates entirely unmolested.

Fen glances at the top of the city's walls, eyeing the guards and their bows just as they eye her and her companions in turn. She turns her back to them, keeping her attention on the horizon, and only relaxing once they are far out of range. Marina and Zinnitzia ride steadily up in front, talking to each other too quietly for Fen to overhear. Neither seems particularly concerned.

'What does that mean?' Cat asks suddenly, voice cracking along the edges.

'What?' She twists, turns. He is pointing at a sign bearing Kreuzfurt's mark and slogan.

'Can't you read it?' she asks in turn. It is probably one of the most well-known epitaphs in all Soleb. *Kreuzfurt: Hope for the Hopeless.*

'Yes,' Cat says. 'But what does it mean?'

'It . . . it's so everyone knows that, inside Kreuzfurt, you'll get what you need. That whatever it is you're lacking, it will be provided. If you have nowhere else to go, Kreuzfurt will be there.' He is still frowning, and she wonders what's troubling him so much. 'Think about it,' Fen presses. 'Nobody wants Givers and Reapers just wandering around. But there's not a lot of options. At Kreuzfurt we're supposed to have the chance at some kind of life. We can walk and work and read . . . study and . . .' She trails off. For years she had fought against every part of this place. Now, trying to defend it, it feels almost hollow. 'It's hopeful,' she presses on. 'That's what the sign is saying. That there's hope for a better life.'

'I don't think it's meant for us,' Cat replies.

'What?'

'That sign, I don't think it's meant for the exalted.'

'It's meant for anyone inside Kreuzfurt,' she insists.

'Then why can it only be read by those *outside* the gates? And only by the ones who can leave? A prison with home comforts is still a prison.'

'It's not a prison.' Prisons are where people go when they do something bad. She hadn't done anything wrong. None of the Givers or Reapers had. They were chosen by the gods, and that was out of their hands. Even if there were guards up top. Even if it was scary to think of their bows aimed right at her. 'It's safer. For everyone. If we're there.' He doesn't agree. She doesn't care. 'So, it's not a prison. But the sign . . . it *is* for the guests too, of course. They only come to Kreuzfurt if they're truly in need. So, they arrive and . . . and Kreuzfurt gives them hope.'

'Yes,' he agrees finally. 'It gives them hope. But not us.'

'Well, how is it any better than Alelune? You actually *were* imprisoned. You were in cells. *Underground.* And they hurt you there.'

'The guards did, yes,' he confirms warily 'My . . . brother too.'

'You have a brother?'

'Yes.'

'But I thought you went to the cells when you were a child? How did your brother hurt you?'

'He visited.' Cat's bell jingles a little as he fidgets, and he flicks it twice before saying, 'He is a cruel boy, my brother. I didn't know brothers could be kind. That you could . . . love them as you do.'

Elician. It seems her brother lives in the shadow of every word they speak, sitting between them, haunting each of their choices and interactions. She thinks, *I'd give anything if he were truly here,* but says, 'My brother's the best person in the world. No one's better than him.'

'I know,' Cat replies. He seems sincere. And he is gentle as he allows a subtle change in topic. 'Elician told me stories on the way here. About constellations, and nightcats. They were different from the ones I knew, but I liked them all the same.' He pauses. 'I can't give you an oath stronger than the one I already gave. My loyalty is to my people–'

'Those people tortured you.'

'The Reapers are my people. My Reapers. I'm sworn to *them.* And . . . there are good people in Alelune too. People worth protecting.'

'Then why did you make an oath not to harm Elician?' Fen asks.

'Can I not want both? Your brother safe and unharmed, and my people free?'

He can. But it's a nuance that she's never seen replicated elsewhere. Their countries have been at war for so long that the idea of wanting something good to happen on both sides of the border at once feels almost absurd. 'What about the King?'

'What about him?'

'You could hurt him. You could hurt . . . a lot of people. There's a *reason* it's better if your – if Reapers are kept away.'

'Yes,' Cat agrees. 'But I swore not to harm any member of Elician's family. Trust me,' begs the enemy soldier her brother had wanted her to befriend. 'Please?'

She wants so badly to say yes. That she had truly meant it when she had offered her friendship. They have spent months learning so many things at each other's side. Despite herself, despite her prejudice, she wants to trust what he said as true. *He scares me*, she thinks. *He destroyed that garden with a thought.* He could do so much worse.

'I'm trying,' she whispers. It feels like a defeat.

'I won't let you down,' he replies, his conviction as cast iron as his vow.

She nods, hoping it will be enough. Then, lowering her voice and glancing furtively at Marina and Zinnitzia, she asks, 'Do you want to learn how to drive?'

It's a long way to Himmelsheim, and they can at least do this together. When he smiles, small and subtle as it is, it still shines like the bright of day.

She hopes she hasn't made another mistake.

CHAPTER TWENTY-THREE

Cat

Travelling to Kreuzfurt had been strange. Elician and Lio had not been in a great rush. They'd ridden without paying much attention to their surroundings. They'd chatted to each other, laughing loudly and unselfconsciously – without any of the shamed silence that had been his lot. That journey had felt like a beginning, an opening salvo, an opportunity. Here was a language he'd been taught but had never been able to hear in all its rhythmic perfection. Here were the colloquialisms, jokes and sayings of a land he had heard about in hushed whispers from cells where learning only happened when the guards turned their backs.

Leaving Kreuzfurt is not the same. Fen chatters, she complains, she tells stories. She describes Himmelsheim and the road to the capital. She teaches him how to drive the wagon, then lies outstretched in it so the sun can burn patterns onto her bare skin. She wraps ribbons up and down her arms to achieve a unique crisscross sunburn that only she seems to understand. She sometimes uses leaves to accent the ribbons' effects, creating starlike imprints that she coos over in the evenings when they stop for the night.

But conversation by this campfire is not joyful or exuberant. No one stands up and makes animal noises or acts out the scenes of a story. No one talks about nightcats and what it would be like to find one in the dark. He misses the friendly camaraderie Lio and Elician displayed. Misses, too, sitting up with Soleb's often sleep-deprived prince, just to look at the stars and watch the moon travel across the night sky.

Zinnitzia and Marina sit shoulder to shoulder, speaking with their heads dipped close. On the first night, Marina settles an arm around Zinnitzia's waist and her nose nudges against the back of Zinnitzia's neck. Fen's face twists as she looks at them, muttering about adults and not needing to *see* it. 'What do you mean?' he asks her.

Her face burns redder than her sun-kissed skin. 'You know they're . . . *together*, right?'

'Together?'

'In a relationship . . . in *love*.' She uses the Soleben word *vak*, and he knows that it would translate to 'love' in Alelune, but the meaning is muddled. There's an implication he cannot remember. 'You do have love in Alelune, don't you?' she asks.

He scowls at the needling. 'Of course we do. But *you* have too many words for it. What does *vak* really mean?'

'*Vak* is . . . when you just want to be with that person, for ever, no matter what. You never want to be alone again, and if you see a world where you might be alone in it, you say and do anything to keep the person you love with you at all times.'

'The person who keeps you from being alone, when you would have been otherwise, even when times are at their worst?' Cat queries.

'Yes. That. That's *vak*. It's the person you marry and stay with until the end of time.'

'Then why did you make that face, when you saw Zinnitzia and Marina together just now?' he asks.

Fen flushes, shaking her head and covering her eyes with her hands. Embarrassed. 'They're just *old*, okay, and I . . .'

'She's a child,' Zinnitzia calls out, clearly listening with amusement. 'And she'll grow up and learn to deal with this herself one day.

Now shut up, both of you, and go to sleep.' Fen throws herself into her blankets, tugging them over her head to hide her shame.

Cat lies down and stares up at the stars. He wonders whether he might one day have room for a love like that. 'Do you love someone?' he whispers to Fen.

'Mind your own business!' she hisses back.

He lies there, cold and unguarded, hands unbound, and tries not to imagine either Elician or Lio in the place he knew of as home. They wouldn't like it there. Lio would hate the lack of stimuli. But Elician . . . at least he wouldn't be alone. At least he has Lio and all the people Cat loves most in the world.

Rolling on his side, Cat hugs his arms close, and watches the forest for a creature that no one ever sees. Hoping, dangerously, for one good thing to tell Elician when they next meet. He listens to the general chirping, screeching, staccato squeaking of the outdoors after the sun has finally gone to bed. He listens until sleep takes him, and he dreams of nightcats swimming across the river, coats bleached white under the moonlight.

In the morning Marina helps him apply the cooling ointment to his back and neck. Fen wakes up just as they finish and she stares, wide-eyed, at the procedure. '*That's* what makes you all smell like that?' she blurts out after Marina explains what it does. Marina actually rolls her eyes at the comment, huffing audibly. 'What is it made from?' Fen wonders.

'It's a blend. But the main ingredient is charranseed – it grows on the keep's grounds.'

'Charranseed!' It's a large spiny tree that grows near Kreuzfurt's southern walls. One whose seeds are large enough to knock a grown man unconscious if he is foolish enough to wander beneath its branches when it is time for them to fall. 'Couldn't you have added lemongrass to it?' Fen asks. 'Or maybe some water lily? It's . . . not the best smell in the world.'

'I'll let Elena know her concoction doesn't meet approval,' Marina says dryly.

'I didn't *say* that,' Fen gripes. 'Just that it *could* be better if . . . if you wanted it to be better.'

'You are more than welcome to try.'

'Besides, how is Cat going to court a lady one day if he smells like charranseed?'

Marina laughs, rolling her eyes. 'Perhaps we shouldn't find problems for ourselves where there is no need. Do you want to court a lady, Cat?'

'No.' He wants them to stop talking about it.

'There, problem solved.'

Fen frowns, though. She gets her things packed into the cart and asks, 'What about a gentleman?'

Even under layers of ointment, his skin feels suddenly far too hot. He flinches at the next swipe of Marina's hand on his back.

'Do *you* want to court a gentleman, Fenlia?' Marina asks sharply as she finishes rubbing the last of the ointment onto his skin.

Fen sputters, shaking her head quickly. Her freckles almost disappear under her fierce blush before she finally manages to spit out, 'We're not talking about me!'

'We're not talking about any of this,' Marina agrees. She nudges Cat. 'Get dressed. And as for you, Fenlia, I mean it. Enough. Lay it to rest.'

'Well, if you do decide to court someone,' Fen mutters anyway, 'don't wear that shit.'

'Fenlia!'

'I'm done!' But she waits for Cat to promise once Marina's back is turned, and he does because he wants to finish the conversation in its entirety.

They continue on. And as the days slip by, Cat flips through the new books Marina has given him for the journey, practising reading Soleben and studying the tables and scientific illustrations inside. One volume in particular holds his interest. He sounds out the words for Fen to explain when he stumbles over them and reads about the biological effect of hormones and neurotransmitters for most of the journey.

There's a certain kind of frustration in knowing a language but crashing against the shores of incompetence whenever he finds a new assembly of letters. Fen had been right; Soleben's greatest charm is that it is a very phonetic language. He *can* sound most of it out. But it is slow. Very slow. He spends hours on one chapter alone, reading and rereading each word until he is certain he's got it right.

They ride with the intention of reaching Himmelsheim in a week, and on the sixth day they come across a large contingent of soldiers on the march. 'Stay here,' Zinnitzia tells them before guiding her horse into a swift lope along the side of the column. Fen curses suddenly, spitting out a word Cat does not know before swiftly patting down her hair and trying to smooth the wrinkles in her dress. She unwinds the ribbons on her arms to show off the sun patterns she has been developing.

'Pull your hood up, Cat,' Marina commands. He reaches behind his head and yanks the looping hood up and over, letting the thick veil unfold to hide his face from the world. Beneath the fabric, the air is thick and hot. He doesn't usually rub the ointment on his face and his skin prickles uncomfortably as it stays enclosed. Only two narrow slits let him see what is happening beyond.

Oh. This is Lord Anslian's retinue. Elician's uncle and the high general of the army is riding towards them, Zinnitzia at his side. He is dressed in glittering gold and shimmering purple, and his horse is almost as bejewelled and shining as its rider. The general's armour reflects light, blinding any who stare for too long. 'Your Highness,' Marina acknowledges to Cat's right. He cannot see what she is doing. Perhaps she bows, awkward but polite, upon her steed.

'Uncle,' Fen intones from Cat's left.

'Why are you driving a cart?' Anslian demands.

'I . . .'

'You're not riding into the city like a beggar. You two should have known better.' He must be addressing Marina and Zinnitzia now. 'How dare you? Lieutenant! Get the princess a horse.'

'With all due respect, Your Grace, we are not yet at the city gates and–'

Anslian cuts Marina off with a sharp, 'Enough.' Then, 'What is this?'

'Cat, Your Grace,' Marina replies. 'Prince Elician–'

'This is the Reaper my nephew brought you?'

'Yes.'

'Show me his face.' Someone tugs at the back of his hood. Marina, maybe. Cat pulls the hood off himself and Anslian frowns and nods. Then the fabric is rolled back over his face. 'His cheek. There was a scar there once. I presume that's your doing, Zinnitzia?'

'Mine,' Fen cuts in.

'Yours? I didn't think that was a skill of yours.'

'I–'

'She did it,' Cat confirms. From beyond the slits in his veil he can just make out the way Anslian's expression twists and his eyes narrow.

'My, my,' Anslian says. Angry, of course. He glances at Marina. 'Perhaps you *are* capable of miracles, to take that shell of a thing and teach it to speak.'

'He's not a thing,' Fen interrupts once more. Her hand touches Cat's wrist, just over his bell. 'He's my friend.'

'Then tell me, friend of the crown,' Anslian says, leaning forward towards Cat from his seat, 'what do *you* know of Prince Elician's disappearance?'

'Now is not the time for this,' Zinnitzia says.

'Perhaps it's not. But you will tell us more, I'm sure, soon enough. Won't you? Ah. Your horse is here, Fenlia. Get on it.' Fen squeezes Cat's hand and then scrambles from the wagon. She leaves the horses' reins in Cat's care. Anslian turns his steed towards the head of the column, Fen riding with him. She glances back once.

'Can you manage the cart on your own?' Marina asks. Cat nods.

The Soleben soldiers part and let Cat steer the wagon between them. Zinnitzia and Marina ride just inside his field of vision, but the veil stays on.

Thankfully, the journey to the capital is not much longer. Within a day they reach Himmelsheim, though they see it long before they reach it. The great city has been built around a massive hill, not quite a mountain but tall enough to almost earn that title. Its grand sprawl rises ever upwards and its main road coils around the almost-mountain, looping in increasingly tighter rings until it comes to a rest before the palace at the top. Only one road leads to Himmelsheim's main gates and there are no tricks or secrets to the ascent. To reach the palace too, there is only one route – by means of the long Great Lane, which circles ever upwards to its destination.

Cat's fingers tighten on his reins once they are inside the city – and entry is easy with Anslian at the head of their party. The horses snort unhappily, and he forces his stiff hands to relax. Anslian and Fen lead the dusty group. Pedestrians hurry to the sides of the lane, pressing themselves against the buildings to avoid the procession. Some civilians cheer as they pass, waving and clapping their hands. Fen waves back on occasion, dainty hand barely visible as it turns outwards in greeting.

The more loops of the road they traverse, the more word spreads. The clapping gets louder. Loud enough to drown out any other noise. Cat tries to breathe but the reverberations rattle his lungs. *Too loud.* He cannot hear his own thoughts form. *It's too loud.* Panic ricochets through him. *Clap. Clap. Clap. Clap. Clap. Clap. Clap. Clap.* The dark enclosure of the hooded veil is too tight, too close. His skin prickles hot and cold. The noise fractures all other senses. He can barely feel the reins beneath his gloved fingers now, or the bench beneath the thick wraps of his clothing as he sits. The sound rises and rises. *I don't want to be here.*

The loops of the royal lane become tighter. Tighter still. He doesn't know if he's driving the cart or if the horses are just following the march of the others. His vision fades in and out as his lungs and heart continue to rebel.

Then the procession stops. At last.

There are voices and his head feels heavier than his shoulders. He tilts. Someone catches him. 'Cat?' Marina asks. Her arm is around his back. 'Cat, we're going down.' *Down where?* He does not ask. No point in asking. No one ever tells him the truth anyway.

She pulls him, and he can't control the way his limbs slide from the wagon and fold as he hits the ground. A great creaking *something* deafens him in its intensity. The palace gates have shut, and the sound of the clapping and cheers is muffled behind their great weight. Marina pulls his hood off and the world is too bright once more. Far too bright. He squeezes his eyes shut and his sweat-damp cheeks chill at the sudden exposure to air. His teeth chatter as his knees soak up puddle water.

'A friend?' someone asks, high-pitched, accented and grating.

'Yes,' Fen replies. 'He's my friend.' There are footsteps. Footsteps that are muffled even more as Marina presses Cat's face to her chest and turns.

'I apologize, Your Majesties, but–'

'This is the young man Elician brought to Kreuzfurt?' a different person asks.

The King and Queen. They are here.

He pushes back from Marina. He inhales and exhales. He blinks past the bright sun that the people of Soleb worship with far too much glee. He tilts his head up and looks at Elician's parents.

Elician shares his mother's cascading curls, her soft brown eyes and the deep golden-brown hue to her skin. But his height and posture, his beard – which wrapped around his jaw and teased the skin above his lips – match his father entirely. King Aliamon steps forward and it is like seeing a mirage. An older version of Elician, with straighter hair and a larger nose, but who moves with the same stride, stands just to the side. Queen Calissia delicately lifts the edges of her purple gown. She crouches before Cat and holds out her hand. There are whispers, gasps, shocked voices hissing this way and that.

'Welcome to Himmelsheim. Welcome,' she says, 'to our home.' Slowly, carefully, wrist jingling its warning, he places his gloved hand in hers. They rise together.

'Thank you,' he says. She smiles, and it is as beautiful as her son's. Sweet dimples form at the corners of her lips.

'We should go inside,' Aliamon says. 'We have much to discuss.'

The King meets with Fen and Anslian separately to discuss their understanding of what has happened since Elician left the warfront on his so-called 'humanitarian mission' to Kreuzfurt. He sends Cat, Marina and Zinnitzia to a small office not far from the throne room to wait for him. Marina requests some water as they reach the room, and not long after a bowl and cloth arrive. She presses the cloth to Cat's face, wiping his overheated cheeks and head. He is too tired to pull away. When the King arrives, he is cool again, his ears no longer ringing. He can hear his own thoughts beyond the pulsing drum of his heart.

Aliamon comes alone, closing the door to his office with a firm hand. Marina has told Aliamon who he is. There had been two weeks of fevered correspondence between Kreuzfurt and Himmelsheim before Cat took his oath, and through it all, Cat had known there would be no hiding his identity. But still, when the King enters and greets him with, 'Stello Alest of Alelune,' the acknowledgement chafes.

'That is not my name anymore,' Cat replies. He crosses his arms, smothering the bell against his side. Aliamon's eyes still fall to it before travelling up to the top of Cat's head and down again.

'No,' Aliamon agrees. 'My son named you something else. Cat. Tell me, do they talk about nightcats in Alelune?' Cat does not reply, but Aliamon continues, unbothered. 'The story started when Marina was young, if you can imagine that far back. Nearly two thousand years ago. Select groups of Alelune soldiers would swim across the Bask and hide in the wilds of Soleb. They were assassins, at first, and they excelled at sudden ambushes of anyone who strayed too far from the rest of their unit. No one heard them come or go, but witnesses consistently reported streaks of grey or white disappearing in the dark. Leaving behind victims that seemed to be torn apart by the claws of a cat.'

'I heard they were really Soleben assassins,' Zinnitzia muses idly, 'who preyed on soldiers along the borders of Alelune.'

'I heard they were both,' Marina adds. Aliamon shrugs. He smiles. His arms are loose at his sides and he bears no weapon. *Nothing to see here,* the posture says. Cat meets his eyes.

'Eventually,' the King continues, 'the stories grew. Rumours said the assassins were not assassins at all, but a cat, a nightcat, a creature of Alelune's beloved goddess, Death.'

'They really don't exist then?' Cat asks. Elician had been so earnest in his search. Cat had wanted to see one too.

'Oh, a creature *did* at some point, but they have been extinct for generations.' Aliamon walks to his desk. He pulls open a drawer and takes something out, tossing it at Cat. It hits his chest and falls. Marina picks it up, holding it out for him to see. 'It's a claw, one of the newer ones to be found.' Spanning her palm, it curves to a sharp point. It can still cut. It can still hurt. 'These make their way through the markets on occasion, but the nightcats – assassins or monsters or both – those are never truly seen.'

'Why are you telling me this?'

'You were sent to kill my son, weren't you?' Aliamon smiles. 'Cat?' He drags the name out. 'And me too?'

'You,' Cat agrees. 'Your wife. Your entire family were targets.' He clears his throat. 'There is a traitor; someone betrayed your family and–'

'You could kill us all now, I'm told. Just by thinking about it.'

Cat blinks, confused. He nods slowly. 'Yes.'

'Why don't you? It would make your queen proud.'

Elician shares features with his father. But he is not like his father. There is a shrewdness to Aliamon that Elician has never displayed. There is a fierce sharpness to this king that reminds Cat of his queen instead. 'Why did you have a party when I died?' he asks in lieu of answering. Marina shifts at his side, her fingers tightening around the claw in her hand. Zinnitzia does not move.

Aliamon's head tilts. His posture remains relaxed. 'Because it pleased me to do so,' he replies.

Oh. Once a year, when his queen took him from the cells to assess him, she brought him through hidden tunnels and passages. She led him to his former rooms and dressed him in fine fabrics. She hid his face behind a mask and let him slip in amongst the people of Alelune. He could wander the streets, dance with the courtiers, watch the acrobats and listen to the music of their country. She had him kill people, sometimes, during these outings. Women who had betrayed her or tried to place their daughters in the line of succession. Spies or political enemies. Most of the time he sat at the feet of a juggling fool, eating sweets and watching one magnificent spectacle after another. Then, afterwards, on the only night of the year when he was allowed to sleep in the room that used to be his, sometimes he could hear her crying. Cursing King Aliamon's name for everything he had ever done to them.

Elician is kind. That is a fact Cat has known since the day they met. He is kind, and when he smiles that inward beauty is put on display for all the world to see. Honest, generous, loyal, giving, empathetic. Cat feels a pang, almost of loss, as he thinks of the missing prince. Elician is kind, but his father is not. When Elician smiled, Cat never wanted to look away. As Aliamon waits patiently for a response, he too smiles. And yet, despite the pleasing symmetry of his face, Cat does not find it attractive at all. He is the man who took Cat's father hostage and used Marias as a bargaining chip that nearly destroyed Alelune's faith in her queen. He is a man who celebrated a child's death and who haunts Queen Alenée's nightmares. Had Cat met Aliamon that night by the Bask River, he would not have regretted killing the King of Soleb. In fact, he would have relished it. It would have been justice.

Could still be justice.

He would *deserve* it. And now, Cat knows: no one will bring him back.

Cat's nostrils flare. He promised Fen. Made an oath. This is Elician's father. *Fen's*, now. He won't kill him. Won't take another father from her. Not for anything. Taking a deep breath, Cat gives his response: 'I see no joy in celebrating someone's death. And it pleases *me* to let you live.'

Aliamon's smile fades. His brow furrows. 'Does it truly?' he asks. He presses his right hand to his face, rubbing his temples as his palm hides his expression. When his hand falls, he says, 'Marina tells me you believe Elician is in the Reaper cells. But it will take months to find a way in to confirm this. They are better protected now, after Ranio tried to smuggle you out.'

'And then, once you have confirmed this?'

'Then we simply hope my son succeeds in escaping where you failed, Stello Alest.' Cat tries to interject, to deny the title once more, but Aliamon presses onwards. 'I hear you want your Reapers freed, that you will do as we say in exchange for that.'

'Yes, but–'

'If we do find Elician and help him escape, we may be able to help your people too. But unless the Alelunen crown has a sudden change of heart, they will not be able to stay in Alelune after that. If they can make it across the border, they would be welcome to stay in Kreuzfurt–'

'No.'

'No?'

'No. Free. I want them to be *free*.'

'The only way that happens is if you return to Alelune,' Aliamon says. 'Your queen would need to give them an order of protection. Something I doubt she would do given the circumstances. And so, are you willing to depose her? For their freedom?' The word is unfamiliar. Cat struggles to translate, but Aliamon gives him no time to think. 'Are you willing to stand in her place? To take control and give the order that keeps your Reapers free? Are you willing to reshape the country you will inherit, and look after all the people of Alelune – not just your Reapers? Because Queen Alenée will not cede any form of power so long as she lives, and neither will I. This war will only end after she and I die, and our history is laid to rest. What comes after, though, is your world, Stello Alest. The world you and my son will make. While you are here and he is there, think on what type of world that will be. Because when the time comes to choose, you should know the answer you intend to give. And you should be prepared to kill whoever it takes to ensure that goal comes to pass. Even if you swore an oath not to.'

'Fen said oaths are sacred. That you do not break them.'

'Fen,' Aliamon sighs, 'is still young enough to believe in honesty. But you should know better. Do you?' He approaches. His hand reaches out as if to touch Cat's cheek. Cat recoils, stumbling even as Zinnitzia steps between them. Aliamon smiles that ugly smile. 'You remind me of Elician,' the King says. 'I wonder, did you grow fond of one another when you met? I imagine my son grew fond of you.'

'I don't know what he felt.'

'A pity.'

Cat's fingers dig into the palms of his hands. The word *why* burns in his mouth in response to this, begging to be asked. Something in him holds it back, militant and strong. The King turns towards his desk. He says, 'There is nothing you can do to help my son at this time. If Elician is in the Reaper cells, I'll see him released. Until then, wait. Learn.'

'Learn what?'

'Marina trained my children to fight once. Perhaps she should do the same for you. As a Reaper, you should not fear the hand of Death, no matter the form that hand takes.'

'You want to train me to fight?'

'I want you to be of use one day. What form that takes . . . well. We'll see, won't we? I'm told mastering swordplay is a rite of passage in Alelune. At the very least, when the time comes for you to make a decision on what you'll do for the crown, you'll have the tools needed to see you through until the end.'

Cat shakes his head. No. That doesn't make sense. 'What about the traitor?' he asks. 'The one who betrayed your son–'

'Let me worry about that. Go. Be content in my palace. It seems you will be here for a while.'

'But–'

Marina catches him by the arm. She squeezes it, then bows, Zinnitzia copying the motion to his left. They force him from the room. Now is not the time to argue. But Cat twists back to watch the King as long as he can. He knows, deep in his gut: *something is wrong.*

CHAPTER TWENTY-FOUR

Fenlia

Anslian escorts Fen to the residential wing of the palace. He does not have to. She knows the way. It has not been *such* a long time since she was last here. But he leads her, and she keeps her head down and hands at her sides, trying desperately to mimic the perfectly polite postures of the ladies at court.

He walks through the palace as if he is the King, and everyone he passes instantly bows and whispers well wishes to his cause. He does not notice them. He does not speak to them. He walks briskly, too briskly for Fen to keep up without falling into a slight jog.

'I don't want to have a funeral for Elician,' Fen says, hoping he can give her more information than her father had in their brief meeting earlier. It had seemed Aliamon would not be swayed from his path. In three days, a funeral *will* be held.

'Neither do I,' her uncle Anslian replies. 'It's a waste of time and money.'

'And he's not dead.'

'Which is why it is a waste.'

'If he's been captured then we should be looking for him.'

'Our spies in Alerae have reported nothing. Elician is not there.'

'Then he's somewhere else!'

Anslian scowls. He comes to a halt and Fen stumbles to a stop in front of him. 'Where, Fen? Where is he?'

'What about searching the Alelunen embassy? Could he be here, in this city?' Alelune maintains one ambassador and household staff in Himmelsheim and always has. Laure de Gianno is the woman currently holding the station, and all official correspondence between the countries circulates through her at the embassy under a banner of truce. A Soleben guard stands watch with Alelune's guards to observe the ambassador's movements, but the same is true for Soleb's ambassador in Alerae. If there is anybody in Soleb who would know about Elician, it would be the ambassador. Even if he's not physically in the embassy, she would have to be kept informed of his situation to know how to respond. She must have some kind of information. She must.

'Use your head, child. We cannot turn their embassy inside out – or take Ambassador Laure into custody as a hostage for that matter. It would provoke an international scandal. Even our allies in Glaika or the Gold Coast would balk at such a thing, and we cannot afford their reprisals.'

'Alelune took *Elician*! Laure's nothing by comparison. Just a spokesperson.'

Anslian scoffs loudly. He shakes his head and Fen squares her shoulders, ready to fight. Even against a hero. Especially if it is to correct something so deeply wrong.

'You cannot give up on him. He needs our help!'

'Until we know for sure where he is, we can do nothing. Assaulting Ambassador Laure will only make the war tensions worse – not to mention imperilling our *own* ambassador in Alelune.' Fen doubts it is possible for the war to get any worse than it already is. In the four years since Alelune had restarted hostilities, each report had been little better than a running tally of death tolls alongside various military victories and defeats. The numbers are always horrific, despite everyone saying they seem to be coming in at the same rate as they did during the last River War. Adding one more person to the list, at this point, hardly seems like much in the grand scheme of things. 'There's no trail,' Anslian continues. 'There's no sign. Elician has all but vanished into thin air. Unless you know where he's being held, this is our only course forward.'

'To wait. To hold a funeral. To do *nothing*.'

'To use our spies and our intelligence officers rather than provoke a country we are *already* at war with.'

'And you, you're going to be named heir, then?' she asks. 'In the meanwhile?'

'Don't give me that look, girl. I have no wish for the crown.'

'But you're still going to be named heir,' she presses.

'Whether I want it or not,' he mutters.

A door at the end of the hall opens, and a woman steps out. She is dressed in all black, head covered by a long black scarf. Anslian's daughter, and now, presumably, second in line for the throne. '*Adalei?*' Fen gasps. Even when she had been ill as a child, Adalei had never been anything but fashionable as far as Fen could remember. Now, her garb seems threadbare and plain. Unremarkable and brutal in its contrast to the austere halls of Himmelsheim. She doesn't know what to say. She doesn't know what would be best to do.

Adalei walks towards them, hands folded in front of her body. 'Papa.' She curtsies low and flawless, hand over her heart. 'Fenlia. I heard yelling.'

Anslian ignores the gesture and wraps his arms around his daughter. One hand cradles the back of her neck, the other holds her back steady. Fen lingers awkwardly to one side, not wanting to interrupt. 'You're meant to be resting,' Anslian chides, kissing the black silk scarf that drapes over his daughter's head. He pulls back to cup her cheeks and kiss her brow too.

'I have no desire to continue lying about staring at walls, Papa,' Adalei replies. 'Fenlia, there are fresh sheets on your bed. I had the maids in earlier to dust and–'

'Thank you, I'm sure it's wonderful,' she assures her cousin.

'When is Lio's funeral?' Anslian asks.

'Two days ago,' Adalei replies. 'Don't be cross with Uncle Aliamon; there was no reason to wait for you. Lio has never officially been my betrothed.'

'I will be cross with my brother with or without your permission, daughter. Wilion was *my* commander. He deserved my salute.' Adalei's eyes fill with water.

It's good she isn't wearing makeup, Fen thinks, distracted. *It would just smear.*

'Then, perhaps, if you have the time, you could speak with his parents before you leave. They would appreciate it.'

'Of course. Fenlia, if you'll excuse us–'

Fen bows and steps back. She does not want to see Adalei crying anyway. She says, 'I'll see you at dinner,' and continues on to her room. The first door opens into a sitting room, but the ones beyond lead to her bedchamber. The bed has indeed been made up, and all her childhood possessions have been dusted and delicately placed right where she had left them before leaving to train in Kreuzfurt. Fen runs her fingers over the glass horses and beaded dolls. Lio and Elician had given her most of these. Adalei had woven and embroidered the fine cloth they rest on.

Things were far simpler before they all had to move away. For the next hour, she unpacks her valise, which a servant had brought to her room. She checks what dresses she has outgrown and what needs resupplying.

A knock at the sitting room door echoes all the way through her suite, and she bids them enter while she continues her work. There is a quiet shuffling of feet, and she calls out, 'In here.' Cat enters a few moments later. 'Oh, I thought the King would keep you longer,' she admits. 'How was it? He's nice, right?'

'I don't know,' he replies.

'How do you not know?' Fen asks, rolling her eyes. He shrugs, rolling his bottom lip between his teeth, then looks over her possessions. 'He's always been kind to me,' Fen reveals as Cat leans towards the only portrait she owns. 'That's my *real* father,' she explains, moving to stand next to it. 'I'm adopted, you know? But my father and the King were basically as close as Lio and Elician. And my father, he was the greatest intelligencer in Soleb! Or . . . he was until he died. We look alike, don't we?' She knows she does. She has his chin. His ears. His nose.

'Yes,' Cat agrees quietly. 'You are much alike.'

'Have you seen Adalei yet? She's Anslian's daughter and she's . . . well, she and Lio were not really *together*, but they were *together*, you know?'

'No.'

'Well, it wasn't official. But they were courting. They have been for years. Lio used to send her all these love poems, but between you and me – Elician wrote them all for him, because Lio is as romantic as a shoe.'

'I don't understand. Elician did what?'

Fen flushes and backtracks. She waves her hands this way and that, marching Cat through the embarrassing truth. That Elician needed to write love letters to his own cousin to woo her on Lio's behalf.

'But he did not love her himself?' Cat asks.

'I don't think Elician has loved *anyone*. He always had these strange rules. And I guess they made sense because no one could know he was a Giver. But he's never interacted with anyone privately or spent much time with anyone as far as I know. He just liked writing poetry, reading books and getting into trouble with Lio. I think for a while people thought he loved Lio in a romantic way, but then Lio fell in love with Adalei – and Elician never so much as blinked. And he's never grown close to or even seemed to *like* anyone else like that. Even during balls, he'd always dance the exact same amount of time with every person who ever asked. I timed him once; I couldn't believe it. What's with that face?'

Cat winces and shrugs. He shakes his head. 'He was lonely,' he murmurs. 'It's sad.'

'How could he have been lonely? He's the Prince of Soleb. He's surrounded by people all the time. Everything he does is praised by every person he meets. He could have a hundred friends if he just bothered talking to anyone for more than a few minutes at a time.'

'But isn't that how you become lonely?' Cat asks. 'When you are surrounded by others . . . but even still, you are alone?'

'Maybe in Alelune.' She shrugs. 'How did it go with the King?'

'I don't know. I don't understand what he's doing with . . . everything. I need to think. Marina sent me to fetch you. She and Zinnitzia want to go over our education moving forward. We will be staying in Himmelsheim and there will be changes.'

'Good changes?' she hopes, doubtful.

'Just changes,' he replies. 'How are your seeds growing, by the way?'

'They aren't.' She had tried everything she could think of on the ride to Himmelsheim, but the seeds remained, stubbornly, seeds. Better off being fed to the birds. She had spent hours on them some days, sectioning them off into piles based on size and shape. But they did nothing beneath her care. Her failure is not something she will put in her report to Elician when he eventually comes home. 'I think Elena is wrong. There's nothing I can do.'

'There must be a trick to it.'

'Do you know how to do it?'

'Not for certain, just a guess. There must be a way of sparking life in them. If you *can* figure it out, it would be nice to see, wouldn't it?'

'I suppose.' But flowers are not going to bring her brother back. She almost tells him this too. She feels the words on her tongue. But she stops at the last moment. 'Are you all right?' she asks.

'It will be better for everyone, I think, when your brother returns,' he replies. Then he bows his head awkwardly and leaves. She locates her seeds and holds one in her hand. If she could have made them grow, then she would have already. After all, Cat is not the only one who could use something to make him feel better.

But three days later, the nation mourns for its lost prince. And there is nothing she can do but attend the ceremony. Civilians fill every spiral of Himmelsheim, standing shoulder to shoulder, chanting funeral prayers and giving praise to Soleb's lost son. Fen stands beside Aliamon, Calissia, Anslian and Adalei as their people come forward one at a time to express their grief.

She trades her white dress for black for the second time this year, temporarily mimicking a Reaper. No jewels or finery. No embellishments. Unlike with Fransen, who had been an acquaintance and almost a friend, Elician is her family. It will be several weeks before she will be permitted to wear anything other than black again. She already misses her lighter garb, especially because none of it is real. Adalei may be mourning in truth for Lio, but the rest of them are simply playing a game of pretend. It feels like cheating, or a mockery of all the people who are actually in pain. When the funeral procession ends, the royal family retreats inside for their last meal together as a unit. Anslian will leave to return to the front lines in the morning.

All the most highly ranked courtiers are expected to attend this final meal, and though it is supposed to be a sombre affair, the sound of chattering fills the hall as everyone finds their seats. Fen is not sure who created the seating arrangements, but apparently Cat has been given permission to join them. He sits bracketed between her and Marina and seems just as annoyed as he was after Fransen's death. Though he does have the good grace not to complain outwardly about their funeral practices this time around.

It is for the best. Sitting across from them are some of the most highly esteemed members of the Soleben nobility. Fen doubts Lord Hamad and his son Rodans would appreciate Cat's less than fond outlook on their culture. Hamad had made a name for himself in the last River War and Fen has already heard Rodans mention that he is looking forward to being old enough to enlist. Both try to ask Cat his opinion on the current war's tensions. He responds by blinking at them dumbly until they decide he cannot understand Soleben and turn towards Fen instead.

'It is good to have you back in the capital, Your Highness. You have been missed,' Hamad says warmly.

'Thank you, my lord,' she replies as the first course is brought out. It is a creamy soup that Elician favoured. All the meals served tonight will be those that Elician enjoyed. This is their time to remember him in his entirety and grieve his loss together. No one will be permitted to eat these meals again at court until the mourning period is over.

'Do you think you'll stay in the capital long?' Rodans asks next. He is a pretty boy with sand-coloured hair and green eyes. He has a long face and a smattering of freckles that have been fading the older he gets. They used to play together before she became a Giver. Afterwards, like all her other friends, he suddenly became very busy. There was a war on. It was bad timing. Sometimes things just happened. She hasn't spoken to him properly since then. It had hurt, at the time. She had winced, too, when she saw him sit across from her. But his tone is earnest, his expression sweet. Just like it used to be.

She wipes her mouth with her napkin, tries to match the uncertain but casual nature of his inquiry, and replies, 'I'm not sure. It depends.'

'Prince Elician had said he wanted you on his council when he became king. Do you think Lady Adalei would have you on hers? You've been working so hard, training in Kreuzfurt. It must be commended.' She flushes a bit at the praise and tries not to shrug in response. *It's unbecoming.*

'You would need to ask Adalei. I don't believe she's made any decisions . . . like that.' Anslian may appear reluctant to take the crown, but Fen knows Adalei will have at least considered its likelihood. Adalei has always been the type to make six different plans for the future, ensuring that if one path failed, she has another already prepared. She is singularly difficult to outmanoeuvre.

'I am sure she would do well to have you with her,' Rodans says, drawing Fen's attention back to him. She thanks him, trying not to smile too obviously at the praise.

The second course arrives and with it, the memory procession. Queen Calissia begins, telling the story of how, many years ago, Elician and Lio used to enjoy scaling the walls of the castle. Like their fascination with chariots, they had read about this in a book – and had tried to recreate the skillset of an ancient warrior sect, renowned for their ability to climb just about anything. The boys had made it halfway up before they ran out of handholds, and the palace guard had needed to rescue them. Fen still remembers the fierce scolding they'd received from the King.

King Aliamon goes next, sharing another anecdote from Elician's life. This honour passes from person to person as they share memory after memory, recreating Elician in their hearts and minds. They skip Cat twice in the procession, understanding that he is there as a guest but not a member of the mourning party. But at the last round, Cat whispers a memory of his own into Fen's ear. 'On our way to Kreuzfurt, there were nights where he had trouble sleeping. Sometimes we would stay up together, watching the stars.'

'That reminds me of a phrase I heard once,' Rodans says. Cat flinches, realizing the boy had been eavesdropping, and pulls back. Rodans speaks it, but even Fen can tell his Lunae is imperfect. She frowns, trying to puzzle out what he means. Marina clears her throat at Cat's side and repeats the phrase, and Rodans snaps his fingers. 'That's it. My tutor said it's something Alelunens say when they meet.'

'Somewhat,' Marina replies. 'It can be roughly translated as: *May a star fall in your lives.* It wishes the listener good fortune and unexpected blessings.'

'Did you?' Rodans asks Cat. 'Have good fortune and unexpected blessings?' Cat blinks at him, and for a moment Fen thinks he will feign ignorance once more. But Cat does not.

He meets Rodans's eyes and, speaking just loud enough for his voice to carry, says, 'Yes, he was that, for me.'

'I'll drink to that,' Rodans's father says. A chorus of voices chime in, until one by one glasses are raised and King Aliamon stands.

'For the greatest king we will never know,' Aliamon calls out. 'For Elician.'

In that, at least, they are united. Even if some of the grief is a game of pretend.

CHAPTER TWENTY-FIVE

Cat

Cat lingers at the end of the feast, watching as Fen blushes and simpers before a collection of teenage boys and girls. He had thought Elician had been lonely when Fen had described his childhood, but he supposes Fen must have been isolated in a different way. She was older when she discovered she was a Giver, and she'd never needed to *hide* that part of herself since everyone always knew. But there are no other children her age in Kreuzfurt. Not amongst the exalted at least. Here . . . she glows amidst her peers, hopeful and desperate for a kind word and a sign of affection. She has never spoken of them before. But now they flock to her, Rodans most eagerly of all, but with various girls and boys from good families also at his side. All of them apologizing for not properly keeping in touch. And all seemingly very interested in what Fen's future at court will be. Fen cannot inherit the throne herself, but that does not mean she is without power.

'You look upset,' Marina says as she presses a glass of water into his hand. He takes it from her but does not drink. Fen laughs at something, a little too loudly and a little too inappropriately considering the occasion.

'Solebens think to die is the worst thing that can happen to them,' Cat murmurs. 'They eat these . . . meals and create rituals around remembering someone exactly as they were, reading names from lists just so they can never be forgotten. But then they seem perfectly happy to forget the dead just as quickly.'

'Oh, this isn't a Soleben problem,' Marina says. 'It's a royal problem. Elician is dead and Adalei is heir presumptive after Anslian. With Lio gone, whoever can win Adalei's heart will be the next prince consort of Soleb. And Adalei has always been fond of dear little adopted cousin Fenlia. So, Fen has the honour of being a royal who cannot inherit – but who *can* grant access to our future ruler. Anywhere else? This disrespectful mess, at the funeral ceremony no less, would have stopped immediately. But here? This is just politics.'

Rodans touches Fen's arm and Cat scowls. 'So, he does not like her, he just wants to use her?'

'He liked her perfectly well when she was a potential heir in her own right, but after she became a Giver and was knocked from the line of succession? Well, let's just say Fenlia never did receive much mail from the capital that didn't come from her family directly,' Marina says. 'Then again, she was always an odd case. Many of the noble families never quite knew whether Aliamon intended for her to be in the line of succession after he adopted her, or if it was just a general act of kindness. They certainly never encouraged their children to interact, and her companions were often quite limited as a result. When she developed her powers, I'd say more than a few of them were relieved that they no longer had to worry about her ambiguous status. But who am I to say if Rodans likes her or not? I do think he has a vested interest in where she'll end up one day, and always has, but what that means for his sincerity?' She shrugs.

'And Solebens think *we're* manipulative,' Cat mutters quietly.

Marina snorts. 'Well, you can't exactly say we aren't.'

'It's just hypocritical, that's all. For Solebens to feel they are better than us.'

'Yes.' She takes a long sip from her own water glass. Then she switches to Lunae, lowering her voice for only him to hear. 'Fenlia aside, you've been upset since you met with the King.'

He glances at her from the corner of his eye. Then he glances at the room around them. With each passing second, it empties of people, but it still feels far too full. He presses his lips closed, and she nods once. She takes his glass, then sets both his and hers on the table. She flicks her wrist, a summoning gesture, and he falls into step at her side. They walk along the long halls of the palace until there is no one left to listen.

'I don't like your king,' Cat says.

'You don't have to,' Marina says.

'Why did you swear to him?'

'It was expected of me, and I didn't feel like causing a fuss,' she replies. 'I told you why Kreuzfurt was built. And at the time, considering everything else that had happened, I had accepted the decision for what it was. That plague . . . When our god unleashed her fury on Soleb, it seemed absolute. I agreed to Kreuzfurt because I thought it could do well. And I swore to every king afterwards because I feared what would happen if one of *us* attempted to influence too much control over the world.'

'But you don't worry about Elician? You don't fear he'll be another Shawshank?'

'No. I've watched him all his life, from the moment he was born. If there was going to be someone who could change it . . . I'd trust him.'

'He said, once, that Kreuzfurt is a cage with invisible bars. He wanted to destroy it.'

'Perhaps he's on to something.' Marina shrugs. 'There must be some line drawn between the segregation of Givers and Reapers while demanding their forced labour and risking our god's wrath. Perhaps it's time to find where that middle ground lies.' Her hand falls to her sword. She is the only Reaper he has ever seen who carries a weapon, and she does it constantly. Every day, without fail, she dons the blade as if it were the bell on her wrist.

'Why do you have that?' he asks, gesturing to the weapon at her side. 'You can kill anyone around you without it.'

'We wear our black robes to keep the people around us safe from harm. They are afraid of what would happen if we touched them. But how can we protect ourselves, when using our powers against others would see us hanged or worse? By using a sword and knowing how to fight, then even dressed as I am, I can protect myself and those I care for. And while I could kill someone accidentally by touching them with my skin, there is no doubt that if I use this sword – I have chosen to end someone's life.'

Cat looks at it. The pommel is a shiny gold, the scabbard as black as her uniform. She draws it, holds it out to him. He takes it.

'You would have learned how to use it before you died, no?' she asks, watching him handle it with familiarity.

'Yes.' He does not remember his lessons well, but the routine he knows. Waking up with the dawn, eating a quick meal, then it was sword work until lunch. His father had been there. His father's seneschal, barking orders and instructions. He strains to remember the man's name. It has been so long since he tried to place it. It comes just as he remembers a particular exercise that he had drilled time and again, and the way his arms had ached after each successive strike of his blade against the training dummy. *Partho.* Partho had been his teacher. And he had been good at it too. 'Every boy is trained for the army,' Cat says quietly, heart aching at the sudden reminder of how fond he had once been of a man he has never seen again.

'Many girls too. I fought in the River Wars when I was much, much younger.' He cannot imagine what the world would have been like that long ago, but he assumes the fighting had been much the same. And he is grateful for the distraction.

'Why did you come to Soleb?'

'I died. I died and became a Reaper – and when I did, I realized that staying in Alelune would not be in my or my family's interest. I left and never regretted leaving. I did regret that, in the years that followed, the Reaper cells were created and no one else had the opportunity to flee. That . . . I had not expected.' Cat swings the sword once. Twice. 'Aliamon's suggestion . . . the Alelunen rite of passage. What do you know of it?'

'Only that we're always trained to fight.'

She nods her head slowly. 'That's all you're meant to know of it,' she tells him. 'Until it happens.'

'Training me to fight could be training me to fight against Soleb one day.'

'Would you, though, truly?'

He tries to imagine it. Tries to see himself standing on a battlefield, sword raised, leading an army to attack a Soleben force on the banks of the Bask. He sees Elician, in his bright gold armour, impossible to miss amongst all the others. He tries to muster the desire to actually swing a blade and hope to kill. 'No,' he confesses. 'Probably not. But your king couldn't know that.'

'That man . . . I have found it best not to question him. He plans for futures that he designs with a craftsman's patience. I rarely like or agree with his decisions, but I know better than to question the ones I approve of. You should learn. He is right. It might come up. And you should know enough to know how to respond when the time comes. But what about you, do you want to learn?'

He loved training. Once. Loved the thrill of it. The movement. He used to try to repeat the steps in his cage before he grew too tall to manage. *My father would have wanted me to learn*, he thinks, suddenly, realizing with a pang how sorry a thought that is. That his father and Elician's father actually agreed on something. 'I don't trust your king.'

'You don't have to. Do you want to learn?'

'Yes,' he confesses. 'I do.'

Marina nods. 'Then we'll start at dawn.' He grins, the familiarity of the routine swirling happily in his gut as he hands her back her sword. 'And Cat? Perhaps you should think about who and what exactly you'd want to cut down with this sword. Because being a Reaper and using *this* to kill mean different things. Not just to the people you fight, but to you as well.'

'What do you mean?'

She slides her blade back into her scabbard. Then, gently, she cups the back of his neck and presses her brow to his. A faint echo of energy, the pull of a magnet, shivers down his spine. 'To kill someone using your sword is an active choice you are making. It is not an accident, nor a brush of your hand against an unsuspecting party. It is a wilful, intentional and difficult task. And to others, it is a signal of your commitment to that bitter end. Prepare yourself in advance, Alest, because one day . . . I truly believe that you will need this sword more than you think. And when you use it, you should always feel certain that it was worth it.'

CHAPTER TWENTY-SIX

Fenlia

When the two-week mourning period is over, Zinnitzia brings Fen to the palace library and supplies her with a stack of books filled with anatomy, physiology and medicine. 'Elena provided a reading list,' Zinnitzia says. Then she lectures with unending energy, pointing to diagrams and explaining each part of the human body in such horrifyingly precise detail that Fen is often grateful that Zinnitzia doesn't let her eat breakfast before lessons start. She stalks behind Fen as she reads, making sure that Fen stays focused on her task. She even looks over Fen's shoulder as she practises trying to make her seeds bloom the way Elena had wanted.

On the other side of the palace, Marina has fully committed herself to Cat's training as well. For four hours every day, Marina drills him in both Alelunen and Soleben sword routines. During the long hours of mindless repetition, she quizzes him on the books he has been slowly working through. As far as Fen knows, his reading has been dramatically improving as of late. He is still rather slow at it, but his repertoire and interests have expanded from medicinal arts to politics, law and even taxation. Apparently, Marina insists these are all things he should know. Fen just wonders how he can bear to remember all that information at once. It seems like so much.

After dinner, she meets him in an enclosed garden not far from the residential wing of the palace. He practises there, somehow still filled with boundless energy, repeating his lessons even without his taskmaster's oversight. She recognizes his footwork from lessons *she* used to take before she went to Kreuzfurt. The overhead block, the step back, the twist of the hips that leads into a deep lunge. He commits to each movement, bending and turning and stepping confidently into each position. She had never moved as fluidly as Cat. Her stances were never quite as steady, but he moves as if he has been born for the blade and merely needed the opportunity to shine beneath its star.

'You're getting good at that,' Fen tells him after a month of watching him work. She rolls her seeds in her hands, lights them on fire, drops them, then smothers the tiny flames with her shoe. She brings them back to life, fixing all their flaws, but they never evolve past the size and shape of their origins. Her nose twitches unhappily. She does it again.

Cat sheathes his sword as she plays with fire, running a sweaty hand across his face. His hair has started to grow longer. He is taller, too. Not by much – she can still look over his head with ease – but a little taller all the same. His body is filling out, tipping over the edge from emaciated into healthy. Now that he's finally eating a proper diet and isn't curled up in a cage, his body seems to be putting itself back to rights. She wonders if he'll stay short for ever. *I hope he does.* She likes being taller than someone.

'Thank you,' Cat says, wiping his face with his sleeve.

One of the last fireflies of the season flutters and glows just to the left of Cat's face. It illuminates his features with a pale yellow that clashes with the moon's silver-blue. Just for a moment, Fen imagines him shining, representing the liminal space between both her country and his, the Sun of Soleb and the Moon of Alelune both bisecting him down the middle. A duality that started when Elician held out his hand and promised to take care of the frightened man he had met on the edge of a battlefield. 'Do you think your swordsmanship can help me find the traitor?' she asks suddenly.

'The King does not want us looking.'

'That's what he told *you*. No one told *me* that.'

'There is a reason he said not to look.'

'Sure, there probably is, but I don't care. Elician is my brother. And you owe him anyway. Can you help me or not?' He shrugs, fingers tightening around the handle of his blunted sword, shifting it back and forth. 'Ambassador Laure–'

'She won't know anything.'

'She has to know *something*.'

Cat shrugs again before shuffling over to sit at her side. He leaves space between them, but it's not necessary. Since the weather began to cool, he has stopped using the charranseed ointment. He no longer reeks enough to make her nose twitch. But, strangely, now that it is gone, Fen almost misses it. She had grown used to the smell.

'Listen,' Fen murmurs. 'Even if she doesn't know where Elician is, she *must* know who the traitor is. Someone must have written something down. There's got to be a letter, or a notice, or *something*. I just need to find a way into the embassy and I . . .' She frowns, then glances at Cat carefully. There is no denying he hails from Alelune. He could not be more stereotypically Alelunen if he tried. 'Maybe *you*–'

'No,' Cat says.

Fen shuffles to face him. Their knees knock together. 'You wouldn't need to do much . . .' she tries to barter. 'It's only a *little* bit of treason. Besides, you said you were only sworn to your Reapers and the embassy doesn't defend your Reapers – it keeps them in cages. Helping me is like helping them.'

He looks entirely unimpressed by that assessment. He shakes his head definitively and changes the subject. 'How are your seeds growing?'

She sniffs. 'They're not.'

Cat's expression does not falter, even as her shoulders tense and she waits for his disappointment. All she ever does is disappoint the people around her. But he doesn't voice any. He gently places a hand on her knee and says, 'When you figure out how to make them grow – if you still want to go to the embassy – I'll help you then.'

'Why only then?' She feels daunted by the impossible condition he's placed on his help.

'Because by then . . . I think I will have run out of other places to look.'

'You're looking too?' She had not known that.

'I'm thinking, Fen. I'm only thinking.'

In the morning, Fen takes out her seeds. She sorts them back into their groups. She holds them in her hands one by one. She thinks about Elician. She thinks about the embassy. And she wills them to grow.

CHAPTER TWENTY-SEVEN

Elician

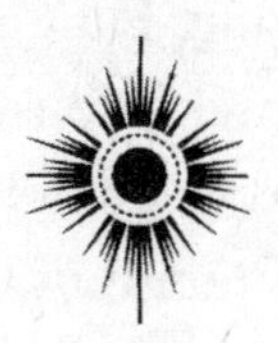

Elician is not used to being alone.

There has always been someone there. Lio, for all his life; Marina, for most of it; his other guards (often serving on rotation at his father's or uncle's orders); Fen, who has been chasing his heels since the day she was born and who he had loved even before she had been adopted. Adalei too; she had been his constant correspondent and confidant. His parents and the courtiers at Himmelsheim had also always been present – all of them had filled the empty spaces of his periphery from the moment he first drew breath. True periods of isolation had been few and far between, confined to segments of his life where piety or official obligation had taken precedence. Even when he wanted to be alone, he had never *actually* been alone. Someone had always stood at the door to his bedroom or lurked in the corners of the hallways, watching for any sign of trouble. To be alone, he'd needed to pretend they weren't there.

He does not need to pretend here.

The room Gillage put him in is brighter than the Reaper cells. He can see the sun. He can feel the wind against his fingers if he holds his hand up to the open window. He can hear movement outside. But the door to his room is always closed and there is never a face to accompany such noises. Even in the cages he had that much. Here, there is never another presence to reflect his own emotions. Whole days pass without any form of human contact. When it comes, it comes in the form of harsh hands and belligerent lackeys who are more interested in standing by and waiting for Gillage's strange doctor to finish her work.

Eline is nothing like the physician that used to care for his cousin at the House of the Unwanting. Eline is not kind or ethical in her ministrations. She is not conscientious about her experiments, nor does she care how he feels at the end of her inquiries. She sheared his curls sometime after his first month in the room, curious to see how fast he could make them grow back, and was annoyed when the pace was slower than she liked. And shamefully, despite that, Elician has learned to look forward to Eline's arrival. Because as exhausting and painful and terrifying as her inquiries are, at least it means that – for a short while – he will not be alone.

The click-clacking of her heels always precedes her presence. The moment he hears them, he crawls out from under the bed he has been given and stands facing the door. She enters with a great sweep of fabric – her skirts elegant and full, far wider and more voluminous than the slim fashions of Soleb. Yet the cloth is equally as intricate and detailed in its weave and patterns. The colours are also vibrant and glorious. He finds himself getting distracted by their hues – bright yellows, oranges or greens – as she speaks.

'Your friend is doing well,' she tells him, baiting him with information while simultaneously reinforcing a threat.

'How do I know you're telling the truth?' he asks her anyway, dancing the steps she has choreographed.

'Let me think . . . what did he tell me this time? Oh, yes, he said your favourite place in Himmelsheim was a rooftop parapet, and you needed to climb the walls in order to reach it. Hand, please?' He holds out his hand and she slices it open with a concealed scalpel. He flinches, feeling the blade slice all the way down to his bones. Tissue splits, muscle tears, and blood flows from his palm in a great gush.

She snaps her fingers and a young girl in a pretty golden dress hurries in with a chair and the lap desk. Eline sits, still watching his hand bleed. She watches until the moment it stops bleeding too – as the skin pieces itself back together, a bruise forms beneath the fresh tissue, and then that too dissipates just as fast. Hastily, she writes her notes. 'Fetch a bowl, Lisène.' The girl hurries out, then hurries back in. 'Hold that,' Eline commands Elician, who takes it clumsily, nerves taking their time reconnecting. She tosses him the scalpel, grins. 'Do it again, into the bowl, please.'

He could kill her. He could kill her and the girl and probably the guard at his door with this knife, but he would not get far. Eventually he would be overpowered. And when that happened . . .

He sits on the bed, the misshapen, uncomfortable bed that isn't even worth sleeping on properly. He balances the bowl on his knees, holds his hand over it and cuts. Blood drains from him into the bowl, and he leans back against the wall to wait until Eline is satisfied. He liked it better when she had been testing the effects of starvation on a Giver. Liked it better, too, when she cut down his curls and made it so he couldn't even play with the ends whenever boredom threatened to overcome him entirely. At least when she did those things, *he* did not have to be a part of it. At least then it wasn't his hand wielding the blade.

Elician loses consciousness at some point. He does not remember when. His body is whole, as always, when he wakes – but the bowl is gone and the moon is at the window, a chill in the air. His back aches painfully after the hours spent slumped awkwardly on the bed. He shuffles off it, onto the floor, curling up in the dark.

The bed in this room is broken, misshapen. There are no pillows, nor is there a mattress. The boards that make up the base pitch inwards towards the middle, and this design appears to be intentional. Painful. It is a joke. It offers an illusion of something but denies it utterly. He cannot lie on it without discomfort. And worse discomfort faces him when he wakes. At least the floor is flat.

There, beneath the horrid bedframe, he imagines himself at home. Hiding beneath his bed on purpose. Drawing pictures on the underside with stolen paints and inks. He imagines chasing fireflies with Lio, and when the thought of his friend hurts too much, he thinks of Adalei. Of sitting with her at Kreuzfurt, talking to her as she plotted her next weaving pattern.

The finest gift Lio had ever given Adalei was a loom he had built himself. Elician had played the role of an informant, and he went back and forth between Lio and Adalei, questioning both and trying to squirrel away answers from each of them to make sure Lio had the correct specifications he needed. When the pieces were prepared, Elician drafted his mother to ensure that Adalei was away from her room long enough for them to assemble it.

She cried when she saw it. Cried and ran her hands over the carefully sanded wood. Later, Elician still worked on his lessons by her side, but he timed his reading to the sound of her throwing her shuttle to the left and right, making patterns out of glorious, vivid colour.

In the emptiness of his room, Elician can almost conjure up the sound of the shuttle as it moves. The *whoosh* of the beater as it swings this way and that. The calming familiarity of quiet days spent in simple contemplation. If Adalei were here now, Elician thinks, she would have a ten-point plan for how to most effectively manage her circumstances. She is the only person Elician knows who can retain her quiet poise and grace even in the most perilous of situations, keeping her back straight and her chin up. Gorgeous in her satins and silks.

'What a load of horse shit,' Elician says to the ceiling. He presses his hands to his eyes. If Adalei were here now, she would be terrified out of her mind, and he would not blame her one bit. Adalei likes order and logic. She likes patterns and sequences she can depend on. She likes strategy and managing expectations. Nothing about his present circumstances allows him to indulge in such things. She would have been homicidal by the second day, and wholly unrepentant and unforgiving after she fully came to appreciate the conditions in the Reaper cells. She and Lio were well suited in that regard. All of Alelune would fall to her wrath if she saw the injustices he's seen here – and Elician must scrub his mind with a figurative rag to force his thoughts away from his cousin's temper.

It is not easy. His only form of entertainment is to sleep and sleeping leads to dreaming. Dreaming leads back to Adalei, Lio, Fen and home. Dreams lead back to memories of a lost Alelune prince, curled against his side at a fire, leaning close as Elician points out every constellation he knows. Round and round his brain runs, pulling up new memories and old – sometimes perverting them into twisted nightmares or outlandish curios that have little logic and offer even less relaxation.

Heels click in the hall. Eline. Again. Elician drags himself out to meet her. 'The first person you ever brought back to life was Lio,' she says, skipping straight to business. 'Lie down, please?' He winces but does as he is told. He lies down on the tortuous bed, hating how his spine bends and aches and his muscles whine in protest. A bowl is placed on the floor beneath his arm. She carves open his artery and he closes his eyes, waiting to die. Again. He wakes intermittently throughout the remainder of the day. Blurred images cross this way and that in front of his face.

He sees her drop a dead mouse into the bowl filled with his blood. Hears her pen scratching against paper on the lap desk. He does not see her results, but hears her say, 'Fascinating . . .' He dies. Wakes up. She is leaving as his eyes open, and his head is still far too dizzy.

'Can I have something to read?' he asks, slurring half the words. Eline hesitates by the door.

'You want to *read*?' she asks him.

'Don't care what.' He is going to lose consciousness again soon. 'Just boring . . . here . . .'

When he wakes up again, hours later, there is a book on the

floor by the bed. A complete history of Alelune. It is not what he had expected.

He reads it anyway.

Growing up, there were times when Elician's father called for *family time*. Lio was released from his duties to go home with his parents. And Elician found himself sitting in his father's solarium, swinging his legs miserably as he waited for something entertaining to happen. If this took too long, and if they were finally given permission to touch, he would let Adalei aggressively plait his curls in whichever style was the current fashion. He would rather have been reading or writing, and she would rather have been at her loom. But his mother, the Queen, insisted such things were work and that they deserved a break. She never did like that Adalei enjoyed weaving in the first place. That was a task for paid labourers, not for *ladies*.

Reading about Alelune is almost as tragically entertaining as *family time*. The learned historian who penned this illustrious tale must have been the least popular member of his academic society. His prose leaves much to be desired and his expressions are dismal. Elician had hoped for something that would infuriate him into an emotion besides his ever-present ennui, and he achieves it. The text is vile, and he spends quite a few lovely hours imagining stuffing page upon page of it down the author's throat. He considers, briefly, doing it to Gillage, but he shies away from the idea quickly enough. He has not quite devolved into fantasizing about brutalizing children just yet. Even if Gillage is slowly inching his way towards the age of majority.

'The pretentiousness alone is enough to strangle a nation,' Elician informs a spider that has crawled through his window to avoid the brisk chill of the outside world. It is a good-sized fellow with long legs and a threatening mark on its back. Elician imagines it would hurt quite a lot to get bitten by it. He keeps to his side of the room and expects the spider to honour their truce by keeping to the window and the window alone. But Elician has also been raised with manners. He acknowledges his temporary roommate and discusses his research as much as he deems appropriate. 'Listen to this.' Elician clears his throat and adopts a particularly affected accent to read, '"Her Holiness, the Graceful Alerina of Nuvola, ascended to the glorious throne of the heavens with ninety-three years of her life spent in dedicated and committed service to the people of Alelune. Her Holiness, the Graceful Alerina of Nuvola, was blessed with fourteen glorious children, ten of whom remained earnestly committed to the War with Soleb, setting aside their own potential prospects in their personal lives to commit themselves wholly and without exception to the glory of Alelune." It's *tripe*!' Elician kicks the bedpost.

The spider does not move and likely is not paying attention. 'It's repetitious, redundant, reprehensible and *wrong*.' Elician waves the book towards the spider as if to get his point across. '"For the betterment of the country, Her Holiness gathered and confined all the Reapers in the land, preventing their loathsome presence from tainting her people to ensure the proper longevity of her nation. No Givers have been born in Alelune following this decree, ensuring that all of Alelune is an honest and pure country with no insidious perversions of humanity amongst their populace." Except that's statistically *impossible*,' Elician grumbles. 'The only reason they *do not exist* is because they do not let themselves be known!'

There's a shuffling by the door and Elician looks up as it opens, expecting Gillage or Eline – readying himself for another of their semi-frequent bouts of medical experimentation. Instead, he finds himself peering at a tall, stocky fellow with a shaved head and a guard's uniform. His brown eyes squint in what can only be described as confusion and, grudgingly, Elician feels a bit ashamed of his spider/history-induced outbursts. He runs a hand over the short hair that still feels wrong after years of having it hang past his shoulders. He tries to make it look good or presentable, to make himself look less like a madman, as the guard asks, 'Who are you talking to?' and peers around the room as if someone might magically appear.

And Elician is forced to point to his eight-legged roommate with as much stoicism as he can manage. The guard follows his finger and winces at the sight of the creature. 'It's not so bad,' Elician suggests, voice cracking. 'Though I admit I'd prefer a mouse.'

'A mouse?'

'They do more . . . and are softer if you want to pet it.' Elician waves his hand as if that could sum it all up, and the guard tilts his head in consideration for a moment before shrugging and closing the door once again. 'Hey! Is someone always standing out there?' Elician calls out, feeling his heart pick up its pace once more. It's several long moments before he gets a reply.

'I'm out here every day,' the guard says quietly, but just loudly enough to be heard. Elician scrambles to his feet. He places his hands on the wooden frame of the doorway. His breaths come faster and faster. The guard goes on to say, 'You can talk if you need to.'

I'm not alone, Elician realizes suddenly. He laughs a touch hysterically at the absurdity of it all. Then he crouches by the doorway, leans his back against the wall and starts to speak.

He has not nearly finished complaining about his book yet.

The guard's name is Jonan Morsen, and sometimes – when Elician misses home more than breath itself – Morsen tells him stories too. They are silly stories for the most part. Stories about lost shopping lists and trips to the market. Watching festival days and old school remembrances. Once, Morsen spins a tale of a lady beautiful enough to make the world stop spinning as it watched her move, it being fascinated by the sway of her hips and the steps her feet took as she danced.

Elician presumes this lady is Morsen's wife, but all he can think of is sweet Adalei and how Lio once tried his best to say such lovely things about her too. *Love,* Elician thinks, *is a game of repetition that replays the same narrative again and again.*

'Your friend said you were a poet,' Morsen chastises through the door after a particularly fierce bout of complaining from Elician.

'My friend . . . Lio? You have seen Lio?' Elician croaks, pressing himself as close as he can to the door.

'When I'm not here, I'm assigned to the cells. I pass him on my rounds.'

'And he's well? He's still alive?'

'He's well,' Morsen replies. 'Young. How old is he?'

Twenty-three, Elician almost says. He doesn't. He thinks back. Tries to remember the number of days that have passed since they left Soleb, since they were separated, since . . . 'How long have we been here?' he asks.

'Nearing nine months.'

'Oh.' Elician squeezes his eyes shut. Which means – 'Twenty-four.' He clears his throat. It hurts to speak. 'Lio . . . Lio's twenty-four now.' And that means – 'My sister's fifteen.' She will be a woman soon. When she turns sixteen, she will be given her first lessons in leadership. If she hadn't been a Giver, she would have been sent to the front as a new recruit. Instead, perhaps a wing in the House of the Wanting would be given to her, as a privilege of her birthright. And Cat . . . *Alest.* Is he twenty-one now? Almost twenty-two, maybe? Marina will have taught him much by now. Or maybe he has not wanted to learn, and spends his days sleeping, warm and content, blissful in the knowledge that he is safe and cannot be harmed anymore. *That sounds nice.*

'Someone's coming,' Morsen warns softly, and Elician stands. He drags himself to the horrible excuse for a bed and sits down awkwardly on the edge where some of the angles aren't as extreme. The door opens and Eline steps in. Her entourage drags someone in behind her. A trembling, pitiful speck of humanity dressed in a tattered tunic, its laces undone, with torn trousers that are cut off at the knee. Another person is pushed in afterwards, covered from head to toe in thick fabric so not one slice of skin is bared. A Reaper.

'Stand there,' Eline orders. The Reaper crosses around to Elician's other side and waits. The prisoner is shoved to his knees between them. 'Touch his skin, Elician.'

'Prince,' Elician corrects her, staring at the man. Eline waits for his cooperation, squinting down at him dispassionately. Sighing, Elician does as he is bid. He places his palm on the prisoner's arm. Closing his eyes, he settles into the familiar sensation of feeling another person's life in his hand.

The prisoner has a few injuries. Skinned knees. Frayed vocal cords from screaming. Elician grimaces as he heals them all. Shock lines the prisoner's face and he tries to pull away, screaming, 'No! Stop – not *you*!' Elician flinches, releasing the man even as Eline's enforcers also shove the prisoner closer.

'Touch him again.'

He does, wilfully ignoring the way the man flinches and twitches. 'It's not like I asked to be your cultural taboo,' Elician mutters as the prisoner sobs.

'Do not let go,' Eline orders, then she turns to the Reaper. 'You. Touch him.' Elician tries not to feel *too* offended when the prisoner does not seem nearly as horrified by the idea of instantaneous death as he is by Elician's far less lethal contact. The Reaper approaches slowly, glancing awkwardly at Elician, who shrugs in return. He has never been party to something like this before and has no idea what is going to happen. He has a feeling that no one, apart from Eline perhaps, will enjoy it all that much.

The Reaper slowly bares a small strip of skin just on their hand. They reach out, pressing the gap to the prisoner's arm, and the man throws his head back in a wordless wail. His eyes stare vacantly at the ceiling. Elician feels the moment the man dies, the way his soul leaves his body, his heart stopping and his brain function ending. A wriggle of discomfort wraps around Elician's mind, and he feels a shiver rattle down his spine. His stomach clenches in anticipation as his own fingers tighten on the prisoner's arm.

He knows it is hard for most Givers to bring someone back from the dead. That they struggle to pull a soul back from the beyond. But Elician has never needed anything more than a touch, a slight press of skin. It is as instantaneous as a Reaper's touch in reverse. Zinnitzia had called him a prodigy. Marina had fretted. Fen, even with all her magnificent talent, still needed a few moments of time. A few moments of prolonged contact to entertain the possibility of cheating Death.

He hates this experiment more than anything else. He cannot control it. The prisoner is now tethered between him and a Reaper, and Elician cannot stop the urge to make this man *live* no matter what the cost. He feels the man's blood moving through his body. He feels sharp pricks of electricity igniting in the man's brain, trying to do something, trying to return to normalcy. And with each physical response that sparks and pulsates, marking the return of *life*, he senses the opposite – the swift and sharp finality of death swatting back.

The Reaper's presence blankets Elician's ministrations, smothering and enveloping them. It's a heady reminder that Elician is the air that fuels the fire of this prisoner's existence. The touch of his skin is the spark that ignites that flame. But the moment Elician releases his hold, he knows that the Reaper's blanketing influence will smother that flame entirely, Death winning out the moment Life cedes the field. And Elician cannot let go.

'Fascinating,' Eline says, taking notes on her ever-present stack of papers.

Elician spares a glance for the Reaper. His eyes have glazed over, lips trembling. His fingers are still holding tight to the prisoner's arm, but the grasp seems almost desperate, as if this contact is causing him some kind of physical harm. Elician has directly touched Reapers before. Marina . . . Cat – Alest. He'd held Alest in his arms and never once felt this strange, sickening spiral deep in his chest. There had been no cosmic back and forth. Life and Death tugging on two ends. Touching Alest had made him think only: *This must be what it's like to feel human.*

But with this prisoner held between him and this Reaper, Elician cannot help but feel the energy it takes to keep the prisoner alive. Elician has become the only thing capable of saving an unwilling man's life.

Suddenly, the Reaper collapses, dropping to the side in a dead faint. The prisoner gasps, head falling forward as his chest rises and falls in a steady rhythm. Elician releases him. He looks down at the Reaper, wondering if he could or should try to rouse him back to consciousness. He doesn't wonder for long.

Eline snaps her fingers. Orders, 'Bring in the next one,' and Elician's head snaps towards the door. Another Reaper is being brought in. The unconscious body of her fellow is left where it fell. The prisoner starts babbling, shaking his head, trying to get away. The guards shove him back in place. Elician feels bile start to climb in his throat. He swallows, trying to ward off a wave of sickness.

'Again,' Eline orders.

Elician closes his eyes, presses his hand to the prisoner's arm, and for the first time in his life thinks, *I do not think you want to live anymore.* But the prisoner's body continues to fight to survive for every second Elician keeps his palm to the man's skin. No matter what they do to him, or how many Reapers are brought into Elician's room: the man keeps coming back to life.

CHAPTER TWENTY-EIGHT

Cat

Cat makes a list of all the people who know Elician's secret:

Elician
Lio
Fen
Marina
Zinnitzia
King Aliamon
Queen Calissia
Lord Anslian
Lady Adalei
(Lio's parents???)

He puzzles over it for hours, pen hovering over each name as he wonders who to cross off as potential traitors. Most have reasons for wanting Elician gone, but who would actually do it? Marina and Zinnitzia both wanted Elician to stop fighting the war. Him being captured would accomplish that. Anslian and Adalei have moved up in the hierarchy with Elician's death, but both seemed genuinely in grief about Lio. Lio's death could have been unintended, but Anslian had purposefully asked Lio to go with Elician. Cat remembers that clearly. Why would he send Lio somewhere if he knew there was a chance he could die? And why would it benefit King Aliamon and Queen Calissia to dispose of their only son now, after spending *years* lying to the world just to ensure that Elician ascended?

And what of Lio specifically? Could he have been involved? His full name, Wilion d'Altas, means his family comes from the best-known border town on the continent. Anslian secured Soleben ownership of the city twenty years ago, but Lio is twenty-four now. Even if Lio had been born and raised in Himmelsheim, his *family* had come from an Alelune-ruled Altas. Perhaps *he'd* betrayed Elician and is hiding in Alerae even now, successfully integrated within the ranks of the Alelunen army.

No. Cat shakes his head, pressing his ink-stained fingers to his eyes, rubbing away fast-growing fatigue. Lio had been nothing but loyal to and worried for Elician during their ride to Kreuzfurt. He can't imagine Lio betraying Elician. Not for anything.

But who else is there?

King Aliamon does not seem interested in sharing his investigatory methods with Cat. He says they are trying to find someone who can get to the Reaper cells but refuses to offer any additional information beyond that. Progress, Cat has been informed, takes time.

It took Ranio nearly a year to smuggle you *out of the city*, the King had said, sneering when Cat flinched at the reminder of Ranio's death. *How long do you imagine it will take us to find a way to smuggle out my son?*

Do you even know if he's there yet? he had asked in turn.

King Aliamon had refused to answer. He refuses to answer many things Cat wants to know, and Cat's impatience grows with each stunted inquiry.

It festers. It festers as the seasons change and cold winter wind slices its way through Himmelsheim. Snow and ice cling to the highest peaks of the palace, creating dangerous patches of stone where it is far too easy to slip and fall. Inside the palace, blue stones are placed through the halls, each radiating enough heat to keep everyone warm through the night. Braziers burn near each outside entrance and all the doors are sealed shut. Thick cloth pads are pressed against cracks in the windows, and curtains made of the same material as Cat's Reaper garb are used to block the biting chill. The occasional cocklestove (some ornately built as miniature replicas of Himmelsheim) supports the blue stones when needed so there is nary a draft to be felt. But outside, the city is frozen, and its people are quiet.

It feels like everyone is waiting for something. Though what, Cat does not know.

He practises his swordplay with Marina. He pretends not to notice Elician's father watching his progress. And he tries not to give too much weight to the few conversations he has had with the King that do not revolve around Elician directly. *Have you thought about taking the crown? Of being King of Alelune? Would you make a claim? There is no law forbidding a Reaper from ruling.*

Each time Aliamon presses him for an answer, Cat asks a question. *Have you found your son? Does he have a way out?*

Keep training, Aliamon says in turn. *My son will need someone competent on the throne when he rules.*

'He wants you to be Soleb's ally,' Marina suggests when he tells her of the talks. 'Someone will take Queen Alenée's throne eventually. He'd prefer to choose who that will be.'

'He wants to buy my affection,' Cat translates. 'It's insulting.' She does not disagree. Instead, she gives him more lessons. This time, on oration. He memorizes them all, reading famed speeches out loud, trying to mimic the cadence and tone of a statesman. He listens in on a few parliamentary sessions when he has the opportunity, watching the order of business as the assembled lords and ladies make petitions to the King or debate proposed rules of law.

The latitude he is given grates. No guard follows his footsteps. No watchful eye traces his movements. It's another infuriating test. Kill

Aliamon, like Cat's queen demanded, or play the perfect pet hostage, granted all the rights and privileges as a full citizen of Soleb but meant to return to Alelune and undo a government that has long stood the test of time.

More infuriating: Cat is not sure what he truly wants to do.

Instead, he goes back to his list, folding it and unfolding it so often that the paper tears slightly in the middle of the crease. He explores as much of the palace as he can in hopes of finding an answer, and he finds Elician's rooms.

Well, he finds Lio's first. An unattended door that leads to more questions than answers. For a boy that had not been a prince, Lio had lived like one. His furnishings are fine, his clothing rich. The weapons on his wall are well made, sharp and beautifully decorated. A few wooden figurines, shaped and painted like Soleben soldiers, stand vigil on his writing desk, all in various stages of combat or repose.

There is nothing damning in Lio's room. But he had gone to war at twenty and never returned. Perhaps the truth lay on the battlefield and not here. All Cat finds here are the signs of a boy well loved. Lio wanted for nothing while living in the palace. And when Cat presses open a door near Lio's bed, he finds himself in Elician's chambers. A level of trust that almost takes Cat's breath away.

Elician's bedroom is far bigger than Lio's, of course. The prince could have swung his sword through all its many steps and forms and still would have found it difficult to accidentally strike a wall – though there is a suspiciously shaped gash tastefully hidden behind a curtain. His bed, massive in all respects, seems minuscule in the great emptiness of the open floor sprawling out before it. And one wall is entirely covered in books.

Cat pokes through Elician's things, not entirely sure if he is looking for something specific or if he's simply interested in knowing more. He opens the nightstand beside the prince's bed and finds a small blue stone in the corner. It glows faintly, good for little more than a light in the dark. *That shouldn't be here.* It should be in the hands of the people to whom it was originally gifted. Not stolen and kept in a drawer like a forgotten token. At least the ones in use throughout the palace are obvious in their purpose. Cat despises the sight of those too, but he can accept that they are being used with intention. This . . . this feels far more absentminded than that.

Cat reaches for the stone, tracing his fingers over its warm surface. Only the Master of the Blue Palace had permission to give them, and his father is long dead. Tears press at his eyes. He closes the drawer, hiding the stone from view. *Take it, Elician,* he thinks. *I give it freely to you.* But it is not his stone to give. Not anymore. He does not know who sits in the Blue Palace, now that his father is gone and he has been set aside. But whoever reigns over the Blue Lands is the only one with the authority to gift each precious stone mined from the earth.

Turning slowly, Cat lowers himself to Elician's bed. He presses his hands to his eyes again and breathes slowly. He wishes he could have given it to Elician directly. Explained what it meant. Why it was important. Why it was wrong that it had been stolen in the first place, but how conceding it as a gift now felt somehow *right*. Leaning back, he lays his head on Elician's pillow. He looks up at the ceiling far above. He wonders what Elician would have said. Wonders, too, how Elician could even stand such a grandiose room with a mattress so soft that–

'What are you doing here?'

Jerking upright, Cat throws himself from the bed. He struggles to find his footing as he whirls towards the voice at the door. Adalei, the Lady of Himmelsheim. Heir apparent after Anslian, now that Elician has been declared dead. Dressed in black, head still covered by a long fabric scarf that encircles her throat and trails over her shoulders – she clashes badly with the bright and glittering gold accents of Elician's room.

'I–' He has no excuse. He had not been in the process of

uncovering anything useful, save for the knowledge of what the prince's bed felt like. Like him, Adalei has entered from the connecting door that leads to Lio's chambers, and Cat flushes in shame. She had gone there to see her beloved's things and discovered Cat's impropriety by accident. 'I'm sorry.'

'Have you done something wrong?' she asks.

'I . . .'

'Far be it from me to tell any young man to leave my cousin's bed.' It is the heart of winter, but a sharp heat snaps through Cat, leaving him breathless. 'Though I admit, when I thought of finding someone in my cousin's bed, I imagined him there as well.' His cheeks burn. Words fail at his lips. Useless. 'Apologies,' she says, smiling wryly. 'I meant no offence, only he gave me so few opportunities to tease him properly. I would have enjoyed it.'

'I'm not offended.'

'No? Most days I cannot tell your face from the snow outside our windows, yet now you've turned darker than the poppies in spring.'

'I . . . I'm not offended.' He can feel his blush deepening.

Her eyes narrow slightly before her smile grows. 'Not offended – charmed, perhaps? Tell me truthfully then, what *are* you doing in my cousin's bed?'

'I just . . . wanted to know what it felt like.' Adalei hums thoughtfully. She glides past him, elegance personified. She straightens some of the wrinkles on the silk bed cover until there is no sign that he had ever been there at all.

'It's a fine bed,' she drawls. 'Though I'll tell you a secret: he spent more time under it than in it.'

'Under it?'

'He drew pictures on the bottom. A whole world just for him. You should look sometime. They might interest you.' She trails her fingers along one of the large bed posts. 'Have you seen his portrait in the memorial hall? It was just raised last week.'

'Yes.' He had found it by chance. While walking to meet Fen, he had caught sight of Elician's name on a placard beneath the new installation. The prince had been draped in regal shades of white and gold, kneeling with sad eyes turned up towards the sun. The background depicted duelling armies, the foreground showed only flowers and fields. One of Elician's hands rested on the golden pommel of his sword. His other was a closed fist over his heart. 'It doesn't look like him.'

'I hear they made him more handsome for the painting,' she replies, shrugging.

'No.' His nose scrunches. 'They didn't.' The artist had chosen to flatten Elician's lovely curls, turning them into a subtle wave that feels simply *wrong* to look at. Elician's skin had been painted just a few shades lighter, and his eyes had been given a strange golden hue rather than the warm and comforting brown that always felt so charmingly sincere. There had been no sign of Elician's dimples either, but perhaps more egregiously, Cat notes, 'There's no beard. He has a beard.'

Adalei laughs as if she had not expected to and covers her lips with her hand. 'He didn't have one before he left for the war. The artist wouldn't have known.'

'He looks better with it.' Cat's brows furrow, his lips twist. 'And . . . he is not . . . that is not how he should be positioned.'

'Oh? How do *you* think a portrait should display my cousin?'

'He would often sit with his knees up and his hands on the ground, leaning back. He would tilt his head, and when he *did* look at the sky, he . . .' Just breathed in sweet fresh air, simply happy to be alive.

What do you think, Cat? Elician's voice echoes in his head. Sweet and content. *Is today going to be a good day?*

'You became quite fond of him on your way to Kreuzfurt, then? Even though he was your captor?'

'He was kind.' So few people in his life have ever been that way from the start.

Adalei is quiet for a long while. Finally, she nods her head. 'Yes,' she says softly. 'He has always been very kind. I imagine he would have become rather fond of you as well by the time your journey was done.' Aliamon had said the same thing when Cat first met him. Unlike the King, Adalei genuinely sounds pleased by the knowledge. Her eyes sparkle, and she leans in like she intends to tell a secret. 'We used to tease him, tell him he could make friends with anyone and anything.'

It was what Elician had wanted more than anything. To have friends. Cat stares at her, numbly, as he remembers Elician speaking about how hard it had been just to find time to talk to another person. 'That was cruel,' he says, words falling from his mouth before he can think to stop them.

Her eyes narrow infinitesimally. But her expression does not alter. 'You're right,' she admits. 'He could make friends in seconds, but keeping them . . . that was always difficult.' She shakes her head, sighing a little. 'Often, it wasn't allowed. But in truth, he worried about what making friends with someone mortal would mean in the long run for him too. Something you won't have to worry about. *You* could be his friend for lifetimes . . . if you wanted.'

She moves, and his attention is pulled to her long black dress and covered arms. Her only visible skin is her face and hands, but she wears no bell. 'You are not a Reaper,' he says as she straightens her back and flexes her hands in a kind of absentminded stretch. The black hem of her dress swishes to one side. She shakes her head.

'No, I am not.'

'But you wear that colour, still.'

'It is a tradition for one to wear the colours of Death when a loved one is lost. I will exchange this for something else when I no longer grieve.' The rest of the household has already done so. There are periods of mourning, arbitrarily set to mark the length of the commitment and relationship to the deceased. It has been months since the funeral, memories have been spoken, and all the household has moved on. Yet Adalei's mourning dress remains the same.

'We celebrate death in Alelune,' he says.

'I've heard. You're happy someone has embraced their chance to change and wish them well in their futures.'

'Yes.'

'It's a kind sentiment, but I miss my loved ones. I will grieve for them, even if they have changed into something better.'

'It's selfish,' he points out.

'Sometimes it's important to be selfish, from time to time.'

He bows his head, accepting. When he looks back up, she is carefully adjusting her headscarf. As far as he has been able to tell, the women in Himmelsheim seem to take great pride in their hair, braiding it, coiling it, setting it into designs. The cloth draped over Adalei's head is not flattering, according to the fashions of her people. It hides her hair; it also hides much of her neck and throat. 'What does it mean?' he asks, indicating her scarf, searching for something to say.

'Nothing cultural, if that is what you're asking,' she replies. 'I am simply vain.' She traces the edges of the fabric along her forehead, then lowers her hand to her side. 'I spent many years in Kreuzfurt. Did you know that?'

'Yes.'

She nods consideringly and turns to look at Elician's bookcase. It reaches high up the wall – high enough that a stool waits patiently at its base, to help a reader reach the upper shelf. Adalei trails her fingers along a few spines. 'As a member of the royal family, no Giver was allowed to heal me, and so I went to the House of the Unwanting . . . waiting to die. There was some hope, of course, that I could find some comfort there. Or at least a painless end when I was ill. After he became a Reaper, Fransen stayed with me quite often . . . reading to me, teaching me things. I was sorry to hear of his passing.' She grins over her shoulder. 'I hope he changed into something he enjoys.' Cat cannot help it. He smiles in return. 'Elena was my physician from the very start. And she worked tirelessly to make me whole. You see, Alelune has its blue stones, and we have our greys.'

'Greys?'

'They're difficult to understand,' Adalei responds. 'Fatal to use or interact with in most circumstances. It's forbidden to mine them as a result. But there had been some observations regarding their powers to heal, in the past, and when my health took a sharp turn for the worse, Elena was willing to try. A Reaper needed to hold the stone, and so Fransen did it for her. He held it above me, and Elena talked him through how to use it. I'm not sure what her methods were, but when the treatment was done, it would leave me more drawn out and ill in ways I could not imagine for hours. But, always, there was improvement in the days that followed. Until one day, I no longer needed the treatments at all. But the stone leaves its mark, and it's permanent. In my case, it affected my hair. It never grew back and my scalp . . . well . . .' Her fingers brush where the scarf meets her brow. 'I'd rather hide my . . . *deficiencies* from the court.'

'You're not deficient,' Cat argues.

'Lio would have loved you dearly for saying that.'

'We were not close.'

'Shame.' Lowering her voice, she leans towards him. 'I *am* insecure about my appearance, but in truth, our king is equally not someone who enjoys being reminded of his potential heirs' lack of suitability. If I am to be considered a viable member of this family, I must look a certain way. Act a certain way. And so, the scarf ensures I meet expectations of outward propriety that suit our family's reputation. Do you understand?'

'Your king expects a lot from you all.' He wonders if she would bother with the scarf had Aliamon not insisted upon it first. Cat does not ask, and she does not offer the answer on her own. Instead, she glances back to the books lining Elician's wall.

'A long time ago, Elician, Lio and I made a plan for our future. What we wanted to do once Aliamon had passed on.' Plotting for what comes after a monarch's demise sounds almost Alelunen of them. He's surprised she would confess as much to him now, but she shows no equal sign of uncertainty. She speaks calmly, coolly. 'Elician named me his heir. He expected to abdicate after a certain amount of years, so as not to affront Soleb with his status as a Giver overlong. And then Lio and I . . . we had plans. On what the kingdom could be and how it needed to change.'

'He loved you,' Cat says. Her lips quirk. She nods but says nothing. *She already knows.* A thought comes to him then, sudden and unexpected. Beyond anything he has ever seriously considered before. 'Lio . . . His funeral was before we arrived.'

'Yes.'

'And the remembrance dinner?'

'That too.'

'I have . . . Is it too late to share a story for him, in memory?' The custom is meaningless to him. But not to her. She meets his eyes.

'It is never too late to share a story,' she entreats, voice wavering as she beckons him to speak. 'Tell me. I would like to hear.'

'He went fishing for us. One night, for dinner, as we were on our way to Kreuzfurt. He waded into a stream, and he put his hands in the water. And the fish seemed to just go to him, as if they didn't know or care that he meant them harm. He caught them, and he tossed them up onto the bank and he . . . he asked me to be useful and to kill them swiftly. So I did.' He pauses, unsure. 'I killed Lio, too. When I first met him. But Elician brought him back and afterwards, Lio was never once afraid of me. Of what I could do. Even though I could have killed him again at any moment. He still asked me to help with the fish and believed I could be useful. I don't think I treated him well on our journey to Kreuzfurt, but . . . I liked him. I thought he was a good man.'

'I liked him too,' Adalei replies. 'And he was. Thank you for telling me.' She touches his gloved hand. Squeezes his fingers.

'I'm sorry I killed him.'

'It was not the first time he had died,' she says gently. 'Death has been chasing him since he was a child. But Elician never wanted to let him go.'

'Why?'

'They are brothers, in all ways that matter. Queen Calissia struggled giving birth to Elician, and afterwards, she was too weak to nurse him. Lio's mother was hired to care for my cousin. In return, Lio was considered a natural playmate and confidante. They grew up together, here, and were always at each other's side. Elician was still a child when we realized he was a Giver, and his life was arranged to ensure no one ever knew the truth. Lio helped make that happen.'

'Do you trust him – Lio?' Cat asks her. She frowns, meeting his eyes and holding his gaze until the intensity forces him to look away.

'You want to know if he would have betrayed Elician, if Lio is the reason my cousin is gone.' He nods, still incapable of looking at her, still feeling the weight of her eyes upon him. 'It's possible,' she replies. 'Anything is. But if I were to judge it, I would say no. Lio is fanatically loyal to my cousin, and he was a part of Elician's plans for the future, every step of the way. He has nothing to gain, but everything to lose. I do not imagine Lio is the culprit you are looking for.'

'What else did Elician plan?' He knows the broad strokes. Kreuzfurt freed, an end to the war (somehow), and now even a succession that would appease his people. But there had to be more than that.

'Ask him when you see him,' Adalei demurs. 'It is meaningless coming from me. I could be lying.'

'Are you?'

'I could be. But for what it is worth, I believed in his plans too.' When he dares to glance up at long last, she's still looking at him. Back straight, chin up, hands folded neatly. She is delicate and frail in her black dress with her too-thin wrists and thin body. She reminds him of *his* Reapers, in Alelune. Emaciated, weak, and yet filled with power. Unfathomable power. For appearances mean nothing in the face of what they can do – and Adalei commands power simply by existing. He is compelled to speak to her, prompted by shame, and tempted into revealing the truths he had not intended to speak. Never has he seen someone this perfectly in control who holds none of the physical means to enforce that control. 'Ten people know Elician's secret,' Adalei says.

'What about Lio's parents?'

'No, they were never informed. Ten alone know the truth. Two are missing. One is a young girl who influences nothing. One is a prisoner of war, so couldn't have used his knowledge. Two are sworn members of the Houses of the Wanting and Unwanting, but as clerics of the Kingsclave, they are neutral parties and would see no point in getting involved in politics. One is myself.' She smiles. 'And I have no tangible defence. Queen Calissia is frail and far removed from the true running of politics within Soleb. All this leaves only my father – who failed to write to Kreuzfurt when Elician did not arrive at the front, doing so only after he'd been missing for months – and our king, who is the first person my father contacted. He equally did not confirm with Kreuzfurt if Elician had been delayed in any way.' Cat had been right. Something *had* been wrong during his initial conversation with the King . . . and all the ones that had come afterwards.

'Do you know who the traitor is?' Cat asks, chest aching at the thought.

'My father or Aliamon. Perhaps both. Only . . .' She smiles again, but it's sardonic and twisted. 'I have no proof. So, until I do' – she picks up the hem of her black skirt – 'I will haunt them until they concede. And even then, I will never forgive them for what they've done.'

'What will you do, if you find out who it was?'

Adalei bows. 'Elician is a king who cannot die. We have time to watch them fall.' When she straightens, she walks towards the door. 'Be careful, Stello Alest.' Cat's fingers spasm. His bell rings anxiously at his wrist. He hadn't realized that she knows his true identity.

'Secrets are like Reapers,' she tells him. 'They never stay dead for long.'

She leaves, closing the door behind her. And when she's gone, he goes for the drawer once more. He takes the blue stone in hand and crawls beneath Elician's bed. He lets the stone's subtle light flood the darkness of the world beneath. And it *is* a world. It is a glorious world. A collage of fantasies stretches from one wooden pane to the next, with childish words looping and squiggling in all their glorious triumph.

Silver suns and golden moons. Even written apologies for a party thrown after the Moon Prince's death. *If he had lived, maybe we could have changed this world together,* Elician had written around the body of a boy who held the moon in his hands.

'I think I would like to change the world with you, Elician,' Cat whispers, pressing a hand to Elician's dreams. 'If, after all of this time, you still want to try.'

CHAPTER TWENTY-NINE

Fenlia

Laure de Gianno is a tall woman in her late forties. She dresses in the extravagant gowns of her people, with a wide skirt that extends from her hips. Her colour palette is varied, and her costuming bizarre, and it is made all the worse by the fact that the woman appears physically incapable of smiling. 'That's how all the emissaries from Alelune are,' Adalei explains when Fen goes to her for more information. Fen fidgets with one seed after another in her pocket as she watches Adalei weave a tapestry in her sitting room. Fen is not sure what the final image will be, but Adalei has more than thirty colours ready for use and she switches between them with uncanny intuition.

'Is *anybody* ever happy in the west?' Fen asks. She has only really interacted with Cat, but it seems that anyone born in Alelune is also born with a permanent frown.

'I have been reliably informed that it's just their culture,' Adalei explains as she moves her strings this way and that. 'They're not a particularly effusive people. They prefer straightforward gestures without excessive pageantry. Physical contact in public is generally frowned upon.'

'And yet they enthusiastically insist on going to war with us and kidnapping our prince,' Fen mutters.

'Yes. Well. We did the same to them not too long ago.' Adalei chooses a new yarn spool and begins to weave it into position.

'Have you ever been there?'

'Been where?'

'To the embassy?'

'Fen.' Adalei finally meets her eyes at long last. 'You're not being particularly subtle, you know.'

Fen's cheeks burn hot. She crosses her arms over her chest. 'I don't have anything to be subtle about,' she insists boldly.

'At least pretend you're asking because you're interested in courting your little Reaper friend.'

'I'm not!'

Adalei sighs loudly. She sets her strings down and turns. Her hands fold politely in her lap. 'You want information,' Adalei says. 'You really *should* be careful about who is aware of you wanting this information. You need to learn how to ask about one thing when you mean something else.' Fen blinks at her, mind blank. She can think of no other topic at all worth discussing with Adalei, and Adalei seems to realize it too. The older woman sighs once more, shaking her head as she drawls out a perfectly polite, 'For instance . . .' and smiles in the vapid way court ladies must always smile. 'I shared some of Elician's poetry with your Cat recently. He seemed very interested.'

'Elician's *poetry*? Why would Cat care about that?'

'Oh, I'm sure I couldn't begin to guess. But after travelling all the way from the Bask to Kreuzfurt with only our dashing prince and Lio as his companions, *perhaps* Cat took a shine to our prince after all.'

Fen is not sure she is following this conversation well. She squints at Adalei, who continues smiling blandly, offering nothing until Fen asks which poems Adalei had given him. 'Well, the only poems I had that were *officially* written by him were the ones he used to write about the long-lost Moon Prince. I thought he might like those, so I passed them to him.'

'You *gave* them to him?'

'He seemed like someone who should read them – he is fascinated by Elician, after all. I didn't see any harm in showing him what Elician had thought about the Moon Prince who died too young.'

'What does that have to do with anything?'

Adalei very delicately plucks a piece of invisible something or other off her immaculate dress. She flicks the speck off into the distance and asks, 'Do *you* think your Cat took a shine to our prince while they travelled?'

'No. I don't know. Also, he's not my Cat. And what does any of this have to do with–'

'It's about finding answers to questions that haven't been asked, Fen,' Adalei chides lightly. 'For instance, I know *you* haven't taken a shine to Cat, at least.' Fen's face burns even hotter as she shakes her head, spluttering and denying the accusation that had not even been voiced.

'How can–? How do you–?'

'Your reaction for one. You don't seem to mind the idea that Cat may have feelings for your brother.'

'They barely know each other!'

'Or perhaps you do mind it.'

'I don't!'

'As you say. In any case, you're angry with Cat about something. Did he tell you not to go to the embassy too?'

'He–No. Not really. I mean, yes, he did, but–'

'You're awful at this,' Adalei tells her. She turns in her seat and goes back to her weaving.

'You're the one making things mean things they don't mean. It's very . . . *Alelunen* of you.'

'Perhaps it is. But I'm not the one plotting a crime. You are. And you're hiding it very badly.'

'I promised Elician I would help him. That I would do what I could to help him with anything he needed. And then they *stole*

Elician! *And* they did something to Lio. Someone in Alelune must know what happened, so why won't you help me find out?'

'To what end?' Adalei asks. She continues weaving, back straight and her attention seemingly only on her threads. 'Say that somehow, for some reason, there is confirmation in that embassy that Elician and Lio are in Alelune. Undoubtedly, they're somewhere we cannot reach them. What happens then?'

'Cat says there's a traitor in the palace. Someone who betrayed Elician and got him caught.'

Adalei pauses in her task. She cuts Fen a look. 'There is.'

'Then *maybe* that confirmation also shows who that traitor is.'

'You're risking a lot on a maybe.'

'Tell me the truth, though. If we did find something, wouldn't it be worth it? To you? To know?'

Adalei pauses for a long while. Then, slowly, she nods. 'You're too loud, though.' She continues weaving. 'Leave it with me.'

'Or you could–'

'Fen. Leave it with me.'

Fen watches her cousin. Watches Adalei's jaw as it clenches. Watches her nostrils as they flare. Watches her delicate fingers working expertly on the tapestry she is designing based on memory and intuition alone. 'What would you do . . . if you did find out?' Fen asks next.

Adalei's lips twitch. 'Finally,' she says, 'you're asking the right questions.'

On the coldest day of winter, Marina and Zinnitzia are summoned by the King to discuss plans for the coming spring, and so Fen and Cat are released from their duties. Fen leads Cat through the city, showing him all her favourite places. These just happen to be near the Alelune embassy. Their journey ends at the Temple of Life, which stands just outside the embassy's gates.

Nobody bothers them the whole while. The streets always clear when Cat walks down them, nervous civilians all but slip-sliding across the frozen cobblestones to get out of the way when they hear his bell and see his black garb. He keeps his new fur-lined hood pulled down too, when they wander the city streets. She cannot see his expression, but she hooks her elbow around his after his jingling bell makes a parent quickly yank their young child away from the road – as if Cat had intended to murder her on sight. She squeezes his arm and ignores everyone. If they want to flee, it just means she and Cat will have a better view.

Side by side, they look up at the largest statue of Life. 'He always looks up at the sun,' she explains, pointing high above them at the carved features of their country's god. Life's face is long and angular. His nose is a narrow shaft that curves outwards around the nostrils, charmingly quaint and eerily reminiscent of the line of kings. Honourable Ricgard, the ancient artist commissioned with designing the statue, seemed to have borrowed a few features from the royal line in his work. Thousands of years later, those similarities still hold true. Fen had even teased Elician about it when they were younger. At a quick glance, sometimes he even looked just like the statue. The comment never failed to make her brother blush.

'During the day,' Fen continues, 'Life's head turns so he can watch the sun move across the sky.' No technology guides the statue's movement. Ricgard certainly never admitted to how he managed to carve a living statue that turned its head, centimetre by centimetre, all throughout the day, never once failing to keep its watch. 'Elician, Lio and I tried to find the gears, or weights, or levers, that make it move. But we never found anything. There is no spring, no coil, no mechanism. It is all pure stone.' The boys had climbed the statue itself, hand over hand, until they sat on the god's shoulders, inspecting every part of it, scrambling back to the ground only when Fen had hissed someone was coming.

'"Life made all things,"' Fen recites from childhood lessons memorized long ago. '"He shaped the world and all that is in it, but when the creatures he made wanted more, Death came to release their souls, unmake their bodies and give them the chance to reform or try again."'

'Death leads to Life, then,' Cat murmurs. A nearby family quickly shuffles away, kicking up tufts of snow as they go. Fen hopes Cat didn't notice.

'In a way. But somehow, dying stopped being a choice somewhere along the way. It comes whether people want it or not, are ready or not. But I think it should still be a choice . . . and we should choose what we're remade into.' Fen crosses her arms. 'I wouldn't have chosen *this* life. And now I can't even die – so I can't *be* remade into something else. I'm stuck like this until the gods have decided it's my time. Same as you.'

A few more people wander inside the temple and Fen guides Cat away from the statue and the crowd, still watching the statue slowly turn. 'What happens at night?' Cat asks.

'The head looks down, and then it turns back to the east.'

'Why?' he asks.

Fen pitches her voice to match Elena's accented tones. 'I can show you the how, but as for the why?' Cat huffs, shaking his head with a smile. 'I have a why for *you* though,' Fen says. 'Why does Alelune use the moon as their symbol – and worship Death – if they don't like Reapers? Reapers are *made* of Death. Isn't hiding you away . . . disrespectful? At the very least?'

Cat shrugs. He does not look at Fen. His head is angled only towards the turning statue, hands and arms tucked in close to his body. Children yell and run this way and that. Parents call their names. Worshippers bow and pray to the statue and all that it represents. 'Alelune respects change,' Cat murmurs eventually.

'The change of shape. Of the next becoming. Of evolving into something new. That is what we worship. Death represents the . . .' He says a word Fen does not understand. He tries another word, but she still does not recognize it. 'Machine? Mechanic? The thing that sparks – that does the change?'

'Catalyst?' she offers. He nods.

'Catalyst. Death is that catalyst. Reapers bring change too soon. Unasked for. Unwanted. Change should be natural. Without the influence of Reapers *or* Givers.'

'Change on its own terms,' Fen guesses. He nods.

'Death is a god we question. She is not a god we worship, as such.' He tilts his head towards the men and women bowing and praying to the statue of Life. 'We ask questions of Death, we accept her answers, but we do not ask *for* anything. We wish, rather, to change on our own. Like our moon.' He curls his hands together and makes a shadow puppet on the wall behind them. She watches his hand twist and turn, precisely shaping the journey of a moon as it waxes and wanes.

'Where did you learn that?' she asks, awed.

He shrugs, letting his hands fall. 'We played games in the cells sometimes, when none of the guards could see. *Even in the dark, there is light,*' he murmurs.

'That sounds like something Elician put in a poem once,' she tells him.

'It is,' he replies.

Fen tilts her head back up to the statue. Its gaze is fixed towards the sun, not once looking down at the meagre folk below. Even at night, with its head bowed and eyes lowered, the statue's gaze is not for *them.*

News of the war has been steady and constant. Battles have been won and lost, but no ground has been ceded. Nothing has changed. No one has mentioned Lio or Elician or anything related to where they might be.

'I miss him,' she murmurs. 'No one is saying anything. They just keep pretending as if everything is fine. But it's *not* fine, and if someone *did* betray him, then why hasn't anything else happened?'

'I don't know,' Cat whispers.

'How could they keep him somewhere where *no one* would see him? Unless he really is dead?' He does not say anything to that. Perhaps there is nothing to be said.

The sun starts setting, slowly at first, then faster. Tourists begin to leave the temple; clerics begin to clean the grounds. Fen and Cat find a bench to sit on and watch as the statue's head follows the path of the sun. Its chin tucks inwards as its body moves in the opposite direction. Fen stares up at it. She waits to feel something, anything. Two women and their young baby, bundled up with care, are all that remain at the statue's feet. They hold the baby up and say their prayers, offering gratitude to their god. Fen tries to feel something similar. Gratitude, affection. Some deep, resonating reason to pray or offer praise to an all-powerful being that *blessed* her and her brother just like this. She feels nothing.

Nothing, save an even greater desire to know *why*.

Why her? Why Cat? Why Elician?

The statue does not answer. It just continues to turn. The couple and their child make to leave, and she catches Cat watching them as they walk by, his head turning to follow until they're out of sight. 'Cat?' He turns back to her. 'Do you know them?'

'No. Not really. I thought that woman looked familiar, but . . . it's nothing. Must have passed her at some point on the road.' It doesn't sound entirely like the truth. Especially not when there is something almost pleased in his tone that had been absent moments before. She cannot begin to guess what he might be pleased about. She does not really want to ask to find out.

Looking back at the statue of Life, it still offers no guidance, nor taste of inspiration. Shaking her head, Fen slides her hand into her pocket and pulls out one of her seeds. What is the point of living, really, in the first place?

Maybe Alelune has a point. She certainly could see the value of questioning Life, in trying to ascribe meaning to it. The seed on her palm is alive, yes. And yet . . . it should not stay like this, given its purpose. It would not stay like this if left to its own devices. If put in the ground and provided with nutrients, water and a good temperature . . . it would grow. It would change.

Closing her eyes, Fen wills it to do just that, then. Not to live; it is already living. But to do more. Be more. To grow to—

Something soft and smooth slides across her palm. Cat shifts at her side. Her eyes open. There, small and white, is a root growing from the bottom of the split shell on her palm. A bit of life, in a world made quiet by the chill.

'Well done,' Cat says.

She meets his eyes through the veil. 'Help me find my brother,' she commands. Cat hesitates only for a moment, but he is, and always has been, true to his oaths. He nods his head as the plant in her hand continues to grow.

CHAPTER THIRTY

Fenlia

It is almost impossible to find enough time to slip away from the palace. They have to choose their moment carefully. Cat trains dutifully with Marina, Fen does the same with Zinnitzia, and when their lessons are done, they each take a different route and try to get as close to the Alelune embassy as they can. Fen knows they might not find anything. Knows that the risk is high. But none of the embassy's mail or shipments are monitored by Soleb. A plot between a Soleben traitor and the Queen of Alelune *could* take shape on Ambassador Laure's writing desk. And if it has, Fen owes it to her brother to try to find out how.

Cat is insistent on staying out of sight. They cannot be caught, not for anything, and Fen can guess what the punishment will be if they are. She, at least, would likely be returned to the King. But Cat is an Alelunen citizen – if he is found on their grounds, there would be no need for Laure to hand him back. He would be returned to the Reaper cells and all the horrors therein.

They need to be quick, and they need to be careful. Their reconnaissance takes weeks. They write detailed observations of Laure's guests whenever possible, and Adalei grudgingly provides updates on any court sessions where Laure speaks to King Aliamon. She does it with a shrewd eye and a curled lip, making it clear that she thinks Fen is playing a dangerous game. Still – she helps.

She helps, and though it takes another three months of feverish planning and late-night preparation, eventually Fen and Cat manage to slip away from the palace one evening when there is no moon in the sky. All they take with them is a couple of candles and a great deal of hope.

Fen waits for Cat outside the palace gates. She stays hidden in the shadows, keeping an eye on her surroundings. He appears next to her as if he steps from the shadows themselves. She hisses, tripping backwards, startled despite herself. He is not dressed in black. He wears no bell.

His brown hair is tied behind his head with a cord, and his outfit is eerily familiar. 'Where did you get those clothes?' she asks, eyeing the intricate weave and delicate embroidery ornamenting the front of his purple tunic.

'Elician's room,' he replies. 'They fit.' They had been straining on Elician's shoulders before he went to war, but they do fit Cat now. Though the tunic sits far too loose around the shoulders and waist, it's the right length on him, and the brown trousers are tucked carefully into his boots. He could be anyone like this. And no one would know.

We're going to be in so much trouble if we're caught, Fen thinks.

'Let's go,' she says. Then, turning, she takes a deep breath and leads the way. Together, they hurry down the spiralling streets towards the embassy. A tall stone wall with a wooden awning separates it from the other buildings on the row. A large wooden door is the only entrance that they will be able to use, and guards stand in front of it – bracketed by braziers. Both are lit exceptionally bright tonight, illuminating each adjacent structure.

Fen's heart beats fast in her chest as she quietly slips from one shadow to the next. Cat is deathly silent behind her. She cannot even hear him breathe. When they reach the outer limits of the firelight,

Fen leans against the stone siding of the luxury apartments that are always afforded to foreign dignitaries. When she had first started plotting, she had hoped maybe they could slip in through the apartments, but there would be far too many witnesses. Far too many guards and possibilities that were too uncertain or unknown.

Fen's fingers press against the sandstone wall. It is a dark night tonight. Very dark. Spring has started, summer is on its way, but here in Himmelsheim the nights are cold. And the guards are huddled very close to those braziers. Slowly, Fen reaches out with her hand. She tries to imagine the fires growing bigger. Brighter. Too bright. Out of control.

The guard closest yelps loudly when flames burst high into the sky. He stumbles and falls back, but then the other fire is burning just as brightly. Bright enough, and hot enough, that the flames begin to reach towards the awning. The guards yell; the door opens. Two more guards step out, this time to help mitigate the fires before they catch on anything important.

Fen wills the fire to burn more, more. Even more. She pushes it to go hotter, faster, stronger. Someone needs to run to get a bucket and they return only a few moments later with water pumped from the well. The bucket is upended on the first brazier, and Fen lets her attention shift from it to the second. She lets the first fire die out in order for the second to burn even more. The guards all have their backs turned. They are all focused on the task of the great inferno that is licking and biting and chewing at the wooden awning of the embassy.

Taking a deep breath, Fen glances over her shoulder. They need to time their attempt carefully. Cat nods at her and she nods back. She focuses on the guards once more. The fire is burning brightly. She tilts her weight forward onto the balls of her feet. She takes a deep breath and–

Cat drowns the world in darkness.

They run.

The guards are shouting, stumbling, bumping into each other. They try to light a torch, but the flames refuse to spark. They try to find themselves in the shadows, but by the time they manage, Fen and Cat have already slipped past them and through the great wooden door. Cat takes Fen's hand. They hurry through the courtyard, away from the yells of confusion and concern. The walls are lined with large fruit trees, and Cat pulls her to a stop behind one very thick trunk.

They wait.

The smell of fresh leaves wafts all around them. Leaves and smoke. The trunk of the tree they are crouching behind is not very wide, but its foliage is thick. Leaves hang down from its great boughs, and in the shadows they hide from the cautious eyes of the nervous staff members doing a quick check of the grounds.

Even so, Fen cups her hands over her mouth to keep from making any noise at all when she hears someone approach. Cat is as rigid as a statue at her side. They listen as the footsteps draw closer, then as the footsteps pass them by. They wait. They wait. They wait.

Eventually, Fen lowers her shaking hands from her lips. She breathes in deeply. She lets out a long breath of air. Slowly, she straightens. Cat hesitates only for a moment before he rises too. He points towards the left, and she follows him without question. They sneak ever closer towards the building proper and a small window just out of reach.

If Elician were here, Fen knows he could have climbed the wall himself. His clever fingers always seemed to know where to find purchase even when there was barely as much as a centimetre of possibility. Fen squints at the wall, and the distance to the window up above. It is far too high to reach.

Cat lowers himself to his knees. He motions for her to climb on, and she flushes as she carefully straddles his neck to sit on his shoulders. He braces his hands on the wall as he stands up. When she reaches this time, her fingers can just barely touch the lip of the window ledge. Cat's hands get under her feet and push one of her legs up. It is awkward and uncomfortable. She nearly knocks them both off balance, but she gets her foot up onto one of his shoulders, then the next. And from this height she can just manage to address the window properly. She opens it, pulling back the shutters and peering into the darkness of the room beyond. Her arms burn as she hoists herself up, one small crawl at a time. Cat gives her legs another shove once she gets going.

The ledge on the interior wall, however, is barely wider than the one she has just navigated. She's off balance and top-heavy. She falls. It isn't far, but pain ricochets through her as she lands awkwardly, falls and bangs her head on the hard stone floor. Her shoulders and knees scrape painfully on the ground. But she is inside.

And she cannot hear any guards approaching.

She waits for a moment, feeling her body piecing itself back together. Then she stands in the darkened window and looks back down at Cat. His shoulders sag with relief as he sees her leaning out. Then he seems to be inspecting the problem of the wall himself. Fen looks around, but there is nothing she can pass down to him. She doubts most embassies keep ladders around for thieves to appropriate. That would be far too convenient. She is tempted to tell him she will meet him in a few minutes when he draws back from the wall. Seems to nod to himself as encouragement, then runs.

Fen scuttles back. She misses the sight of him making the attempt, but she hears three soft scrapes against the sandstone and then Cat's hands are on the ledge. He scrambles, and she dives forward to catch his arms and tug him inside. She pulls him in quickly and they close the shutters behind them. They wait in the darkness of a room Fen cannot identify just yet. The world outside remains silent.

Reaching into her pocket, Fen pulls out one of her candles. She presses her fingers to the wick and lights the flame. Around them, the room glows in faint oranges and yellows. Brooms and buckets line one wall, a table and a rack with folded linens line another. Fen walks to the door and leans against it. Nothing. No one. No footsteps at all. She opens the door as quietly as she can, then peers down the hall. First left, then right.

Adalei had said that Ambassador Laure's office is on the northern side of the embassy. That it overlooks the palace and has a view of the Temple of Life too. It takes Fen a moment to reorient herself, but she turns right and hurries as silently as she can. Fen hears her heart beating in her head, her sweat forming on her brow. Everything she does feels too loud by far. When they reach the office door in question, Fen is half certain they are only moments away from getting caught.

Fen presses her hand to the doorknob and tries to turn it. It's locked. Cat reaches past her, nudging her trembling fingers out of the way. Then, he presses his bare hand to the door, lightly stroking the lock. This time, when he turns the knob, it opens. Dust or ash flutters from the keyhole as he pushes it wide. She doesn't get the chance to investigate before he hurries her inside, closing the door behind them.

It is the right office. Two rows of bookcases stand parallel to the wall, and a grand desk covered in paperwork is affixed just before grand windows which peer out into the city. And in the centre of the room is a large box. Cat stands still just before it, frowning at its lid even as Fen tugs on his arm. 'How did you do it?' she asks.

'It's the same as what I did with the apple back in Kreuzfurt,' he replies. 'The inversion of what you do with your seeds. You bring life, make it grow. I end that life, and all dead things decay.'

'Metal isn't alive,' she points out. 'It never was to begin with.'

'But its *existence* is something. All things must die. Nothing lasts for ever. Metal rusts. It disintegrates. Its components break down and are used as ingredients to help something else take shape. It is a death in its own way, and if it's a *death*, then I can influence it. I just needed to learn how the bindings that kept it whole could be broken. And then . . .' He waves his hand.

He can destroy anything. Fen shivers, biting her lip as he steps closer to the box. He reaches one hand towards it. She thinks he's going to break it down too, collapse wood and metal into a dusty pulp just because he willed it to exist no more.

But there are footsteps in the hall. Footsteps drawing near.

Cat hisses, turns. He snatches at her wrist and tugs her behind one of the rows of shelves, killing the flame of her candle and drowning them once more in darkness. The door opens barely a second later. Fen holds her breath as she dares to peek around the edge of the bookshelf. Her heart sinks to her stomach.

Despite all their careful planning and all their attempts to ensure things went smoothly, clearly something has gone wrong. Ambassador Laure has returned early from the overnight business meeting she had been scheduled to attend. Laure stands in nearly the exact same place Cat had stood, overlooking the large box in her office. She holds a lantern in her hand, and from the rigid set of her shoulders and an angry *tsk*, she is not happy.

CHAPTER THIRTY-ONE

Cat

We cannot be caught here, Cat thinks, squeezing Fen's hand as they hide. *I cannot go back. Not yet. Not now.* What will happen if he does? They don't know who the traitor is. Fen would be left here, alone, to find them, and then what? *I could find him.* The thought strikes him hard between the ribs. His heart lurches in his chest. *If I get brought back to the cells . . . if he's there . . . I could find Elician. I could free him.*

King Aliamon's taunting questions circle around his throat like a vice. Is Cat actually willing to betray his queen? Just for Elician? And even if he did find the prince, what then? What would that mean for his Reapers? For all of Alelune in return? He would likely have to kill hundreds of Alelunen men and women, his brother, his mother, everyone in his mother's court, anyone who stood in their way. And for each person he killed, it would create another person who would stand against him. Alerae would flood with the blood of the dead and . . .

He would have to destroy his own kingdom to save one man.

He will not do that.

There has to be another way to get Elician free and to find the traitor within Soleb. Another way to end this war and free his people without a death toll that would rival Shawshank's historic plague.

Ambassador Laure slams her lantern on her desk. It echoes loudly in the room. 'When did it arrive?' Laure asks sharply. Another voice answers, someone out of view – a man.

'Only an hour ago, my lady.'

'An hour is too *long*. I should have been informed *at once*.'

'You left us orders to not disturb the fête, my lady–'

'This was a missive straight from our queen.'

Fen tugs Cat's hand in alarm. He glances at her. But she only shakes her head in confusion, points to her ear.

She doesn't understand what they're talking about, Cat realizes. They are talking too fast, and their accents are too thick, far from the practised schooling Fen is used to. Laure is moving, walking to the box.

'I did not know it was of such importance,' the man babbles.

'Get out!' Laure howls, and he goes, door slamming shut in his haste. Then there's the sound of metal on metal. Cat nudges Fen to the side so he can take a look for himself. Laure is kneeling, turning a key on the padlock that keeps the box closed. She slides the metal loop free and lets it fall to the ground with a *clank*. Then the box opens, and Laure steps backwards.

There is a shuffling. Fabric moving. Limbs knocking against wood. *I know that noise.* These were the sounds of his life when he had been taken from Alerae to the warfront in a barrel. *Someone is in that box.*

Laure's back obscures the view, but slowly the body reveals itself. Hands at the edges of the box. A swish of dark fabric, designed to conceal the wearer. Laure steps back, lantern swinging in her hand. Still, Cat cannot see the other person's face. Laure speaks. 'You have your orders. Go.' The light shifts. The body moves. It is a woman, all in black, and she steps past Laure and walks through the office door.

Cat jolts to his feet. Laure starts to turn – *Die*, he thinks. Laure collapses into a heap on the ground, eyes staring up at the ceiling.

Fen curses. 'Cat, what the *fuck* are you thinking?'

Too much. He is thinking too much. He rushes to the desk, shuffling hands over papers, trying to find his queen's seal. '*Cat!*' Fen hurries towards him, very nearly tripping on Ambassador Laure's body in the process, then stops when she sees the box is lying open.

'You can bring her back when we leave,' he says, barely remembering to respond in Soleben. 'She didn't see me. It was too fast; she won't know what happened.'

'What did she say? What happened?' Fen rushes to him and looks at the papers he is sifting. 'We can't just kill people and bring them back . . . Zinnitzia says there are consequences!' Of all the times to listen to Zinnitzia.

'She just sent an assassin into the city,' Cat replies. He opens another set of papers. Nothing. Nowhere. The order had to have come from his queen, and she always stamps the pages with–

'This one.' He slaps it on the desk and Fen presses to his side to look down at the curved and swirling letters of the Alelunen alphabet. At the top of the page is Queen Alenée of Alelune's half-moon and star emblem.

'What does it say?' she asks, squinting at the page. 'No, wait . . . hang on . . . that doesn't make any sense.' She is faster at reading than him. More familiar with the spelling that still catches him off guard and the too-similar letters that he struggles to fit to the right phonic. He can read it. He *can*. But he doesn't have time.

'Read it out loud.'

'I– Fine, it says: Apples have been planted in the water, but they are taking too long to – go bad?' She does not sound certain, but she carries on. 'The . . . the gardener will handle the immediate shipment of fruit once you confirm delivery.' She looks up at him. He mouths the words, trying to make sense of them. He reaches for the paper and stares at the squiggles and curls. Fen is right. She read it perfectly. But the meaning is not truly about apples or gardens.

My queen had plans, but they are taking too long. He puzzles it out.

She is going to give something to someone once the assassination takes place. Over a year ago, Cat had been sent to Soleb to kill the royal family. He failed. And when he met with King Aliamon, the King had seemed almost disappointed that Cat had no interest in killing him. And in every moment afterwards, he has given Cat ample opportunity to rectify that. No guard. No overseer. Private meetings and training, constant training, cast alongside questions asking him where his loyalties really lie. *Something is wrong,* Cat had thought then, and he thinks it now. He shoves the letter into a pocket sewn into Elician's borrowed tunic. He takes Fen by the hand and pulls her around the desk. 'We need to go.'

Fen stumbles, desperate to keep up. 'What about Elician? Is there anything about him in there? What about–How are we supposed to *escape* from here?'

'Quickly,' Cat tells her.

'Wait – don't forget *Laure*!' She nearly trips over herself to get to her knees and press her fingers to Laure's outstretched hand, but she makes the contact she needs. Laure gasps back to life even as Cat pulls Fen out the door.

Cat does not try to be subtle. He takes the main stairs, and he runs down them. Heads are swivelling and turning. Fen tries to cover her face. Cat does not bother to do the same. Someone shouts, but Cat keeps running. Faster now. Fen trips again as she tries to keep up. He is faster than her, and he drags her after him each time her steps fumble. They burst out the main entrance and five guards immediately turn towards them. He imagines their lives on a thread, and he yanks that thread taut. All five drop to their knees. Fen screams.

'I didn't kill them!' he calls to her over his shoulder, still running towards the embassy's main gate. He slashes a hand through the air and those guards fall too, mouths frothing, eyes rolling back. Fen yanks her wrist free just as they cross the main road. 'We need to *go*!' Cat insists.

'What did you *do*?' she screams back.

'I just stopped their hearts for *a moment*,' he replies. 'They'll be fine. Fen, that box? The assassin inside it? She's a Reaper. And she's going to the palace.'

'How do you know?' Fen asks, head spinning. 'And how could you stop a heart for a *moment*?'

'Elena *taught* us, Fen. I just need to kill the signal from their brain that keeps their hearts beating. When I let the signal flow again – they return to normal. That's it, that's all. Now, Fen, *please*?'

Her hands curl into fists, and she pumps her arms as she runs. They are not too far from the palace.

That doesn't make him feel any better.

Cat does not kill the palace guards when they approach, momentarily or otherwise. But they are more than a little taken aback when they hear what he has to say. Fen tells them to raise the alarm despite their uncertainty. Even if they wouldn't have listened to Cat, they *do* listen to Fen. Once they are back inside the grounds though, the rush continues.

'Tell me how you know . . . that the assassin is coming here,' Fen gasps as she still tries to keep up with Cat as he races through the palace halls.

'*I* was the apple meant to spoil your barrel.'

'You were a what?'

'It's a saying,' he says. 'It doesn't matter. It was my duty to kill Elician and I failed. The Queen must have sent someone else–' He slides to a stop at one of the balcony windows. Fen crashes into his side. The gate guards that have been following them slow more gracefully, but Cat is already pointing up.

Someone is climbing the walls.

'There!' she yells, pointing too, directing the guards to see. 'Gods,' Fen chokes out. The assassin – the *Reaper* – hoists herself inside a window with far more grace than Fen and Cat had managed only hours before. There is no time to lose. Cat turns and Fen manages to outpace him just this once, and only because she knows exactly which route is the fastest.

She skids around corners, throwing open doors that Cat did not know connected to hallways that split across the palace. She keeps screaming the whole time, attracting every guard they pass in the process. They jostle from their posts, blinking at her as she continues shouting about an intruder. Lanterns are lit, soldiers draw their swords. The guards at the King and Queen's bedchambers startle and try to stop her from advancing, but when she yells, 'Assassin at the window!' they burst into the rooms for her.

The Reaper is there already.

Cat had guessed who it would be. Assumed, based on the body shape and movement. She is dressed all in black, but her hands are free. She moves with deadly purpose. The guards charge forward but all it takes is a swivel of her wrist. A bare palm to bare skin. Fen tries to scream a warning, but the guards drop dead from the frighteningly fast attack.

On their bed, Aliamon and Calissia are struggling to untangle themselves from their sheets. Fen dives forward and tackles the Reaper, tucking in her head and driving her shoulder into the Reaper's chest. They fall to the ground and the Reaper slaps and shoves at her, bare hands slapping uselessly against Fen, who gasps a deep, choking breath as one blow connects and she curls to one side. Cat snatches a fallen guard's sword. He steps forward. The Reaper turns towards Aliamon and Calissia, but Cat is there. He aims a sword at one of *his* Reaper's chests. He hisses his intention. *Stop.*

And she stops. This is their tongue. Their voice. One voice starts the chorus, a hiss with an intention, and another echoes it, matching the intention, then adding their own emotion to denote a change. He hisses it again. *Stop.* She echoes it this time, properly, profoundly, but then: an inquisition.

Are you sure?

There are people watching them. Aliamon, Calissia, Fen. Cat keeps his hand on his sword, and he meets the eyes of the Reaper who had lived in the cell directly opposite his for half his life.

'I defend them, with my life and death,' Cat swears in Lunae. 'Stop, Cieli.'

'You *know* her?' Fen asks, dumbfounded. She rises to her feet. And as she rises, Cieli kneels. She kneels and bows her head.

There is rustling at the door. Marina is there. Zinnitzia too. Marina takes in the scene with a swift glance and then looks immediately to her ward. 'Cat?' she questions softly.

And Cat turns his back to Cieli to look at the King and Queen, standing close together and looking no worse for wear despite the chaos. 'Please don't hurt her,' he asks, shifting to Soleben.

Instead of answering properly, Aliamon sighs. He lifts a hand to his eyes and shakes his head. Pinching the bridge of his nose, he says, 'I think we're going to need another private talk, you and I.' Cat bows his head but does not deny it.

Marina binds Cieli's wrists gently but firmly. Calissia peers towards the guards Cieli had killed. 'Zinnitzia, please?' she entreats quietly.

'Your Majesty . . .'

'Just this once won't hurt anything,' Aliamon says. And Zinnitzia crouches, pressing her hand to the guards' bare skin, raising them from the dead.

Which leaves Fen to slowly, anxiously, raise her voice and ask, 'What the fuck is going on?'

CHAPTER THIRTY-TWO

Fenlia

Cieli is much, much older than Cat. She is just as thin as he was when he first came to Kreuzfurt, and the mark on her face makes Fen's fingers twitch in discomfort. Cieli had stayed perfectly still when Marina bound her wrists, but Fen keeps expecting her to move again. To do whatever she had done when Fen first tried to stop her. Cieli does none of that. She stays loose and pliant as Cat murmurs to her in soft Lunae. Too soft for Fen to make out, too smooth for her to identify.

Aliamon and Calissia don robes and request that their antechamber be used to discuss the present business. Guards shuffle this way and that as they try to determine how many of them are required for the task of monitoring the assassin in their midst. Marina resolves the situation well enough. With the King's permission, she starts giving directives. Patrols are organized and sent out to look for any more intruders. From what Cieli and Cat say, there will be none. But it is possible. Anything is possible.

Fen stands awkwardly amongst them all, shivering even though the room is not cold. Calissia notices. She fetches a spare robe from her boudoir and wraps it around Fen's body. 'It was incredibly foolish of you to do what you did tonight,' the Queen tells her softly. She strokes the tangled coils of Fen's hair. In the fuss and the chaos, some of the locks have sprung free from their braids. Fen will need to redo them. She shivers again, and Calissia sighs and pulls her close. She holds Fen as Fen's teeth start to chatter. It isn't cold. She shouldn't be cold. But she is. 'Come,' Calissia murmurs. 'Let's get you to bed, yes? It is late.'

'No,' Fen replies. She shakes her head against the comforting warmth of the Queen's body, the familiar safety and relief her touch provides. 'No, I need to stay. I need to be a part of . . . this.'

'Fen . . .'

'It was my choice – to search the embassy,' Fen says. She speaks loudly, loud enough to draw the King's attention towards her. For Cat to turn as well, his sea-green eyes almost glowing in the firelight. 'It was my decision to break in there. And if we hadn't gone–' She glances towards their Reaper prisoner. 'We wouldn't have known and . . . no one had even *noticed she was here* until we said something.' She takes a deep breath in. She steps back from Calissia and tries to stand as tall and proud as her brother would have. 'I will be a part of this discussion,' she says. 'I deserve to be a part of this discussion.'

Aliamon's expression doesn't falter. He looks just as stone-faced and unflappable as before. But he looks to Calissia, who dips her head. Then he looks to Cat, who directs his attention to the floor. 'Tell me why,' Aliamon says at long last. 'Why did you ignore every order, every command, every rule that was set in front of you that forbade you from doing what you did tonight?'

Fen's stomach hurts. Her fingers tremble at her sides. She shivers. 'I swore an oath, Your Majesty,' she says. 'When you adopted me and called me "daughter", I swore an oath to this family that I would do all in my power to protect it and its future. I swore an oath to *Elician* too. And no one was doing *anything*.'

'No one was *telling* you anything,' Aliamon corrects. 'There is a difference.'

'And I found an assassin. *We* found an assassin.' Fen points to

Cat, who still will not look at her. 'You didn't have to adopt me, sire,' she continues. 'You did not have to take me in. You swore to protect me after my father died and you could have done it without making me a part of your family. But you did, and you have, and I am here. And if I am a part of this family then I want to *serve* this family. Not Kreuzfurt, not the people clambering for Givers to heal them. But *this family*. The way my father served *you*.'

'Your father trained for *years* before attempting anything close to what you two did tonight.'

'Then train me in what my father did for years, instead of giving me "life lessons" at Kreuzfurt,' Fen argues. Her cheeks flush with sudden rage. 'We did everything right. We took precautions, we had a plan, it all *worked*, and in the end, we saved your life because of what we did!'

Aliamon shakes his head repeatedly. 'You are still a child.'

'I will be sixteen soon. If soldiers can be recruited at sixteen then I can be recruited for this now. I want to help my brother. I want to serve this crown; let me serve it. Elician believed in me. You can too.' She swallows thickly. Her stomach squeezes tight with coiled anxiety and warring emotions she could not hope to name. 'Unlike my father, *I* will not die.'

Cat flinches at the claim. The Reaper behind him makes a noise, a hissing sound that is wordless, formless, just noise. Cat repeats it back at her, slower and quieter. Aliamon glances at them both from the corner of his eye before murmuring, 'There are things worse than death, Fen.'

'Then train me to face *that*.' He shakes his head. She presses on. 'I will outlive you. I will outlive Adalei, and all the members of your bloodline save Elician. I will live for maybe hundreds of years, and you adopted me into this family for a reason. Let this be my reason. I don't need to know how to *heal* people, others can do that. I need to know how to keep this family safe. To keep myself safe too when things go wrong. Please. Tell me what's going on.'

Calissia steps closer. She places a cool hand against Fen's cheek, then kisses her brow. When she pulls away, she slides her arm around Fen's back. 'Tell her,' Calissia requests. Aliamon sighs again and shakes his head. Pinches the bridge of his nose. Then, strangely, he looks towards Cat.

Cat looks back at him. His head ducks a little. His long hair has slipped from its tie in the rush of the night, and it falls into his face even as his shoulders hunch. As Fen watches, a strange hush seems to fall over the room as they wait for Cat to speak. 'My name is Alest, son of Queen Alenée of Alelune.'

Fen's breath catches in her throat. *No,* she thinks. *That's not possible.*

Cat keeps speaking, slow and steady, *still* refusing to meet her eyes. 'I was sent here, to Soleb, to kill your family, starting with Elician. But someone *in* your family is the only one who could have set up the opportunity, to make it worthwhile for my queen to send me in the first place. And only two people could have orchestrated what followed: the King or Lord Anslian.'

'Lord Anslian–' Fen exclaims, and twists, but Adalei is not in the room. She is not in the room, and she should be. Adalei is always in the room when there are discussions of matters of state. But here, now, her father is being accused of treason, and she is nowhere to be seen. Fen finally manages a half-hitching inhale, but it is not enough. Not truly.

'What you don't realize,' Aliamon says, 'is that I have known for some time that my brother orchestrated Elician's abduction, which was successful, and my death, which . . . was not.' He smiles a little at Cat, who does not share his joviality. Cat – *Alest* – remains hunched over and uncomfortable. Fen's eyes fall to the Reaper prisoner. Cieli. The one who had immediately fallen to her knees the moment her crown prince told her to stop.

'You . . . No, that . . . You can't be a *prince*. You can barely read,' Fen says, shaking her head as she tries to imagine Cat in Alelunen finery: sharp white and silvers, glittering blues, a white-gold circlet on his head, black trousers with a shimmering moon above his heart.

'I hadn't had a *chance* to read in nearly twelve years,' Cat – *Alest* – corrects. 'I forgot . . . a lot.'

'But you memorize everything!'

He shakes his head. 'I taught myself how after I died.' He motions to the Reaper they have caught. 'Cieli taught me Soleben, Brielle taught me history and mathematics, Chisenia taught me science. Any voice that could reach me, taught me. I learned. I had endless time to learn. And when all I had was my memory . . . I depended on that more than anything that came before.' He lists the names like they should mean something to her, but she does not recognize them. Does not understand the point or purpose. She shakes her head, trying to clear the roar of thoughts rising to a crescendo too loud to make sense of.

'But . . . your *mother* put you in those cells? Your *mother* took Elician?'

'I did not know Elician would be taken,' Alest continues. 'I was supposed to kill him. That's all I was told. If there were other plans . . . it is not in my queen's custom to consult me on decisions she makes.'

His queen. The possessive burns. Fen's fingers clench at the sleeves of her robes. 'That's why you refused to swear an oath of fealty to Elician,' Fen breathes out. 'You – *you couldn't*! Because you're a prince yourself. But why didn't you complete your mission . . . ? You could have killed *everybody*. It was your duty!'

And duty must always be followed.

Alest scowls at the ground. 'My duty is to my people. Killing everyone I was sent to kill . . . I do not see how that will help my people.' He had asked Aliamon to leave the Reaper assassin unharmed. Fen glances at her and swallows at the look of pure devotion on her face.

'That's not an answer,' Fen tells him anyway.

'Isn't it?' he breathes out quietly. She waits for him to say more. She waits, and it seems Aliamon is waiting too. And the Queen. And Marina, who stands guard, vigilant and quiet behind her prisoner's back. They wait, and Alest does not bother to look up to see how they watch him. He keeps his focus on the ground. He keeps his words quiet when he does finally speak but makes no other token of respect to exhausted company. 'Your brother is kind. He is . . . the kindest man I have ever known. And I did not want to repay that kindness by harming those he – unknowingly – put in danger by entrusting me to their care.'

'But what about your queen? Your people?'

'I let them down.'

The prisoner hisses something. Alest glances back towards her and shakes his head.

Fen does not know what else there is to say. She looks to her king, and Aliamon just looks tired. Drawn. He pats Alest's shoulder, squeezes it, before pulling away. Then Aliamon meets Fen's eyes.

'Anslian will try again,' he says. 'And you will not be here when he eventually succeeds.'

'But if I *am* I could keep anything from happening to you!'

'It is *forbidden* for a Giver to resurrect a member of the royal bloodline. When we die, we die. We will have no more kings clinging to power by refusing to know their time is done. One day, in the end, my brother *will* succeed. And *you will not interfere*. Nor will I give you the *chance* to interfere. Not after you and Stello Alest have bungled through every other plan I've made. I want you out of this palace. You will leave. Tonight. Your former tutor – Elena – has a practice in Crowen that serves as a cover for a safehouse in the city; you will stay with her there.'

'Elena goes to Kreuzfurt in the summers,' Alest says.

'This summer, she will not. You will go, and you will stay in Crowen. You will continue learning, and you will *wait*.'

Fen shakes her head. Her fingers curl into fists. 'If Anslian is the traitor, if you've known about it all this time, why are you doing *nothing*? Why are you just . . . just *letting* him kill you?'

'I don't owe you every answer you seek, girl. Things have been set in motion, and this whole mess would be resolved far sooner if you simply *stopped* getting in the way.'

'You were angry I didn't kill you before,' Alest says suddenly. 'You are angry now.'

'I know where my son is,' Aliamon replies. 'And I know, when Anslian manages to kill me, my son will find his freedom. One will follow the other.'

'How do you know?' Alest asks.

'Because it is my duty to know. Just as it was yours to follow orders.' The prisoner, Cieli, hisses something sharp and furious. She moves to stand, but Marina forces her back to her knees with a heavy hand to her shoulder.

'Do not talk to him like that,' Cieli barks out in strangely precise Soleben.

'I will talk to him as I like. That is *my* prerogative,' Aliamon snaps. Then, to Alest and Fen both, he declares, 'All either of you has accomplished by delaying the inevitable is ensuring Elician stays imprisoned far longer than he needed to be. You're the ones who failed him, not me.' Fen's breath catches. She shakes her head, trying to find the right words, but he doesn't give her a chance to think. 'Elician will be freed after Anslian takes my crown. Afterwards, I've made sure Elician will know to go to Crowen. You will meet him there. And perhaps then you will truly understand what it is I have done for you all.'

'You . . . you want to die?' Fen asks, struggling to understand.

'I want you out of the way,' he repeats, firm and resolute. 'Once, you might have been a queen in your own right, a proper heir I would have proudly led to the throne. But as a Giver, you are never going to be what I hoped for you.' Tears spring to her eyes. She bites her lip to keep from saying anything even as grief strangles her heart.

I never wanted to be a Giver, she does not say. *I only wanted to serve you faithfully,* she cannot say.

'But that plan will never go through, and so this one must be in its place. You're right, Fenlia. You will live a long while. And when the time comes, you will ensure Elician succeeds. Yes, you confirmed there is treason. Yes, you stopped an assassin. But it is a treason I was aware of, and a plot I had anticipated. All you have done tonight is prolong an eventuality that could have been resolved far sooner. But you will study. And you will learn. You will do better. You will not *fail* this crown again. When you are given a command, you will *follow* it despite your grievances. Swear it.'

With tears still streaking down her cheeks, she takes a swift breath in, puts her hand on her heart, and bows. 'I swear.'

'Then go. Both of you, prepare to leave the city. I will speak with you again before you depart. I need time to think.'

Fen takes a few steps back. Alest does not. 'Cieli,' he says quietly.

'Will remain unharmed,' Aliamon replies. 'Go. I will speak to you of the future later.' Alest does not bow. He bends his neck slightly, then follows Fen towards the door.

When it closes behind them, Fen looks into Alest's face and tries to hold the name in her mind. For a long while, he had just been Cat. But now . . . he looks back at her. His lips part like he wants to say something, but he says nothing. He just turns and walks away.

PART IV

As each new being walked the earth, some earned the gods' particular favour. To the Givers, Life blessed them with the chance to heal and protect all those not yet ready for death and the change of the time after. He cast his great light upon these Givers, granting blessings and protection from Death and her attempts at subversion.

But Death would not be outdone, and in turn, she gave her grace and power to those she called her Reapers. She asked only that they take for her those who have lived for too long. Or those who needed to stop, restart, and one day live again. Death took lives for herself too. Often and without remorse – even those who were not yet ready to change. She took them, and reworked them, all to test and tease and tempt the great followers of Life and his golden sun. Always asking the question: why must you stay still, why must you stop? Why can you not do more?

And so, the world was made. Life and Death painting lines on the canvas of a world ever changing, granting grace and giving colour to lives that never stay the same. The Sun and the Moon were always slipping in and around one another, and always working towards one goal: to ensure there was never again another void, and that the cycle of life and death remained constant in the world.

– *The Origins of the Gods*, Anonymous

CHAPTER THIRTY-THREE

Elician

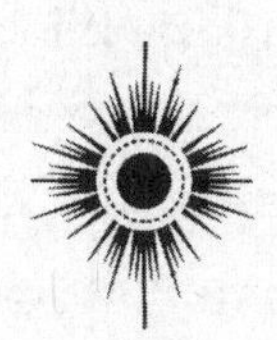

Elician's spider companion survives the frigid winter, the uncertain spring, and manages to last all the way until the end of summer before finally curling its little legs inwards and dying on the sill. Elician wakes to see its body just as the first chill air of a new fall begins to curl through his room. A flutter of wings at the window announces the arrival of a sharp-eyed sparrow who snatches up the spider's remains and flies off with it. 'Such is life persevering,' he murmurs, wishing the spider a good life when its soul returns.

'Morsen . . . are you there?' he asks. There is no response. Someone else must be on duty. Tucking his knees closer to his chest, he imagines himself somewhere else. At Soleb's harvest festival, watching Lio and Adalei laughing, dancing. Then at their wedding, surrounded by oranges and yellows, autumn at its finest. *They will have the most beautiful children,* Elician knows. For years, he has known that he will never sire any child of his own. That he has no intention of creating a family just to watch them die. He couldn't, and wouldn't, stop Lio and Adalei from forming the family they want though, so he has resigned himself to loving their descendants just as he loves them. The future princes and princesses of Himmelsheim will want for nothing; they will giggle and run and play without fear or self-doubt. He will read to them. Make the world beautiful for them. And then he will leave it in their hands to build before the pain of losing them too becomes too much to bear.

He hears footsteps in the hall. Not Eline's heels though. Someone else.

Gillage throws open the door. Elician opens his eyes slowly, wearily, from where he rests on the floor. 'Get up,' the prince orders, kicking under the bed and striking Elician's shoulder. Pain blossoms then fades. Slowly, Elician crawls out. He looks up.

Gillage is dressed in the finest garb Elician has ever seen on him. The fabric of his tunic is a deep midnight blue. It glitters with silver sequins and reaches down to his mid-thigh. He has a wide belt around his waist and an almost comical-looking sword at his side, though Elician doubts the boy has ever used it before. Gillage's curls have been flattened too, with some kind of substance that seems to have adhered each lock to his scalp. He is wearing a circlet.

'Are we going somewhere?' Elician asks, standing slowly, eyes fixated on the silver band. His knees creak as he rises. His body aches.

'My mother has summoned you to court,' Gillage replies. 'I'm to escort you.'

'Efficiency in this country really leaves much to be desired. She *just* discovered I'm here now?'

Gillage slaps him across the face.

'I'm starting to think that's just how your people say hello,' Elician mumbles.

Gillage's guards drag him out of the door so roughly that Elician trips over his own feet. Gillage laughs, kicking Elician's knee to compound his difficulties, then daintily jumps over Elician's crumpled body.

'And *I'm* starting to think your people should stay on your knees, since you're so desperate to get down there,' Gillage says, affecting a bored undertone that gets right under Elician's skin.

'Well, why wouldn't we?' he grits out, struggling to stand. 'Your flooring is the only thing worth mentioning in your entire country.'

Gillage's face has returned to that splotchy purple-red that precedes most of his tirades. 'If we were not on our way to my mother, I'd cut your heart out of your throat.'

'Wrong part of the body, Your Highness, but it's always a good idea to practise your anatomy.'

'Your Highness?' Nured asks, interrupting the boy before he can say or do anything else.

'We don't have to keep your little plaything alive, down in the cells,' Gillage reminds Elician. 'Remember that the next time you think about misbehaving. I won't hesitate to send you bits and pieces of your *friend* until every inch of him lines your room.'

Elician nods, forces his expression to something approaching courtesy. 'Yes, Stello.' Gillage grins wide enough that Elician almost retracts the honorific that does not belong to the boy. Instead, he keeps his lips pressed shut and follows Gillage to the Queen.

They have not blindfolded him this time. Gillage and his entourage walk with such confidence that Elician half wonders *why*. He does his best not to appear obvious, but with every twist and turn they take, he memorizes the route and some unique feature to ensure he doesn't lose his way. He spies one path that leads down to the courtyard of the palace. Another that leads out to a garden.

One hall is permeated with the smell of food. His mouth waters as he imagines juices on his tongue, savoury sauces, wines, vegetables. He has eaten nothing in months. There has been no need to feed him. He cannot die. He would call Gillage 'Stello' again if it ensured him even an apple. He also knows it is not worth the exchange. There are other, bigger things he would exchange for conferring the honour. Lio's life and well-being aren't comparable to an apple.

The doors leading to the throne room are massive. They are made of wood, intricately carved with beasts of legend. Griffons and dragons, phoenixes and harpies, a nightcat lurking in the shadows just behind. Two members of Gillage's escort open the doors. He walks in first, head held up and smiling widely.

The hall is similar to the great hall in Himmelsheim. For half a moment, he is disoriented. Then, he realizes: the halls are inverses of one another. Twinned, even. Something hard shoves Elician in the shoulder, and he stumbles after Gillage along the mirrored hall. An assemblage of finely dressed men and women stand on either side of the Queen's dais. Some carry marks and banners that denote their territorial allegiance. Elician's book on Alelunen history gives him some perspective there, at least. He looks for the one that had interested him the most, but as far as he can tell, there is no representative from the Blue Palace here.

As they draw closer to the dais, the Queen quickly becomes his only focus. She sits on her throne wearing an elegant gown. Its shimmering fabric and the glistening embroidery speak to the finest craftsmanship in Alelune, potentially the world. Silver leaves on white branches climb from her skirt to her chest. The base colour is a deep midnight black, offsetting the glittering design so sharply and beautifully that Elician's fingers twitch from the mad desire just to touch the fabric and feel how it's been woven. Her collar is low cut, and an intricate necklace cradles her neck as a pendant nestles just above her bosom. A moonstone. Multi-coloured and glimmering.

Elician lifts his eyes higher, and when he meets hers, he cannot help but stare. Cat – *Alest* – looks just like her. Far more than Gillage does. Alenée's brown hair is naturally straight, though styled into an intricate arrangement on the top of her head. Her chin rounds out towards a jaw that is perhaps a touch too wide to be considered conventionally attractive. But her eyes – she shares the exact same sea-green eyes as her oldest son. Elician had spent days looking at Alest's eyes. They had been beautiful then, and the same shade pierces him just as brutally now.

'I know your son,' Elician says, not waiting to be introduced or bothering to care about protocol. He has been her prisoner far too long to care. He has no more patience for such a thing.

'And I knew your father,' the Queen replies. She snaps her fingers, and a chest is brought forward. The lid opens, and Elician glances inside. He wishes he had not. There is a head there. Drained of blood. Set with preserves. Someone is talking, but the words are washed out and unintelligible, drowned by a great echoing tunnel of noise that reaches its crescendo in a sharp ringing that leaves no room for anything else.

He knows that head. Knows that face. The attendant reaches down and plucks it out by its hair. Holds it before Elician's eyes as if he needed it upright to recognize features not so unlike his own.

His father's mouth hangs open. The skin around his eyes sags, mishappen and ringed with dark purple circles. Blood mars the flesh beneath his nose. No one had bothered to clean that during the preservation process, and his father's usually richly tanned skin has lost its natural vibrancy, turning an unpalatable waxy sand colour. Aliamon's long hair is a spongy mess of black, the locks sheared and shorn at the neck from whichever strike severed the skull from its body.

Sound returns.

Queen Alenée is speaking. 'I sent the Reaper boy–'

'Your son,' Elician murmurs, unable to take his eyes from his father's misshapen face. His own head tilts slightly, the weight of his body suddenly too heavy and too light in turn.

'What was that?' the Queen asks, not hearing him. Elician steps towards his father. What is left of his father. Decaying muscle and rotting flesh. He wonders when it happened. Laughs, almost, at the incredulity of that thought alone. Yet, logic is easier to process than anything else. It is safer than anything else.

'Your son,' he repeats, no louder than he had the first time. The hall is silent, though. Silent save for his footsteps. They echo. They echo like the beating of a drum, the steady thumping of his heart. He reaches out. The attendant holding the head looks back at the Queen in her beautiful dress. She must make some kind of gesture because soon the head is thrust at Elician's chest. He catches it with both arms. It is not heavy. Not really. Shouldn't it be heavier? He holds it close. 'Not the *Reaper* boy. You sent *your son* to your enemy.'

His hands touch the weathered flesh, but there is nothing there. No soul to call back. No tether to make whole. Without his father's soul, there is nothing Elician can do. He is almost certain he could remake a body if he needed to, reforming it from only a head. But a body is nothing without a spark of Life. And Death has seen to it: Aliamon will never return. *It's forbidden to revive a king,* Elician thinks hysterically. Vertigo tips him forward. Militant determination keeps him upright.

'The Reaper's job was to–'

'Alest.' Elician looks up. *Don't look back down. Don't look and see!* He meets those sea-green eyes. The skin on his father's face shifts beneath his touch. Nausea spirals through him. He does not want to think of his father. Does not want to have this conversation. Not at the same time. Not all at once. But he must. He has no way out. He meets her eyes and says, 'Alest, Stello of Alelune, heir to your throne. That is who you sent to Soleb. Your *son*.' The head feels so wrong in his hands, and he can't bear it a moment more. Elician places it on the floor, tears off his filthy shirt, and then swaddles the head tenderly like a babe. Shocked and surprised voices burst out all around him. 'You sent your son to murder the Soleben royal family. And yet, he did not do this. This is not the mark of a Reaper's work.' Alest did not kill his father. This, he *knows*.

'You're quite certain,' she says. But she does not sound surprised.

'A Reaper doesn't need to commit this level of violence to kill someone. Stello Alest would not have *needed* to do this.'

'The head was severed after death.' She shrugs. 'But you are right. Your father died falling from his horse. Though, with some help. Your uncle was kind enough to do this' – she flicks a hand towards the swaddled head – 'as confirmation of his work.' Elician blinks slowly, trying to check definitions of words he *knows* he knows. His understanding of Lunae fails him, though; her words spill forth and he can only stare at her, uncomprehending. Syllables arch across his consciousness, and all his mind can do is skip back to the last thing he truly thought he understood correctly. *Uncle.*

'My uncle killed my father?' he says in the most basic conjugations he thinks he can manage. He must have interrupted her. The Queen stares at him for a moment, lips pursed in displeasure before returning to that placid predator's smile.

'At my request. A sign of friendship, to end this bloody war.' No. That does not make any sense. His uncle loved his father. Loves their family. Elician blinks. Hard. He shakes his head.

'Why send Stello Alest to Soleb if my uncle was going to kill my father?'

'That *thing* is not the Stello. *I* am!' Gillage hisses. Elician had forgotten all about him the moment the head had been revealed, but now he finds the boy. He's lurking like a gargoyle at the base of the dais leading to Queen Alenée's glittering throne. His face has gone purple as he clenches his fists and trembles visibly. Elician wonders if the boy will slap him again in front of all these people. He cannot find it in him to care.

The Queen intercedes. She says, 'Enough, Gillage,' as if her child is little more than a yapping dog. But, like a yapping dog, Gillage ignores the command.

'Mother, *I'm* the Stello.'

'Alest is your firstborn son,' Elician says, talking over Gillage. 'He is alive. He is alive and in Soleb, and you know this.' He glances at the courtiers, the guards, the people who are all in attendance before their queen. None of them are surprised. 'You all know this,' he murmurs.

'My son is dead. The Reaper I sent to Soleb is that which replaced my son when he died.'

'And yet he lives, and breathes, and speaks . . . and he did not kill the king you sent him to kill.' Murmurs start up around him. His head spins. Vertigo swivels his senses, producing a violent tremor. He is shaking, he realizes.

The Queen persists, dogged in her relentless pursuit of something Elician cannot quite understand. 'Your father is a traitor to his country by not seeking terms to end this war.'

'To end it? You're the one who breached the Marias Compromise!'

'And you're the ones who forced that compromise into place. You're the ones who broke the Night Accords that granted us the Bask in 876–'

'But that's all we ever do! Both of us. You take the river, then we take the river, then–' Elician shakes his head. He shakes it again. He squeezes his eyes shut, struggles to regain control of his emotions even as his father's *head* is nestled against his chest, and when he opens his eyes, he meets Queen Alenée's unflinching gaze. 'Do not speak to me of traitors when you abandoned your *rightful heir* to be tortured in your own prisons.'

Gillage begins to screech, 'I am–'

His mother cuts him off. 'Silence, Gillage.'

The whole court is silent. It is as if no one dares to even breathe. *She isn't denying it,* Elician thinks dully. *Alest is still her heir.* He glances at the little goblin prince, the cruel and desperate boy at the bottom of the dais. *It must burn, to be so unwanted.*

Queen Alenée raises her hand and flicks her delicate fingers to the left. 'Bring him in,' she commands. Elician waits. All he has done since he was captured is wait. A side door opens to the right, and he hears the sound of dragging steps, making him turn to watch who enters. He'd been determined to stare at the Queen until inspiration somehow struck on just how to murder her on her precious throne. Until he could find a way to sever her head from her body, just like his murdered father. But the steps are getting closer, and the Queen is watching the door–

'Lio!' His oldest friend is dragged across the floor and thrown to the ground at his feet. Elician kneels at his side. Lio struggles to push

himself upright. Their hands collide, then Lio's fingers shift to grasp Elician's forearm.

'You're late,' Lio tells him in *their* tongue. Not Lunae. Soleben. Their own language. And even the relief of hearing it, in its remembered beauty, is overshadowed by Lio's *evident* decline in health. Lio is emaciated and filthy, and his hair has started to fall out in clumps, leaving bald patches along his scalp and behind his ears. Elician places a hand to the back of Lio's neck and touches their brows together – offering comfort. Lio is the one who pulls back first, staring down at the horrible token Elician has wrapped in his own shirt. 'What . . .'

'My father's head,' Elician explains breathlessly. Lio's lips part. He stares at it even as Elician repeats himself, 'I'm holding my father's head,' and laughs, hysterical suddenly, at the realization he has no idea what else he is meant to do in this circumstance. *It is possible,* he realizes, *that I've lost my mind.*

'As I was saying,' Queen Alenée announces. Elician flinches. He glances her way. He holds the wrapped head closer and squeezes Lio's neck just a little. Feels every ailment in his friend's body through his palm. He is starving, dehydrated, malnourished – and several muscles are in various states of atrophy. Absently, Elician starts healing the muscles first. It feels so *good*, healing something and experiencing the sensation of success for a change. Each muscle stitching itself back into working order sends a thrill through Elician's body. There is no Reaper here tearing his work apart. There is no Eline writing on her clipboard, taking notes and blood – and studying, always studying. This is the way it is meant to be. The *only* way it is meant to be. 'Due to your own reported demise, Prince Elician, your uncle Anslian is now King of Soleb. In a matter of days, we will sign a peace treaty at the Blessedsafe neutral zone. The terms are still in negotiation.' *Blessedsafe.* That's not what it's called in Soleben. It's the Kingsclave. She intends to meet Anslian at the Kingsclave.

'Elician's not *actually* dead, and you both know that though,' Lio bites out. The Queen's eyes snap to him. Elician's heart pounds faster. He digs his nails into Lio's neck in warning.

'Here are *my* terms prior to the signing.' The Queen stands. She leaves her dais, and her courtiers bow their heads and avert their eyes. Elician and Lio do not do the same. They watch her as she approaches. As she crouches down to their level. Her skirts fold outward like the lapping waves of a perfect pond. The moonstone shimmers gloriously as it dangles between them. She dips her voice low, a quiet conversation between her and them. An appeasement to their circumstances, a bargain over the head of her enemy laid in the hands of a king without a crown. She says, 'You are a Giver. Thus, it is within your ability to *give* me a child using your . . . unique talents.'

And Elician, expecting land or fiscal benefits, says, 'What?'

'I have tried for twenty years to have an heir worthy of my throne. Instead, I have a dead thing and a monster. Give me a child, and you will be returned to Soleb. You can take up your throne, and the peace between our countries will remain. Giverborn are *always* female. I'll have my heir and you'll have your kingdom.'

'And what of Alest? You already have an heir.'

Alenée pauses only for a moment. Then, with perfect precision, says, 'With a female child, he would no longer be my true heir.' Gillage gasps; some of the assembly murmur, talking amongst themselves, but Alenée ignores them. She presses on. 'He may stay in Soleb and live a long and happy life far from our borders, never to return.' Elician falls still. This woman, a mother twice over, looks back at him. 'We each have our roles to play, young prince. Give me this daughter, and you can go back to playing the role your family set out for you. You can keep Alest, you can keep your kingdom. The war will not reconvene. It will be over.'

It would not take long. A hand pressed against her abdomen. A desire for life to bloom in her already capable body. He would need to stay for the gestation. Stay until the Stella was born and first drew breath. After that . . . he could go home. Alelune would have its heir. Lio and Adalei would finally have a chance to be together and have a child of their own. Both countries' futures would be secure. Anslian . . . He does not know what Anslian would do, but would that matter? He could manage the chaos his uncle has caused once he gets home. *Home.* He could go home. Elician glances past the Queen, towards her son.

Maybe culture and custom demanded the Queen's actions towards Alest, her son and heir. She is the leader of both faith and country. Maybe she was not in a position to deny centuries' worth of tradition just because her son had unfortunately become a Reaper. Their laws demanded she imprison him. Their laws demanded she keep him separated from her people. Maybe she *had* arranged for Alest to escape to a better place. Maybe she *had* known all along that he would not kill Elician or his father, but that he could find a better life in Soleb.

But that does not explain Gillage.

That does not explain why Gillage is so brutal and violent. Why he has no clear confirmation of his position in court. Nor how he can be allowed to torment the Reapers in the cells below, and relish in his cruelty. Gillage is so desperate to prove himself, and so lacking in any kind of alternative path forward, that he still clings to his ill-fitting title of Stello with hands and teeth.

Queen Alenée may not have had a choice with Alest, but she did have one with Gillage. And *giving* a child to her would be condemning that child to the same kind of life her brothers have faced. A potential for abandonment, exile and torment. A life that, Elician is certain, would have no peace. 'No,' he says quietly. 'I won't do it.'

The Queen does not seem surprised. He doubts *anything* could surprise her. 'The agreement with your uncle necessitates a child,' the Queen says. 'My line secured, for the war's end. He promised this to me . . . either by your hand, or by your sister's.'

'My sister's not very good at being a Giver,' Elician tells her. 'She cannot give you what you want.'

'It does not matter if she can only fix a broken bone or a runny nose, she is a Giver one way or another. If I cannot have a daughter, then . . . I will give your *sister* to Gillage as a bride. She just turned sixteen last month, isn't that right?' Lio stiffens beneath Elician's touch. The muscles that Elician has just healed turn rigidly tense once more. Elician's senses flare in discomfort as he feels Lio's limbs beginning to tremble under their sudden strain. 'And one thing that's certain about Giver-mothers . . . they *always* bear healthy children.'

'Gillage and Fen are still children themselves,' Elician murmurs. It is a terrible argument. It is not even *an* argument. The words slip out and he is too exhausted and worn low to know what he is supposed to say. But Gillage is . . . fifteen now? That is insane. It has to be insane. This cannot be right. This cannot be. 'Nineteen is the marriageable age in Soleb–'

'The truce your uncle and I are brokering begins when my heir is born. How long that takes is up to you and your sister. But one of you will provide me with a *proper* Stella.'

'But she can't give you that either. She's not your blood and Death's line has to pass down via a female heir – or you can't prove their child is Death's chosen line.' Cat's explanation, from well over a year ago now, rings through Elician's mind. Alelune requires proof. Proof that the line is unbroken. A child born from a woman's body is undoubtedly the blood of that woman. Gillage is Death's line, but even if he were to lie with someone there would be no way to *prove* that the child that woman gives birth to is his. She could have taken another lover. And the line could be broken. In all past circumstances, another queen was chosen, from an earlier break in the line. Or, failing that: Death herself chose a new queen. Perhaps she should now. Perhaps a god's intervention is exactly what they all need.

'We could prove that it's his child,' the Queen says slowly. Elician thinks of the option Cat had suggested, abandoned because it was an unconscionable decision then, and still is now. Imprisoning the woman. Keeping her under constant observation to *make certain* no one but the Stello has access to her. 'We would only need to prove that she truly carries *his* child. Then the line is unbroken.'

'No,' he says again. 'You cannot have her and . . . I will *never* give you a child.' His child. Made because of him. He . . . he cannot. He will not. He *will not* think about it.

The Queen sighs. She stands up. Her skirt moves in a fluid wave, fabric folding beautifully back into position. Her hands fold charmingly in front of her, and she nods to Elician. A bargain struck whether he wished it or not. He has no control over the former and she cannot pursue the latter. It does not matter what he says. He cannot stop this.

'Then I have no need to keep you comfortable,' she informs him. 'Kill the spare.'

The Queen turns back to her dais. Her courtiers lift their heads. 'What?' Elician asks, stupid and slow. He cannot die. She *cannot* kill him. He will survive any blow they give him.

His fingers spasm on Lio's neck. The Queen sits on her throne and Elician meets his best friend's eyes. The guards are coming.

His father's head falls from Elician's grasp. Elician stumbles to his feet, pulling Lio up with him. He swivels on his heel. There are too many and they advance from all directions. Marching like ants to a rotted fruit waiting to be carried back to their nest. 'No.' Elician shakes his head. He pulls Lio closer. He does not know where to go. Does not know what to do.

'Elician,' Lio murmurs.

'No!'

Somewhere, he hears Gillage laughing. Laughing and clapping his hands in glee. But how can Gillage be pleased, when earlier he had been delighting in the chance to give pieces of Lio to Elician as a gift? Enjoying the prospect of his slow torment? If the guards kill Lio now, Gillage cannot torture him later. They cannot find a way to escape either. They cannot get out of this.

Swords are being drawn. A hand grabs at Elician's arm. He whirls about and punches the man who tried to restrain him. More bodies are coming. More hands. Blades are swinging through the air. Elician shoves Lio out of the way and feels one slice brutally through his own arm. Blood splatters all around them, but the wound heals quick as can be.

'*No!*' Elician yells. He fights with every ounce of energy he has. He throws himself at them, kicking and scratching. He twists a sword out of one guard's hand and takes it for his own. He spars. Dizzy, and without having expended this much energy since he last fought on the front lines, Elician throws himself at the men who come to end Lio's life.

He thrusts his blade into their bellies. He parries and ducks and dives under their relentless brutality. He carves open arteries and veins, and he beats them all back from where Lio lies, weakened, behind him. '*Idiot,*' Gillage laughs.

Elician turns. The would-be stello has drawn the ceremonial sword that he has been toting about as if he knows how to wield it. He grins, savage and wrong. He swings it down, and Lio mouths a word that never sees the light. The blade lands right against the soft expanse of Lio's throat. Blood gushes and spurts from the terrible wound. And Elician is falling forward, hand outstretched. *Heal, heal it, I can heal it!* But hands and blades descend on his body.

He is crushed to the ground, Lio just out of reach. '*NO!*'

'You know my terms,' the Queen says, bored and uncaring.

'*NO!*'

She flicks her hand. 'Clean the mess, take him away. Congratulations, Gillage, you're engaged.' She stands once more and seems to float from the room, her dress shimmering with each step. Elician screams after her. Screams as they drag him back. Screams as Lio's body is lifted by its ankles and pulled farther and farther away.

'Lio! Lio!'

'Oh, shut him up,' someone grumbles.

A sharp pain slices through Elician's brain, a mockery of his first day in captivity, and he knows no more.

CHAPTER THIRTY-FOUR

Elician

Elician's mother fell ill the moment he was born. She lay in bed, burning from fever and unable to lift her hands to hold her babe to her chest.

Elician remembers the story as he sits, once more, in the cold dark of the Reaper cells. In Alest's cell. In Lio's. His father used to tell him that Verine d'Altas had only given birth to Lio a few weeks before Calissia gave birth to Elician. That she came to the palace to nurse the infant prince, and when the rest of the court fluttered fitfully around the Queen, she watched over Elician and her son. Never again had either boy been parted.

Even when his mother recovered and could tend to him on her own, Elician screamed and howled and wailed for his milk-brother, only calming when he could cling to the chubby baby he had known from his first day alive. Then it simply became accepted. Lio became the youngest sworn member of the royal court, and Elician was given the most precious gift he had ever had.

Lio had been there when Elician first fell and noticed his hands healing before his eyes. He had lied to everyone they'd ever met about who and what Elician was. He fought harder and faster than anyone Elician knew, desperate to be a guard worthy of a prince. Worthy of Adalei, too.

Adalei. Elician presses his hands to his face. He can almost imagine the feeling of Lio's skin beneath his palm. The sweat that had beaded on his neck as they'd listened to the Queen's demands. *Adalei's going to kill me,* Elician thinks. He almost feels relieved at the notion. He is too tired to live anymore. To face a future existence that goes on for ever, knowing Fen is soon to be deposited in Alelune – forced to bear a child for a sadistic prince far from home. Also knowing that his father had died at his uncle's hands. Knowing that he could not even save one person. Not one person he actually cared about. *What was the point of all these years of lying?*

Even the guards he killed while defending Lio had been brought back to life while he had been unconscious. A trick Gillage had delighted in informing him of. They had only needed to move Elician's hands to their bodies, and without conscious effort at all, the guards sprang to life as if nothing had happened. The mere thought is more violating than it has any right to be.

The Reapers watch him in their cells. Some had been singing when he first awoke, half-naked and cold in Alest's cell. Their song was a strange kind of celebratory relief that hurt worse than any funeral dirge he has ever known. *Finally, it's over,* the song seemed to suggest. Finally, Lio was at peace. And they were glad for it. He swipes at the tears on his cheeks. He thought he didn't have any more crying left in him, but he supposes his body is healing that too. Providing them endlessly, to show his misery is real. That it is ever present. That it cannot be taken away by Gillage, the Queen or Alelune.

'Where do they take the dead?' Elician asks the Reapers of Alerae. Somewhere, someone, maybe Morsen, is walking down the endless hall. Footsteps echo, but no voices. 'If someone dies' – Elician wipes his wet cheeks – 'where do they take them?'

'You mean, where did they take Lio?' Brielle corrects from his left.

'Yes.' A childhood memory of skinned knees and lies floods him. Promises made under fireflies. Poems written in the night for a girl Lio had been destined to marry. Thoughts run through

Elician's mind. Images and memories, shattered dreams and desperate prayers. His desperation seems fitting, as he lies where Alest once lay. Where a frightened boy had been sentenced by his mother. The same mother who wants to turn Elician's sister into a broodmare and call it peace.

'There's a pit.' Brielle points down the hall. Points as though her finger could spear through wall and stone and darkness, emerging into the world above and reaching a target with the accuracy of a seasoned hunter.

Elician shifts to his knees. He places his head on the ground, his palms shoulder-width apart. His brow kisses the alabaster stone, and he turns towards where Lio's body lies, and he stays there. Eyes shut. Hands cool against the earth.

This is not a prayer.

Come back, Elician wills. He reaches out with his mind as much as he can. *Come back.*

The first time Lio died, they had been climbing the walls. Elician had just reached the top and Lio was right behind him. Then the crevice he had been using as a handhold failed. Elician watched, horrified, as his friend plummeted back to the earth – shattering his spine and his skull in the process. He had been too stunned to scream. No one had been watching them. Why would they need to? They could not get hurt.

Except.

They *could* get hurt. Lio could get hurt. Elician had scrambled down the wall as fast as he could. He pressed his palms to Lio's body, trembling as he thought *what if . . . what if . . . what if I can't . . .* but Lio jerked upright only seconds after Elician made contact. His spine straightened, his veins filling with the exact amount of blood he needed to survive. And Lio held Elician as he sobbed apologies and promised never to climb the walls again.

(That, like promising to never again bring someone back to life, was a lie.)

Elician has resurrected Lio far too many times since. Sometimes, he felt like he was in a constant tug of war with Death. Death wanted to take Lio for her own, but Elician refused to let him go. Refused to part with the only person he had ever felt truly comfortable with. Who had always known every part of Elician's soul and who had never once turned his back on him.

I'm going to die of old age one day, Lio had told him once, years ago, covered in blood from a day of fighting a war without end. Elician, too tired to say anything, had only rolled over to look up at him. Waiting. Expecting. Lio smiled. *I'm going to leave you with a couple of kids who'll take care of you, just like me.* His smile grew bigger and bigger. *And you'll never be alone, little brother. You'll always have someone there with you, no matter what.*

Elician squeezes his eyes shut. He breathes in deep through his nose and out through his mouth. He grinds his brow into the alabaster. He pushes against the earth, commanding it to bend to his will and his will alone. Lio's skin is a feeling Elician memorized years ago. His heart a steady *thump thump . . . thump thump . . . thump thump . . .* that speeds up only in combat or when he looks at Adalei. *Adalei.*

I promised to bring him home to you, Elician thinks. *Come back. Come back, brother, come back. I promised Adalei you'd come back. So come back. Come back.*

Two hundred and six bones, six hundred and fifty muscles, one hundred and eighty-seven joints, oxygen, carbon, hydrogen, nitrogen, calcium and phosphorus, but most importantly: soul. The soul. It rests in the body. It shines and sparkles with life more than anything else. It is the first thing that shatters under a Reaper's touch. The precious ether that keeps everything running, dissipating the moment a Reaper begins their trade. But so long as there is a soul Elician can reach . . . then anything is possible. Anyone can return.

Elician has spent enough time lately fighting Reapers for control over a person's soul, and he can trace the exact form and shape of Death's influence. He can picture it like a painting formed of shadow. The feeling of a soul: electric and vital. It is pepper and mint, hot and cold, sweet and salty. It is clashing flavours and wondrous sensations. Rain before it falls. Ozone right before lightning strikes. It is the feeling of resting your head against a warm chest and listening to a heart beating right beneath your ear. It is an invisible force, constantly in motion, felt but never seen.

Come back.

Gillage's blade cut Lio's trachea, his jugular and his carotid. He bled out in seconds. Elician is still drenched in the blood that should be in Lio's body. He can feel it. Every atom. Every molecule. Every twisting strand of unique matter that makes Lio *Lio*.

Come back.

Elician's palms become warm. The blood that has soaked into his clothes, Lio's blood, feels suddenly fresh and vibrant with life . . . and falls onto the stones. He breathes in through his nose, out through his mouth. He presses his hands even harder against the ground. In his mind, he sees Lio lying in a mass grave. Sees him with his star-bright eyes staring up at the heavens. The moon. Staring up at the moon. He sees Lio's torn throat. His lax posture.

Come back.

He imagines the wound closing. Elician's hands burn against the alabaster. Someone hisses. The Reapers always hiss when they want to pass messages, but Elician does not care. Cannot care. Everything is meaningless. Everything except for the thread between him and his friend – his brother.

Come back.

The throat closes in Elician's mind. The wound heals itself perfectly. There is not even a scar. Blood replenishes itself in Lio's body, produced by will and dedication.

Come back.

Lio's heart starts to beat. Even at a distance, his heart starts to beat. Elician sees it in his mind. Feels it in his hands. He can even feel the ground trembling beneath his palm. *Thump thump, thump thump, thump thump.* Electricity sparks within Lio's brain.

Come back.

And the soul. Lio's soul . . .

Elician presses his head as hard as he can to the ground. His tears mix with Lio's blood, fresh and wet against the alabaster. 'Please, brother . . . come back.'

Lio's eyes snap open in that other place. He jerks for air, and Elician throws himself backwards in his cell. His head clangs against the bars behind him. He gags, trying to breathe but finding no air. His body is burning. He is on fire. He is on *fire.* His clothes are alight, and he beats his palms against them, coughing against the smoke and trying to catch his breath.

He gags as the fire is finally put out. The Reapers are hissing louder and louder to each other. Something *clunks* at the far end of the hall. Something loud. A guard. Elician coughs and tries to find fresh air. He swings his hand through the smoke. He does not know where it all came from or how. The footsteps are approaching faster now. Voices are sparking all around.

Elician slaps his hands against his eyes. He rubs as hard as he can, and when he finally manages to see, a figure has positioned itself in front of him. Keys jangle loudly as the cell is unlocked.

Morsen kneels down to look at him. 'Your Majesty,' he says softly. *Majesty.* Not *Highness.* Because his father is dead. And that would mean . . .

'But my uncle's king now,' Elician says, correcting him.

'*You* are the rightful king, Your Majesty.' The bars swing open. A hand is extended. 'I can get you out.'

'Out?' The words do not make sense. Elician presses his palms to his face. He rubs the tears from his eyes. Slowly, he returns to a crouch. He crawls, on hands and knees, towards Morsen, and lets the man pull him the rest of the way out of the cage. When he stands, his head spins. He loses his balance and leans against the bars behind him. His breath shudders.

Morsen braces him. Keeps him upright. 'Come with me.' Morsen motions down the endless hall, peers into a darkness where Elician has never been. Elician shakes his head in response.

'Lio . . .'

'He's dead, Your Majesty. You are the Soleben king. You need to return home. The Queen is leaving for the Kingsclave to meet with your uncle. If that new treaty is signed–'

'*Fen.*' Elician's brain feels like it is a step behind. Many steps behind. He tries to conjure an image of his little sister, still in the middle of growing up, her limbs too long, her joints too bony, her anger entirely justified. He trembles as he thinks of her in any state of captivity. Of her being *here*, under Gillage's sadistic care.

Adalei is going to kill him, Elician knows this, but hopefully she will do it after he keeps Fen from suffering an even worse fate than Lio. He shakes his head again, like a wet dog throwing loose every stray droplet of pain and despair. He tries to get his feet to cooperate. His legs. He shifts on his heel and looks up. Brielle.

Brielle's brown eyes are staring straight at him. She emerges from the shadows, glowing in the faint light of the torch that Morsen has brought with him. Her lips are pressed together. Her hands wrap around the bars as she looks straight into Elician's soul. 'Unlock her cage,' Elician murmurs.

'What?'

Elician makes a haphazard grab for the keys in Morsen's hand. He gets them on his first attempt, and it is likely the shock that has Morsen just give them to him. Stumbling a little, Elician lets himself fall, boneless, before the lock to Brielle's cell. He tries the first key. It is not a good fit. He goes for the next.

'Your Majesty–'

'Can you . . . can you get them out?' Elician asks Brielle, gesturing to the many cages. 'Get them all out?'

Her hand reaches through the bars. She touches his knuckles. Wraps her fingers around his palm. 'We took care of Lio as best we could,' she tells him softly, her wizened voice resonating in his soul. He nods, tries another key. It does not fit. He goes for another. 'He was a good boy . . . a sweet boy.'

He pushes the key into the lock. Hears Morsen shifting about, nervous and unsettled. 'He was my brother,' Elician says. He turns the key. The lock slips to the side. The cage opens, and Brielle shifts to wrap her arms around Elician's neck. She holds him close, maternal and kind. The kind of hug that Alest should have had growing up. The kind he knows from the bottom of his heart that Brielle would never have given Elician had she not deemed him worthy of receiving it. He asks again, 'Can you get them out?'

'They may not wish to leave,' Brielle tells him. 'Where would we go?'

He does not know. He cannot even begin to know. He feels like he has never known anything in his life. As though every year of his past has been a useless charade of experiences that have led him to a point of pure stupidity. He is at the top of a wall he wanted to climb in his hubris, and Lio is down at the bottom: shattered and broken. Only this time there is no fixing him. There is only imagining a resurrection that is impossible to achieve.

'Why stay *here*?' he asks instead. 'Here, like this . . . for ever?'

'Because there is nowhere else to go. And there are *countless* cells just like this all over the country. We will be caught and returned either to these cells or another. There is no other life for us.'

That cannot be it. That cannot be good enough for her. For them. He trembles in her grasp. He cannot just leave her here. Like this. He cannot seek freedom without all the rest getting theirs too. He cannot face Alest and tell him he left them all behind. 'Brielle–'

'Tell *our* stello we follow *him*,' Brielle says. 'And we will wait for the day he comes back to us.'

No. That isn't fair. Elician pulls away. He meets Brielle's dark eyes. 'He's free,' he whispers. He cannot imagine finding *Cat* in Soleb and ordering him home. Cannot imagine sending him back to his mother and this viper's nest. 'You can be too, *please*! Let me help you.'

'You're not our king,' Brielle tells him. 'But he will be.'

'You don't know that. Gillage–'

'I believe it. I believe in him.' She places a hand on Elician's cheek. She kisses his brow. Then she pushes him back and closes her cell door. The lock snicks closed. All around them, voices rise in unison, all saying the same words. *Our king. Our king. Our king.*

Elician shakes his head. He tries to speak, but no words form on his lips. It isn't fair. It isn't *right*. But the Reapers hold their faith. And they will not be swayed.

Morsen pulls Elician to his feet, takes the keys from his hand and places them well in reach of Brielle – in case she changes her mind. In case any of the Reapers change their minds. He pushes Elician gently down the hall. Elician's feet trip and stumble, but all around him the voices keep speaking.

Our king. Our king. Our king.

It is not him they are talking about. It will never *be* him. These people will never be *his* people. But their words resonate through him anyway. They fall in line with the beating of his heart, the step of his feet, the breath in his chest. Morsen leads him down the hall without end. They pass cage after cage. Reaper upon Reaper. Each one chants the same words, hollowing out a promise that Elician is not sure he will be able to keep. He cannot force Alest to return. He wouldn't even want to.

They keep walking. On and on they go. Time flutters across Elician's consciousness. His legs burn from the strain. His feet shuffle-slide the whole way, but he moves. He has to move. He has to reach Fen, has to stop his uncle, has to stop the Queen. He does not know how he is going to do any of that, but he knows he needs to do it.

A ladder finally descends from one of the stone pillars, one without a torch. Morsen gestures for Elician to wait as he climbs up. Elician waits. He leans against the ladder and his eyes are wet again. He'd held his father's head in his arms. His *brother* had been nearly decapitated only a few moments later. His sister–

'Your Majesty . . .' Elician looks up in a kind of shock. Morsen has reached the top of the ladder. He throws open a trapdoor. He peers down at Elician and Elician knows he is supposed to climb. So, he climbs. Hand over foot, he climbs. He gets to the top and wipes his face. He lets Morsen continue to lead him. He does not know what else he is supposed to do.

They are on the main level of the palace now. The gardens are nearby. The courtyard. The kitchens. The throne room where Lio died. Elician flinches away from it, keeping his head angled downward as Morsen hurries them along. It is pre-dawn. The guards are few and far between. At each vague sound of a possible interloper, Morsen huddles him into an alcove. They hide until they are certain it is safe, then keep walking.

They stop only once. Once, where Morsen hesitates before a wooden door, glancing over his shoulder at Elician. 'This leads to the pauper's graveyard of Alerae,' he says carefully. He waits as Elician processes that bit of information, as Elician imagines the line that Brielle had drawn in the air, from her finger . . . straight to here. 'He was buried hours ago,' Morsen continues. 'I am sorry for your loss.' Morsen says it bluntly. Too bluntly. For a moment Elician cannot fathom if he is talking about his father or Lio. Maybe both. Maybe his father was buried in Lio's arms. Maybe in death, at least, they are not alone. 'We have to pass through it, but we cannot stay there long; it is too open. There are palace windows that look out across this land. Do you understand?'

'Do not try to find him,' Elician translates quietly. 'Just keep going.'

'Yes. I'm sorry, Your Majesty.'

Apologies mean nothing. Morsen did not order Lio to die. He had not been involved with them getting taken in the first place. His greatest crime has been serving Alelune. Perhaps, technically, from Alelune's perspective, his greatest crime is what he is doing tonight. 'Why are you helping me?'

'Ranio Ragden was my mentor,' Morsen says.

The words echo through Elician like the snap of a slingshot and he stares at Morsen as the name pierces his mental fog. 'Fen's father,' he murmurs. 'He died in Alelune . . .'

'He died trying to rescue Alest from the Reaper cells. They followed this exact route. They made it almost to the border when something went wrong.'

'What?'

'I don't know. Alest was put back in the cells and Ranio's body was put on display. He was my friend for many years. I took his place after his death. I'm sorry it has taken this long to free you. I was not sure where to find you and then . . . I wasn't sure how to get you out.'

Elician shakes his head. It doesn't matter. None of it. He pats Morsen's arm. Says, 'Let's go home.' He does not want to think anymore. Does not want to think about the chain of events leading up to this moment. Does not want to think of Ranio Ragden's death. How Ranio had come *incredibly close* to saving that terrified child – who somehow had become wrapped up in all their lives, despite the odds against him. Does not want to think how, all those years after Ranio died, Elician had been the one to place Alest into Ranio's daughter's care. A daughter who had become a Giver.

Morsen opens the door to the graveyard. They step out into the half-light of the muddy field. In places, rough grave markers have been erected. Others have fallen in the ill-tended grounds. Elician keeps his eyes on his feet. He cannot trust himself not to look. Cannot trust himself not to stare desperately at each patch of soft earth and wonder if that is where Lio is buried. If that is where his father is buried.

They walk, slow and steady, down the rows. Their feet quietly plod across the mud. There is an outer wall and a gate not far ahead. Elician can see horses on the other side of the gate. His heart clenches at the sight. It really is an escape route. A way out. His eyes burn one last time. Pain lances through his chest. He should not look for Lio. He *should not*. They are almost out, and yet:

He looks anyway.

He turns and scans the entire expanse of the graveyard. He lets his eyes roam over the lumps and pits and valleys and all the good and bad and possible options that there can be. He trembles under the weight of the knowledge that he will never bring Lio home. Lio's body will never be burned, his ashes scattered by the hands of those who loved him most. Elician will likely never come back to Alerae. Even if he does, there will be no chance to find the body. They would have to dig up the whole graveyard to manage it. Even then–

'Your Majesty?' Morsen murmurs from the gate. It is time to go. Time to leave.

Something moves at the corner of his eye. He stops. Stops and tilts his head back. The earth on a grave mound is moving. No, not the earth, something *on top* of the earth. A shape is shifting about, awkwardly. Perhaps trying to push itself up . . .

Elician is moving before he can think about it. Morsen hisses his title behind him. It does not matter. He runs, feet slapping loudly on the earth. He skids to his knees and his hands snap out. His fingers dig into the mud-stained flesh of the man who is doing the best he can to pull himself from the ground. The man's face lifts.

'*Lio.*' He is alive. He is *alive*. Elician drags him up to his knees. He clutches Lio's face even as Lio's eyes blink blearily in his direction. Clumsy hands clap Elician's sides. His arms. His wrists. Every part of Lio is coated in mud. It streaks through his tatty hair, paints his face, stains his naked flesh and hides his skin from sight. He has never looked better. Elician tugs him forward and chokes on a sob, wrapping his arms around Lio's body. Feeling Lio's breath against his neck. Hearing the hitching gasp as he breathes in Elician's ear.

'If you've turned me into a Giver *or* a Reaper,' Lio warns hoarsely, 'I'm going to be extremely upset.'

Morsen is there now, crouching at their sides. He pulls off his outer coat and wraps it around Lio's body. When he touches Lio's skin, he does not die. 'Not a Reaper,' Elician informs him dully. He reaches forward and presses his fingers against the place where Gillage's blade had ended Lio's life. The wound has healed. But when Elician touches him with purpose, he can sense that there are other wounds. Nails torn from digging himself out of his own grave, skin shredded against rocks, trachea still damaged from the blade. Not lethally damaged but strained enough to cause pain. 'Not a Giver.' All of that would be healed if he were. Lio is as he always has been – perfectly human, with a soul that Elician could recognize from all the way in the Reaper cells.

'I brought you back,' Elician whispers. 'I didn't touch you but I . . . I brought you back anyway.' Shock threatens to overtake relief. Uncertainty wars with elation. Elician clings to Lio, feeding him every ounce of energy he has to fix every problem his senses can pick up. And Lio can do nothing to stop him because that would require Elician to stop touching him. Although, maybe not. *Maybe I could heal him from afar.*

'Stop,' Lio croaks. 'Stop.'

'You're alive . . . you're alive and I–' How far away had they been when he'd saved his friend? The graveyard was on the complete other side of the palatial compound, and besides that: how long had it been since Lio had been buried? Long enough for the Queen to have prepared for her journey to the Kingsclave, and long enough for Morsen to arrange for their escape. And yet still – *still* – Lio lives. Elician has never heard of a Giver trying to resurrect someone after that length of time . . . and yet now that it's happened, he cannot help but wonder: is there a limit? If the soul could still be retrieved . . . would any of the rest truly matter?

'We need to leave, Your Majesty,' Morsen says. 'We cannot stay here.' Elician looks up at the tower windows. At the palace looming just to his right. He shivers unconsciously, then grasps Lio and hoists him to standing with all his strength. Morsen wraps Lio's right arm around his shoulders, clasping him to his body to help support him as they go. There is no question of leaving him behind, no murmured complaint about only having prepared two horses. If nothing else, Elician is grateful that Morsen understands that leaving Lio is *not* an option.

They flee through the back gate. Morsen holds on to Lio as Elician mounts his horse. 'Do you want me to hold him?' Morsen asks only once, but Elician rejects the idea with a firm shake of his head. He fully intends to fix every part of his brother's body before they leave the outer borders of Alerae. He does not want to test if he can heal from afar either.

It takes a great deal of pushing, pulling and hoisting – the poor horse shuffling unhappily the whole time – to get Lio seated in front of Elician. When there, though, he leans back against Elician's bare chest. Elician rearranges Morsen's coat to drape over Lio's front. Neither of them is dressed for the weather or for a ride, but there are few options in an escape such as this.

Morsen loosens the ties keeping the horses in position, mounts his own horse and leads the way forward to freedom.

CHAPTER THIRTY-FIVE

Elician

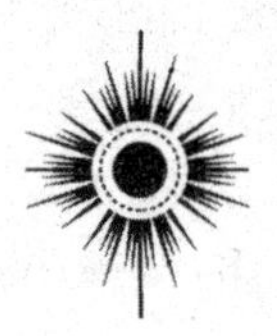

The Kingsclave is a meeting place designed to broker treaties between two nations that rarely have a reason to be civil. Its physical location rests on the permanent border between Alelune and Soleb (the only part of the border that never changes, no matter what ground is won or lost in the war) on top of a rocky outcrop that reaches high into the sky above the river. Two long paths, one from each country, lead up to the top. A single tower rests there, with an outer ring and an inner sanctum. By sacred decree, no blood can be spilled within the Kingsclave's walls, and no death can occur on its grounds. For generations, members of both Alelune's and Soleb's clerical communities – distinguished leaders from Kreuzfurt, as well as from the sacred temples set up in praise of Life and Death – have tended to the Kingsclave as guardians of that same oath.

The fugitives move as swiftly as they can, reaching the Kingsclave without being discovered, but they are only just in time. As they reach the cliffs leading to the meeting grounds, royal retinues from both sides are already marching up their respective paths to the tower. It is uncomfortably obvious that they will not be able to walk up the path to the building without drawing attention to themselves. If they try the trail from Alelune, they will be captured in an instant. If they try to cross the border first, then double back from the Soleben side, there is no telling how Anslian's chosen supporters will react.

There is no telling how they will react once Elician reveals himself at the Kingsclave either, but the clerics and the oaths they all share should keep them from slitting his throat immediately. 'You'll have to stay here,' Elician says as they make their way to the only other path to the top: up the cliff wall itself. With sharp and jagged edges poking out on either side, he can easily hide from view if he just stays quiet in the shadows.

It is a steep climb, but the rocks and cracked edges offer just enough handholds for Elician to climb. He can make it. The food Morsen provided during their journey invigorated him more than he had expected. His muscles are still weak, but if he goes slowly, his body will heal the exhaustion as he climbs. He will make it to the top.

'I always go with you,' Lio argues.

'You're not strong enough to make the climb.' Lio will need months to return to proper shape, and Elician cannot afford the distraction or energy he would need to heal Lio and climb at the same time. 'I cannot watch you fall and die again,' he says, to add weight to his argument.

'Elician–'

'If you *must* do something, then *carefully* scout the way across the border. We may need a quick retreat.'

'But–'

'That's an order.' He says it without looking at his friend. Says it knowing it will hurt him.

Still, despite the hurt, Lio's voice is clear and calm. He says, 'I understand, Your Hi–Majesty.' Then, 'Take a blade with you, at least.'

'There are no weapons allowed in the Kingsclave,' Elician says.

'The actual order is that weapons must be held at the door,' Morsen pipes up. He takes a dagger from his belt and slides it into place at Elician's side. 'You're not going through the door.' He is not. And yet the distinction feels wrong. He pushes it back to Morsen.

He says, 'No,' and this time, Morsen does not argue.

Even so, as Elician prepares himself to leave, he still does not know what he is meant to do once he gets there. *I'm just going to go, tell them my sister's not for sale, and that we need to renegotiate the terms of the truce.* And hope that, after all this time, his own people will still recognize him once he emerges from the inner sanctum with that news.

Taking a deep breath, Elician presses his hands to the stone and begins to climb. The cliff offers poor handholds, but he digs his toes into every possible slant. He presses his fingers into the slightest grooves. His knuckles burn, and he relishes the journey upwards as he trusts his limbs to hold his weight steady and firm. Fraying muscles heal and strengthen with each action. The burning pain of exertion becomes a familiar friend.

There is a peacefulness in climbing. Any fall could delay or destroy his progress. In a mortal man's life, a misstep could end it. To climb, and climb well, his mind can only be on the rock. He cannot let a single stray thought distract him from his task. He cannot allow even a moment's uncertainty. The moment he presumes to know better than the rock is the moment he will lose his grip.

He cannot think of Anslian or the Queen. He cannot think of Fen. There is only the climb. One hand, then a foot. Then the other hand, and the other foot. He scans his path with an architect's eye, looking for the most accessible route while also scouring for impediments. He puts his trust in his experience and grips hard on to jagged edges that threaten to tear open his palms.

The ascent is slow. Wind bites at his back as he climbs. The pungent smell of the Bask River tickles his nose. He shoves that thought down too. It's unnecessary. Unhelpful. Still, when the wind blows it chases away the smell – and he finds that he times his more determined manoeuvres for when the wind is taking a breath. For a long time, it is just him and the cliff face. And, eventually, it is just him and the outer wall of the Kingsclave.

The wall rises from the cliff, made of stonework battered by the wind and the elements for thousands of years. He digs his fingers into the gaps between the stones. Carefully, slowly, painfully. He climbs. The higher he goes, the more he hears. There are voices now, speaking in both Lunae and Soleben. They guide him further. They beckon him close. One hand, one foot, one hand, one foot. He goes on.

The wall surrounds a great courtyard, and at the centre of the courtyard is the inner sanctum where only the monarchs are permitted, to discuss terms in private. Honoured guests are to wait inside the wall. They witness their monarchs enter the sanctum and witness their return. But the conversations held inside the sanctum are for the eyes and ears of the monarchs alone. Whatever the final terms of any contract are, they are to be determined without influence from outside factors. And if either emerges without the other, or if any blood is spilt, they will have no choice but to face the consequences of their actions by stepping into the courtyard to face the judgement of the opposing side's forces. Without weapons, that judgement is expected to take the form of an arrest. But Elician has little doubt that the assembled party would find a way to enact their vengeance.

The assembly grows louder as he reaches the top. He breathes deep as he pulls himself up by his fingertips alone, holding the position just until he can confirm that no eyes are on him. The clerics responsible for ensuring the honour of the Kingsclave are going about their final preparations. Their white garb covers them from head to toe. Alelune despises Reapers and Givers, but clerics from Soleb include both. As is custom, all clerics in the Kingsclave are dressed in order to not be identified as one or the other, either as from Alelune or Soleb, or as baseline human or something more. From the sounds of the processions coming up the main lane, it will not take long before the Alelune queen and his uncle Anslian arrive.

He needs to be inside the inner sanctum before then. And from there . . . what? His head aches as he pulls himself up that final stretch. His elbows dig into the wall and leverage him just enough to swing his legs over the top. He spares one glance towards the bottom. Lio is just barely visible now, but when Elician waves once, Lio waves back, and it is enough to confirm he and Morsen are still free for the time being. He watches as Lio ducks into hiding, then he rolls over the top at last, getting a better look at the path to the inner sanctum.

There are three clerics lighting lanterns and making the final precursory rounds. They are talking quietly to each other, familiarity breeding distraction. Elician squints at his path of descent. It will take him several minutes to climb it. The whole while, light will illuminate his body. He would be spotted even by the most unobservant fellow.

No. He cannot climb down yet.

Licking his lips, he sends up thoughts of gratitude that Lio let him do this on his own. He carefully crawls along the top of the wall until the ground directly below him is open and unoccupied. He waits. Waits. Waits. The clerics manoeuvre to the opposite side of the sanctum, their white clothes making them beacons, easy to track as they move. They are fiddling with something. With a deep breath, Elician bunches up his borrowed shirt, stuffs it into his mouth and rolls off the wall. He plummets. It takes barely a second before he smashes hard against the earth. His teeth snap against the shirt as his body tries to scream. He gags and feels his bones shatter and piece themselves back together again. All the while his ears ring perilously, meaning he can't hear if his fall has been discovered.

Before he has even finished healing, he drags himself away. His legs snap and creak beneath him. His ribs pop back into place. His shoulders wriggle into position. He goes left, then forward, stumbling behind the wall of the inner sanctum just as one of the clerics rounds the corner and starts searching for the source of the sound. 'It was probably the procession, they're making enough of a racket,' one of the clerics excuses. 'Just ignore it and help me with this.' Tears streak down Elician's face as blood drips down his brow and onto his shirt. He presses himself into the shadows, fixing himself bit by bit even as the clerics mumble amongst themselves.

Finally, he is whole again. He spits his shirt from his mouth and takes a few steadying breaths of air before daring to inspect his position better. Taking the main door to the inner sanctum is too obvious. He will not make it there unless the clerics and the earliest of the royal retinues leave. He looks the building over, up and down and – *there*! A large vent graces the upper wall. It requires more climbing, but this time the pillars that decorate the exterior are set close enough together that he can brace himself upon them. He will not need to freehand it.

He presses his shoulders to one pillar, takes a deep breath, then sets his feet on its opposite twin. Slowly, so slowly, he ascends. At the top he uses his own weight to push against both pillars, lungs heaving with exertion, and holds his position. His hands search, his fingers digging into the grate covering the vent. A few tugs and it swings silently open on well-oiled hinges. He thanks the care of attentive clerics who are dutiful about their work. Moments later, he angles his head and shoulders through, and shimmies onto the wide ceiling beams that crisscross the top of the sanctum's dome.

As soon as he's pulled himself through, the grate snaps shut behind him. He lies on the beams, breathless and sore, and lets himself heal once more. He is finally alone, and without anyone there to see, so he takes a few moments to simply breathe. Breathe, and get his bearings.

There is a table in the centre of the room. Two chairs. No food or drink is permitted in the Kingsclave for fear of poisonings, and blue stones are used as light sources to avoid anyone trying to light someone on fire by way of candle. Apparently, someone had tried once. Elician cannot remember which side started it.

He does not have time to remember. Even as he assesses the

layout, he hears the herald announcing *King* Anslian's arrival. Then Queen Alenée's. Elician looks in all directions. The beam he is lying on is not a good place to hide. While it is high enough to obfuscate him should someone not be looking his way, if anyone were to glance up, he would be spotted in a moment. It is a matter of placement then, and luck. Slowly, he shimmies along his beam until he is pressed into the darkest corner, right above the door itself.

It opens as soon as he settles. He holds his breath. Queen Alenée and King Anslian step inside. The door closes behind them, and the two monarchs approach the table. They sit. For the first time in nearly two years, Elician looks at a member of his family. His uncle's appearance . . . is not what Elician had expected.

Anger had fuelled much of Elician's journey to the Kingsclave. Anger, and no small amount of desperation. He could not let his sister fall into the Queen's hands. He refused to let it happen. But that *Anslian* of all people had been responsible for setting up the bargain to begin with – for *Anslian* to have *murdered* his own brother to take the throne – it was still unthinkable. And Elician had always thought he was a better judge of character than that.

Elician's mind had conjured no shortage of fantasies of what his uncle would look like as king. Proud, victorious, strong. Elician had seen him in countless battles. He had listened to his endless rally calls. He had watched as Anslian walked through the camp, inspecting the wounded and managing his soldiers. Anslian knew how to lead, and how to look like a leader. His version of a king should have been nothing less than exhilarating to behold. And yet—

At some point since Elician has been gone, Anslian's hair has turned grey. There are dark circles beneath his eyes. Wrinkles that Elician cannot remember having ever been there before. Anslian also now walks with a limp. One of his hands is wrapped in a bandage that seems out of place compared to the other fine clothes he is wearing: clothes that Elician recognizes as his own father's ceremonial robes. And they have not been tailored for Anslian's more muscular frame, sitting poorly on his uncle's body – too short at the sleeves, too long at the waist. Adalei almost certainly would never have let her father attend such an occasion in so poor a state, but she clearly had no involvement in his attire.

Beside Queen Alenée, who is dressed just as decadently as when she'd ordered Lio's death, Anslian appears wilted. Unkempt. He does not seem the kind of man who betrays for power. Even though his posture is perfect, his head up. Even though he looks at the Queen with the air of military discipline he always wears like a cloak.

'There are final matters to be settled before we sign,' the Queen starts, regal and refined. Her voice is calm and neutral, and yet . . . she sounds almost bored. Elician wonders if her emotional capacity only ever extends that far. If she can experience boredom and nothing else.

'Are there now?' Anslian asks, sitting across from her.

'Your nephew refused my request for a child, therefore it is your *niece* I expect you to give to me. You have her, I presume?' Her hands remain calmly folded in her lap. She sits and speaks with such unnatural stillness that it casts an illusion of unreality over the scene.

Anslian nods. Elician's heart quickens. 'I do. Though I'm surprised. I had been expecting to hear word of your pregnancy since the day Elician arrived in Alerae.'

'And I had been expecting to hear news of Aliamon's death for the same length of time.'

'Your son didn't kill him when given the chance. He even interfered when you sent that other Reaper to finish the job.'

'I told you Alest's actions would always be his own. You're the one who wanted to be king. You should have murdered Aliamon from the start.'

'And I told you, it would have been neater if a Reaper had managed the job. Fratricide is frowned upon in Soleb.'

'Yes, you're all very quaint about that.' *Coward*, her voice seems to say. Elician imagines if given the chance, she would have murdered her own sibling herself to secure her throne. There is a horrible history book in an abandoned room in Alerae that details countless generations of Alelunen monarchs doing just that. Anslian's attempt to not get his own hands dirty would look weak to Alenée. It looks weak to Elician too. 'Your nephew was quite upset when I took the liberty of informing him of your involvement.'

Elician does not think he makes a sound. He does not think he has moved. He has been holding his breath since their 'negotiations' started, and yet, despite all of that, Anslian's eyes flick up in his direction. He looks at Elician, *sees* him. Elician freezes in shock. His uncle's lips form a small smile. He turns back to the Queen before her attention is drawn upwards. 'I'm sure he was. He's always believed in justice.'

'What a pity for him.'

'Indeed,' Anslian says calmly. He stands and produces a long roll of parchment from his sleeve. 'All the terms and conditions, just as we agreed.' He hands it to her, and she reads it carefully before nodding. Standing. She flattens the paper on the table and collects the ceremonial pen, prepared to sign. Elician glances about, trying to find the best way down.

I'll just jump.

'I'm sorry,' Anslian says suddenly. The Queen glances up. Too late, and too unprepared. Anslian moves with a soldier's speed and power, arms and hands in perfect position. Her neck breaks with a sickening crack before Elician can think to shout a warning. Elician leaps, landing on the sanctum's floor far too late. He shoves Anslian back, only to watch the Queen's body fall: dead.

CHAPTER THIRTY-SIX

Elician

'You . . . killed her.' Elician glances at the sanctum door, half expecting the clerics to burst in and begin their retribution. It is the most sacred law of the Kingsclave. No violence can happen here. It is neutral ground. It is meant for the most difficult of negotiations to proceed without fear of *exactly this*. The Queen had come because she had known she would be safe and . . . Anslian killed her.

'Yes,' Anslian says. He steps towards Elician. Elician steps back, tripping over Alenée's legs. But his uncle is persistent, certain, and when his weathered hands touch Elician's face he means him no harm. He merely cups Elician's cheeks between his palms and looks at him. *Looks.* 'I'm so sorry, my dear boy.'

'Uncle?' Elician asks.

'I was not sure I'd see you again. I'd hoped, but I . . . I was not sure.' Anslian's hands shift, falling to Elician's shoulders. He pulls his nephew into the gentle glow of the blue stones in order to see him more clearly, and Elician stumbles after him. Then, once there, he finds himself unable to move. He's trapped by confusion and uncertainty as Anslian gives him a proper examination. 'You've lost so much weight. Oh . . . your hair.' His fingers touch the ragged and torn edges.

It is too much. Elician shakes his head. He closes his eyes and tries to banish the sight and smell of this place. He tries to find some semblance of calm, of understanding. But there is no understanding. Nothing makes sense. 'What are you talking about?' he asks, tired of manipulation and secrecy. Tired of lies and plans that he had never been told.

Elician's first memory of Anslian had been the feeling of his arms. Of being picked up and carried back to the palace after he had become lost in the city of Himmelsheim's many spirals. He had rested his head on Anslian's shoulder and smelled the perfumed sweetness of his uncle's clothes. From that moment on, his uncle had always made sense to him. He had always been a loyal, stalwart, fierce man who placed the good of Soleb above anything else.

Killing his own brother, arranging a peace treaty with the Queen, even arranging for Elician to be taken out of the way . . . If Anslian had thought it was all for the good of the people, Elician could almost understand it. It was twisted and wrong, but he could force himself to adapt to that reality. But this . . . to have committed all these atrocities to create a treaty that was meant to ensure a lasting peace, and then just *murder* the only other person required for that peace to take place–

'You killed her,' Elician says again. 'You've . . . This war will *never* stop if she is dead, here, like this . . . I–What are you *doing*?'

'I'm sorry, Elician.'

'Stop *apologizing*.' Elician flinches at the volume of his own voice. He glances back over his shoulder, but the door stays closed. No one is coming to check on them. No one is interfering. It is just them, a torn treaty and the corpse of the Queen. Alelune will be furious. Gillage – *Gillage* is going to be king. Alenée was cruel, but at least she wasn't *him*.

'I can't stop apologizing,' Anslian murmurs. He smiles, but it is too sad. Too tired. His face creaks under the weight of the emotions and he leans back to rest against the table behind him. 'I owe you those apologies more than anyone else.'

Elician feels ill. He presses a palm to his forehead and tries to stave off a spasm of pain as it spears through his skull. Too much. It is too much. The past few days have been more than he has been able to bear, and it is only getting worse. He is *tired* of there always being one more thing. He wants this to be over. 'She gave me my father's head,' he says. 'I held it . . . You cut off his head and I had to see – why would you *do* that?'

Thankfully, his uncle does not apologize again. Anslian waits long enough for Elician to catch his breath, then quietly responds, 'It was the *only way* to convince Alenée to leave Alerae for the Kingsclave. She had to believe I was on her side.'

'You killed my father for a *meeting*?' Not even for a certain and sure collaboration. Just a chance at a face-to-face.

'Your father killed himself for a meeting,' Anslian corrects. 'I . . . I was taking too long for his liking. *Her* liking.' His shoulders curl inwards, protectively, as his head bows. 'We had been trying to find a way to reach Alenée for years. But she never left the city. Our spies could never get close enough to her. She had no interest in peace unless it was on her terms . . . and her terms were exacting. She wanted unfettered access to the Bask and Altas, and Aliamon dead. She never forgave us for what we forced her to do for Marias. Aliamon suggested I reach out to form an alliance with her, ostensibly without his knowledge. It would be believable if I appeared to crave the throne.'

No. That doesn't make any sense. Elician shakes his head. The stabbing pain is getting worse. Pressure builds behind his left eye, spreading across his skull. He shoves his fingers onto the pressure points at his nose, his temple. Nothing stops the agony as it builds. Anslian keeps talking. Now that he has started, he cannot seem to stop, as if he is desperate to reveal all their manoeuvrings. Elician barely has the wherewithal to understand the savage tale.

'The negotiations have been going on for years. And I *tried* to stop them, to stop your father, Elician. You have to believe I tried. I never wanted your father dead or you – you in her control.'

'Stop. Stop, none of this– *Start over.* Explain it to me properly. Like I'm *stupid.*' Because gods he feels stupid right now. He cannot understand this trajectory or how they ended with his father beheaded and the Queen of Alelune dead on the ground of the Kingsclave. 'How did we get here?' Elician asks. '*Tell me the truth.*'

Anslian glances towards the door. No one has heard them, and no one will interfere. This room is meant for negotiations, and those negotiations will take as long as they need to take. They have time, and Anslian nods. Resigned.

'Your father and Alenée hated each other long before they took up their thrones. The source of that rage, I don't know. He never told me. But I know that I made it worse when I took Marias hostage when we were fighting to take back Altas from Alelune twenty-two years ago.'

'Why did you?'

'Because I believed taking him hostage would end the war. And it did. She conceded the city and the river, and her reign was continually besieged by challengers ever since, cousins and distant relatives who thought they could rule better than the woman who let Altas slip from her grasp. Where Soleb had seventeen years of peace following that victory, Alelune nobility waged silent and deadly civil war amongst themselves. She needed a daughter to secure her line, but Marias was hated for his part in losing Altas and she was pressured to divorce him. Gillage was born after a hasty marriage with a more suitable lord, and another son still was not enough. Then . . . when Alest drowned, and came back as a Reaper, she had little choice but to imprison her own child. And still: her grip on her throne became weaker. Her deciding to restart the war in an attempt to reclaim the Bask was only a matter of time.

'And it was time that your father spent attempting to create a legacy that could not be undone. He tried first to retrieve Alest from the cells, believing he could use Alest as a bargaining chip once Alelune's succession crisis came to a head.'

Elician's fingers clench tight. 'He would have saved Alest only because he could have used him against Alelune? Not because it was wrong Alest was there to begin with?'

'When did your father ever do anything out of the goodness of his heart?' Anslian asks.

Never. Elician knows he had never done anything just because it was right. It was only ever for glory and recognition. For the praise and acknowledgement that he, the benevolent ruler, had done well.

'Ranio believed that Alenée was trying to find ways to remove Alest from the cells. Aliamon gave him the order to make an attempt, believing it would be a successful heist.'

'What went wrong?'

'We don't know. But after he failed, Aliamon changed focus.' Here, Anslian hesitates. He closes his eyes, preparing for a blow he knows will hurt, but finds the strength to deliver it anyway. 'He adopted Fenlia in the hopes that should your own secret ever be revealed, someone else could stand as heir.'

'I know.'

'You know?'

'Adalei and I heard you arguing about it.' It had been a painful day. He could at least understand why his father doubted *him* so completely; there were laws forbidding his ascension. But to know that his father loathed Adalei for something far less tangible was simply inexcusable. Aliamon found Adalei too ill, too weak, to be a viable candidate for the throne, hence the need for another heir. For Fen. 'He was furious when Fen became a Giver too,' Elician murmurs. Within hours of Fen's discovery, she had been sent from the only home she had ever known to Kreuzfurt.

Her place in the family all but rescinded.

And she never knew why.

Elician had promised to bring her back. To make sure Kreuzfurt could never hold her or any other Giver or Reaper against their will again. But he had never told her why, in the moments after her life changed for ever, her world had *needed* to change so drastically too.

'I always felt it was the gods cursing him,' Anslian reveals. 'He tried so hard to hide his Giver child from the world, and when he feared that secret might be undone, he tried to choose another, and the gods would not forgive him his hubris.'

'He could have adopted someone else.' Even as he says it though, Elician doubts his father would have stooped so low. His father loved Ranio like a brother. Adopting Fen would have felt like justice, vindication to him. But to take in an unknown? Someone unworthy or unproven? It would have disgusted Aliamon. It would have ruined his dream of a legacy he could be proud of.

'He never would have countenanced such a thing,' Anslian confirms.

Elician shakes his head, tries to clear his thoughts. 'Why did he arrange for Alenée to take me hostage?'

'Because he saw one way to destabilize Alelune for generations. A way that led to Alenée's death. With her dead, Alelune would be too busy fighting amongst themselves on who should be their ruler to stand in the way of Soleb's continued improvement and growth. Even if they eventually sorted themselves out, they would never be able to challenge Soleb militaristically again.'

That doesn't answer the question. Not really. 'Why did he arrange for me to be taken hostage, Uncle?' Elician repeats, firmer this time. 'How does *that* fit into his plans for legacy?'

'The path to Soleben stability was built on Alenée's death. But she was too well protected by those loyal to her. She needed to be in a place where she would be alone. Unprotected.' He waves his hand around them. The Kingsclave, where honour forbade violence, and for Solebens a vow was absolute. Alelunens called it *Blessedsafe* because that's what they should have been. Safe. 'She would only come if she believed it was *worth it* to her. If she believed that she would truly walk away the victor.

'So, he would give her everything that she wanted, by making her believe it was what *I* wanted too. Morsen confirmed what Ranio had suspected: that Alenée had been making opportunities for Alest to escape. It seemed worth it to try that tactic again. This time, with Alenée's involvement. I proposed to her an equal exchange. She would send her son here. He would make an attempt on your life, and you . . . in your kindness, would do what we all knew you would do: offer him a chance to live in Kreuzfurt instead. And once you ensured that her son had a life, one he would never have received in Alelune, I would ensure that you were delivered into *her* custody. She needed a child. A female child. And as a Giver you could give her that. It seemed so simple. Neat.'

Nothing about this was either simple or neat. Elician shakes his head. 'She told Alest to kill you and Father. He told me that.'

'Me as well?' Anslian doesn't sound entirely surprised. 'I suppose she didn't trust us either.'

'Considering she's *dead*, that's not an entirely unjustified belief.'

They were lucky. They were all lucky that Alest had looked at them all in that moment, in Himmelsheim, while he was surrounded by the ancestral enemy to his people, and had done *nothing*. Had Alest followed through with his mission, killing Aliamon, Anslian and anyone else in the royal family who stood in his way, he could have created all the same instability that Anslian had just condemned Alelune to instead. Soleb's royal family would have been decimated, and Elician would have remained her prisoner. For ever.

Alenée had played two hands at once, letting the pieces fall where they may. She told Alest to kill the Soleben royal family, but even without that, she had gained all the benefits that the original plan had offered. Alest safe in Soleb. Elician imprisoned, peace seemingly at hand. She had come here, just as Aliamon and Anslian had planned, to sign a peace treaty. She had believed them. And now she is dead. Just as they would have been dead had her son acted with any more malice in his heart.

They have all been so incredibly lucky.

And the people of Alelune, now, are far less so.

'I knew she told him to kill Aliamon,' Anslian continued. 'I even told her the opportunity could arise. At your funeral, it would be easy enough to bring him to Himmelsheim. And it was. Easy enough to put them in a room together and wait to see what he would do.'

'And he chose not to kill him. Father must have been furious.'

The half-smile that crosses Anslian's face is bittersweet, his eyes wet with unshed tears. 'He was. It would have been convenient. For all of us. Alest killing him would ensure I had no hand in his death. I would have ensured Alest vanished without being captured, free to go wherever he pleased, and no one would have questioned my succession. And yet, Alest didn't kill him. And that . . . that returned the responsibility back to me.'

Elician cannot find it in him to feel grief for his uncle's plight. Not in that. Not when his uncle had participated in the negotiations in the first place. It may have been easier for Anslian to let Alest do the deed, but Anslian had still gone to the negotiating table at the start promising Aliamon's death.

'I was . . . stunned. I had not expected it of that boy. And when I realized what it would mean . . . what I would have to do . . . I couldn't bring myself to do it in the end. I dithered. Delayed. I left the capital and insisted I needed to be at the border, only to be summoned back time and again. Months passed. Alenée was growing impatient. I told her I was unable to act and that it was her son who had failed to accomplish the task she had given him. She sent a second Reaper. Aliamon had purposely set a lax guard to enable that assassination to succeed but–' Anslian laughs. 'Alest stopped that too. And with every day that Aliamon stayed alive, you remained in Alerae. We couldn't remove you until she had left the city.'

Of course not. Their plan had been to entice Alenée to a place where they could kill her. And letting Morsen get Lio and him out sooner would have entrenched her in Alerae that much more. Anslian's eyes fall to the Queen's corpse.

'I thought she would be with child. I waited to hear the news. Your father – he was almost resigned to the fact a child would be born. Once, he thought it was amusing that it was you who would have done it. Another Soleben victory in its own way. But the news never came. And she . . .'

'She only asked after my father died.'

Surprise flickers across Anslian's face. He frowns, glancing towards the dead queen. 'I wonder why.'

It is far too late to ask now.

'Maybe she didn't find it as amusing or as appealing as you thought.'

'She needed a female heir.' Elician wonders if, at the end of everything, she had needed Aliamon to die to motivate her into actually doing something about that. She could have remarried. She could have found any number of suitors. She didn't. She had known her duty, and she had still waited until the final moment to push for it. Even in the end, she couldn't have forced him into compliance. She had been willing to exchange Elician for Fen. Resigned to contingencies, and far too easily.

'Would you have murdered her if she came to you months pregnant anyway?' Elician asks.

'Yes.' Anslian meets Elician's eyes, unflinching in the face of condemnation. 'After all of this . . . yes. But you never did give her a child, did you?' That shouldn't matter. Not when the risk had been so real. That shouldn't have mattered at all. But Anslian continues. 'When we planned everything from the start, we hadn't thought it would be a concern. You were never meant to stay there as long as you did. Your father . . . he had it arranged. As soon as Alest was brought to the palace, your father would be murdered. I would take the crown. I would meet her here. And this would be done with.

A few months at most. Never long enough for her to give birth to the child she would have begotten even if you had agreed.'

'I wouldn't have made that same choice,' Elician replies.

'No. I don't think you would have made any of these choices.' Perhaps worst of all is how Anslian says those words. Calm and gentle, filled with love and a deep respect that is counter to all the meticulous plans and machinations Anslian and Aliamon had put together. Elician's refusal is something to be proud of. Elician wishes he could understand how Anslian had got to this point, where he could do so many things he *didn't* agree with, only to be proud that Elician would never do the same.

Anslian's attention remains on Alenée's corpse. There is nothing close to guilt in his expression. But he looks tired. Tired and old beyond his years. 'Lio,' Anslian says slowly. 'We heard that Lio . . .'

'I brought him back,' Elician replies. His uncle jerks back, meets Elician's eyes at last. 'He's alive. I . . . brought him home. I'm going to bring him home.' Tears stream down Anslian's cheeks, sudden and dramatic. He presses a palm to his face and cries. His shoulders shake as tremors shudder down his spine. Elician has never seen his uncle weep before. Not after his wife's death. Not when they stood vigil by Adalei's mother's casket. Nor even when Adalei had first fallen ill and had been taken to the House of the Unwanting. He had always stood tall and proud, face seemingly carved from stone.

'You were meant to go to Kreuzfurt alone,' Anslian says, his voice cracking. 'I should have sent you alone. You would have been captured and . . . it would have been better.'

'But *you're* the one who sent Lio with me,' Elician murmurs. '*Why?*'

'Because I was still trying to stop this damn fool negotiation from the start. This plan that led to *all these deaths* . . . and countless more. I had hoped your father would not risk both of you. While it may never have been official – Lio's betrothal to Adalei was almost certain. It was my last attempt to delay all of this, in the hopes Aliamon would not be willing to risk a second member of this family. I told him weeks before Alest even crossed the border what I would do, hoping it would forestall him. I hoped too that even one more blade would make the difference, that you would never be caught in the first place.' But they *had* been caught.

His father had not hesitated. He had accepted Lio's loss and what it would mean. Elician imagines the epic history book written in his father's honour. Praising him for his sacrifices, his planning, his willingness to risk the continuation of his line, just to destroy Alelune's chance of thriving on its own. What did Aliamon care about Adalei's happiness? What was Lio in the face of potentially destroying Alelune's monarchy? An afterthought, perhaps. Not even strong enough to defeat the soldiers sent to kidnap Elician, and therefore: not worth mentioning at all. Aliamon would be a king whose careful schemes saw the end of Alelune as a territorial threat. None of the rest mattered. Least of all the brave soldier who had sworn his life to Elician from the moment he knew the proper words to recite.

Fuck him.

'I'm sorry, Elician,' Anslian says. 'I'm so very sorry.' The apologies mean little. They are not coming from the right person. It is his father who should be apologizing. But his father is dead. 'I thought I'd die, and Adalei would never be happy again. That I'd truly failed everyone I loved.'

No.

No. He hadn't.

He had done wrong. So much wrong. But in all of this, he has been the only person who seemed to care that it was wrong. And that, in its smallest form, is something Elician can find forgiveness for.

Elician wraps his arms around his uncle and holds him close. He presses his face into Anslian's throat, smelling the perfume that had always meant warmth and safety even on the darkest days of the war. Anslian's arms hold him. He weeps into the shorn mess of Elician's curls, before drawing back to cup Elician's face once more. 'Will you tell Lio something from me?'

'Tell him yourself,' Elician says, though it is a token protest. He glances at the Queen's body. At the door. 'How – how are we getting out? We have to get out. They'll kill you for what you did.'

'Elician,' Anslian sighs.

'No. No, we need to leave. The grate – can you fit?' Elician's already working the maths, the angles. He can swing himself up, and then pull Anslian up with him. They could escape together. Somehow. They could do it.

Anslian says, 'I killed the Queen of Alelune at a Kingsclave, Elician. It's my duty to die for that transgression.'

'*No.*'

'I was never meant to be king, Elician. *You* were. Always. We hid who you were for years, bent law and sense to get to this point. Your father arranged for you to escape, to get free, knowing Alelune would collapse without its queen, and knowing that you would have your chance to rise. You were always meant to wear this crown, to stand as the leader of Soleb and end this war. He wanted that. And so do I.'

'*No.*' Elician shakes his head. He looks back to the ceiling beams. He is going to find a way out. 'I'm not leaving without you.'

Anslian takes his hand in his. Then, reaching into his borrowed clothes, removes a bundle of envelopes. Names are inscribed on the front, each written in his father's hand. His own, Lio's, Fen's, Adalei's . . . even Alest's. The bundle is passed securely into his care. 'I don't know what he wanted to tell you in the end. But he said his spy would ensure you were brought here, and that everything would end the way it needed to.'

'And you still have faith in him? After all of this? After *everything*?'

'Yes.'

'*Why?*'

'Because I made a vow.'

'Fuck your vow!'

'You don't mean that.'

'Come with me, come. We can go. We can go, and we can figure this out and no one else needs to die.'

'Elician, everything your father and I did, every moment we fought and argued – then conceded to this negotiation – was to put you in a position to end this war. And now we are on the edge of that victory. The Queen is dead, and her throne is weak. Alelune's rightful heir is more sympathetic to us than he has ever been, and there is a chance here for you to make sure that all of this ends the way it needs to end. No more manipulation. No more interference from others. It is your time now. I cannot be there for that.'

Not good enough. It is not *nearly* good enough. Elician shakes his head. He grasps Anslian's robes and shakes him, his other hand squeezing his father's packet of letters. 'You cannot do this.'

'There's only one way you're going to get out of here, Elician. That's if I walk through that door and give you the opening you need to leave.'

'I held his head,' Elician says. 'I held his head in my arms. I watched them kill Lio. I watched their . . . their *prince* cut Lio's throat. I cannot sit here, again, and *wait* as someone else makes a choice that I can change. I cannot just stay here and watch you *die*.'

'Let me do this,' Anslian replies. 'Just this one last time. Let me finish this, please.'

'I'll bring her back. If she's not dead, then you cannot be harmed.'

'You cannot bring her back, Elician. She is a queen. It's not allowed.'

'I don't *care*! It's not allowed to *kill* someone at the Kingsclave *either*,' Elician yells. He grasps his uncle's shoulder.

'But it's done. All of this is done. Everything we worked for, everything we did. All the sacrifices we've made—'

'Have been *bullshit*.'

'But they're done.'

'You cannot do this. You cannot lay this on me, the culmination of all your planning, and then tell me to just sit here and watch as they kill you. You cannot.'

'Let me act one last time,' Anslian whispers. 'And when I die, I'll be with my wilful older brother and my wife.' Carefully, very carefully, Anslian takes Elician's hands in his. He folds Elician's palms inwards, forcing him to cradle his father's letters between them. Slow and soothing, he says, 'Please, take care of my daughter . . . watch over her and Lio. Tell him he's everything I could have hoped for for her. That he has my blessing, now and always. Please. Follow this last command.'

'Don't make me do this,' Elician begs. The fog is returning. The pain in his chest. Despair climbs through his body, squeezing his insides tight. But the choice has already been made.

'Fen and Alest are *not* here . . . they're in the safehouse in Crowen. Aliamon said you'd know the way.'

'Yes . . . I know it.'

'Adalei should be with them. I sent her there before I left. Go to them when you leave here. They'll need you just as much as you'll need them.' Then, Anslian presses his lips to Elician's brow. 'I have always loved you, my boy. *Always*.' It is too much. It is not enough. It is too soon. Anslian pulls the letters from Elician's hands and tucks them into Elician's shirt. He guides him beneath the rafter he'd dropped from and offers his hands as a boost to help Elician hoist himself up. But Elician cannot bring himself to move. He stands, staring at Anslian, memorizing his face. His bearing. His countenance. Everything about him. It is that last look from his uncle that ends any thought of protest or resistance. That last look that makes everything evidently clear.

He's ready. The world has wreaked havoc on this man. It has torn him to shreds and left him at the end of a terrible path, with no way to move forward. And in the end, he'd not even been the one to land his brother's fatal blow. Aliamon had killed himself, when Anslian proved too slow at fratricide. He had killed himself and forced his brother to sever his head. Forced him to send the butchered remains of his body to Alelune as proof of a treachery that had never happened, to inspire or traumatize those it needed to influence. *He's ready to go.*

Braced by his uncle's strong arms, Elician swings himself up to the broad beams criss-crossing the top of the sanctum. Anslian wipes his face free of tears, then straightens the garments he'd borrowed from his brother – knowing there had been no need to tailor his own. He would not be King of Soleb for long. In death, as in life, Anslian wears his brother's influence with love and pride.

Anslian takes a deep breath. He removes his crown from his head. He places it on the table next to the torn treaty. He looks up one last time before bowing to his nephew. One hand over his chest. He speaks, and Elician's heart breaks. 'I wish you good fortune, as the new Sun King of Soleb. May your journey be far kinder than ours has been.'

Anslian steps towards the door, reaching for the ornate handles.

'Uncle . . .' Anslian waits. He glances up. 'You're not going to be a villain in the history books. I swear to you. Adalei will know what you tried to do. That you tried to stop it. She will be proud of you. As . . . am I.' It is the only thing he can say. It does not feel good enough. 'I forgive you,' Elician adds on, softer still, but heard nonetheless. His uncle closes his eyes. Takes another steadying breath, then nods to himself. He opens the door.

Elician presses his back against the wall as he balances on the supporting beams, hiding deep in the shadows. He presses his hand to his mouth as Anslian steps outside. As he announces, in the booming voice of a veteran general, 'The Queen is dead. She kept my nephew, Elician, son of Aliamon, prisoner for these past few years, and this is my justice. I accept my punishment and my fate but say this: Elician is the rightful King of Soleb, now and always.'

Chaos descends.

The Alelunen troops rush forward, calling for Anslian's blood.

The clerics just barely manage to keep the Soleben contingent back when they try to intervene, ordering them to leave the Kingsclave and return to Soleb. The Queen's body is removed from the inner sanctum and Anslian is taken away, to be dealt with by the Alelunen party. There is no trial; there is no need for one. Anslian admits his guilt and, by sacred oath, he is handed over to Alelune to face whatever punishment they deem fit. There can be no recourse. Even his own people don't argue with this judgement.

The shouts and yells echo through the inner sanctum. With the door thrown wide, Elician can hear *everything*. He can hear how they shout for Anslian's head. How they tear at his father's clothes, wrapped poorly around Anslian's body. He can hear the crowd growing more enraged with each passing second.

Elician clenches his eyes shut. He squeezes his palms over his ears. He breathes in and out as slowly as he can, waiting for the chaos to fade into nothingness. But the furore only grows. The Alelunen contingent makes haste as they remove Anslian from the Kingsclave grounds, shouting about assaulted honour and decency betrayed. They, unlike the Soleb *traitors*, intend to follow neutral-zone protocols. No blood will be spilled inside the sanctuary. No harm to its delegates will be permitted. But the same cannot be said for *outside* it . . .

They have started chanting their anthem as they march. Their voices swell in a vicious tide, carrying on and on until there is nothing left save the echo of their fury. The courtyard beyond falls quiet. There are some stragglers in their wake, but far fewer than before. They are milling about, murmuring to themselves about the failed Kingsclave. Some are clerics, worrying about what this means for their position *as* clerics. What does it mean for them, that they allowed a monarch to die under their watch?

Elician waits for as long as he dares. When he moves, his legs cramp badly. He breathes through the tingling pins-and-needles pain that slithers up his thighs and calves. Soon, the pain eases and he navigates towards the vent, across high beams, with careful ease. He hesitates before he slides out.

The crown is resting on the table, right where Anslian had left it. It glistens gold. Each careful thorn is a masterfully sculpted sunbeam in the candlelight, curling over at the edges just as the sun curves its light around the world. It should not be left here, at the Kingsclave; it should be returned to his people. Perhaps the clerics had not seen it before their judgement was enacted. Perhaps there simply has not been enough time yet to take it. The Queen's body has been hastily collected and ferried off. But everything else has been left as it was. *The crown should not be left behind,* he thinks again. Yet, if he goes down now and removes it . . . they will remember that it had once been there. And how will he ascend to the rafters again without help?

Leave it, Elician thinks. He squeezes his eyes shut. *I'll get a new crown,* he decides. *One not steeped in my family's blood.*

Pushing open the grate, Elician checks below. No one is there – so he slides through the gap to hang precariously by his fingertips, then drops to the earth with a thump. He waits until his body heals the damage from the fall.

Turning, he presses himself against the wall of the inner sanctum. He listens to the clerics as they settle the keep for the night. Lanterns are going out. Whispers are falling silent. He doesn't know how long he's been here, but knows he needs to leave soon. Lio will be worried.

He glances around the corner again, only to jump back when a cleric rounds it to face him. His voice catches in his throat as he tries to come up with some sort of excuse. Some sort of terrible excuse that explains away his presence. Then the cleric pulls down the white cloth obscuring their face. Raises one finger to her lips as her features are revealed. '*Zinnitzia!*' he gasps.

She motions for silence again as she continues behind the inner sanctum – circling the tower to return to him. Once her circuit is complete, she speaks, her voice pitched low. 'All clear, no one left.' Then she disappears, and he waits for her, frozen against the wall.

His heart thunders behind his ribs and his hands have started to tremble again. He can't stop thinking about his uncle's farewell kiss. More lanterns go dark. The sanctuary is now draped in the shadows of the evening. He still does not move.

He waits, and waits, and finally Zinnitzia returns. She is not alone. Another cleric is with her, tall and slender. She also removes her head covering, and he tumbles forward to embrace Marina. She holds him close, wrapping her arms around him as she has done since he was a child – never once letting him come to harm.

'He did not betray Soleb,' Elician whispers into Marina's neck. 'My uncle was not a traitor. He did not kill my father.'

'We know, little king,' Marina replies. And that is not right. It cannot be right. He has always been her *little prince*. But now – now he is something different. Something wholly different. He pulls back and she lets him go. She squeezes the back of his neck, tender and fond. 'We were informed just before it happened. Your father sent us here to wait for you – for however long it took. But he said to trust that you would make your escape in time.'

'In time for what?' Elician asks. Zinnitzia steps forward, holding up the crown he'd left behind. The one that had caused all this despair, all to protect a king without the right to rule. He is a Giver. He never should have been given this chance. And yet here it is. He realizes he hates the crown, hates it more than he has ever hated any inanimate object in his life.

'Your father failed as a king and a father,' Zinnitzia says. 'Your uncle did as well.' He clenches his fists, confused by her words, awash with emotion.

'But they sacrificed themselves for their country–'

'They put their personal preference, for you to rule, above their own duty to the people,' Marina cuts in. '*All* life is sacred. Including their own. They should have served their people – not sacrificed themselves for you. Nor bent laws or common decency just to ensure you had a place to rule. One cannot make choices to sacrifice those in the present for a future that might not come to pass.'

'But what if they're right? If this war *does* end under my reign?' He thinks, then, of Alest. Who refused to kill his family. Who had every right and reason to want to, but still hadn't. And who, by Anslian's own accounts, has been manipulated this entire time, but is still the true heir to the Alelunen throne. He swallows, hating himself for volunteering someone he hasn't spoken to in years, someone just as condemned as he is. But still, he asks, 'What if Alest and I *can* halt the bloodshed, stop the war?'

'They were still wrong to do what they did.' Zinnitzia holds the crown up again. 'I, Zinnitzia of Kreuzfurt, proclaim you, Elician, son of Aliamon, first of your name, Sun King of Soleb. To uphold the sacred oath of your office, and your country.' She lowers the crown onto his head. 'Long may you reign.' She steps back, one hand over her heart. In unison, she and Marina bow to him. 'May it all be worth it.'

'What are your orders, sire?' Marina asks.

'Fen,' he murmurs. 'We need to find Fen. Then . . . home. I want to go home.' Marina and Zinnitzia nod.

They do not need to ascend the walls to escape the Kingsclave. No one is watching as they exit through the door to Soleb. They walk the long and lonely path to the bottom of the fortress. Then, Marina goes to collect Lio and Morsen as Zinnitzia stays at Elician's side.

Together, as they wait for the others, they stand under the blood-red moon that had risen upon the Queen's death. *The gods are watching.*

Gillage will be proclaimed king in the coming days. Elician does not know what started the war aeons ago, but he knows what will drive it forward now. Queen Alenée is dead. Her forces will rally in her name, and they will be led by a sadistic child who relishes doling out pain to those he finds wanting. And somewhere, between now and then, his uncle will face Alelune's fury. He will be executed in the name of vengeance, and Elician must allow it to happen.

'All life is sacred,' he murmurs to the night sky.

'Even yours,' Zinnitzia murmurs back. He had not wanted her opinion. But now that he has it, he feels the weight of the world crash onto him once more. All life may be sacred, but some people still must die. He presses his palms to his face and weeps for all he's lost. Zinnitzia offers no comfort. He does not expect it. No word or touch could offer relief here. He can only cry. And when he runs out of tears, after Lio, Morsen and Marina rejoin them, he mounts his horse and guides them all towards Crowen.

He just wants to go home.

CHAPTER THIRTY-SEVEN

Elician

They ride in silence.

They are a mourning party as well as a royal host. Marina and Zinnitzia had taken three horses from the Kingsclave stables to join Elician's and Morsen's steeds, so everyone has their own mount. Elician is in front, the weight of the crown growing heavier with each hour it rests on his head. He does not want to wear it, but cannot bear to take it off. Not now. Not yet.

Marina must have explained what transpired at the Kingsclave for Lio does not ask him any questions. And Morsen keeps to himself. He rides at the back of their party, sombre and easily forgotten. Elician almost wishes someone *would* say something. But even as he thinks it, he realizes that he doesn't have the patience for conversation of any kind. His nerves are rubbed raw. His temper lingers at the tip of his tongue. He seals his mouth shut so he can't speak any of his harsh thoughts out loud.

It is all for the best.

Their horses plod eastward, across plains and sparse forestry. There are few places to hide, to disappear. It doesn't matter. Elician has no desire to hide anymore. This is his country. *His* in every sense that matters. This earth is *his* earth. If they did pass someone, and they do not, they would be *his* people. The crown grows heavier.

Anslian's words, and his father's actions, squirm in Elician's mind. He squeezes his reins rhythmically, tries thinking of something else. Fen. How tall she is now. How strong. He doesn't understand why she was sent to Crowen, but then again, he does not understand much of anything his father put in place. Legacy. All for a legacy Aliamon would never live to see. Elician squeezes his reins again, deliberately shifts his thoughts. Alest, the rightful King of Alelune, is in Crowen too. He can still ascend the Alelunen throne but how would he claim it? And would his people even accept a Reaper wearing the crown?

Then again, when has what the *people* wanted ever mattered much in politics? When have *those* people mattered to Soleben politics in particular?

Should they just let it lie? Let Alelune tear itself apart, just as his father planned? What would Alest want? Does he care?

His horse carries him onward into this future. 'You're not breathing, my King,' Lio murmurs. Elician flinches at the voice, and he snaps his head about, glaring balefully at his friend. Lio takes it without complaint. Elician releases the last bit of air in his lungs and inhales long and slow. There are apples nearby. He smells them, mouth watering for a taste even as his stomach seizes at the thought.

If he is going to engage in creature comforts, he would much prefer sleep to an apple. He imagines a proper bed with warm blankets and pillows. He doesn't think it is too much to ask for, for a king. But at the same time, when their group sets up camp each night, he finds himself lying on his back with his eyes open. Sleep eludes him as he stares at the sky, at the moon. Its light shines down upon him. The domain of Death, bathing him in her glow. He tilts his head towards his companions, and past them all, he sees eyes staring back.

A creature, crouched low to the earth, ears pressed flat, eyes narrowed. A muzzle and teeth, and white fur streaked with grey.

A nightcat.

He blinks, throwing himself upright, but it vanishes. Slipping out of existence like a mirage. 'Your Grace?' Morsen asks from where he had been uselessly keeping watch. Elician does not reply. He stares out into the shadows, waiting for an illusion to become real.

In the morning, there are no footprints in the earth. There is no sign that the creature had been there at all.

It takes them nearly a week to reach Crowen.

The city's walls are high and well defended. Elician can see the guards walking the tops of them, armed and prepared for an assault. Considering their current political circumstances, he is not entirely surprised. Even the gates to the city are tightly closed, barring any entrance. He stops his horse well before they reach the gates, though. He stops and watches the guards. His people. The first strangers who will know that he is there as king. He thinks again, *I'm not ready*. But diverts his thoughts once more.

'There's a tunnel,' Morsen suggests the longer Elician stares up at the wall. 'A hidden one.'

Elician glances back at him dully. 'I know where it is,' he replies. 'You know of it too?'

'Yes,' Morsen replies. 'It was how I could make certain reports unseen.' Slowly, Elician nods. He steers his horse away from the city. The others follow. No one asks him why he wants to take an alternate route. No one asks why he wants to effectively *sneak* into the city when he could walk through the gates the moment he declares his presence. They just follow. His word is law now. His decisions are meant to be listened to as if they came down from the gods themselves.

He thinks about the tunnel. It is not tall enough or wide enough for the horses. Of them, he would rather leave Morsen behind to mind the animals, but one man might not be enough to handle them all. Someone else will need to stay behind with him. The choice is not an easy one. 'Marina, you and Morsen will take the horses back to the city gate. We'll continue towards the tunnel. If we find no trouble, I'll send a message to the gate and have them open it for you.'

'Yes, Your Grace.'

Elician dismounts at her words and Zinnitzia and Lio follow his lead.

Marina is the better fighter should the party run into trouble inside Crowen. But he barely knows Morsen beyond the knowledge that he is a spy who trained with Ranio Ragden. Trust is not something he is keen to give at the moment, but he trusts *her* to take care of *him* in case Morsen does anything *un*trustworthy while they are gone. Elician doubts that will be the case, but his uneasiness doesn't subside.

It is a long walk for him, Lio and Zinnitzia. Perhaps not compared to their ride *to* Crowen, but long enough that the sun has dipped behind the horizon by the time Elician spots the landmark that identifies the tunnel. The scraggly tree is dead and decrepit and its trunk has been nearly cleaved in two by a storm – or a particularly vicious sword strike. Its roots are sound though. And after scraping away a few palmfuls of dirt, Elician reveals a buried trapdoor.

It takes a bit more time to shift the earth so the trapdoor can be loosened and raised. Once he has done so, it takes even longer to gather enough dry branches and earth to balance atop the entrance so their route is obscured. He'll have to send someone back to better secure it another day. Darkness wraps around them as Elician cautiously drops down into the hole, adjusting his crown to keep it firmly in place. The tunnel is only slightly taller than he is, and he helps the others scramble down – then trails his fingers along the rough walls, feeling for the path forward. 'This way,' he murmurs softly. He reaches out behind him until he finds Lio's arm. 'Take Zinnitzia's hand,' he instructs, and hears them shuffle, then their affirmation that they're now linked too. Elician leads onwards.

They walk slowly. Each step is a shuffle-slide into the deep. There are no blue stones down here. More's the pity. With no air vents, lighting a torch would only lead to them choking in the dark, and who knows if there are pockets of gas or animals who might be attracted to the light.

No one speaks.

Elician tracks their progress primarily through a vague mental map he had created while they manoeuvred from the entrance. He knew of the tunnel from lessons on safety and security trained into him as a child, but using it is an altogether different sensation. His sense of direction, at least, continues to insist that they are heading the right way. And when they cross under the city walls, something changes. He stops for just long enough to tilt his head up. He can *just* make out the sound of movement up above. Carriages and city dwellers going about their business.

Keeping one hand to the wall, Elician continues on. By the time his fingers come to rest against a ladder, his whole body is aching with tension. His hands are scraped and his knuckles bleed from their journey though the dark. He does not care. 'We need to climb,' he tells them.

Even without a torch, the air quality in the tunnel is poor. He can feel his own chest struggling to fill and so knows that Lio is in a worse position. But Zinnitzia is like him. She will heal. Lio will not. Not unless he is healed by them. He is *always* healed by them, and Elician feels guilty all over again at the trouble he brings to his friend.

He squeezes the rungs of the ladder. Thinks of something else. Starts to climb.

One hand after the other, he ascends. It is not a tall ladder, just meant to take them from the deeper underground to a slightly more acceptable underground: a basement cellar. His fingers find the outline of a hatch over their heads. Pushing up, he grits his teeth as he heaves at the stiff wooden trapdoor. It gives suddenly and the door crashes onto the stone above. Elician flinches at the horrible clanging. He continues upwards. Once in the cellar, he helps Lio and Zinnitzia climb the rest of the way out. It's still pitch black but the air is less oppressive.

'Now what?' Lio asks when the hatch is closed behind them once more. His voice is hushed in an effort to keep their party hidden.

'If anyone was going to hear us,' Elician tells him at a far more regular volume, 'they'd have heard us when we opened the hatch. Zinnitzia?'

'Here.'

'Clasp hands with Lio again and keep close; I'll get us to the door.' There is some fumbling. Zinnitzia loses her footing and nearly falls, but they stumble onwards through a cellar that smells of mould and hay. Elician finds the stairs and they cautiously make their way upwards. He finds the cellar door by smacking his shoulder against it, sending his teeth rattling in the process. Cursing to himself, he fumbles at the latch and the door swings open into another dark room.

A window lets in some moonlight and his eyes start to adjust. Yet when Elician steps through, a bell rings. It is the only warning he has before a sword slices through the air towards his face. He throws one hand up instinctively, unable to do more while unarmed. It is too late, and too useless by far. But the blade stops mid-strike, sharp silver hesitating a breath away from his throat.

Elician turns his head to squint through the gloom. But just as he thinks he might be able to make out his assailant, a light flares and fire erupts on his sleeve. He yelps and jerks backwards, slapping at the flame that – vanishes quick as it came.

'Fen–' someone starts to say. And before Elician can react to his sister's name, the faint glow of several lanterns fills the room.

Blinking up from his arm, the fabric still smouldering, he finally sees his assailant. A man, lanky and short, but with a straight back and features cut from alabaster stone. Sea-green eyes stare at him from an unblemished face that Elician recognizes all too well. 'The Queen is dead, Stello Alest,' Elician murmurs. He pulls off his crown and lets its weight carry it to the ground. It clatters with a noise that rings in Elician's ears. Even so, he places his hand on his heart. He bows. 'Long live the King.'

'Elician?' someone says just beyond Alest's shoulder. He wearily lifts his gaze.

The girl standing before him cannot be his sister. She wears a deep purple dress embroidered with gold. Her hair is tied in a long braid that hangs over one shoulder. She is taller than Alest still, but she has somehow lost the gangly limbs of youth. 'Elician!' She pushes past Alest. Throws her strong arms around Elician's neck. He catches her, and his head spins. He feels his vision fade a little as he staggers under the weight of her. His sister sobs into his shoulder. She speaks to him, but he cannot hear her words. His knees buckle and Lio's arm comes around his back and holds him up. Voices go back and forth over his head. He can barely keep track of any of it.

Zinnitzia retrieves the crown, speaks to Alest about something Elician barely understands. She calls him Cat still. Why call him Cat? Everyone knows who he is now. Everyone *must* know. Does Fen not know? After all this time? The voices begin clamouring louder and louder. More people are approaching. Lio makes a noise, sharp and almost pained. It forces Elician to attention and he turns, ready for whatever threat that–

Adalei.

She is dressed for bed in a plain nightgown and shawl. Sensible as always. It is late. Everyone should be dressed for bed, but only Adalei seems to have taken that notion to heart. Her headscarf is simple and black – hastily put into place, no doubt, when she heard the commotion. It sits somewhat crooked along her brow. Just out of perfect alignment. That is not like her at all. She does not seem to notice.

Her eyes are wholly focused on Lio. And Lio is wholly focused on her. His arm trembles at Elician's back. 'Go,' Elician murmurs. Lio stumbles forward awkwardly, as if in a dream – his hand touching his chest in his habitual gesture. And even with his back to Elician,

Elician knows full well what Lio must have remembered. Adalei's headscarf had not been with him when he'd been pulled from his grave. Three years of fighting a war, and nearly two years in captivity, he'd still kept that slip of fabric safe and treasured. Yet, after all that, it had been mislaid when his naked body had been thrown into a pauper's grave. 'I'm sorry,' Lio chokes out. 'I lost it . . . it's not here.' Tears press against Elician's eyes. Adalei has still not said anything. She is silent, staring at Lio as he rubs his chest. 'Your scarf . . . I promised I'd give it back to you but I–'

Adalei's lips part. Her hands rise. She unravels the scarf on her head, pulling it free. Her scalp, hairless and scarred from countless treatments and surgeries in her youth, is bared. Fen gasps quietly at Elician's side. He wonders if she has ever seen Adalei like this. She would have been too young to visit her in the House of the Unwanting, and perhaps she has never known what she looks like without it. Adalei has never wanted anyone to know.

Adalei steps towards Lio. She presses her black scarf to his heart, where the previous one had once rested. A treasured promise of things to come. 'There is no need to return it,' she whispers to him. 'I have you.' Then she arches up on her toes and kisses Lio featherlight on his lips. Fen gasps again. She says something to Alest; Elician is not sure what.

Lio folds his arms around Adalei's body. He ducks his face to her throat even as she kisses his cheek. He holds her, shoulders shaking, and she holds him in turn. She breathes him in, one hand losing itself in the patchy remnants of his hair.

Spots dance across Elician's vision as his last bit of energy threatens to leave him. For a week, reaching the Crowen safehouse had been the only thought keeping him moving forward. And finally, it is done. They are here. And almost home.

Adalei looks at him over Lio's shoulder. 'I promised I'd bring him back to you,' he murmurs.

'Thank you, cousin,' Adalei says, voice thick with tears.

Elician nods to her. His head spins. The spots grow worse, blinding. His limbs move awkwardly. He says something slurred and nonsensical. A warning, maybe. Fen yelps, but this time he cannot summon the strength he needs to respond. Someone leans forward to help support him. Alest, maybe. They are saying something, but the sound is fragmented as if underwater. He feels his legs collapse underneath him.

This time, he lets himself fall.

CHAPTER THIRTY-EIGHT

Elician

Somewhere, someone cooks something that smells like childhood. He does not know what it is. It is warm and savoury. He can imagine the taste on his tongue. People are talking. They sound happy. Beloved voices making noises that speak only of joy and relief.

It is a good sound.

He thinks it might be real, but he must be asleep.

For once, it is a good dream.

Elician finally wakes to the sound of a fire crackling. He is lying on something almost unbearably soft. He isn't used to it. The room around him is simple and neat. There is a desk to one side where sheets of paper with anatomical drawings have been collected and deftly organized. A dresser with a bowl for washing, a blade for shaving and a mirror are on the opposite side of the room. But right in front rests the glorious fire. It burns sweetly, and someone tends to it quietly. Elician thinks it is Lio at first, but as he sits up, he realizes he was wrong.

It is Alest.

The rightful King of Alelune glances back at him, dropping the poker and standing. Alest hands him a glass of water, murmuring his excuses for his presence. 'Fen wanted to check up on Lio. I told her I'd let her know when you woke.'

'How is he?'

'Lio? He's . . . he's fine, I guess. He hugged me.' Alest sounds rather mystified by that – somewhere between fond and uncertain. He touches his shoulder absently, as if recreating the gesture. Elician can imagine Lio wrapping his arms around Alest's body and pressing his face against Alest's shoulder to avoid the risk of accidental contact.

'Were you offended?' he asks quietly.

'No,' Alest replies. 'I know how your people are now. It was not bad.'

'He meant no offence,' Elician insists.

'I know.'

'He just . . . he spent a long time in the Reaper cells in Alerae,' Elician murmurs. 'We learned about your time there.' Alest does not respond immediately. Elician sets the water glass to the side. He swings his legs off the side of the bed and sits there, hands between his knees. The silence is eerily familiar. Comforting in a way that it should not be.

Slowly, Alest leans against the wall directly opposite Elician. He lets his back slide down it, keeping his right arm tucked in close as he sits. The bell at his wrist jingles, an obnoxious sound. 'He didn't deserve to be caged there,' he says eventually.

'None of us did.' It seems the appropriate thing to say, but Alest only shrugs. Perhaps he sees these words for the platitudes they are. Determining who deserves what never really matters in the end. 'How long has Adalei been here?' Elician asks.

'A few days. She told us her father was going to the Kingsclave. She wasn't happy.'

'I doubt she would have been.' She will be far less happy when she knows the truth of all that unfurled. The news may have already reached her. She wore such striking black earlier, even as evening wear. She was already in mourning. He wonders, too, if she knew the totality of the plans their parents had made for them. He hoped not. It would break her heart. But if she doesn't know, he will steel himself and stand steady as her informer. She deserves the truth, as much as it will hurt.

Alest glances towards the door, perhaps wondering if he should alert the others that Elician has finally woken up. When he meets Elician's eyes, he lowers his voice. 'When you saw me earlier, you called me by my real name. And you called me king.'

'It's who you are now,' Elician agrees quietly. 'Does Fen know?'

'She knows,' Alest says. 'That first night . . . on *Tomestange*, do you remember? When we saw the stars, by the campfire . . . I thought I would give it a try, truly being someone else. And it was nice. Being called "Cat". I liked it, even. Stello Alest of Alelune did not have a good life.' His accent comes across when he speaks his name. He rolls the l's in a way that Elician has never managed. 'Cat just wanted to keep his friends safe.' His arms draw in now. They wrap around his stomach as he stares down at his knees. 'That's something Alest could never do.'

'You didn't have a choice, Cat,' Elician tells him. He laughs a little at the absurdity of the assurance. 'None of us had many choices, but you least of all.'

'They said Lord Anslian killed my queen at the Kingsclave.' The statement is not unexpected. And yet, he still does not call the Queen his *mother*.

'Yes.'

Cat hugs himself closer.

'Can I sit by you?' Elician asks. The words leave his lips without conscious thought. Cat seems startled too, but then he nods slowly. His brows furrow, and he watches Elician slip from the bed and join him on the floor. Their shoulders press against each other's. Warmth flares through Elician's body and he relaxes so suddenly he feels a bit dizzy again from it all.

'Your father sent us to train with a physician, Elena Morsen–'

'Morsen?'

Cat's nose scrunches. He tilts his head just a little. He almost looks like his namesake in the picture books Elician had as a child. The effect is oddly endearing. 'Yes? She said she knew you. That she treated Adalei when she was younger, and you had met–'

'I do know her. I just . . . didn't remember her last name.' He presses his hands to his face. 'When I was in Alelune, a man named Jonan Morsen helped break Lio and me out of the city.'

'He's her husband?'

'Yes . . . and he told me about his wife too. I should have realized.'

'You were tired. Hurt.' He *was* tired. Hurt. 'You still are.' Elician huffs at the quiet evaluation.

'Yes, I guess I still am,' he admits wearily, but continues. 'Jonan Morsen was Ranio Ragden's apprentice.' Cat winces at the name. He stares down at the floor. 'Whatever happened that day was not your fault,' Elician says vehemently.

'I killed Fen's father,' Cat refutes.

'On purpose?'

'Does it matter?'

'It might.'

'I never told her.'

'It was not your fault,' Elician repeats.

'You weren't there; you don't know what happened.' There are dozens of questions that Elician could ask as a follow-up. Dozens of ways he could poke and prod at Cat's story. He sees Cat brace for those questions too, awaiting judgement.

'Cat. Was it on purpose?' Elician asks.

Sea-green eyes blink up at him, and the King whispers, 'No.' Elician takes Cat's hand in his. He holds it in his palm. 'I fell forward, touched his horse. It died and Ranio broke his neck in the fall.'

'It was an accident.'

'It only happened because I was there.'

'It wasn't your fault,' Elician repeats. 'But that doesn't make the pain any less poignant. I'm sorry that things happened the way they did. You deserved a better life.'

'You're sad.' Cat's voice pitches strangely. Confused, perplexed, uncertain. He frowns and Elician nods, leaning his head against the wall and looking up at the ceiling.

'I'm very sad. For a lot of reasons,' he murmurs.

Cat shifts. Turns. Kneels so he is facing Elician directly. He touches Elician's face, cupping his cheek. Cat's skin feels *warm*, warmer than anything Elician had felt in the long months of isolation. 'You cannot kill me, remember?' Elician asks, leaning into the touch. 'Though the thought of death seems almost preferable to the mess we're in.'

'Elena taught us biology . . . anatomy,' Cat replies, somewhat illogically. 'Science. She taught us much about science. And . . . we learned that hormones and neurotransmitters affect emotion. I can kill, or stop, the biological process that's causing you to feel so sad,' Cat murmurs. 'I can block the neurotransmitters that are hurting you. I read about it in a book; I know what I would need to kill to—'

'You can be that specific? That targeted?' It sounds unbelievably complex, what Cat is offering.

'Elena . . . she taught us to look at the small, not the whole. Once I understood the theory, I taught myself the rest.'

'All life is sacred,' Elician murmurs absently. Cat does not seem to understand, but Elician does not expect him to do so. 'Have you been working on me now?' he asks. 'Keeping me calm?' If he has, it might explain why he feels no panic at the idea, no anger at the intrusion. He supposes that would be most natural. Cat is offering to manipulate how his body feels. That should be alarming. But Cat looks horrified at the notion of adjusting Elician's biological processes without his permission. He recoils, pulling away so fast that

Elician chases after him, catching his soft hand and holding it close. 'You're not like your brother at all, are you?' Elician asks quietly. 'Somehow, despite everything, you're kind.'

'You were kind to me once, when we first met,' Cat replies.

'Was it kindness?' Elician had captured him, bound him, abducted him and imprisoned him in a gilded cage far from home.

'I thought so,' Cat murmurs. His head shifts a little, just enough for Elician's attention to fall to Cat's unblemished cheek. With his free hand, Elician very slowly reaches up to touch it. To rest his palm against Cat's smooth skin, mirroring Cat's former gesture. And Cat, in turn, mirrors his response. His eyes flutter. His head tilts, leaning into the touch as he breathes deeply. Serene, at peace, and calm beneath Elician's hand.

'Who did it?' Elician asks him, stroking his thumb back and forth over Cat's cheek. 'Who healed–'

'Fen,' Cat says. Somehow, it does not surprise Elician at all. 'She's . . . brilliant, when she doesn't think too hard.' *That* makes Elician smile. He slowly lets his hand drop and Cat meets his eyes again. Patient, calm. So unlike their first meeting.

'I'm happy for you,' Elician says. 'You deserve to be happy.'

It is nice being here, like this. Sitting in the quiet, talking to someone, perhaps the only person in the world who understands the full depth of his anguish. He and Alelune's true heir both have their own personal traumas, but somehow Elician's story has always been intertwined with Cat's. Right from the very beginning.

His imaginary friend, finally made real.

They hold each other's hands. They breathe the same air. 'I killed Gillage's father,' Cat says. Or perhaps, he *explains*. Perhaps this is Cat's attempt at some kind of justification. Perhaps this is the way he has excused all the horrors that have been done to him. Gillage could be cruel because Cat had killed someone important in his life. His happiness didn't matter.

'You were a child,' Elician says. Cat frowns, dissatisfied with the response. Perhaps he wanted condemnation. Perhaps he wanted to frighten Elician away, scare him from the truth that Elician had seen with his own eyes.

'You are quick to forgive me for murdering people. Are murderers always excused based on their age, in Soleb?'

'You did not murder that man. He tried to kill *you*.'

'I dove into that river. It was my fault.'

'He was meant to protect you. He let you drown.'

'Meant to or not, I was the one who dove,' Cat repeats vehemently. 'It was my fault.'

Elician squeezes Cat's hand. He changes the topic. 'Gillage will be a terrible king.'

This time, Cat does not hesitate. He answers with a calm, 'Yes,' but offers no additional thoughts. If he were anyone else, Elician might suspect that Cat was disinterested, but he cannot be. Cat has proven himself incapable of true passivity when it comes to the political turmoil between their two nations. He refused to kill Aliamon. He stayed with Fen after his true identity had been revealed.

'There's no law saying you cannot ascend to the throne. Not in Alelune. Your existence was still acknowledged by your mother in the end. She even called you her heir.'

'I am no king,' Cat refutes.

'Brielle thinks you are.'

Cat's head suddenly snaps up and his fingers grip Elician's in a brutally tight squeeze. His free hand grabs Elician's shoulder. 'Brielle? Brielle, is she all right?'

'She's fine,' Elician replies. 'Or she was when I left her. I tried to free her . . . I unlocked her cage. I tried to get her and the others to leave with me, but they wouldn't. Believe me.' Elician sits up, covering Cat's free hand with his own. 'I *tried*. I swear to you. I asked, and she said . . . she said that they're waiting for you. For their – their *stello*. They would only move at your command. I'm sorry. I'm so sorry for that.'

Tears form in the corners of Cat's eyes. His grip loosens, but Elician still holds their hands steady. He keeps them together, the burden nothing at all to bear. Not compared to the weight of a crown. The weight of the crown he knows he is offering Alest-who-wishes-only-to-be-Cat.

'There are hundreds of Reapers in Alelune. The ones in Alerae are the majority, but not the entirety. Aside from *them*, none would know me. None would recognize me. And the people – they hate and fear our kind. They would not accept me.'

'But Gillage is a monster,' Elician says.

'Gillage is a monster,' Cat agrees. His shoulders slump forward. His head bows. 'I do not know how to be a king. I . . . I do not know if I can be *their* king.'

But if he isn't, Elician knows for certain that one day, Gillage will get overthrown. It's only a matter of time. Someone will replace him. And then someone will replace her. And on and on it will go. The country locked in a civil war as families fight for the chance to reign.

'I do not know if I can be the king my people deserve either,' Elician confesses. Sea-green eyes peer up from under dark brows. Cat's frown is palpable. His uncertainty at Elician's words verges on disbelieving, and Elician says, 'What my father . . . what my uncle did, I cannot make those choices. I cannot do what they did. But if that's what it means to lead . . . how can I ensure I uphold the principle that all life is sacred? When no matter what choice I make, someone is hurt? If all life is sacred, then doesn't the good of the many outweigh that of the few? Aren't I–' Elician breaks off. 'Shouldn't I be willing to sacrifice more?' His chest has started to ache. Pain blossoms in his brain again. He pulls one hand away from their desperate clasp to rub his aching temples.

Cat watches, his gaze serious, and says, 'I can help.' Elician hesitates, then nods. Slowly, the pain stops as Cat had promised. Elician's heart slows. Even so, he now feels exhausted and drained.

Like he had been crying for hours and then came to an abrupt halt. He breathes in, breathes out. For all that he has calmed, he is keenly aware that it came as an enforced peace. 'I don't know how to do this,' Elician admits.

'Elena says, to heal a wound, you need to start small.'

It is on the tip of his tongue to reply that a war is nothing like a wound. He does not. A war is exactly like a wound. A land once whole is separated by chaos and blood. The various armies fight each other like platelets and germs; sometimes they gain ground but sometimes they do not. Sometimes the bacteria wins and the wound festers. The armies fail. The victim dies.

'I want to go home,' Elician admits. He waits.

Cat bites his lip, then offers, 'I want to see Brielle again.'

'I want to see Adalei and Lio get married.'

'I want to see Fen show you what she's learned.'

'I want the war to end,' Elician murmurs. 'Permanently.'

'Permanently,' Cat agrees, then: 'I . . . do not want to be king.'

Elician hates that there is nothing else he can say to that except, 'Neither do I.' He wishes there was another life. A simpler life. Where he could just disappear and be of no importance to anyone. But if he walked away into the wilds now and let the world deal with its own consequences, he would regret it for the rest of his very long life. He has to stay. He has to see it through. But *gods* does it hurt.

'I read a history book, when I was held captive,' Elician says. 'It was the complete history of Alelune. It never said why we had to fight over that damned river. Only that neither country ever wanted to share it, and from there it just became an endless war. A cycle that continued generation after generation, one group laying claim, then the next one. A whole war with no real reason behind it, just two countries wanting to claim a damned river that runs in between them – both too stubborn to let it go.'

Cat shifts and stretches as he sits, but their hands remain clasped tight. 'Perhaps that's what our people have in common,' he suggests.

'Fighting against the unknown of peace, because at least war is familiar?'

'Why not?'

Elician lets his eyes fall to their hands. The tangled mess of their union. Giver and Reaper. Sun and Moon. Soleb and Alelune. Life and Death. 'All life is sacred,' Elician murmurs one final time. *Even those who hate and condemn my people. Even those who live in an enemy nation.* Alelune does not deserve the chaos his father set up for them. Elician shifts, straightening and resecuring his grip on Cat. 'I . . . had this idea that one day I could parlay with the Stello of Alelune, that I could negotiate a peace that would ensure our countries no longer had cause to quarrel. I dreamed that I would go to Kreuzfurt and throw open the doors. That all those in the Houses of the Wanting and Unwanting would be free to choose the lives they wanted and would not be separated or . . .' He tugs at the tie around Cat's wrist. The bell falls to the ground. 'Or treated like criminals simply because they exist.'

'We would need an open border and there could be no restrictions on the river . . .' Cat murmurs. 'And both sides would need time to get used to doing better – they'd need the opportunity to fail, the opportunity to try again, and the opportunity to one day succeed at peace.'

Elician can picture it. Ships flying both flags sailing freely along the river. Commerce. Trade. Possibility. Respect for a place both countries loved, and a desire for both sides to provide and prosper. The doors of the Houses of the Wanting and Unwanting thrown open. No more locked doors, simply lives given freedom for the first time.

'It will take *lifetimes* to make true peace between Alelune and Soleb. But . . . never before has a member of either royal family been *god-chosen*. And here we both are, Cat.'

'Here we are,' Cat agrees.

'If I have to spend the rest of my life making sure that every single person I meet can have the life they deserve to live, it will be worth it.'

'It's a good dream.'

'Would you accept the crown of Alelune, on this basis?' Elician rubs his thumb back and forth across Cat's knuckles. 'Would you take that crown, and lead your country, your entire country, and ensure that peace could last?'

Cat does not answer for a long time. He stays still, holding Elician's hands. He stares at their interlocking fingers, squeezes them gently, and says in soft Lunae, 'Not alone.' When he meets Elician's eyes, he almost looks like he did when they first met, nearly two years ago. Vulnerable and afraid. 'I will not return to Alelune alone. Not for ever. Not to rule permanently. But if you swear you'd go with me, that I would not be there by myself . . . I would do it if I wasn't alone.'

'I swear,' Elician murmurs in the foreign tongue. 'If we do this, if we want to do this well – we will do this together, every step of the way.'

'Alelune will never accept joining as one with Soleb. We cannot be *one* nation.'

'No,' Elician agrees. 'But we don't have to be. One union between the two would be a start. Then one treaty. Then . . .'

'Peace.' Cat leans closer. His breath comes quick.

'Peace,' Elician agrees.

'And all of us will be free, when we are done – the Reapers underground and in the House of the Unwanting?'

'All of us.'

'Do you mean it? *Truly?*' He can feel Cat's pulse. His passion. His belief. The determination here that, a few years ago, Elician never would have thought possible. But this is the man Brielle insisted would come to free them. The man that the Reapers in Alerae wait for still. The man the gods built for this purpose, just as they built Elician.

'Yes,' he says. 'I swear to you, if you take that crown, I will do everything in my power to ensure that there will be peace eternal between our lands. And I swear . . . I will never leave you to face that burden alone.'

Slowly, Cat raises their hands to his lips. 'Then I swear an oath to you, Elician, King of Soleb. And I bind my life to yours.'

Elician leans forward, kissing Cat's knuckles in turn – and sealing the promise on both ends. 'My life is yours too, Alest, King of Alelune.'

Cat's eyes catch a flicker, to their left. He gasps. Elician turns too. Outside, shooting stars are flying across the sky in breathtaking, streaking bursts without end. It marks the moment their fractured houses quietly join as one.

Acknowledgements

I am incredibly grateful for all the support I have received in the creation of this book. My agent, editors, copy-editors and all the people involved in the publishing team have been phenomenal; I couldn't have done this without you. To those in my personal life who read drafts and listened to me fuss about plot points – I am humbled and honoured by your support.

LINDSEY BYRD grew up in New York before moving abroad for graduate research studies. She is an amateur birder and enjoys going for hikes to take photos of nature. Lindsey enjoys all forms of speculative fiction, and is an avid researcher of history.